THE UNDERFOOT

the mighty deep

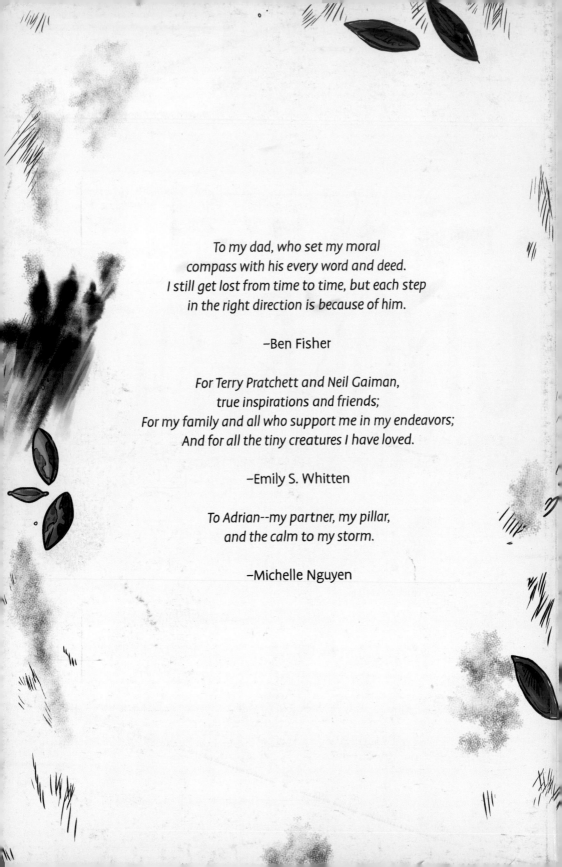

To my dad, who set my moral
compass with his every word and deed.
I still get lost from time to time, but each step
in the right direction is because of him.

–Ben Fisher

For Terry Pratchett and Neil Gaiman,
true inspirations and friends;
For my family and all who support me in my endeavors;
And for all the tiny creatures I have loved.

–Emily S. Whitten

To Adrian--my partner, my pillar,
and the calm to my storm.

–Michelle Nguyen

THE UNDERFOOT

the mighty deep

BOOK 1

Written by Ben Fisher and Emily S. Whitten
Illustrated by Michelle Nguyen
Lettered by Thom Zahler

CARACAL™

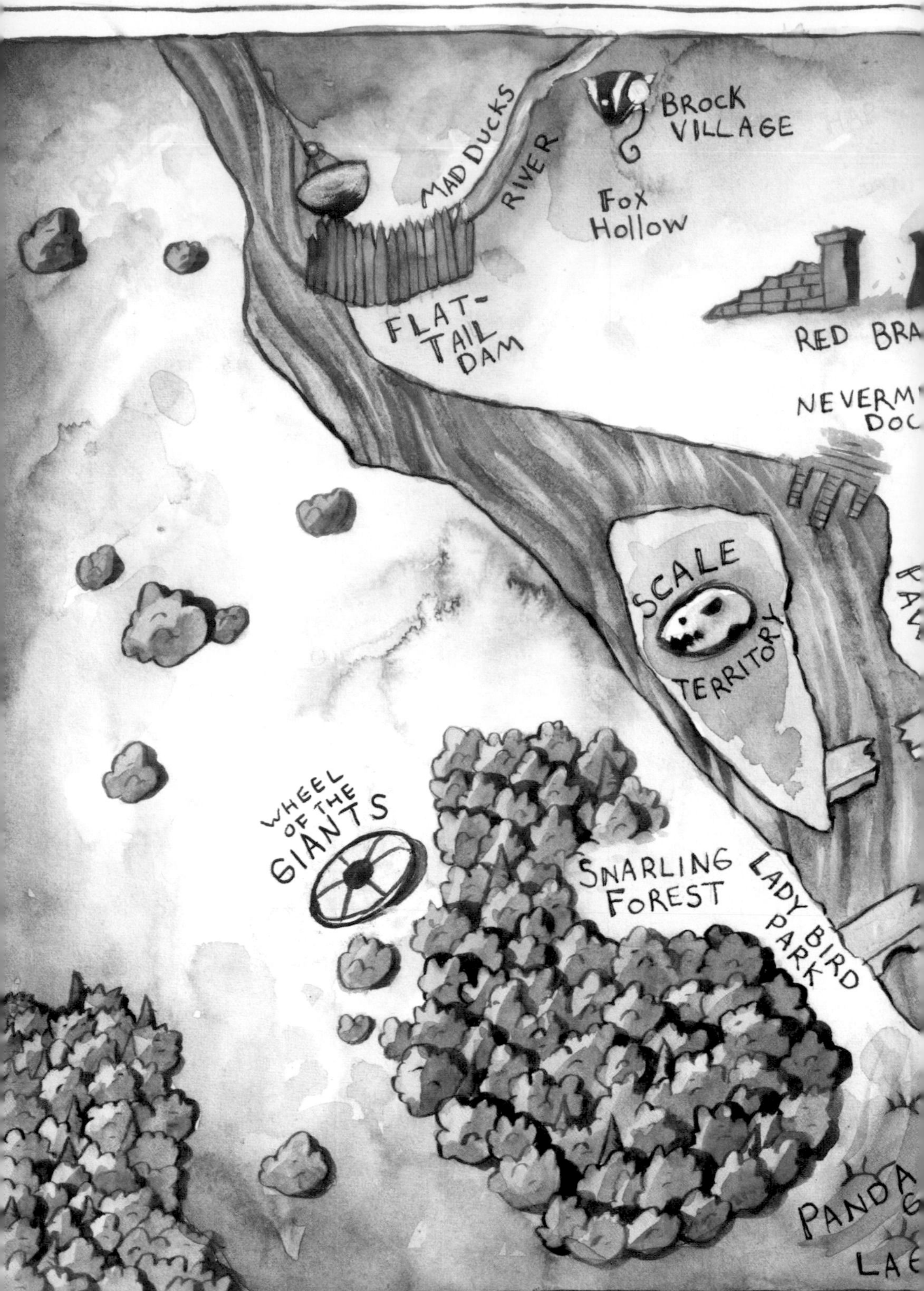

BROCK VILLAGE
MAD DUCKS RIVER
FOX HOLLOW
FLAT-TAIL DAM
SCALE TERRITORY
WHEEL OF THE GIANTS
SNARLING FOREST
LADY BIRD PARK

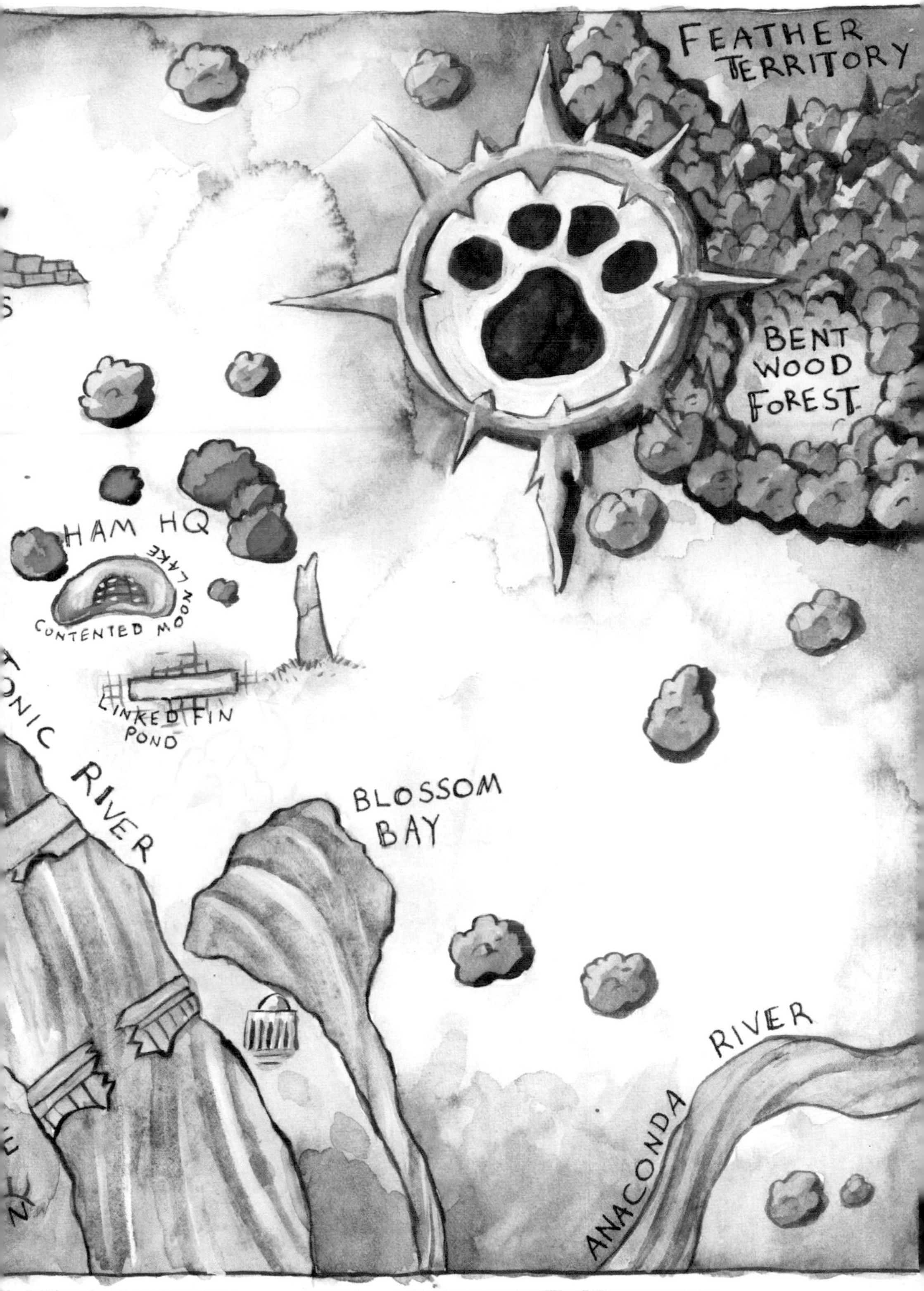
FEATHER TERRITORY
BENT WOOD FOREST
HAM HQ
CONTENTED MOON LAKE
LINKED FIN POND
ONIC RIVER
BLOSSOM BAY
ANACONDA RIVER

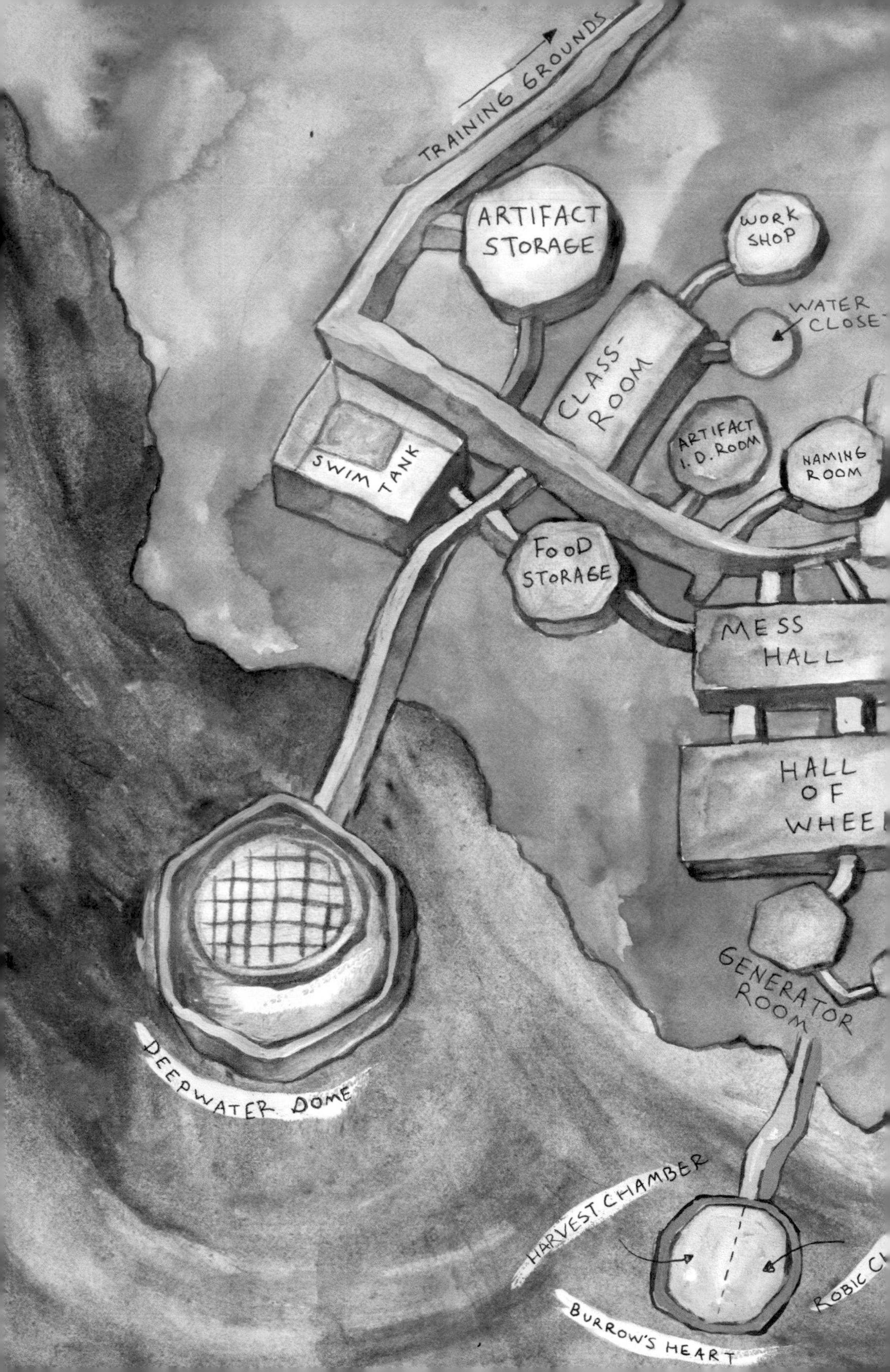
TRAINING GROUNDS
ARTIFACT STORAGE
WORK SHOP
WATER CLOSE
CLASS-ROOM
SWIM TANK
ARTIFACT I.D. ROOM
NAMING ROOM
FOOD STORAGE
MESS HALL
HALL OF WHEE
GENERATOR ROOM
DEEPWATER DOME
HARVEST CHAMBER
ROBIC C
BURROW'S HEART

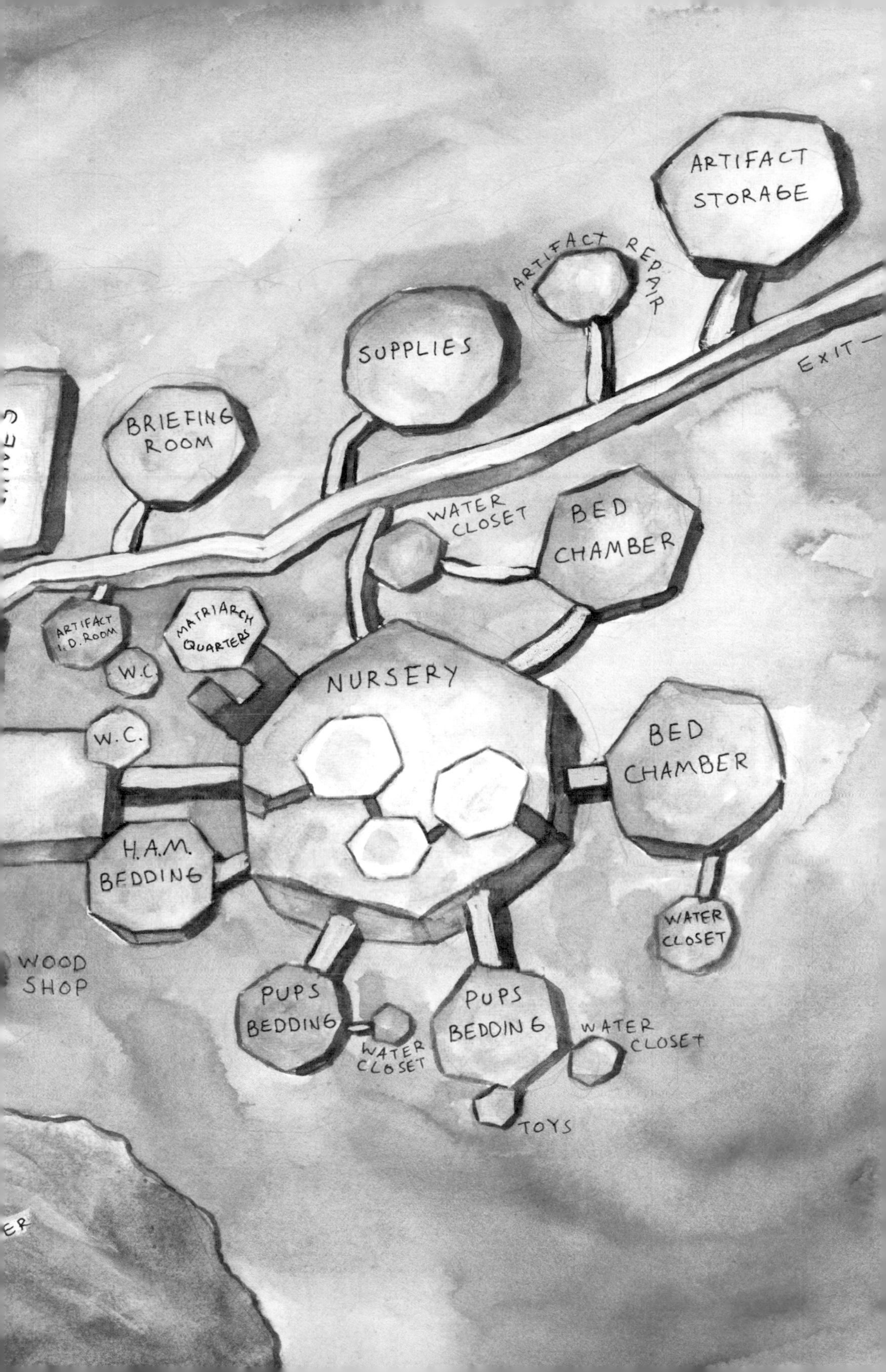
ARTIFACT STORAGE
ARTIFACT REPAIR
SUPPLIES
EXIT
BRIEFING ROOM
WATER CLOSET
BED CHAMBER
ARTIFACT I.D. ROOM
MATRIARCH QUARTERS
W.C.
NURSERY
W.C.
BED CHAMBER
H.A.M. BEDDING
WATER CLOSET
WOOD SHOP
PUPS BEDDING
PUPS BEDDING
WATER CLOSET
WATER CLOSET
TOYS

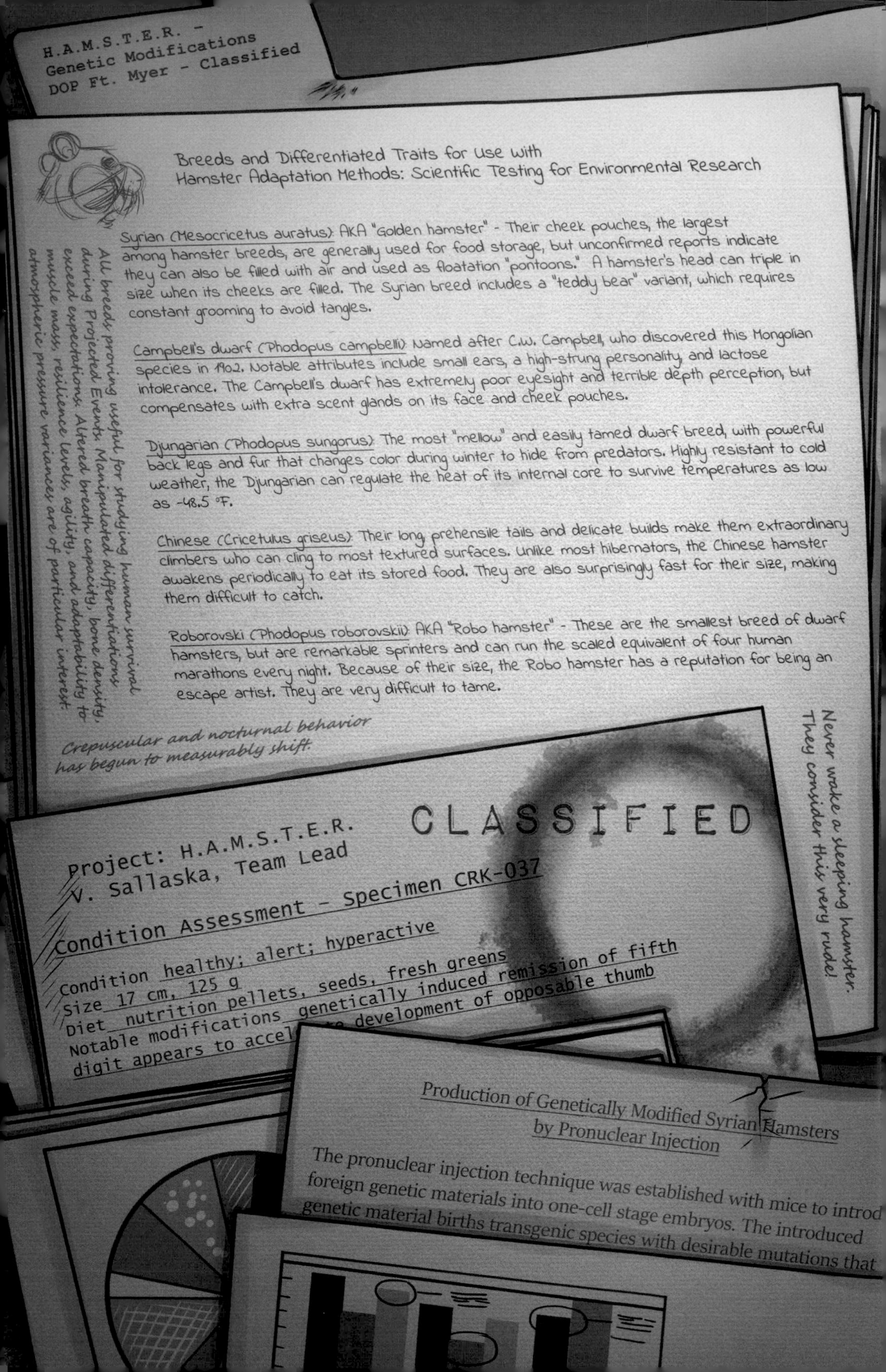

H.A.M.S.T.E.R. –
Genetic Modifications
DOP Ft. Myer – Classified

Breeds and Differentiated Traits for Use with Hamster Adaptation Methods: Scientific Testing for Environmental Research

Syrian (Mesocricetus auratus): AKA "Golden hamster" – Their cheek pouches, the largest among hamster breeds, are generally used for food storage, but unconfirmed reports indicate they can also be filled with air and used as floatation "pontoons." A hamster's head can triple in size when its cheeks are filled. The Syrian breed includes a "teddy bear" variant, which requires constant grooming to avoid tangles.

Campbell's dwarf (Phodopus campbelli): Named after C.W. Campbell, who discovered this Mongolian species in 1902. Notable attributes include small ears, a high-strung personality, and lactose intolerance. The Campbell's dwarf has extremely poor eyesight and terrible depth perception, but compensates with extra scent glands on its face and cheek pouches.

Djungarian (Phodopus sungorus): The most "mellow" and easily tamed dwarf breed, with powerful back legs and fur that changes color during winter to hide from predators. Highly resistant to cold weather, the Djungarian can regulate the heat of its internal core to survive temperatures as low as -48.5 °F.

Chinese (Cricetulus griseus): Their long, prehensile tails and delicate builds make them extraordinary climbers who can cling to most textured surfaces. Unlike most hibernators, the Chinese hamster awakens periodically to eat its stored food. They are also surprisingly fast for their size, making them difficult to catch.

Roborovski (Phodopus roborovskii): AKA "Robo hamster" – These are the smallest breed of dwarf hamsters, but are remarkable sprinters and can run the scaled equivalent of four human marathons every night. Because of their size, the Robo hamster has a reputation for being an escape artist. They are very difficult to tame.

All breeds proving useful for studying human survival during Projected Events. Manipulated differentiations exceed expectations. Altered breath capacity, bone density, muscle mass, resilience levels, agility, and adaptability to atmospheric pressure variances are of particular interest.

Crepuscular and nocturnal behavior has begun to measurably shift.

Never wake a sleeping hamster. They consider this very rude!

CLASSIFIED

Project: H.A.M.S.T.E.R.
V. Sallaska, Team Lead

Condition Assessment – Specimen CRK-037

Condition healthy; alert; hyperactive
Size 17 cm, 125 g
Diet nutrition pellets, seeds, fresh greens
Notable modifications genetically induced remission of fifth digit appears to accel... development of opposable thumb

Production of Genetically Modified Syrian Hamsters by Pronuclear Injection

The pronuclear injection technique was established with mice to introd... foreign genetic materials into one-cell stage embryos. The introduced genetic material births transgenic species with desirable mutations that

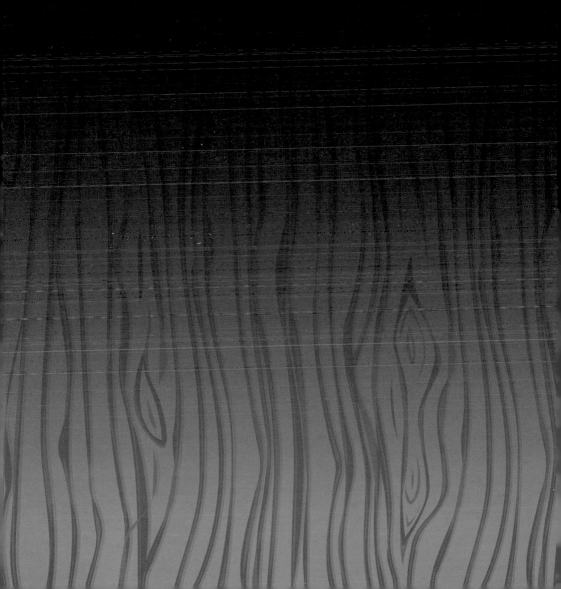

CHAPTER ONE

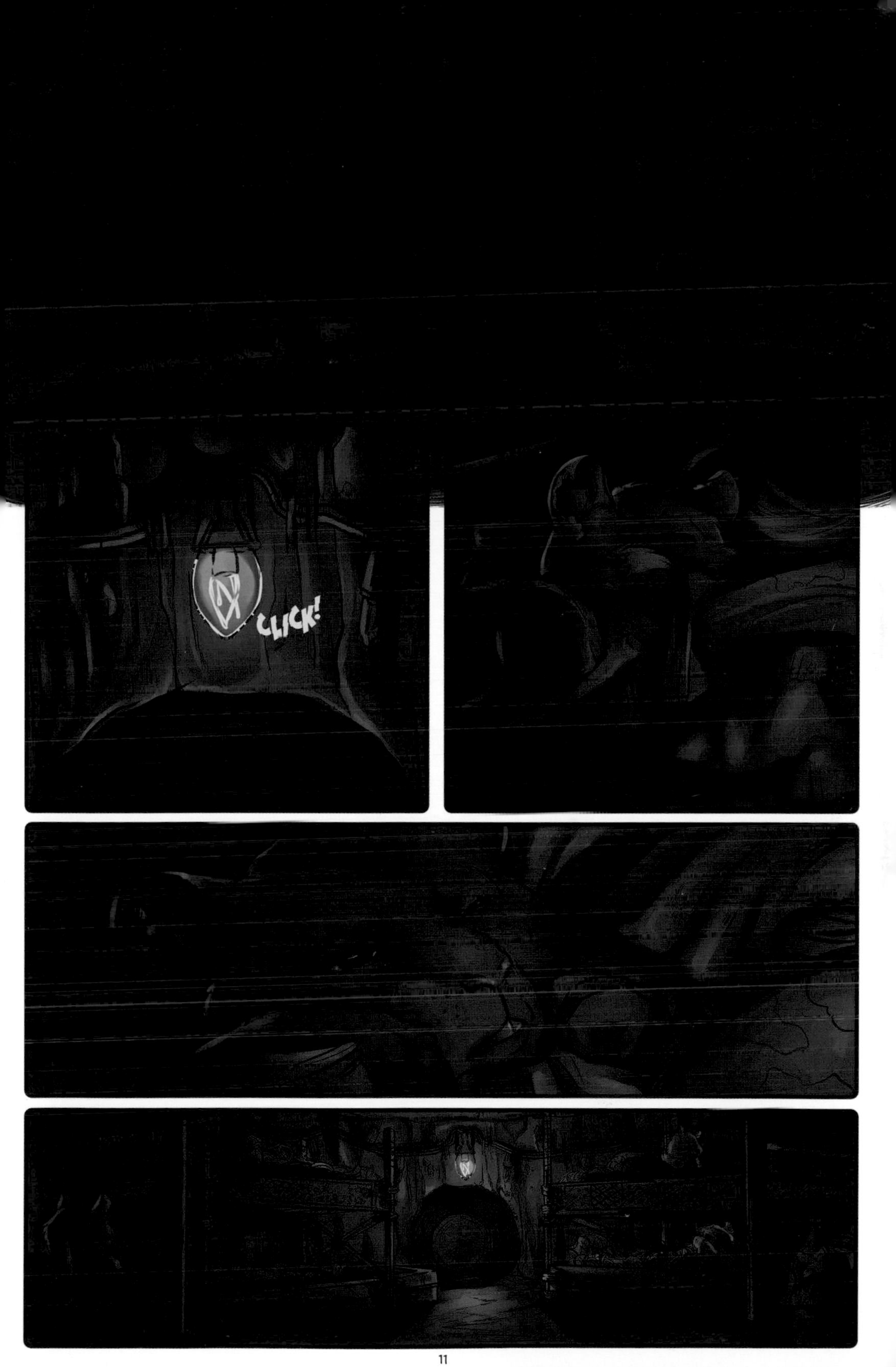
CLICK!

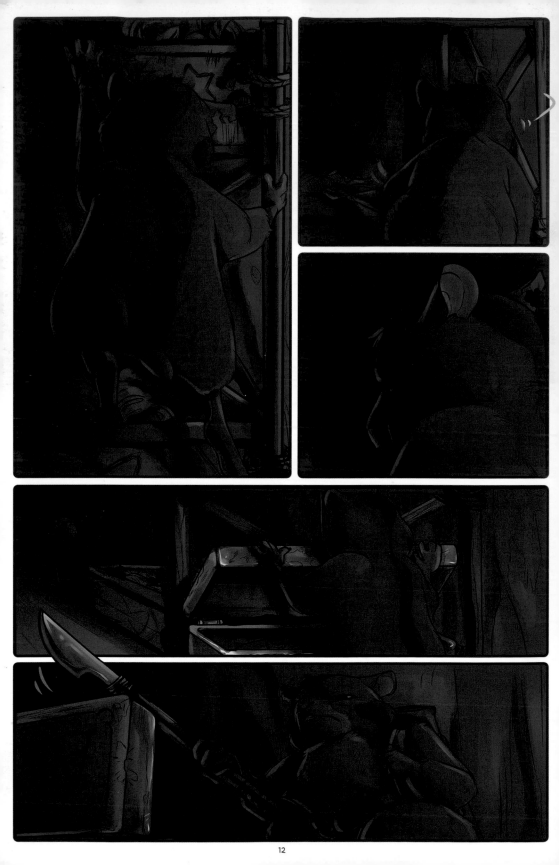

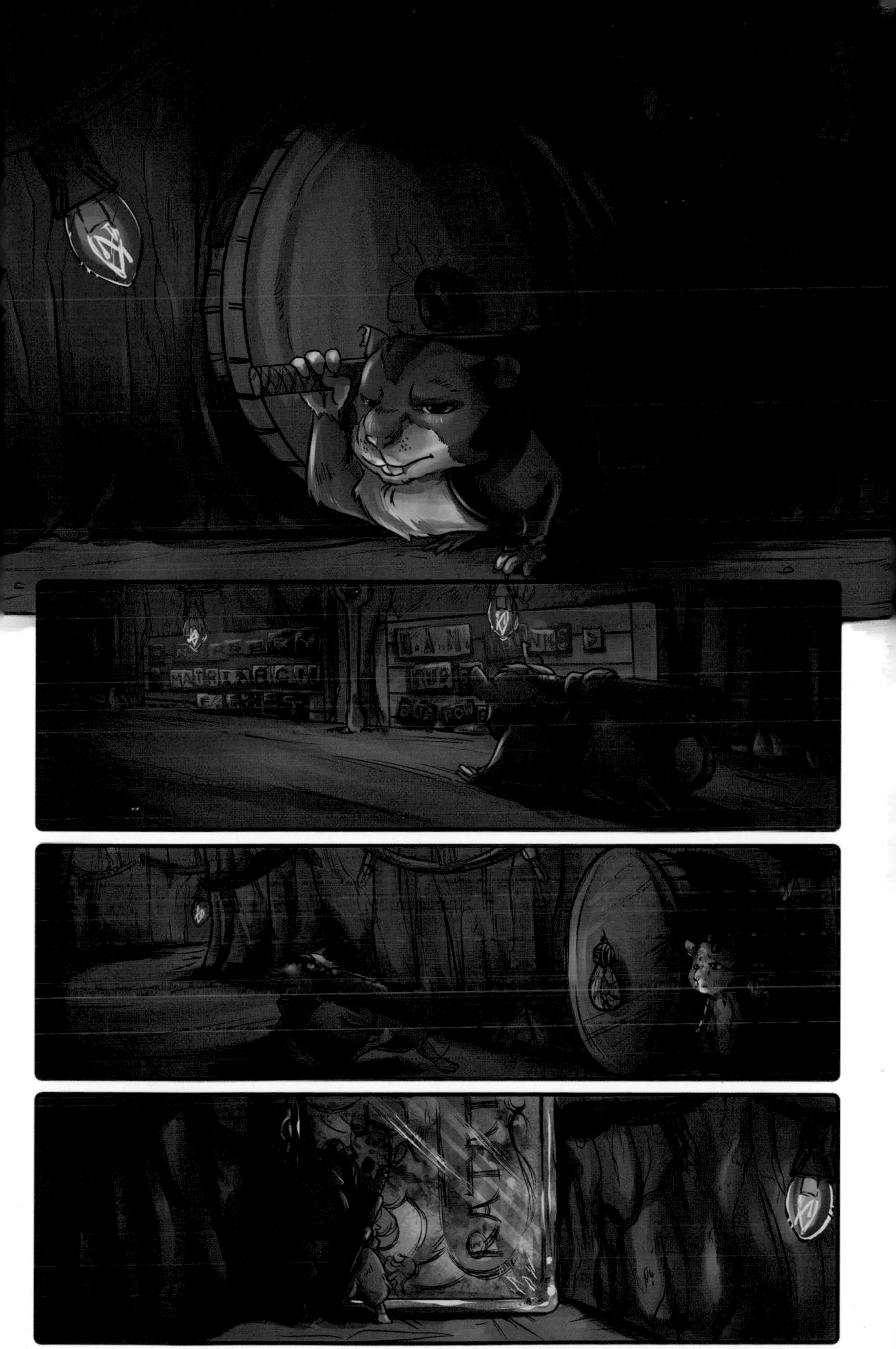

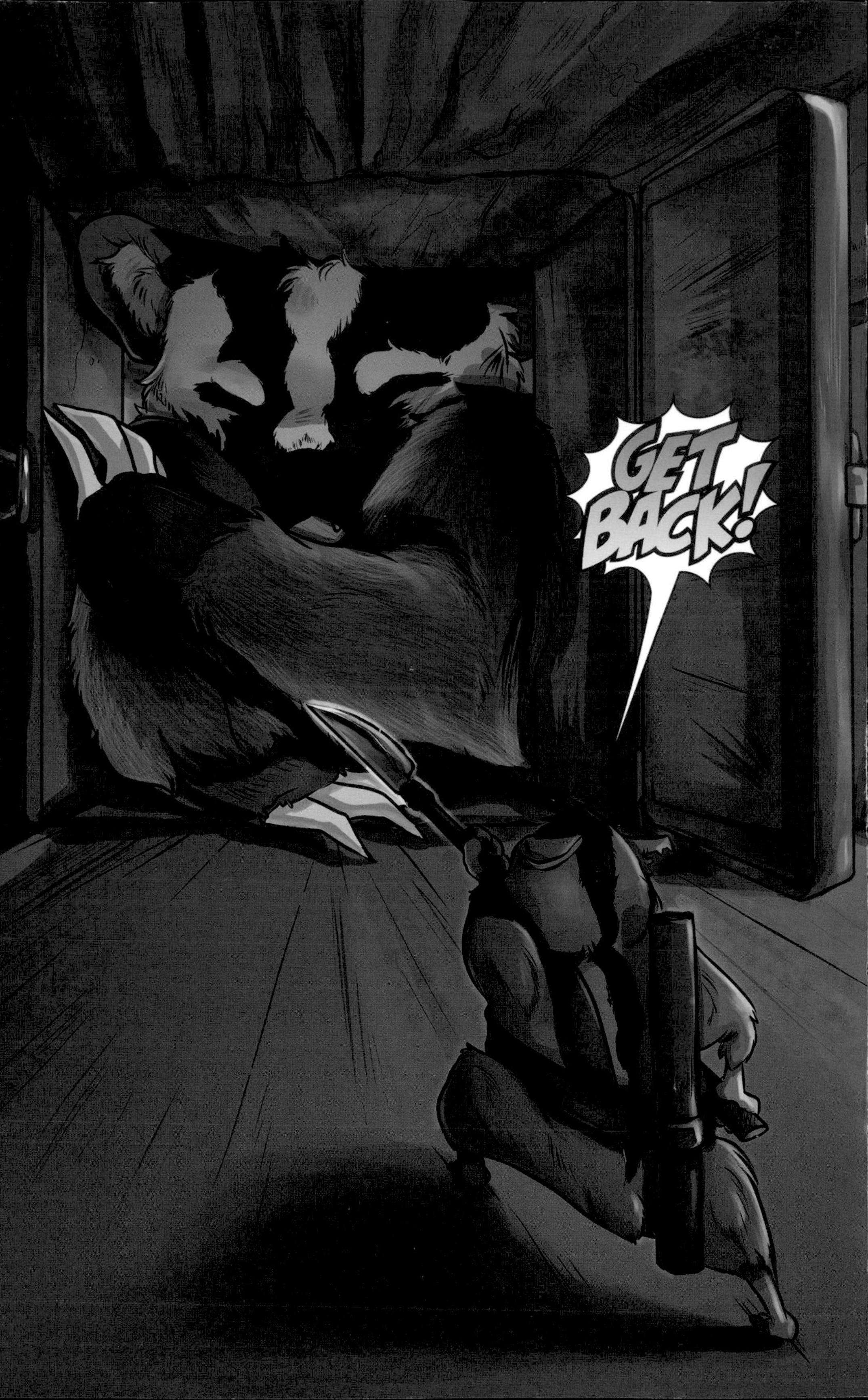
GET BACK!

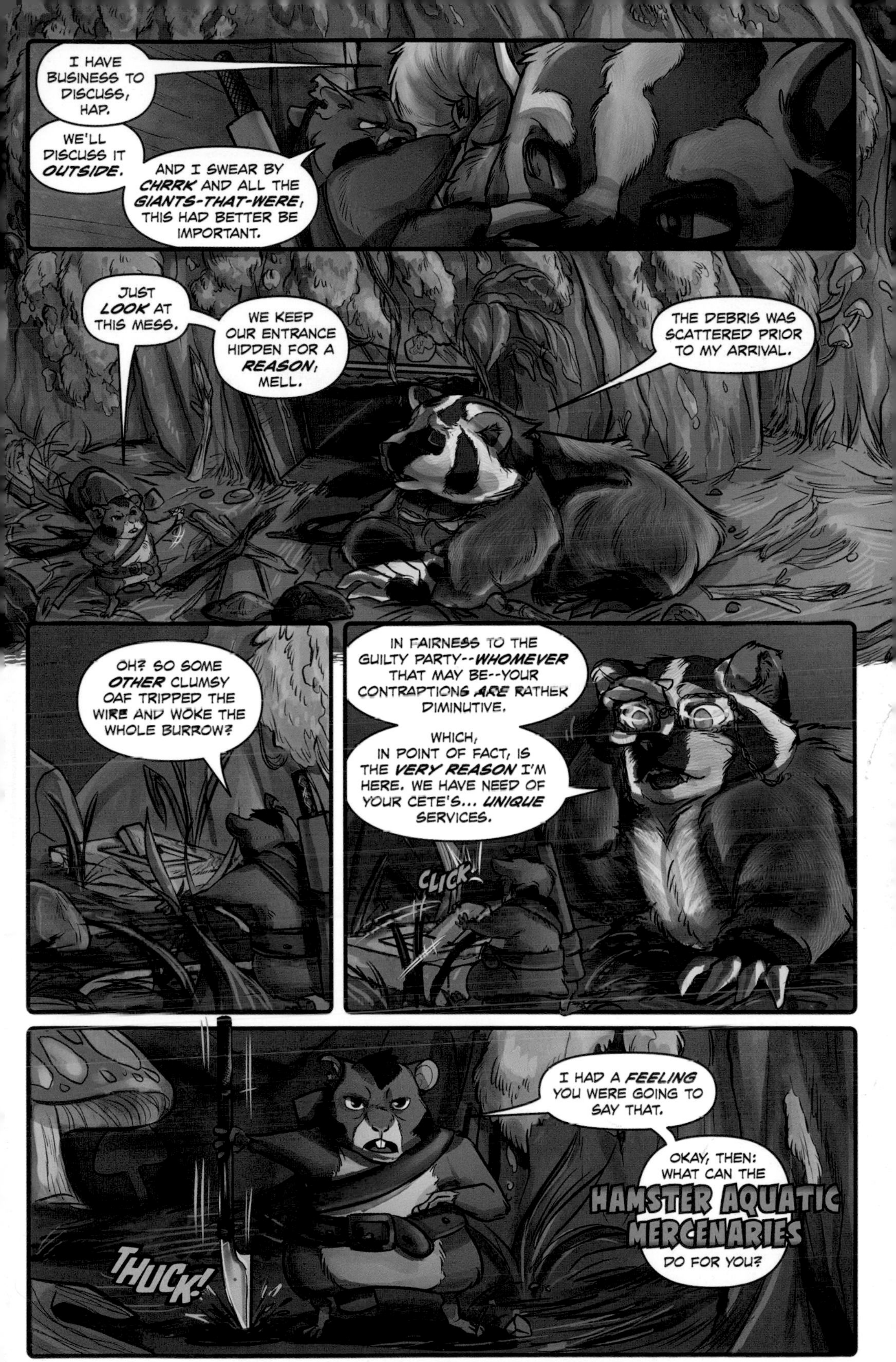

I HAVE BUSINESS TO DISCUSS, HAP.
WE'LL DISCUSS IT *OUTSIDE*.
AND I SWEAR BY *CHRRK* AND ALL THE *GIANTS-THAT-WERE*, THIS HAD BETTER BE IMPORTANT.
JUST *LOOK* AT THIS MESS.
WE KEEP OUR ENTRANCE HIDDEN FOR A *REASON*, MELL.
THE DEBRIS WAS SCATTERED PRIOR TO MY ARRIVAL.
OH? SO SOME *OTHER* CLUMSY OAF TRIPPED THE WIRE AND WOKE THE WHOLE BURROW?
IN FAIRNESS TO THE GUILTY PARTY--*WHOMEVER* THAT MAY BE--YOUR CONTRAPTIONS *ARE* RATHER DIMINUTIVE.
WHICH, IN POINT OF FACT, IS THE *VERY REASON* I'M HERE. WE HAVE NEED OF YOUR CETE'S... *UNIQUE* SERVICES.
CLICK
I HAD A *FEELING* YOU WERE GOING TO SAY THAT.
OKAY, THEN: WHAT CAN THE HAMSTER AQUATIC MERCENARIES DO FOR YOU?
THUCK!

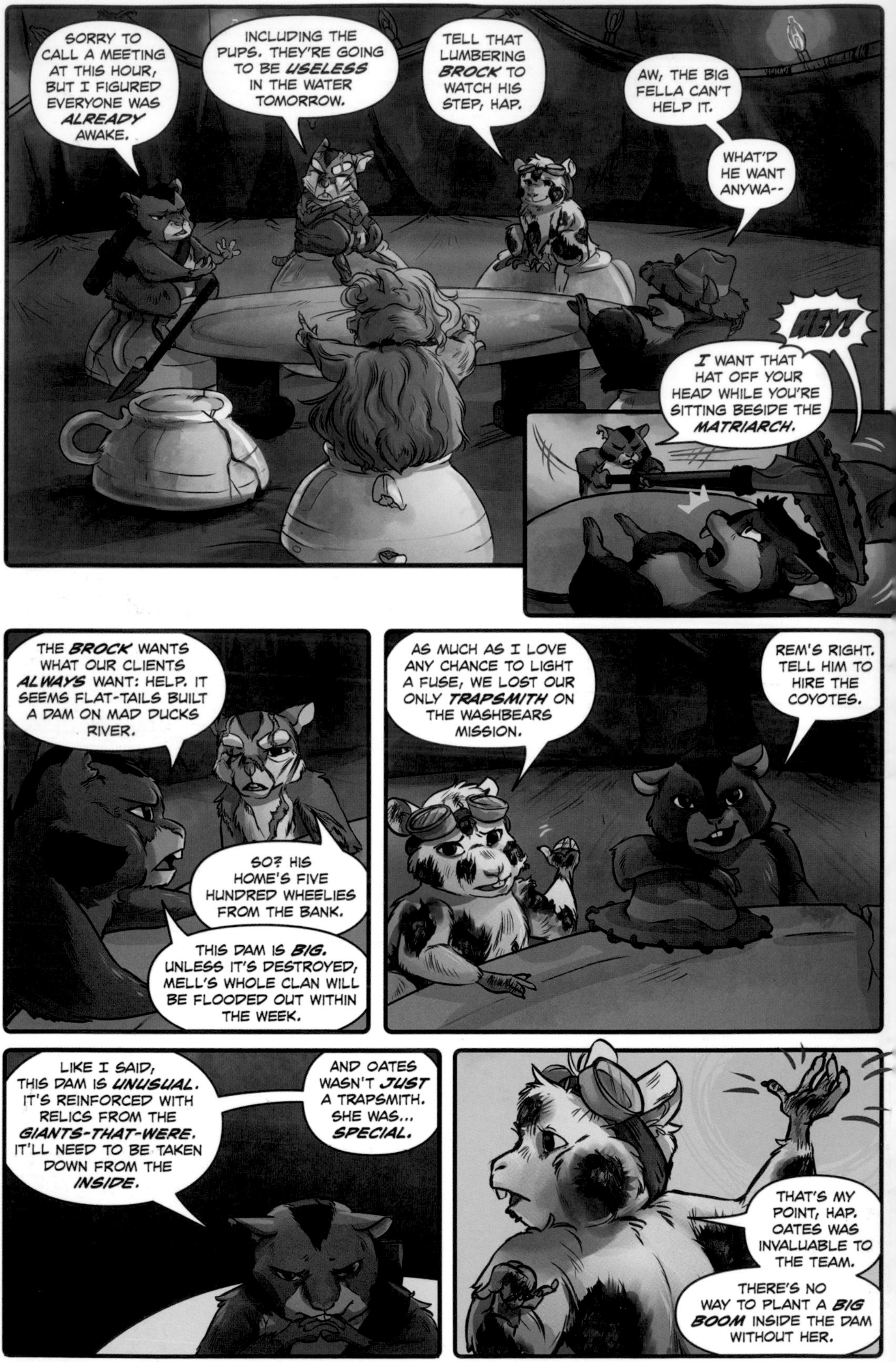
SORRY TO CALL A MEETING AT THIS HOUR, BUT I FIGURED EVERYONE WAS ALREADY AWAKE.
INCLUDING THE PUPS. THEY'RE GOING TO BE USELESS IN THE WATER TOMORROW.
TELL THAT LUMBERING BROCK TO WATCH HIS STEP, HAP.
AW, THE BIG FELLA CAN'T HELP IT.
WHAT'D HE WANT ANYWA--
HEY!
I WANT THAT HAT OFF YOUR HEAD WHILE YOU'RE SITTING BESIDE THE MATRIARCH.
THE BROCK WANTS WHAT OUR CLIENTS ALWAYS WANT: HELP. IT SEEMS FLAT-TAILS BUILT A DAM ON MAD DUCKS RIVER.
SO? HIS HOME'S FIVE HUNDRED WHEELIES FROM THE BANK.
THIS DAM IS BIG. UNLESS IT'S DESTROYED, MELL'S WHOLE CLAN WILL BE FLOODED OUT WITHIN THE WEEK.
AS MUCH AS I LOVE ANY CHANCE TO LIGHT A FUSE, WE LOST OUR ONLY TRAPSMITH ON THE WASHBEARS MISSION.
REM'S RIGHT. TELL HIM TO HIRE THE COYOTES.
LIKE I SAID, THIS DAM IS UNUSUAL. IT'S REINFORCED WITH RELICS FROM THE GIANTS-THAT-WERE. IT'LL NEED TO BE TAKEN DOWN FROM THE INSIDE.
AND OATES WASN'T JUST A TRAPSMITH. SHE WAS... SPECIAL.
THAT'S MY POINT, HAP. OATES WAS INVALUABLE TO THE TEAM.
THERE'S NO WAY TO PLANT A BIG BOOM INSIDE THE DAM WITHOUT HER.

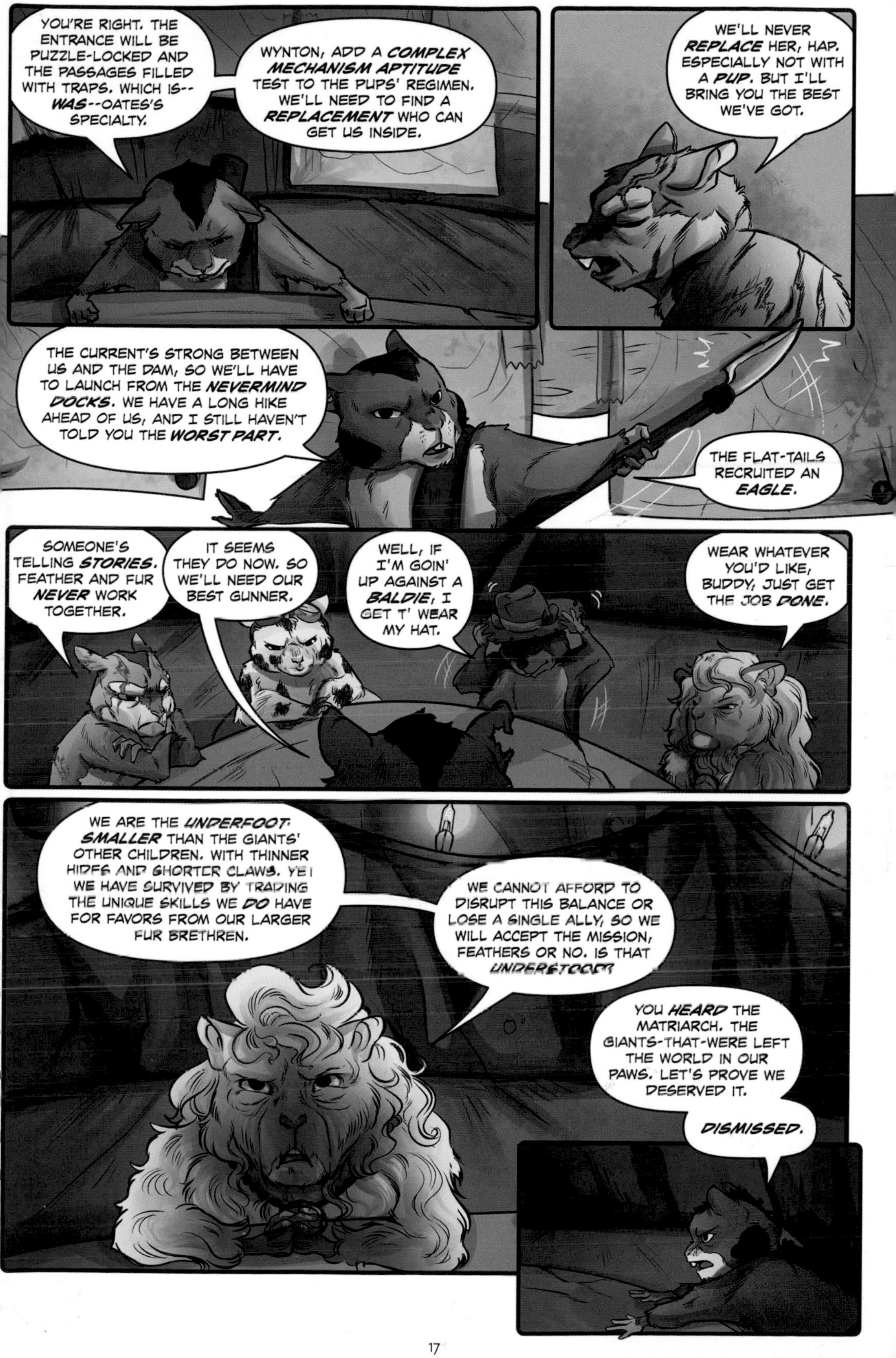

YOU'RE RIGHT. THE ENTRANCE WILL BE PUZZLE-LOCKED AND THE PASSAGES FILLED WITH TRAPS. WHICH IS--*WAS*--OATES'S SPECIALTY.
WYNTON, ADD A *COMPLEX MECHANISM APTITUDE* TEST TO THE PUPS' REGIMEN. WE'LL NEED TO FIND A *REPLACEMENT* WHO CAN GET US INSIDE.
WE'LL NEVER *REPLACE* HER, HAP. ESPECIALLY NOT WITH A *PUP*. BUT I'LL BRING YOU THE BEST WE'VE GOT.
THE CURRENT'S STRONG BETWEEN US AND THE DAM, SO WE'LL HAVE TO LAUNCH FROM THE *NEVERMIND DOCKS*. WE HAVE A LONG HIKE AHEAD OF US, AND I STILL HAVEN'T TOLD YOU THE *WORST PART*.
THE FLAT-TAILS RECRUITED AN *EAGLE*.
SOMEONE'S TELLING *STORIES*. FEATHER AND FUR *NEVER* WORK TOGETHER.
IT SEEMS THEY DO NOW. SO WE'LL NEED OUR BEST GUNNER.
WELL, IF I'M GOIN' UP AGAINST A *BALDIE*, I GET T' WEAR MY HAT.
WEAR WHATEVER YOU'D LIKE, BUDDY, JUST GET THE JOB *DONE*.
WE ARE THE *UNDERFOOT*: *SMALLER* THAN THE GIANTS' OTHER CHILDREN. WITH THINNER HIDES AND SHORTER CLAWS. YET WE HAVE SURVIVED BY TRADING THE UNIQUE SKILLS WE *DO* HAVE FOR FAVORS FROM OUR LARGER FUR BRETHREN.
WE CANNOT AFFORD TO DISRUPT THIS BALANCE OR LOSE A SINGLE ALLY, SO WE WILL ACCEPT THE MISSION, FEATHERS OR NO. IS THAT *UNDERSTOOD*?
YOU *HEARD* THE MATRIARCH. THE GIANTS-THAT-WERE LEFT THE WORLD IN OUR PAWS. LET'S PROVE WE DESERVED IT.
DISMISSED.

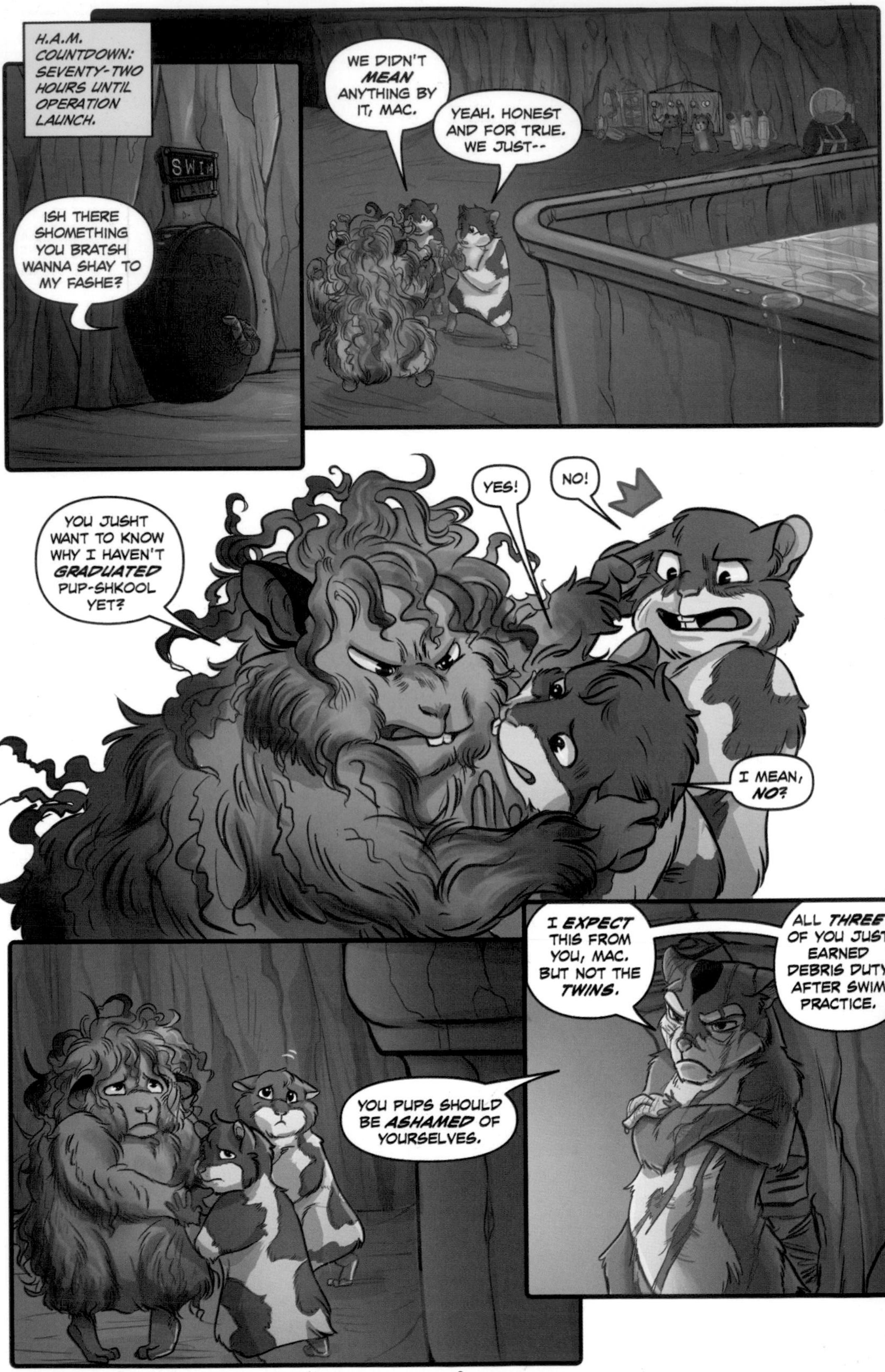
H.A.M. COUNTDOWN: SEVENTY-TWO HOURS UNTIL OPERATION LAUNCH.
SWIM
ISH THERE SHOMETHING YOU BRATSH WANNA SHAY TO MY FASHE?
WE DIDN'T *MEAN* ANYTHING BY IT, MAC.
YEAH. HONEST AND FOR TRUE. WE JUST--
YOU JUSHT WANT TO KNOW WHY I HAVEN'T *GRADUATED* PUP-SHKOOL YET?
YES!
NO!
I MEAN, *NO?*
I *EXPECT* THIS FROM YOU, MAC. BUT NOT THE *TWINS*.
ALL *THREE* OF YOU JUST EARNED DEBRIS DUTY AFTER SWIM PRACTICE.
YOU PUPS SHOULD BE *ASHAMED* OF YOURSELVES.

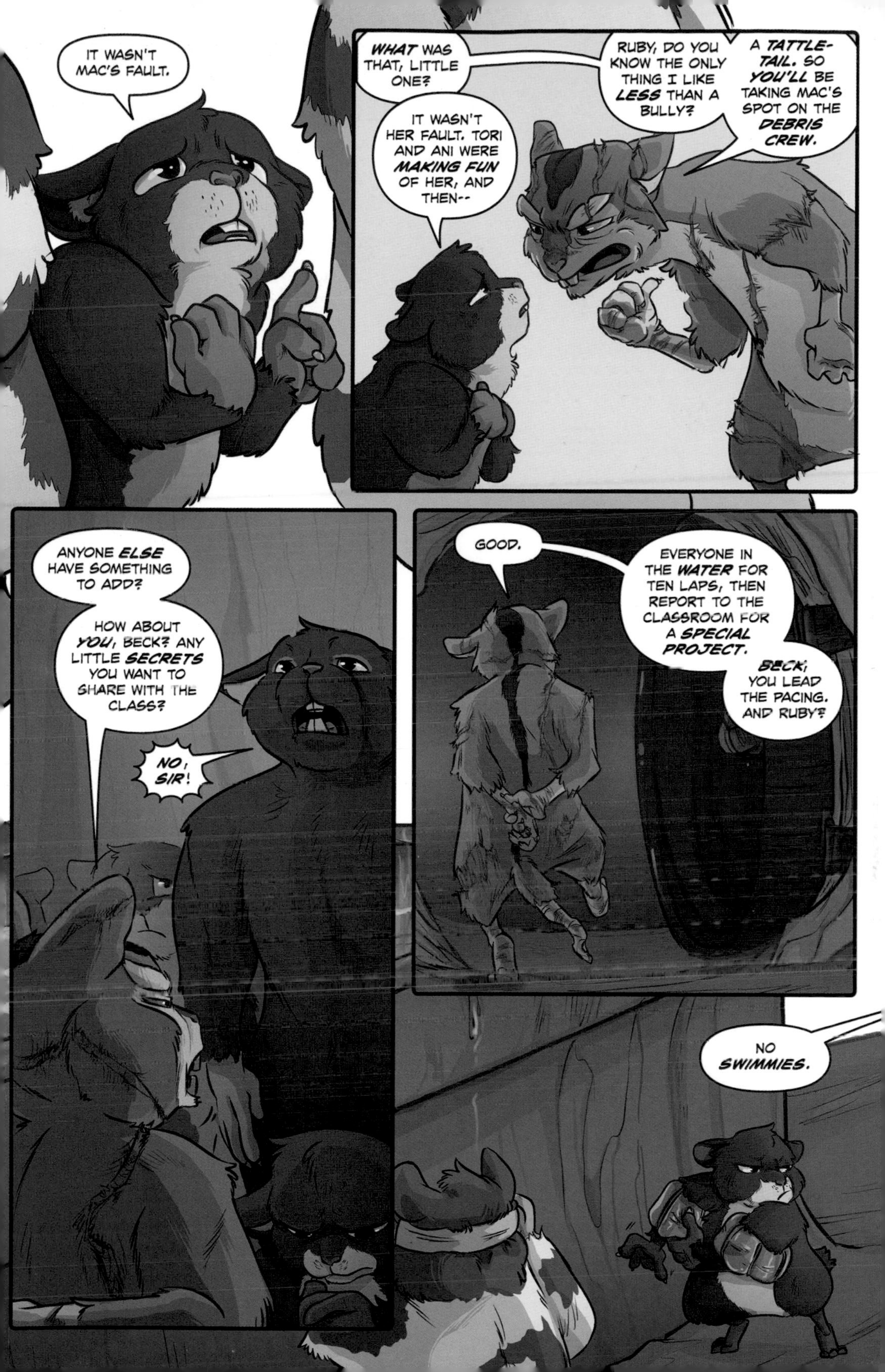
IT WASN'T MAC'S FAULT.
WHAT WAS THAT, LITTLE ONE?
IT WASN'T HER FAULT. TORI AND ANI WERE MAKING FUN OF HER, AND THEN--
RUBY, DO YOU KNOW THE ONLY THING I LIKE LESS THAN A BULLY?
A TATTLE-TAIL. SO YOU'LL BE TAKING MAC'S SPOT ON THE DEBRIS CREW.
ANYONE ELSE HAVE SOMETHING TO ADD?
HOW ABOUT YOU, BECK? ANY LITTLE SECRETS YOU WANT TO SHARE WITH THE CLASS?
NO, SIR!
GOOD.
EVERYONE IN THE WATER FOR TEN LAPS, THEN REPORT TO THE CLASSROOM FOR A SPECIAL PROJECT.
BECK, YOU LEAD THE PACING. AND RUBY?
NO SWIMMIES.

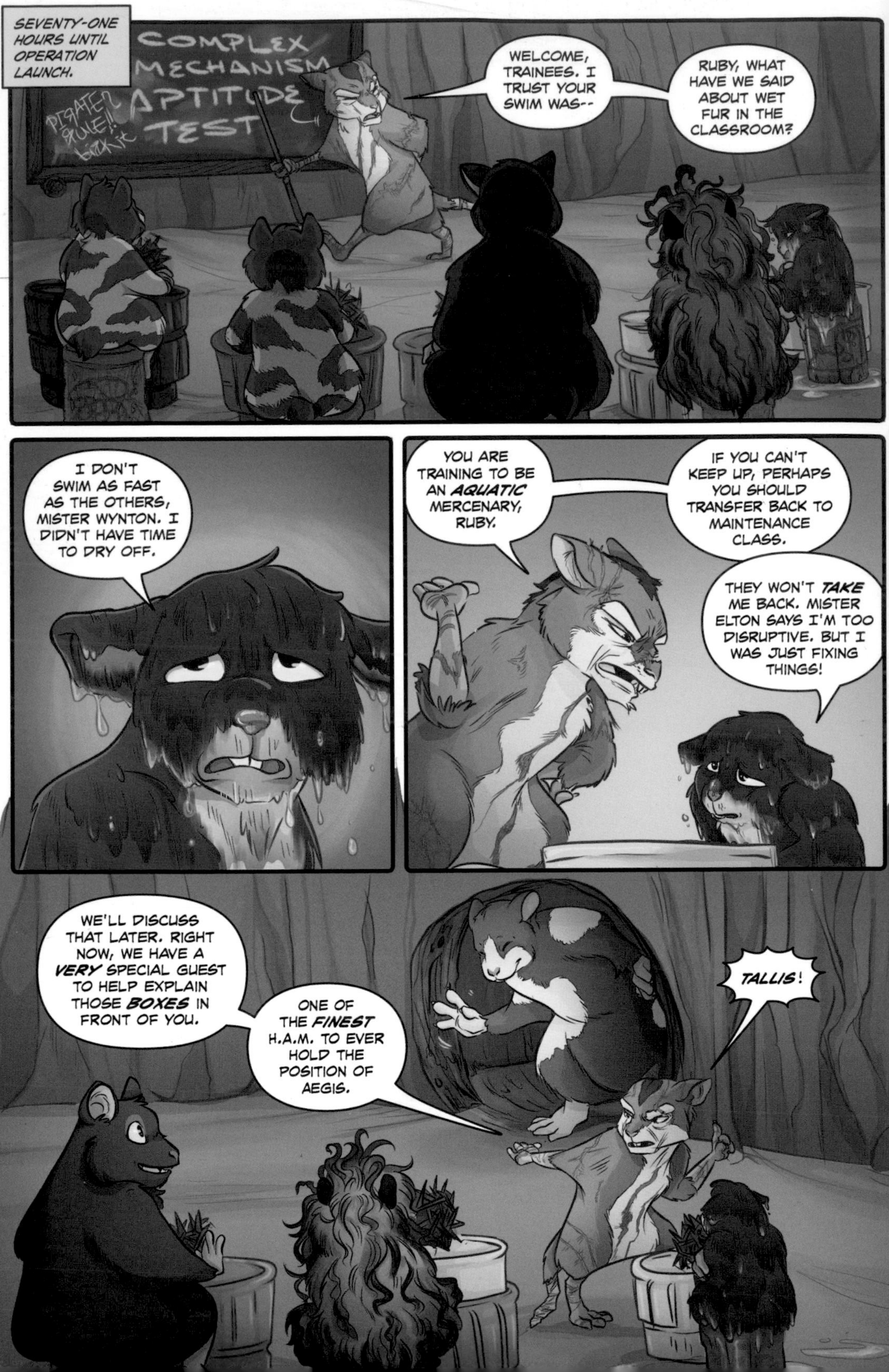
SEVENTY-ONE HOURS UNTIL OPERATION LAUNCH.
COMPLEX MECHANISM APTITUDE TEST
WELCOME, TRAINEES. I TRUST YOUR SWIM WAS--
RUBY, WHAT HAVE WE SAID ABOUT WET FUR IN THE CLASSROOM?
I DON'T SWIM AS FAST AS THE OTHERS, MISTER WYNTON. I DIDN'T HAVE TIME TO DRY OFF.
YOU ARE TRAINING TO BE AN AQUATIC MERCENARY, RUBY.
IF YOU CAN'T KEEP UP, PERHAPS YOU SHOULD TRANSFER BACK TO MAINTENANCE CLASS.
THEY WON'T TAKE ME BACK. MISTER ELTON SAYS I'M TOO DISRUPTIVE. BUT I WAS JUST FIXING THINGS!
WE'LL DISCUSS THAT LATER. RIGHT NOW, WE HAVE A VERY SPECIAL GUEST TO HELP EXPLAIN THOSE BOXES IN FRONT OF YOU.
ONE OF THE FINEST H.A.M. TO EVER HOLD THE POSITION OF AEGIS.
TALLIS!

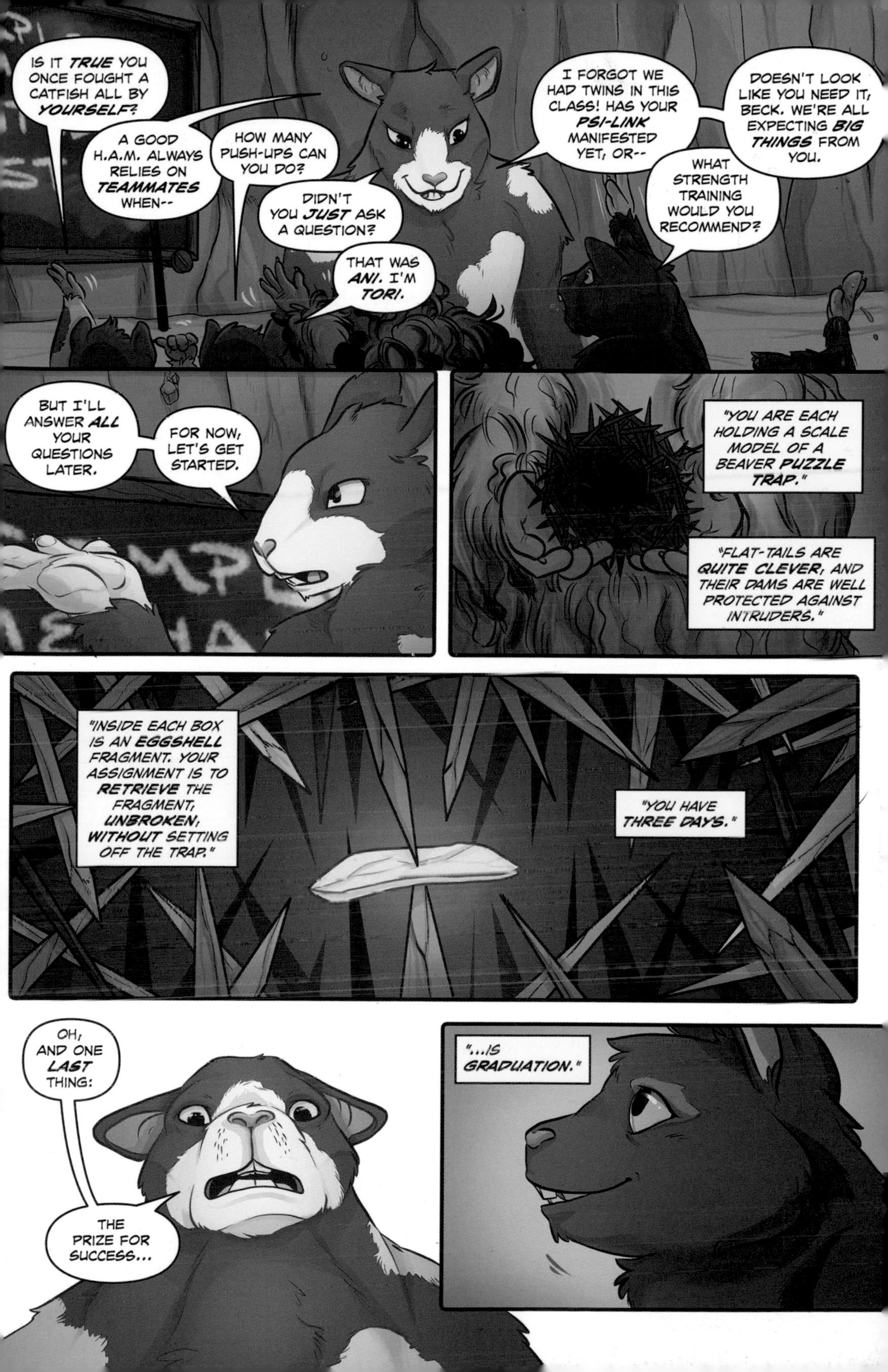
IS IT TRUE YOU ONCE FOUGHT A CATFISH ALL BY YOURSELF?
A GOOD H.A.M. ALWAYS RELIES ON TEAMMATES WHEN--
HOW MANY PUSH-UPS CAN YOU DO?
DIDN'T YOU JUST ASK A QUESTION?
THAT WAS ANI. I'M TORI.
I FORGOT WE HAD TWINS IN THIS CLASS! HAS YOUR PSI-LINK MANIFESTED YET, OR--
DOESN'T LOOK LIKE YOU NEED IT, BECK. WE'RE ALL EXPECTING BIG THINGS FROM YOU.
WHAT STRENGTH TRAINING WOULD YOU RECOMMEND?
BUT I'LL ANSWER ALL YOUR QUESTIONS LATER.
FOR NOW, LET'S GET STARTED.
"YOU ARE EACH HOLDING A SCALE MODEL OF A BEAVER PUZZLE TRAP."
"FLAT-TAILS ARE QUITE CLEVER, AND THEIR DAMS ARE WELL PROTECTED AGAINST INTRUDERS."
"INSIDE EACH BOX IS AN EGGSHELL FRAGMENT. YOUR ASSIGNMENT IS TO RETRIEVE THE FRAGMENT, UNBROKEN, WITHOUT SETTING OFF THE TRAP."
"YOU HAVE THREE DAYS."
OH, AND ONE LAST THING:
THE PRIZE FOR SUCCESS...
"...IS GRADUATION."

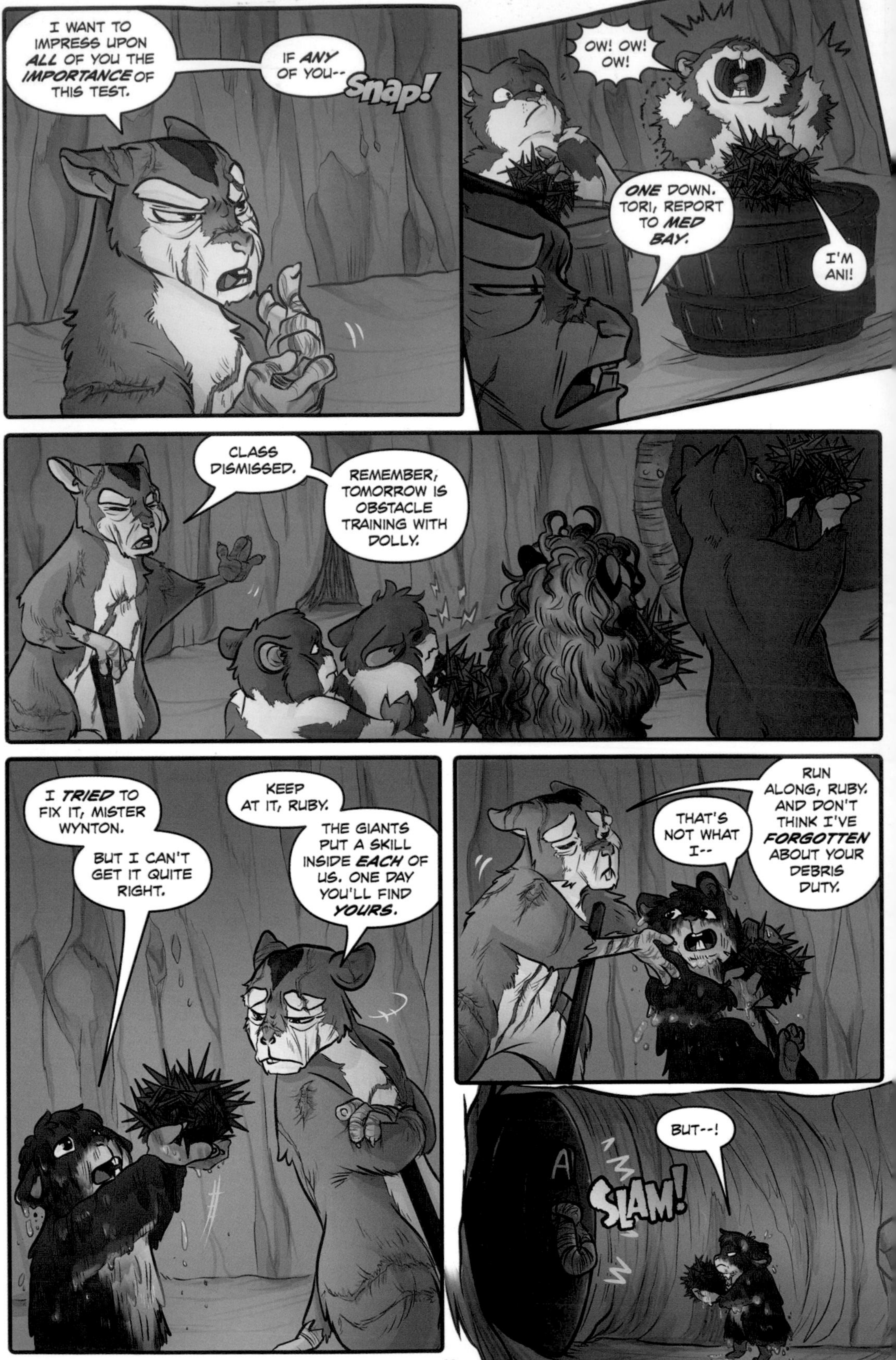

I WANT TO IMPRESS UPON ALL OF YOU THE IMPORTANCE OF THIS TEST.
IF ANY OF YOU--
Snap!
OW! OW! OW!
ONE DOWN. TORI, REPORT TO MED BAY.
I'M ANI!
CLASS DISMISSED.
REMEMBER, TOMORROW IS OBSTACLE TRAINING WITH DOLLY.
I TRIED TO FIX IT, MISTER WYNTON.
BUT I CAN'T GET IT QUITE RIGHT.
KEEP AT IT, RUBY.
THE GIANTS PUT A SKILL INSIDE EACH OF US. ONE DAY YOU'LL FIND YOURS.
THAT'S NOT WHAT I--
RUN ALONG, RUBY. AND DON'T THINK I'VE FORGOTTEN ABOUT YOUR DEBRIS DUTY.
BUT--!
SLAM!

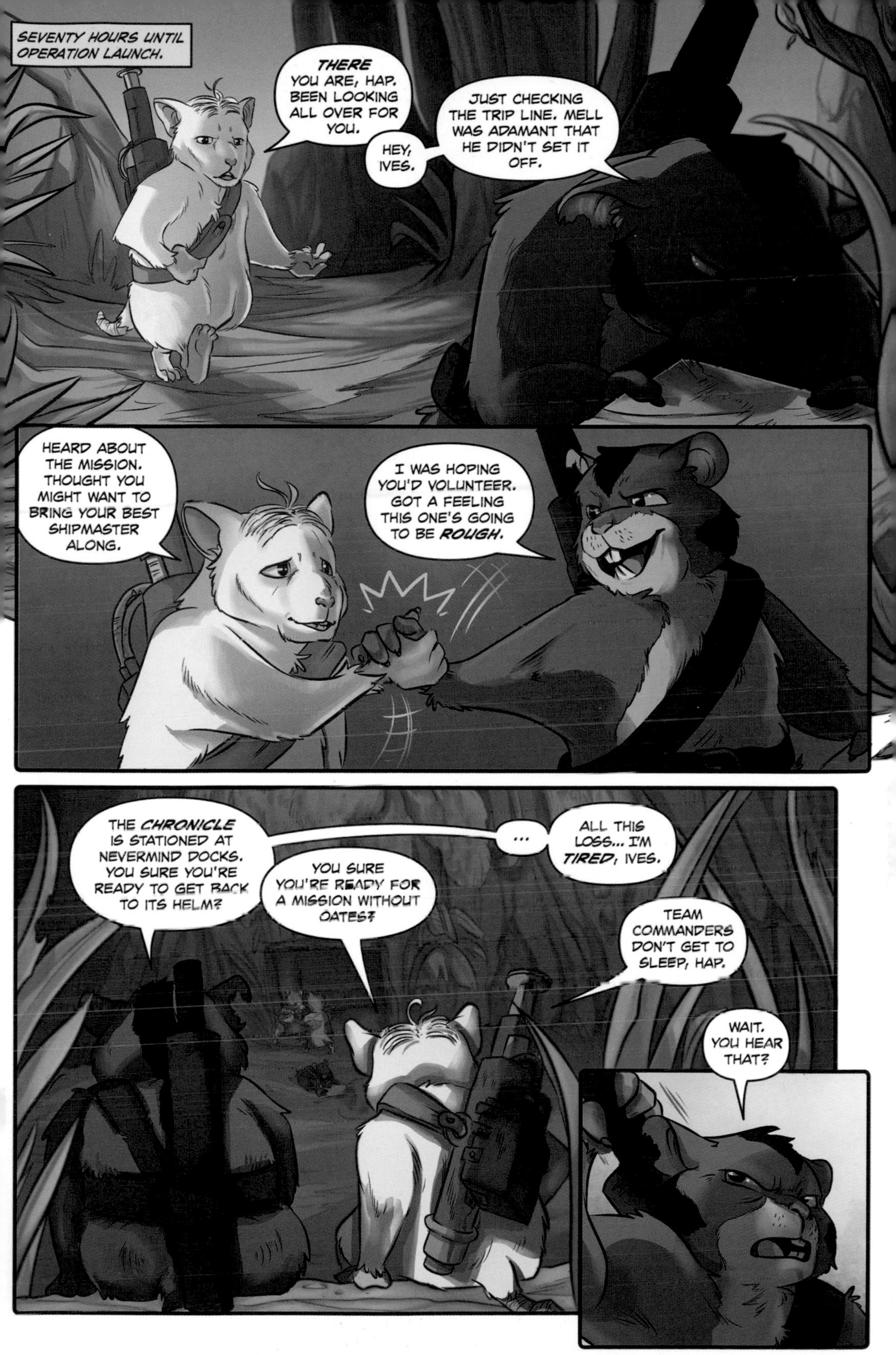
SEVENTY HOURS UNTIL OPERATION LAUNCH.
THERE YOU ARE, HAP. BEEN LOOKING ALL OVER FOR YOU.
HEY, IVES.
JUST CHECKING THE TRIP LINE. MELL WAS ADAMANT THAT HE DIDN'T SET IT OFF.
HEARD ABOUT THE MISSION. THOUGHT YOU MIGHT WANT TO BRING YOUR BEST SHIPMASTER ALONG.
I WAS HOPING YOU'D VOLUNTEER. GOT A FEELING THIS ONE'S GOING TO BE ROUGH.
THE CHRONICLE IS STATIONED AT NEVERMIND DOCKS. YOU SURE YOU'RE READY TO GET BACK TO ITS HELM?
...
ALL THIS LOSS... I'M TIRED, IVES.
YOU SURE YOU'RE READY FOR A MISSION WITHOUT OATES?
TEAM COMMANDERS DON'T GET TO SLEEP, HAP.
WAIT. YOU HEAR THAT?

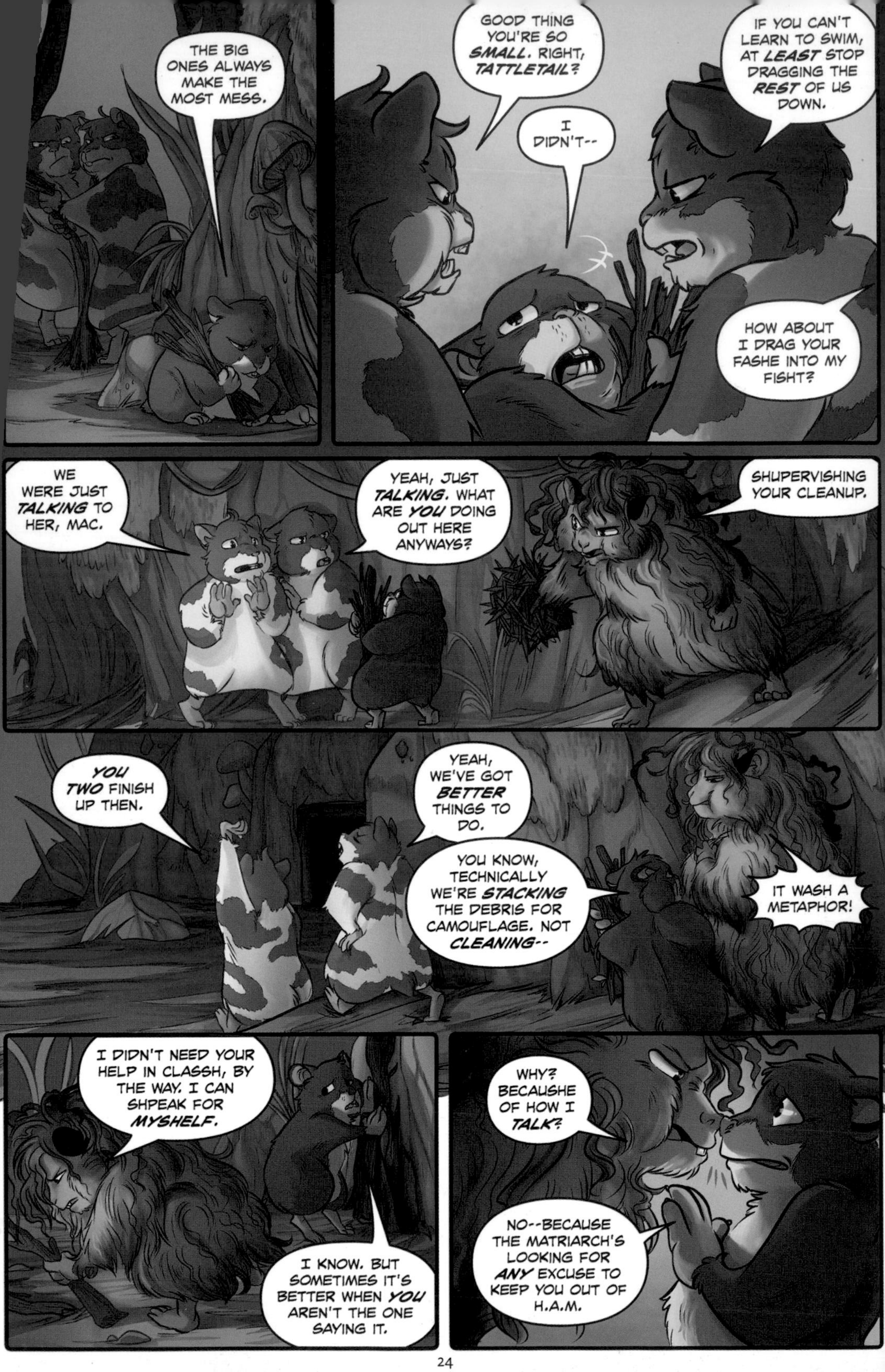
THE BIG ONES ALWAYS MAKE THE MOST MESS.
GOOD THING YOU'RE SO SMALL. RIGHT, TATTLETAIL?
I DIDN'T--
IF YOU CAN'T LEARN TO SWIM, AT LEAST STOP DRAGGING THE REST OF US DOWN.
HOW ABOUT I DRAG YOUR FASHE INTO MY FISHT?
WE WERE JUST TALKING TO HER, MAC.
YEAH, JUST TALKING. WHAT ARE YOU DOING OUT HERE ANYWAYS?
SHUPERVISHING YOUR CLEANUP.
YOU TWO FINISH UP THEN.
YEAH, WE'VE GOT BETTER THINGS TO DO.
YOU KNOW, TECHNICALLY WE'RE STACKING THE DEBRIS FOR CAMOUFLAGE. NOT CLEANING--
IT WASH A METAPHOR!
I DIDN'T NEED YOUR HELP IN CLASSH, BY THE WAY. I CAN SHPEAK FOR MYSHELF.
I KNOW. BUT SOMETIMES IT'S BETTER WHEN YOU AREN'T THE ONE SAYING IT.
WHY? BECAUSHE OF HOW I TALK?
NO--BECAUSE THE MATRIARCH'S LOOKING FOR ANY EXCUSE TO KEEP YOU OUT OF H.A.M.

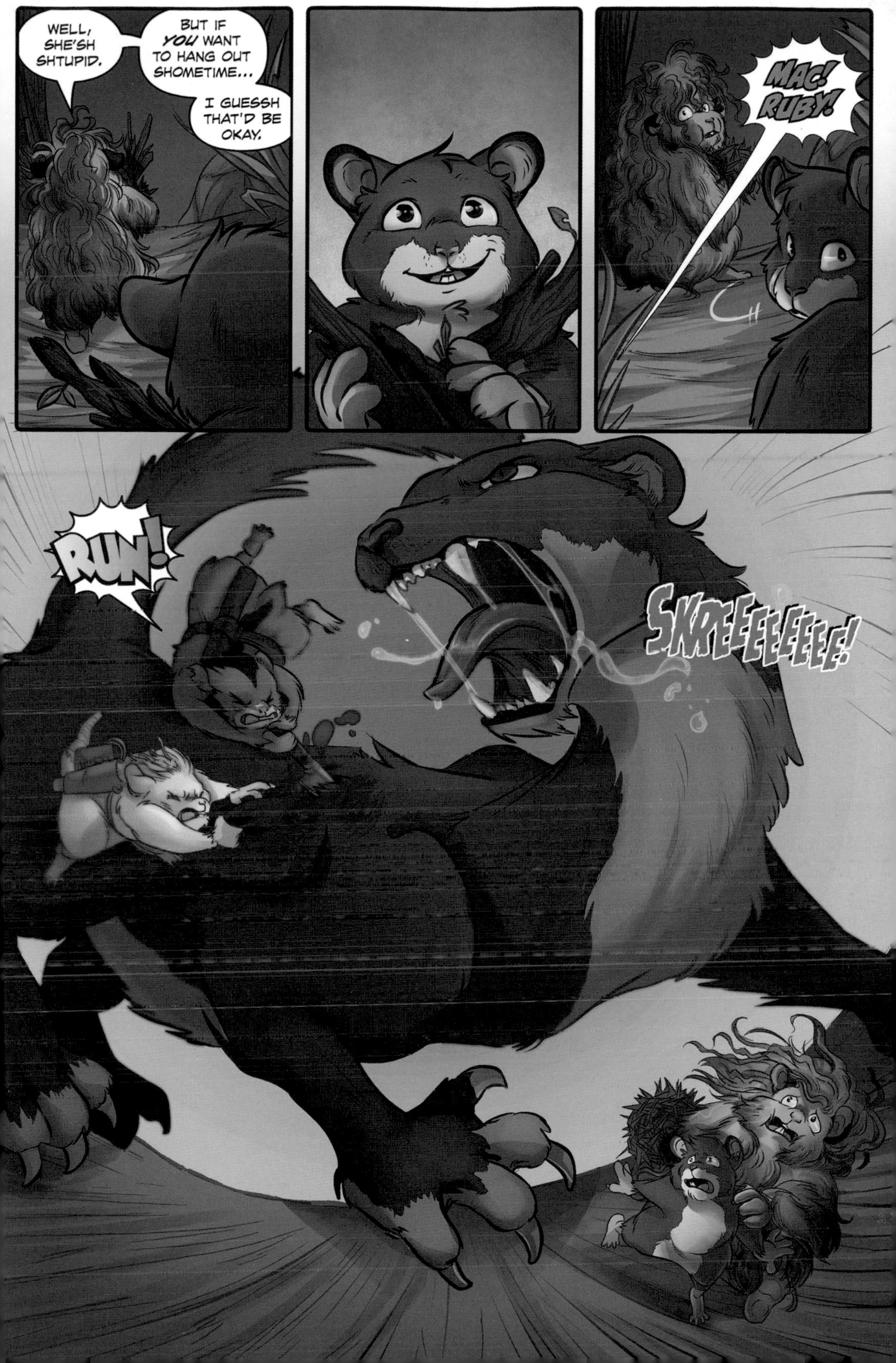
WELL, SHE'SH SHTUPID.
BUT IF *YOU* WANT TO HANG OUT SHOMETIME...
I GUESSH THAT'D BE OKAY.
MAC! RUBY!
RUN!
SKREEEEEEEEE!

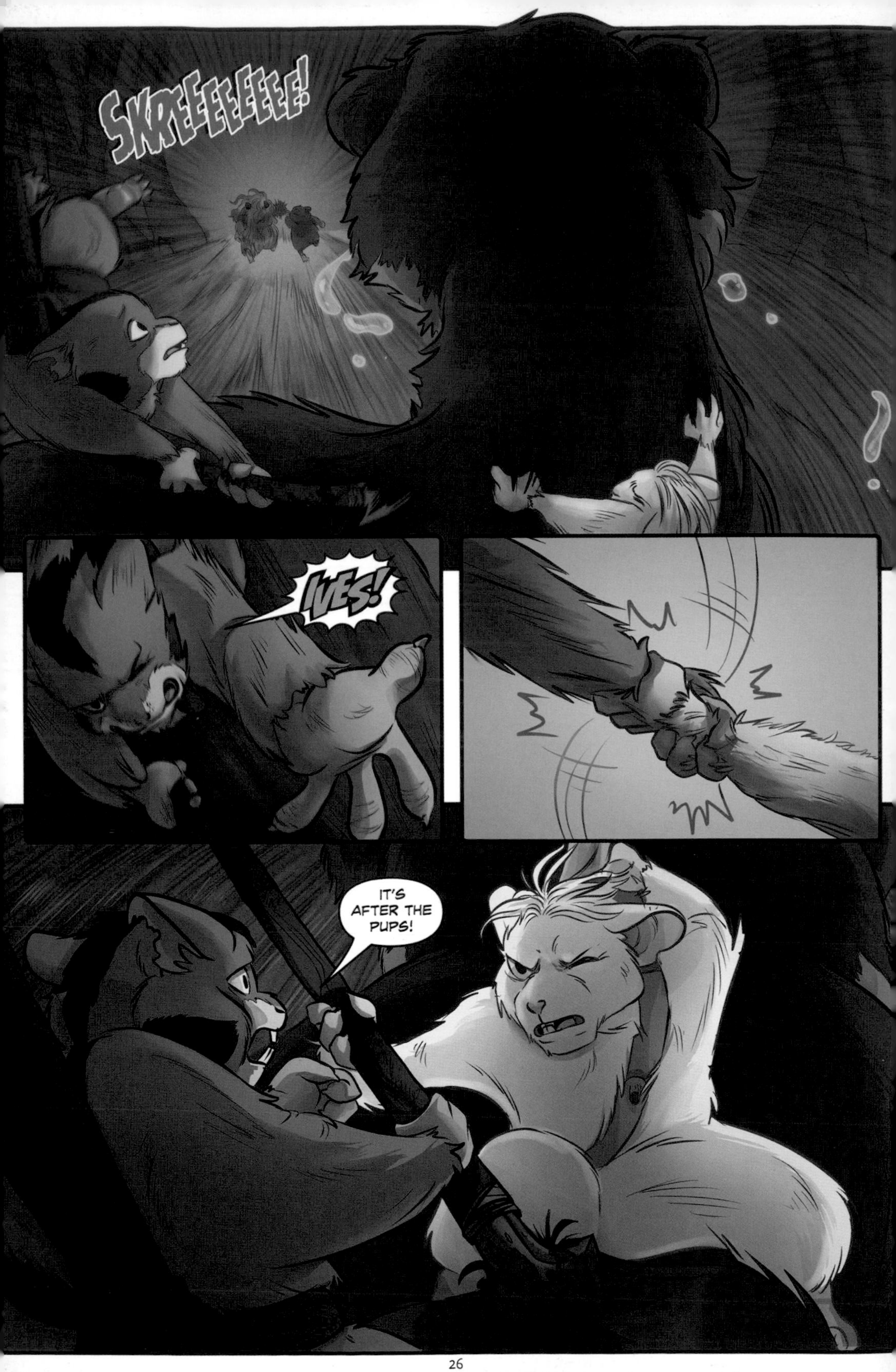
SKREEEEEEEE!
IVES!
IT'S AFTER THE PUPS!

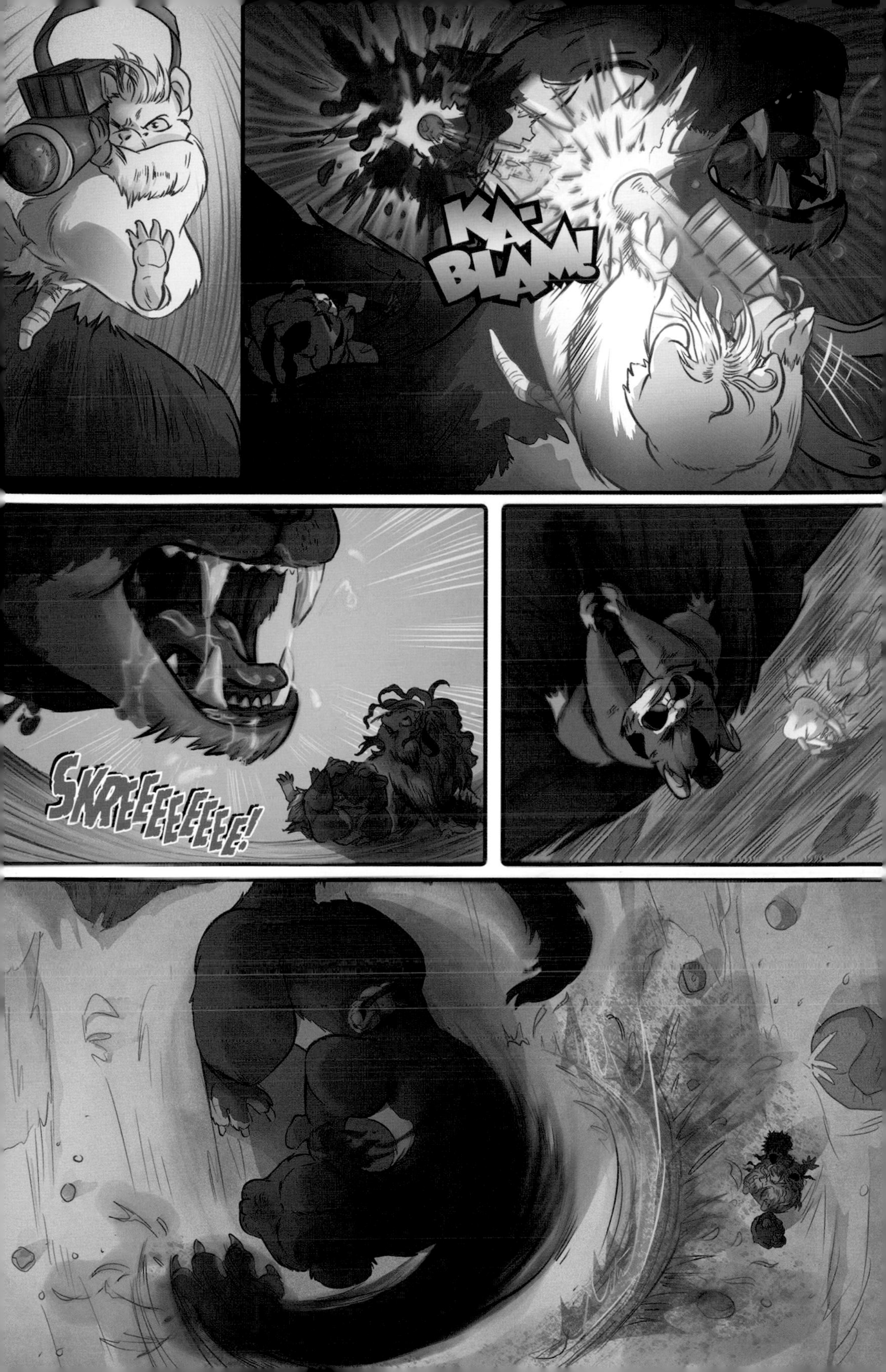
KA-BLAM!
SKREEEEEEEEEE!

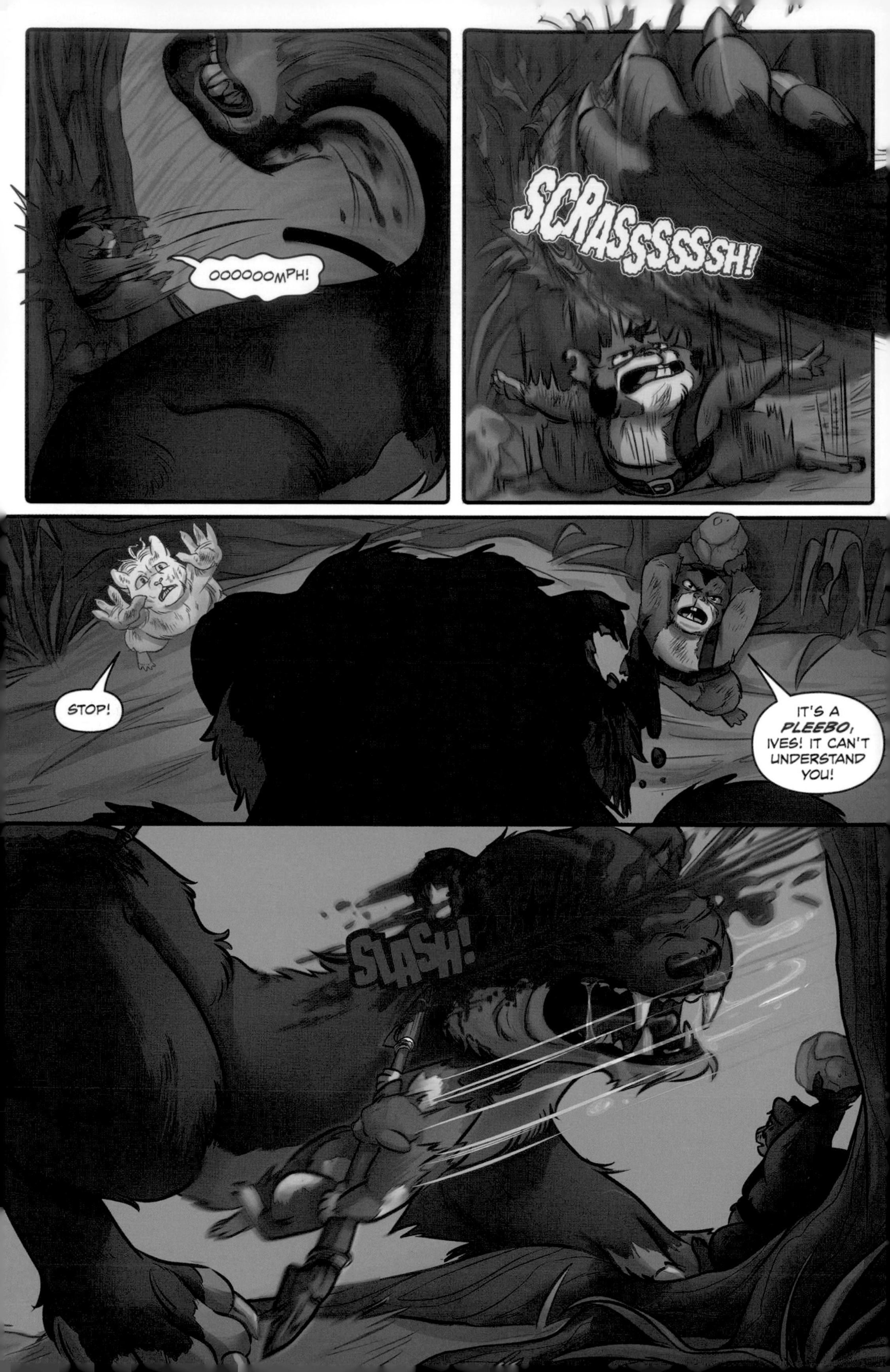
OOOOOOMPH!
SCRASSSSSSSH!
STOP!
IT'S A PLEEBO, IVES! IT CAN'T UNDERSTAND YOU!
SLASH!

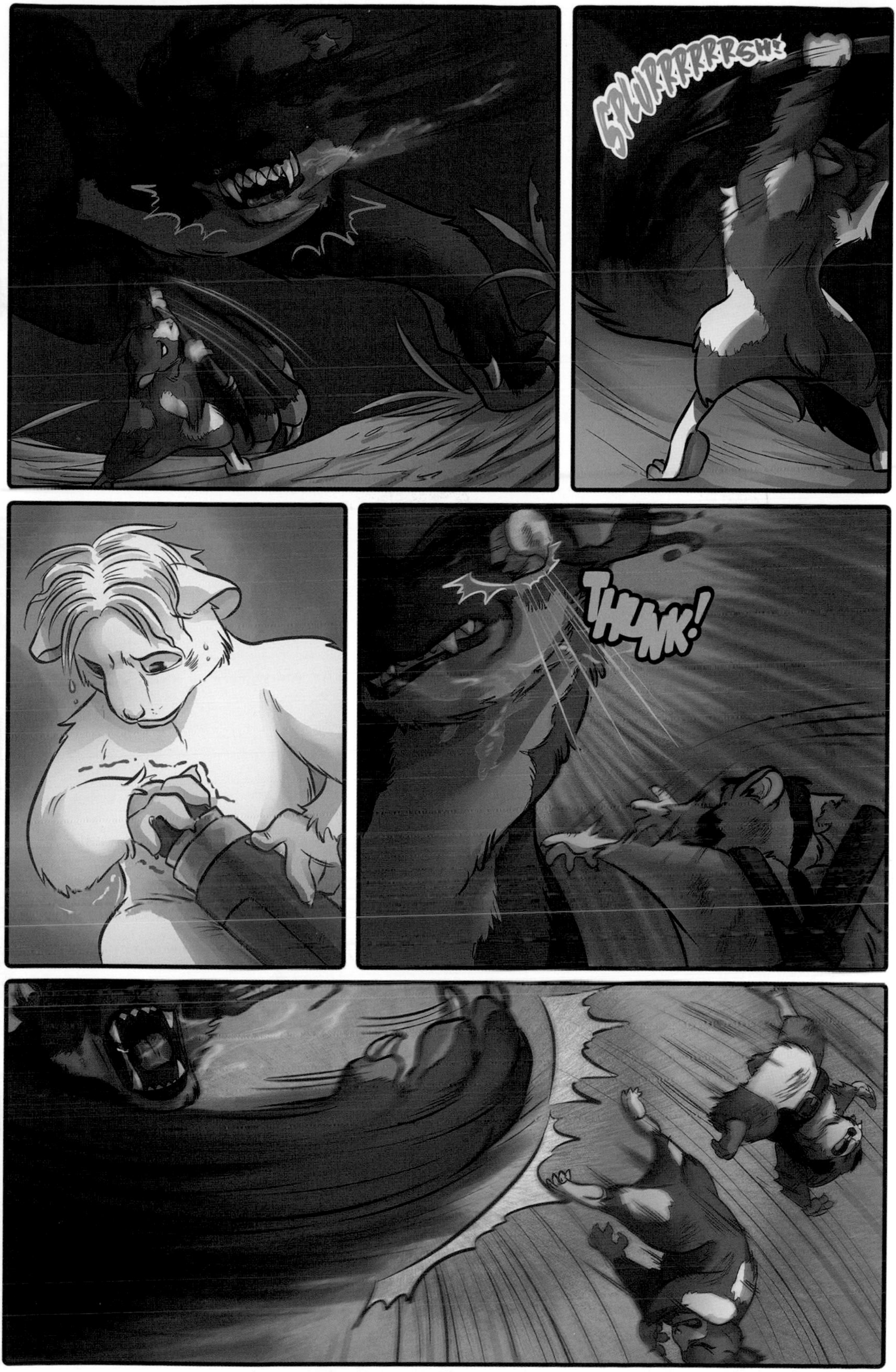
SPLURRRRRRSH!
THUNK!

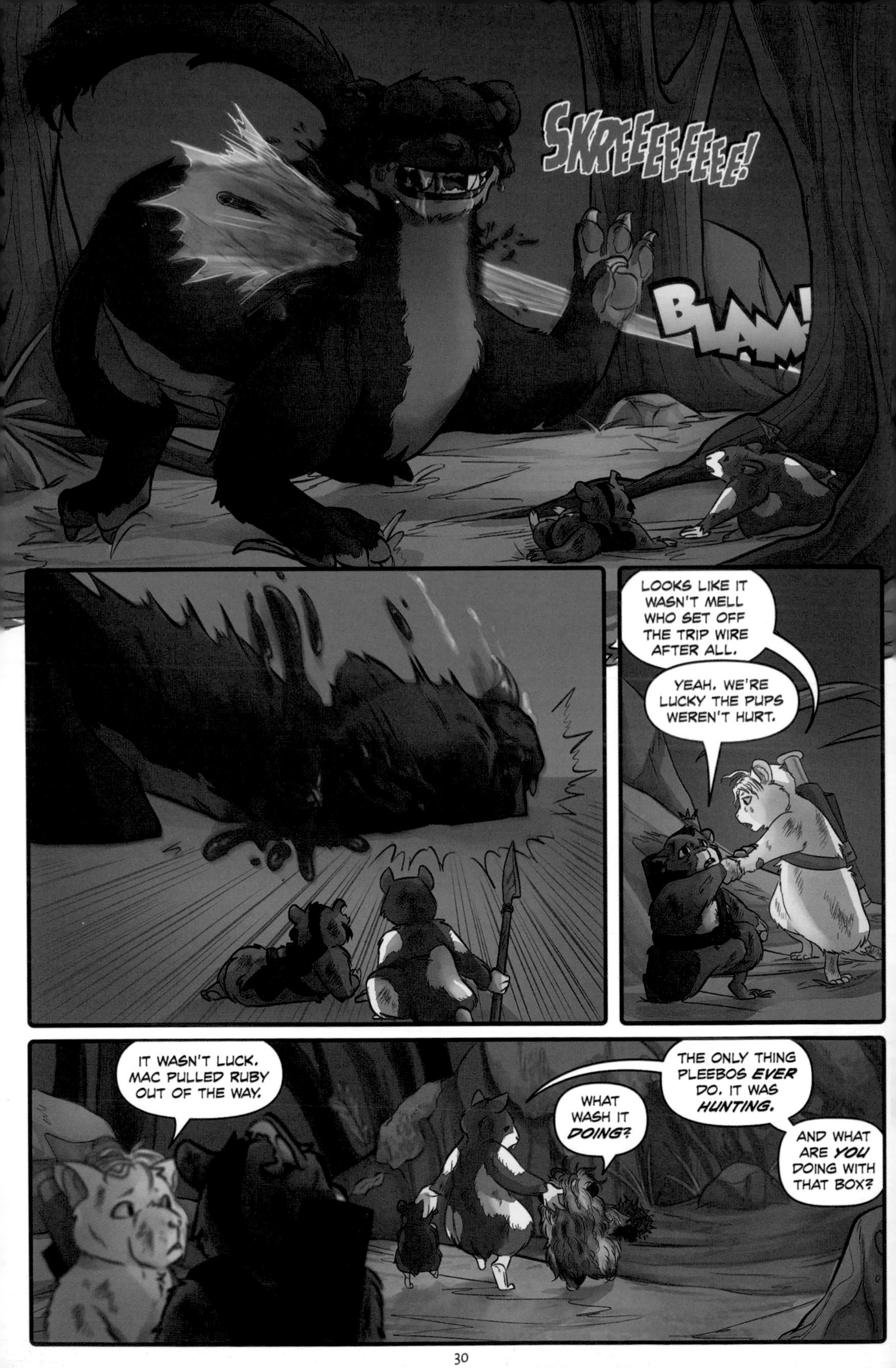
SKREEEEEEEE!
BLAM!
LOOKS LIKE IT WASN'T MELL WHO SET OFF THE TRIP WIRE AFTER ALL.
YEAH. WE'RE LUCKY THE PUPS WEREN'T HURT.
IT WASN'T LUCK. MAC PULLED RUBY OUT OF THE WAY.
WHAT WASH IT *DOING*?
THE ONLY THING PLEEBOS *EVER* DO. IT WAS *HUNTING*.
AND WHAT ARE *YOU* DOING WITH THAT BOX?

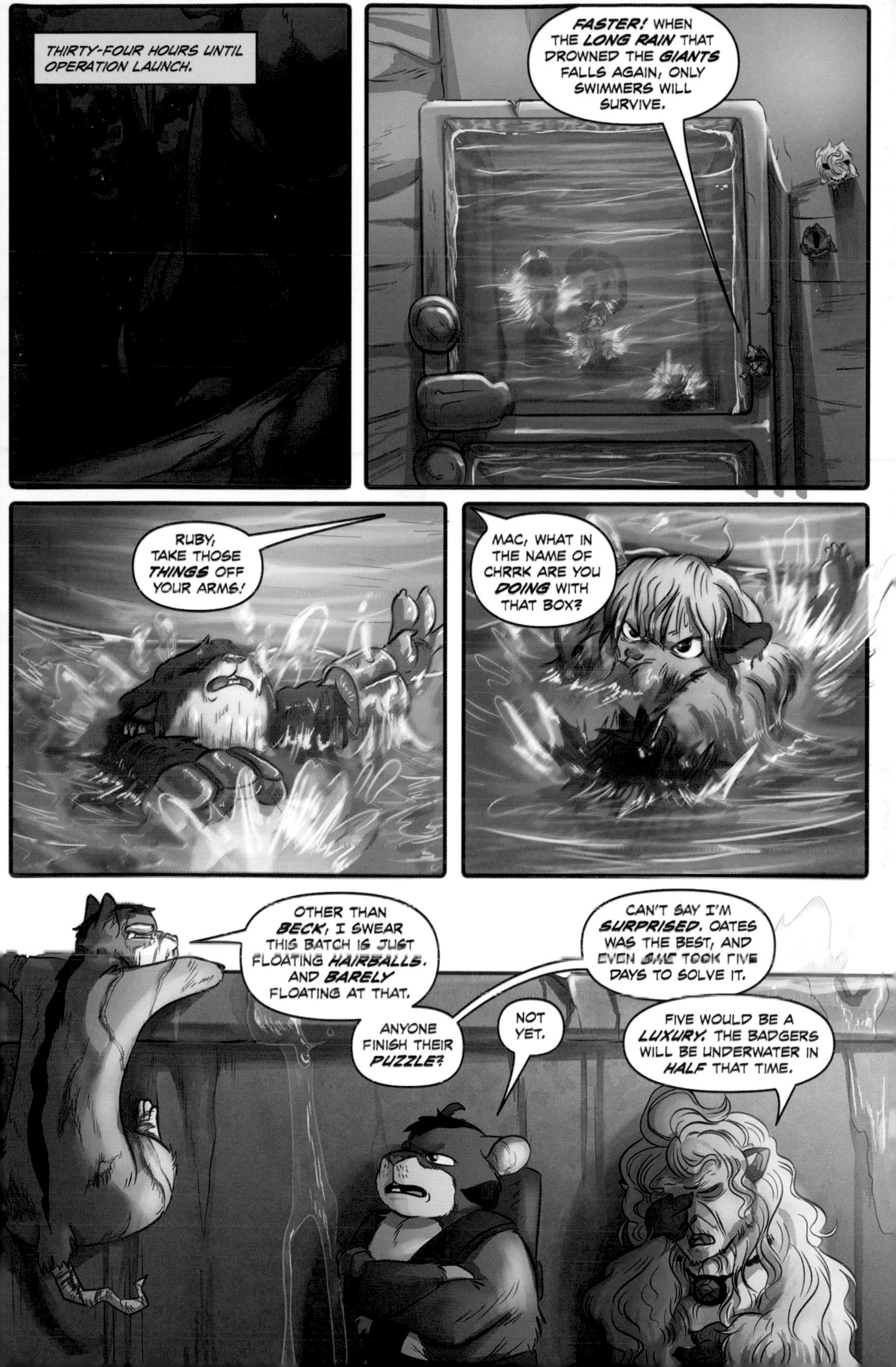
THIRTY-FOUR HOURS UNTIL OPERATION LAUNCH.
FASTER! WHEN THE LONG RAIN THAT DROWNED THE GIANTS FALLS AGAIN, ONLY SWIMMERS WILL SURVIVE.
RUBY, TAKE THOSE THINGS OFF YOUR ARMS!
MAC, WHAT IN THE NAME OF CHRRK ARE YOU DOING WITH THAT BOX?
OTHER THAN BECK, I SWEAR THIS BATCH IS JUST FLOATING HAIRBALLS. AND BARELY FLOATING AT THAT.
ANYONE FINISH THEIR PUZZLE?
NOT YET.
CAN'T SAY I'M SURPRISED. OATES WAS THE BEST, AND EVEN SHE TOOK FIVE DAYS TO SOLVE IT.
FIVE WOULD BE A LUXURY. THE BADGERS WILL BE UNDERWATER IN HALF THAT TIME.

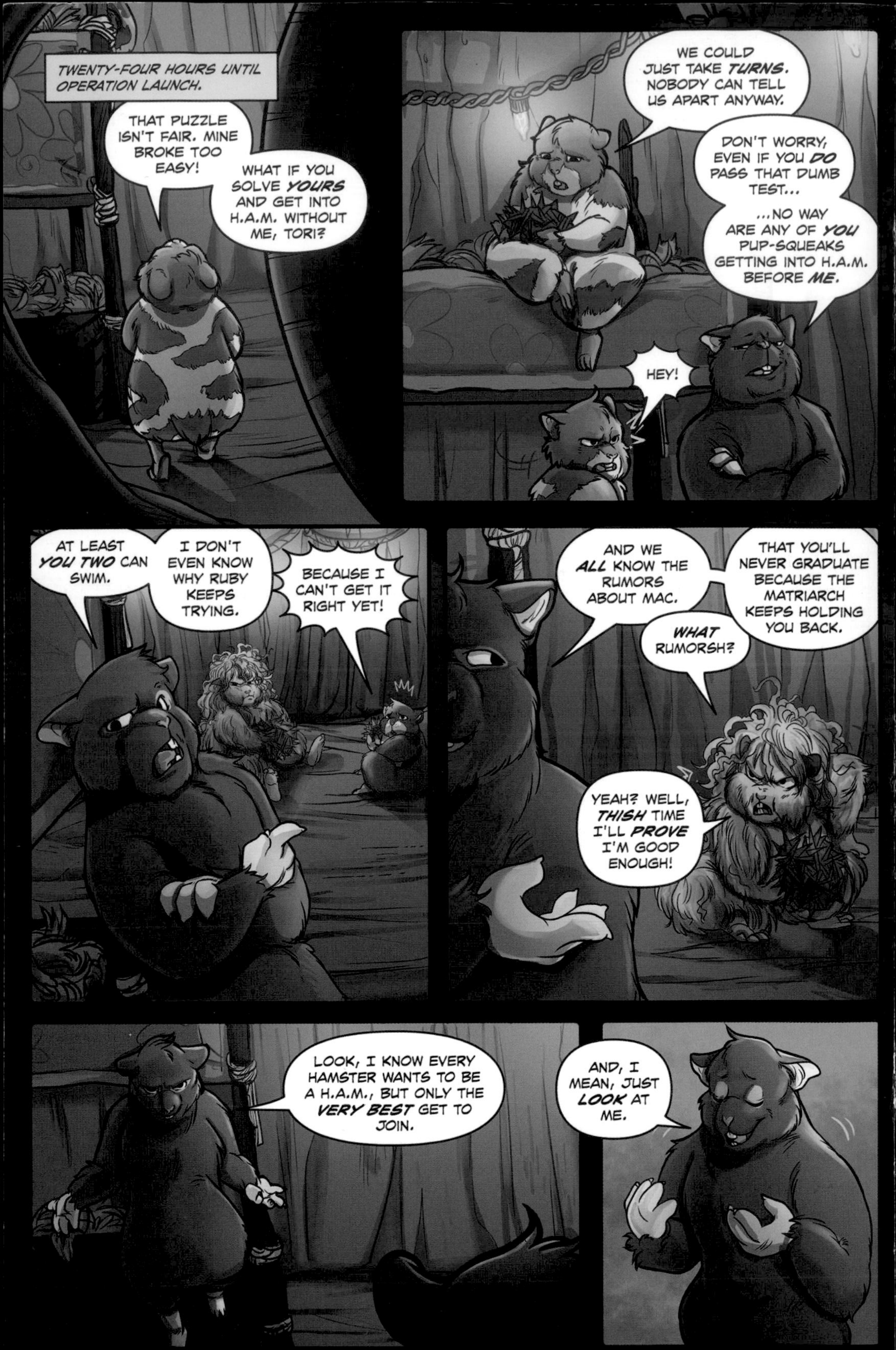
TWENTY-FOUR HOURS UNTIL OPERATION LAUNCH.
THAT PUZZLE ISN'T FAIR. MINE BROKE TOO EASY!
WHAT IF YOU SOLVE YOURS AND GET INTO H.A.M. WITHOUT ME, TORI?
WE COULD JUST TAKE TURNS. NOBODY CAN TELL US APART ANYWAY.
DON'T WORRY, EVEN IF YOU DO PASS THAT DUMB TEST...
...NO WAY ARE ANY OF YOU PUP-SQUEAKS GETTING INTO H.A.M. BEFORE ME.
HEY!
AT LEAST YOU TWO CAN SWIM.
I DON'T EVEN KNOW WHY RUBY KEEPS TRYING.
BECAUSE I CAN'T GET IT RIGHT YET!
AND WE ALL KNOW THE RUMORS ABOUT MAC.
THAT YOU'LL NEVER GRADUATE BECAUSE THE MATRIARCH KEEPS HOLDING YOU BACK.
WHAT RUMORSH?
YEAH? WELL, THISH TIME I'LL PROVE I'M GOOD ENOUGH!
LOOK, I KNOW EVERY HAMSTER WANTS TO BE A H.A.M., BUT ONLY THE VERY BEST GET TO JOIN.
AND, I MEAN, JUST LOOK AT ME.

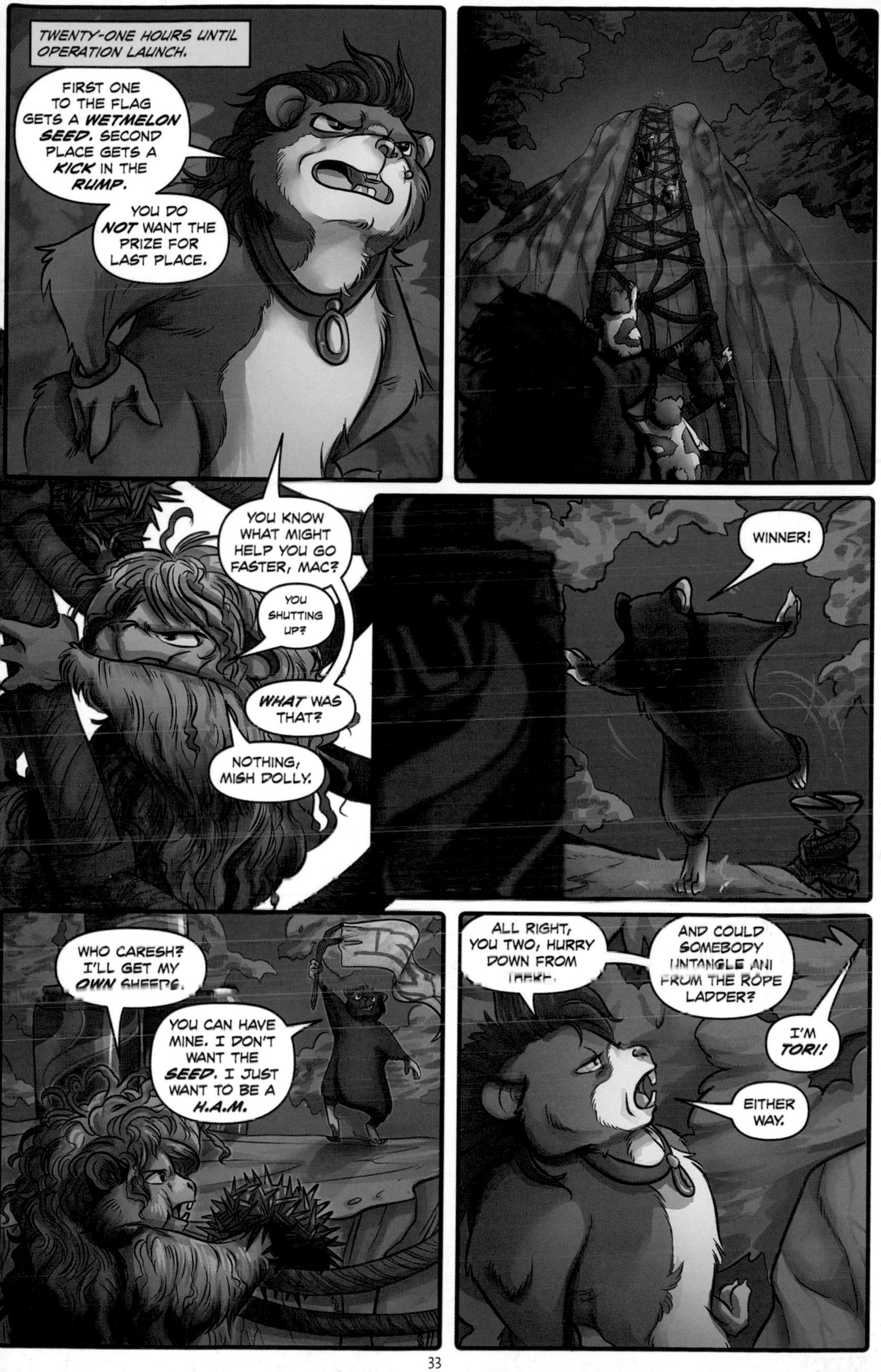
TWENTY-ONE HOURS UNTIL OPERATION LAUNCH.
FIRST ONE TO THE FLAG GETS A ***WETMELON SEED.*** SECOND PLACE GETS A ***KICK*** IN THE ***RUMP.***
YOU DO ***NOT*** WANT THE PRIZE FOR LAST PLACE.
YOU KNOW WHAT MIGHT HELP YOU GO FASTER, MAC?
YOU SHUTTING UP?
WHAT WAS THAT?
NOTHING, MISH DOLLY.
WINNER!
WHO CARESH? I'LL GET MY ***OWN***
YOU CAN HAVE MINE. I DON'T WANT THE ***SEED.*** I JUST WANT TO BE A ***H.A.M.***
ALL RIGHT, YOU TWO, HURRY DOWN FROM
AND COULD SOMEBODY UNTANGLE ANI FROM THE ROPE LADDER?
I'M ***TORI!***
EITHER WAY.

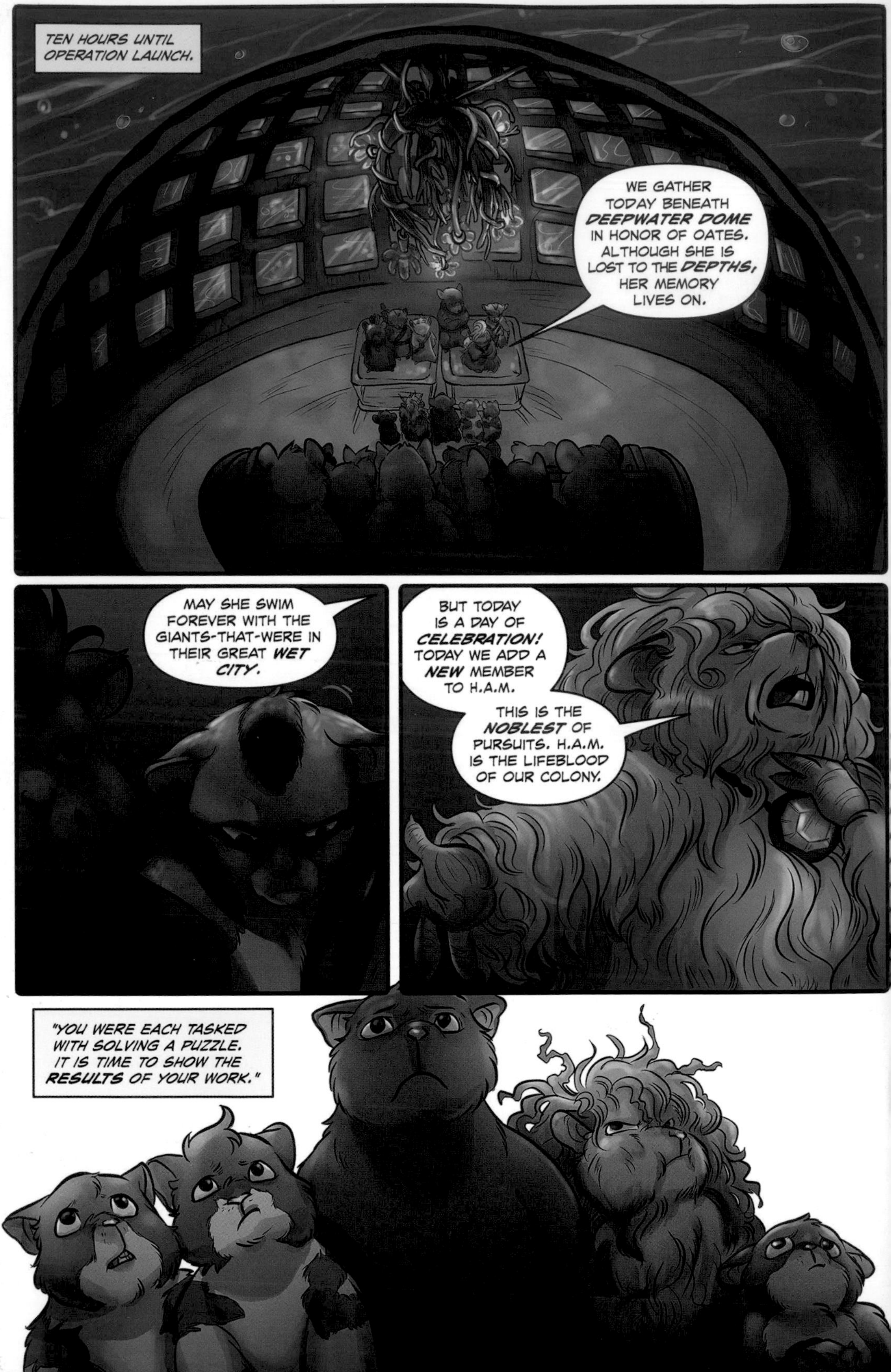
TEN HOURS UNTIL OPERATION LAUNCH.
WE GATHER TODAY BENEATH DEEPWATER DOME IN HONOR OF OATES. ALTHOUGH SHE IS LOST TO THE DEPTHS, HER MEMORY LIVES ON.
MAY SHE SWIM FOREVER WITH THE GIANTS-THAT-WERE IN THEIR GREAT WET CITY.
BUT TODAY IS A DAY OF CELEBRATION! TODAY WE ADD A NEW MEMBER TO H.A.M.
THIS IS THE NOBLEST OF PURSUITS. H.A.M. IS THE LIFEBLOOD OF OUR COLONY.
"YOU WERE EACH TASKED WITH SOLVING A PUZZLE. IT IS TIME TO SHOW THE RESULTS OF YOUR WORK."

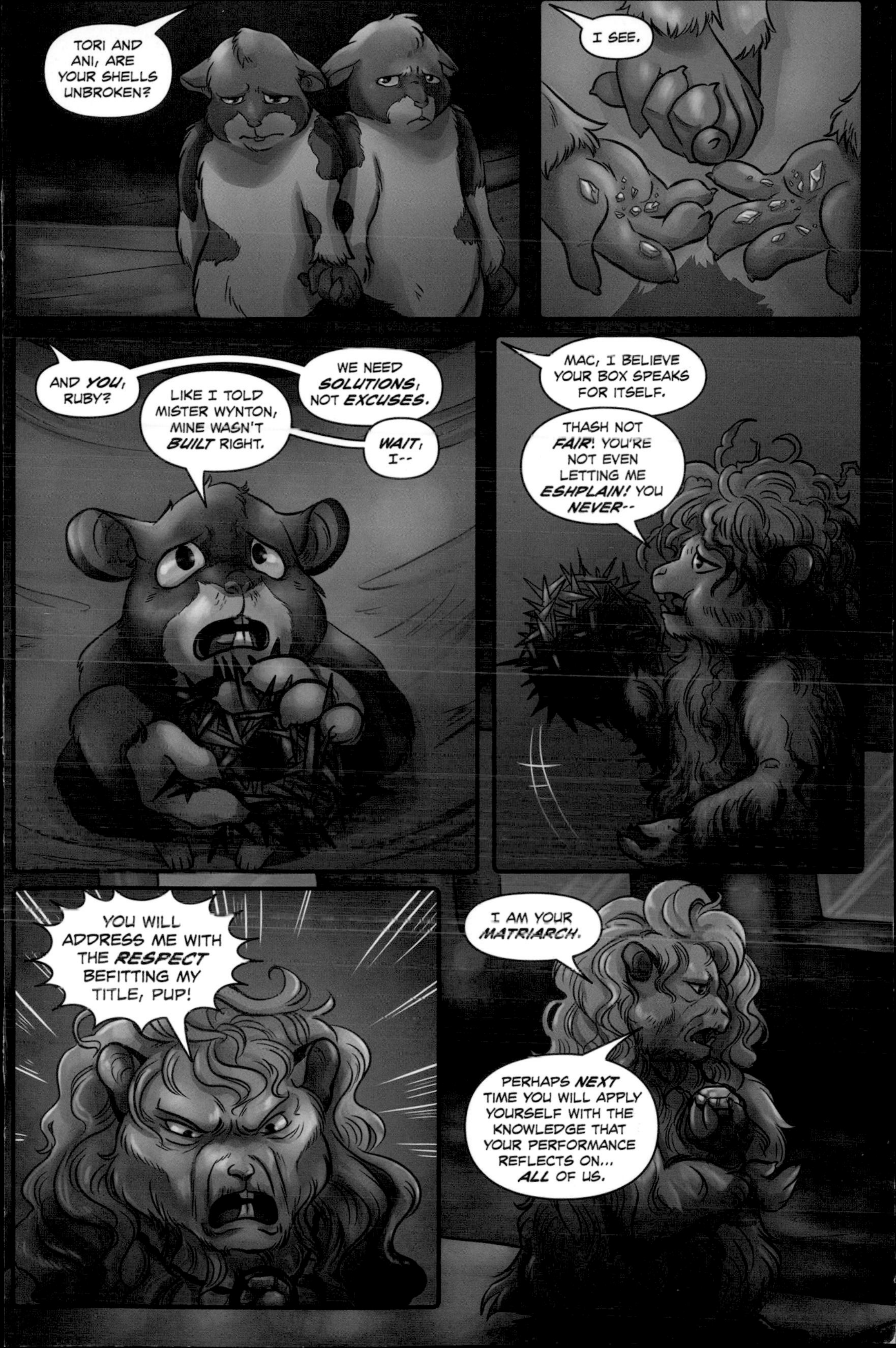
TORI AND ANI, ARE YOUR SHELLS UNBROKEN?
I SEE.
AND *YOU*, RUBY?
LIKE I TOLD MISTER WYNTON, MINE WASN'T *BUILT* RIGHT.
WE NEED *SOLUTIONS*, NOT *EXCUSES*.
WAIT, I--
MAC, I BELIEVE YOUR BOX SPEAKS FOR ITSELF.
THASH NOT *FAIR*! YOU'RE NOT EVEN LETTING ME *ESHPLAIN!* YOU *NEVER*--
YOU WILL ADDRESS ME WITH THE *RESPECT* BEFITTING MY TITLE, PUP!
I AM YOUR *MATRIARCH*.
PERHAPS *NEXT* TIME YOU WILL APPLY YOURSELF WITH THE KNOWLEDGE THAT YOUR PERFORMANCE REFLECTS ON... *ALL* OF US.

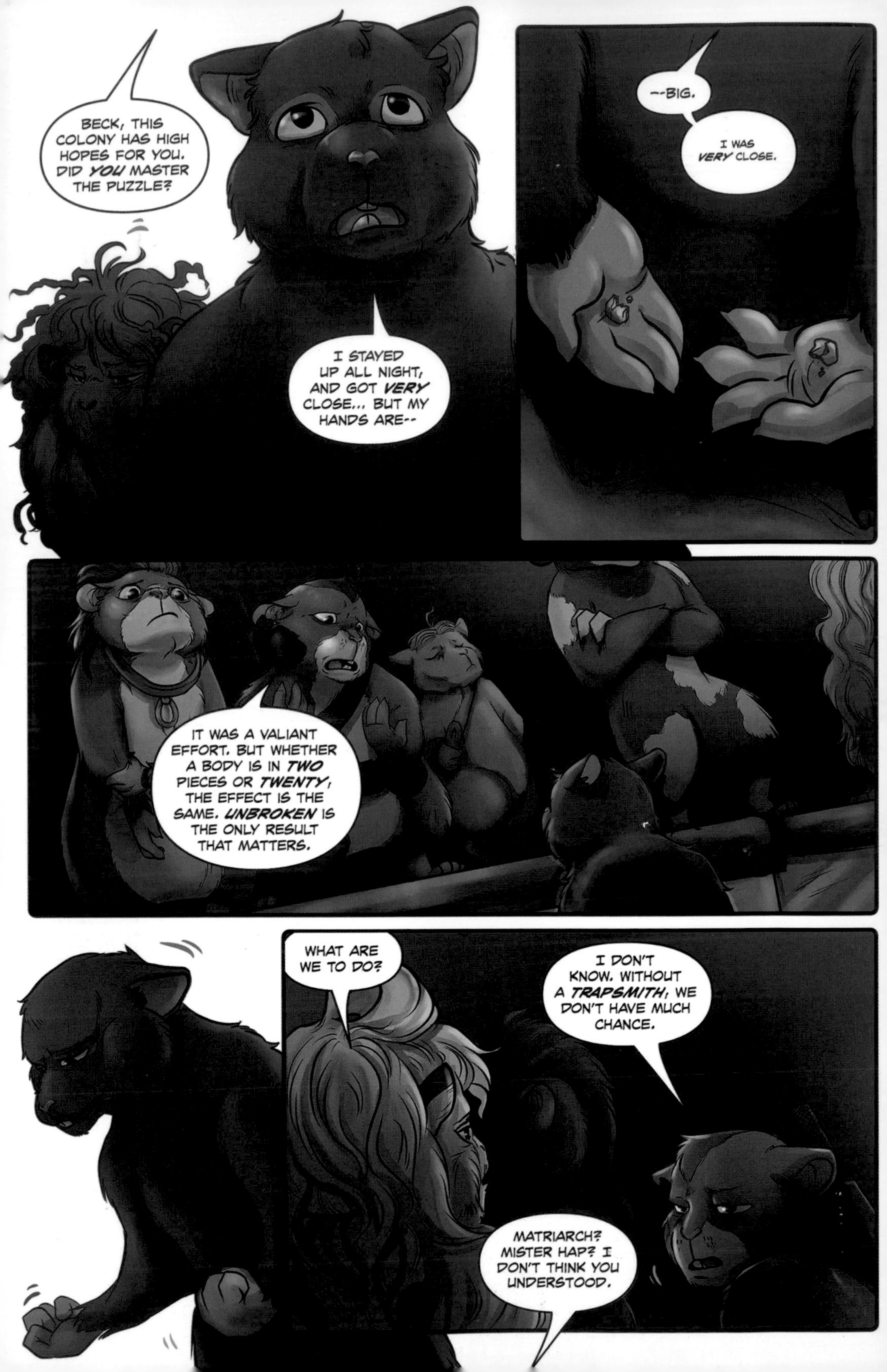
BECK, THIS COLONY HAS HIGH HOPES FOR YOU. DID YOU MASTER THE PUZZLE?
I STAYED UP ALL NIGHT, AND GOT VERY CLOSE... BUT MY HANDS ARE--
--BIG.
I WAS VERY CLOSE.
IT WAS A VALIANT EFFORT. BUT WHETHER A BODY IS IN TWO PIECES OR TWENTY, THE EFFECT IS THE SAME. UNBROKEN IS THE ONLY RESULT THAT MATTERS.
WHAT ARE WE TO DO?
I DON'T KNOW. WITHOUT A TRAPSMITH, WE DON'T HAVE MUCH CHANCE.
MATRIARCH? MISTER HAP? I DON'T THINK YOU UNDERSTOOD.

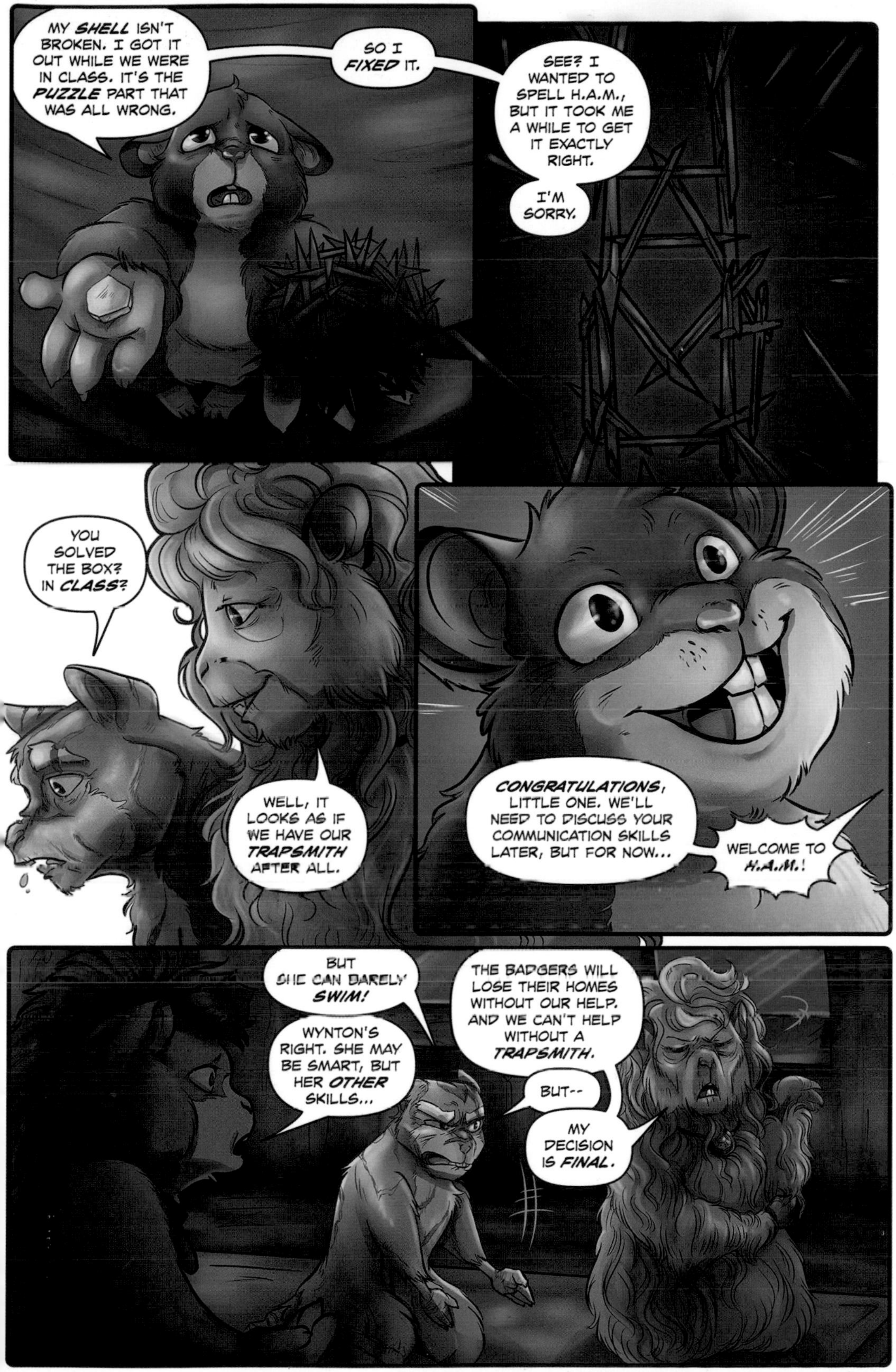
MY SHELL ISN'T BROKEN. I GOT IT OUT WHILE WE WERE IN CLASS. IT'S THE PUZZLE PART THAT WAS ALL WRONG.
SO I FIXED IT.
SEE? I WANTED TO SPELL H.A.M., BUT IT TOOK ME A WHILE TO GET IT EXACTLY RIGHT.
I'M SORRY.
YOU SOLVED THE BOX? IN CLASS?
WELL, IT LOOKS AS IF WE HAVE OUR TRAPSMITH AFTER ALL.
CONGRATULATIONS, LITTLE ONE. WE'LL NEED TO DISCUSS YOUR COMMUNICATION SKILLS LATER, BUT FOR NOW...
WELCOME TO H.A.M.!
BUT SHE CAN BARELY SWIM!
WYNTON'S RIGHT. SHE MAY BE SMART, BUT HER OTHER SKILLS...
THE BADGERS WILL LOSE THEIR HOMES WITHOUT OUR HELP. AND WE CAN'T HELP WITHOUT A TRAPSMITH.
BUT--
MY DECISION IS FINAL.

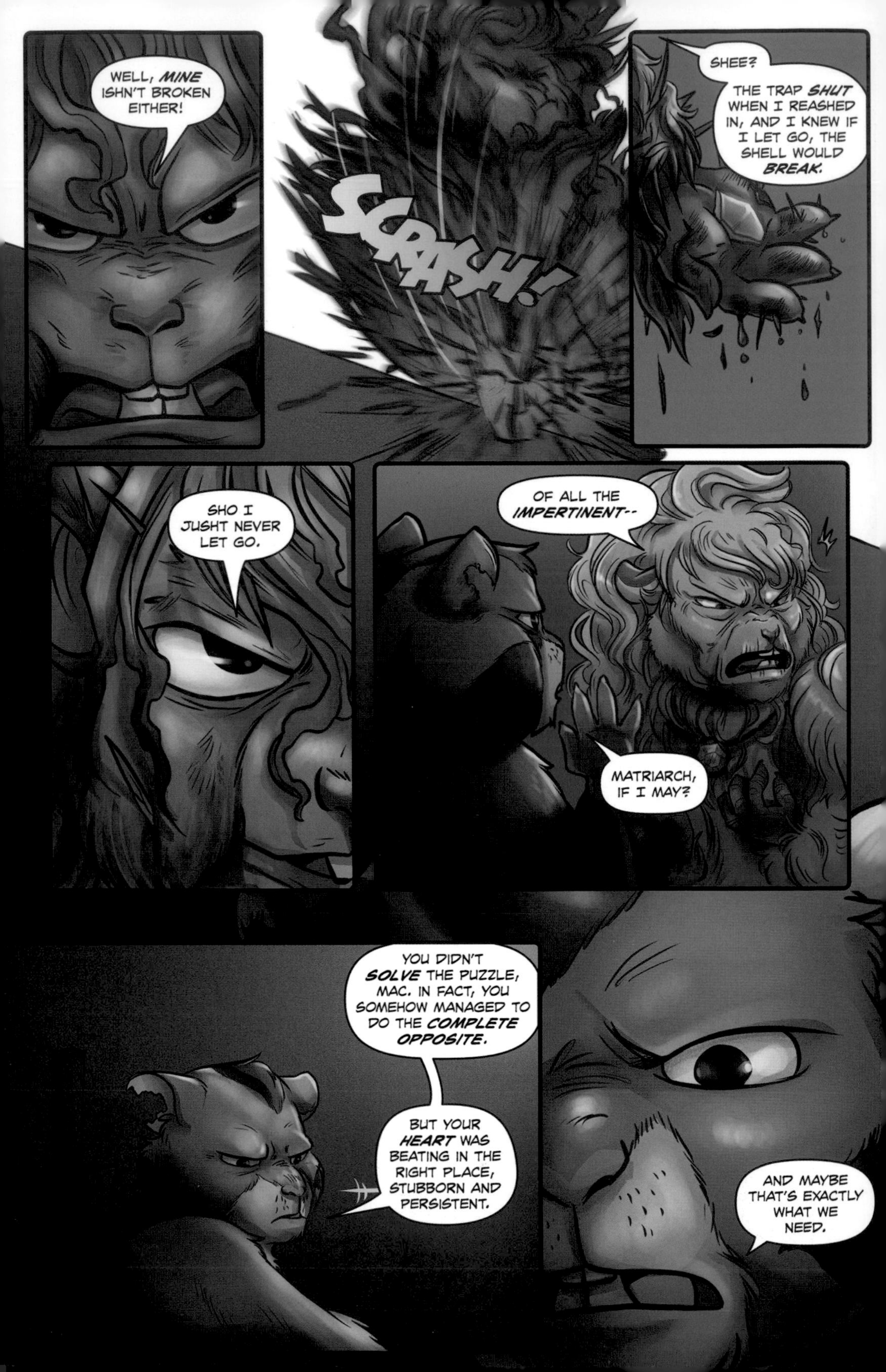
WELL, *MINE* ISHN'T BROKEN EITHER!
SCRASH!
SHEE?
THE TRAP *SHUT* WHEN I REASHED IN, AND I KNEW IF I LET GO, THE SHELL WOULD *BREAK*.
SHO I JUSHT NEVER LET GO.
OF ALL THE *IMPERTINENT*--
MATRIARCH, IF I MAY?
YOU DIDN'T *SOLVE* THE PUZZLE, MAC. IN FACT, YOU SOMEHOW MANAGED TO DO THE *COMPLETE OPPOSITE*.
BUT YOUR *HEART* WAS BEATING IN THE RIGHT PLACE, STUBBORN AND PERSISTENT.
AND MAYBE THAT'S EXACTLY WHAT WE NEED.

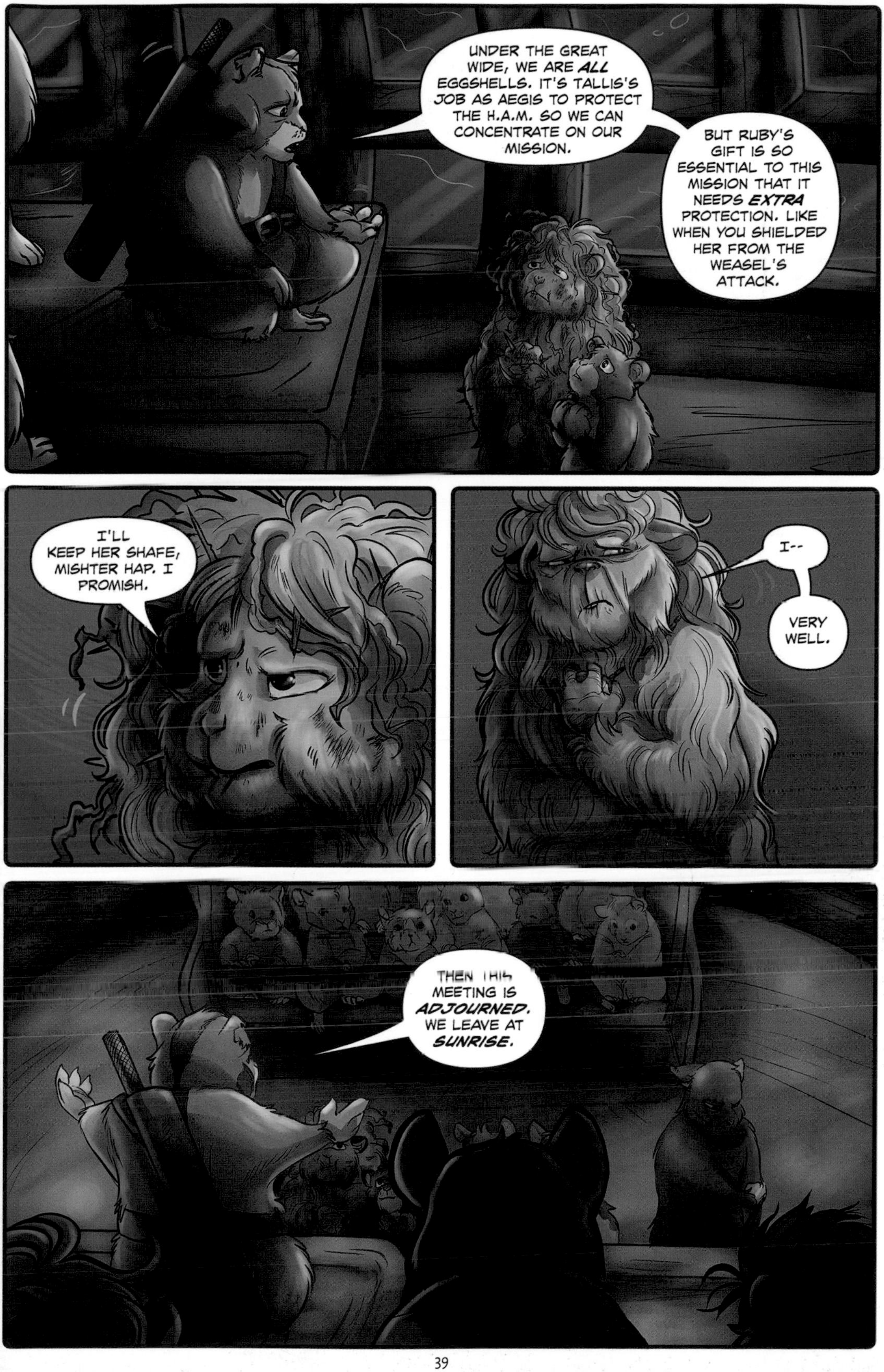
UNDER THE GREAT WIDE, WE ARE ALL EGGSHELLS. IT'S TALLIS'S JOB AS AEGIS TO PROTECT THE H.A.M. SO WE CAN CONCENTRATE ON OUR MISSION.
BUT RUBY'S GIFT IS SO ESSENTIAL TO THIS MISSION THAT IT NEEDS EXTRA PROTECTION. LIKE WHEN YOU SHIELDED HER FROM THE WEASEL'S ATTACK.
I'LL KEEP HER SHAFE, MISHTER HAP. I PROMISH.
I--
VERY WELL.
THEN THIS MEETING IS ADJOURNED. WE LEAVE AT SUNRISE.

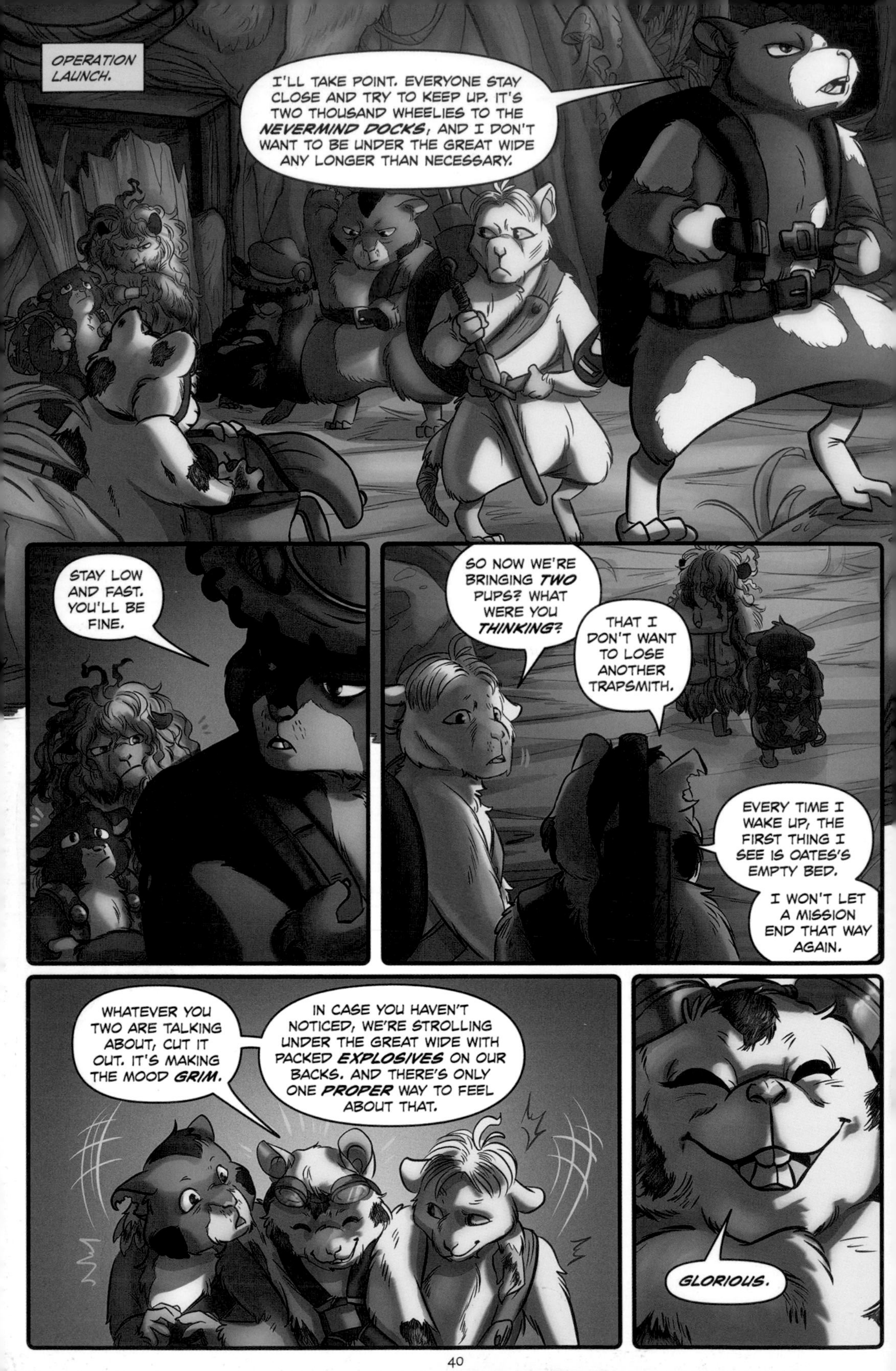
OPERATION LAUNCH.
I'LL TAKE POINT. EVERYONE STAY CLOSE AND TRY TO KEEP UP. IT'S TWO THOUSAND WHEELIES TO THE NEVERMIND DOCKS, AND I DON'T WANT TO BE UNDER THE GREAT WIDE ANY LONGER THAN NECESSARY.
STAY LOW AND FAST. YOU'LL BE FINE.
SO NOW WE'RE BRINGING TWO PUPS? WHAT WERE YOU THINKING?
THAT I DON'T WANT TO LOSE ANOTHER TRAPSMITH.
EVERY TIME I WAKE UP, THE FIRST THING I SEE IS OATES'S EMPTY BED.
I WON'T LET A MISSION END THAT WAY AGAIN.
WHATEVER YOU TWO ARE TALKING ABOUT, CUT IT OUT. IT'S MAKING THE MOOD GRIM.
IN CASE YOU HAVEN'T NOTICED, WE'RE STROLLING UNDER THE GREAT WIDE WITH PACKED EXPLOSIVES ON OUR BACKS. AND THERE'S ONLY ONE PROPER WAY TO FEEL ABOUT THAT.
GLORIOUS.

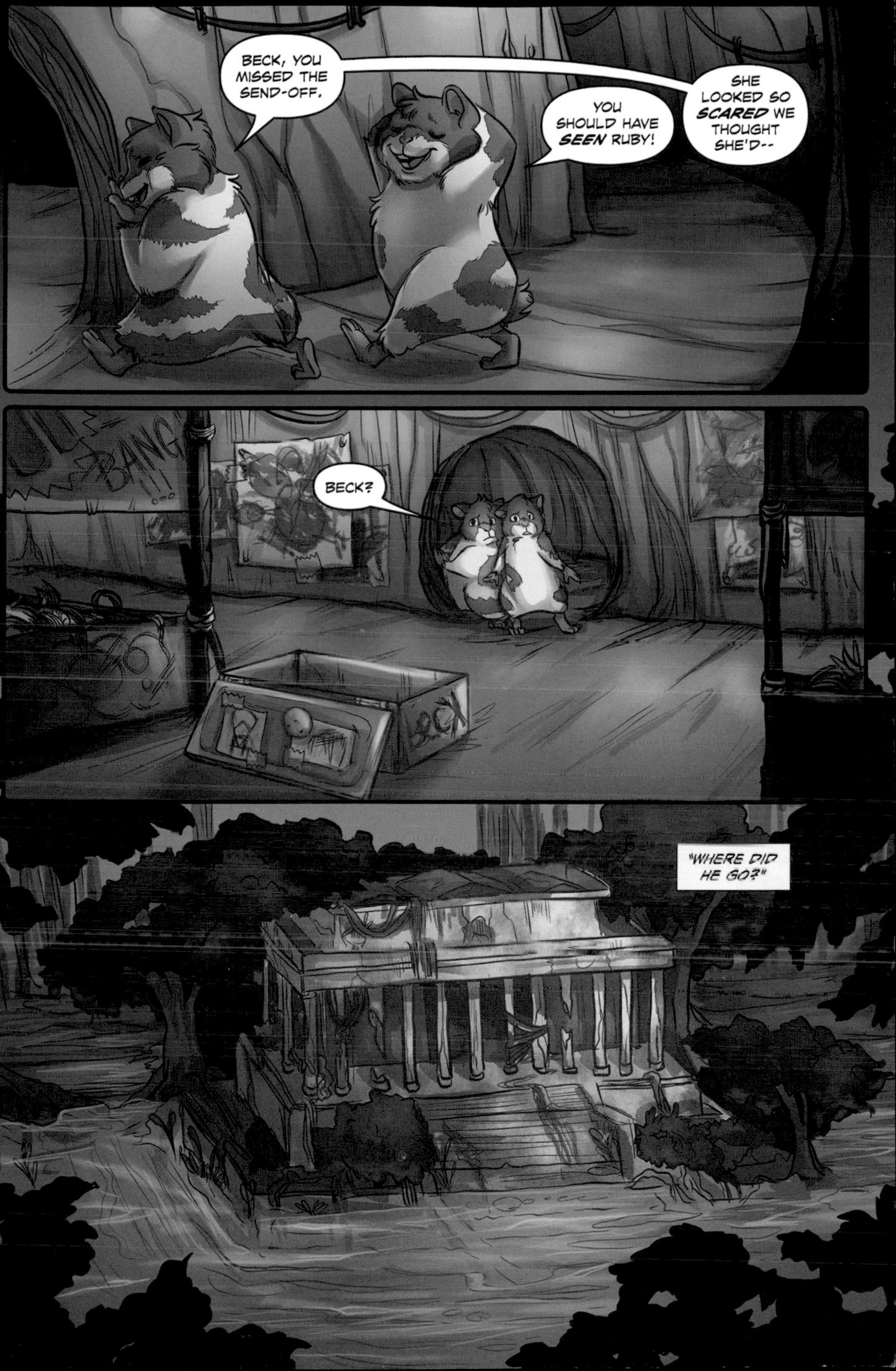
BECK, YOU MISSED THE SEND-OFF.
YOU SHOULD HAVE *SEEN* RUBY!
SHE LOOKED SO *SCARED* WE THOUGHT SHE'D--
BANG
BECK?
"WHERE DID HE GO?"

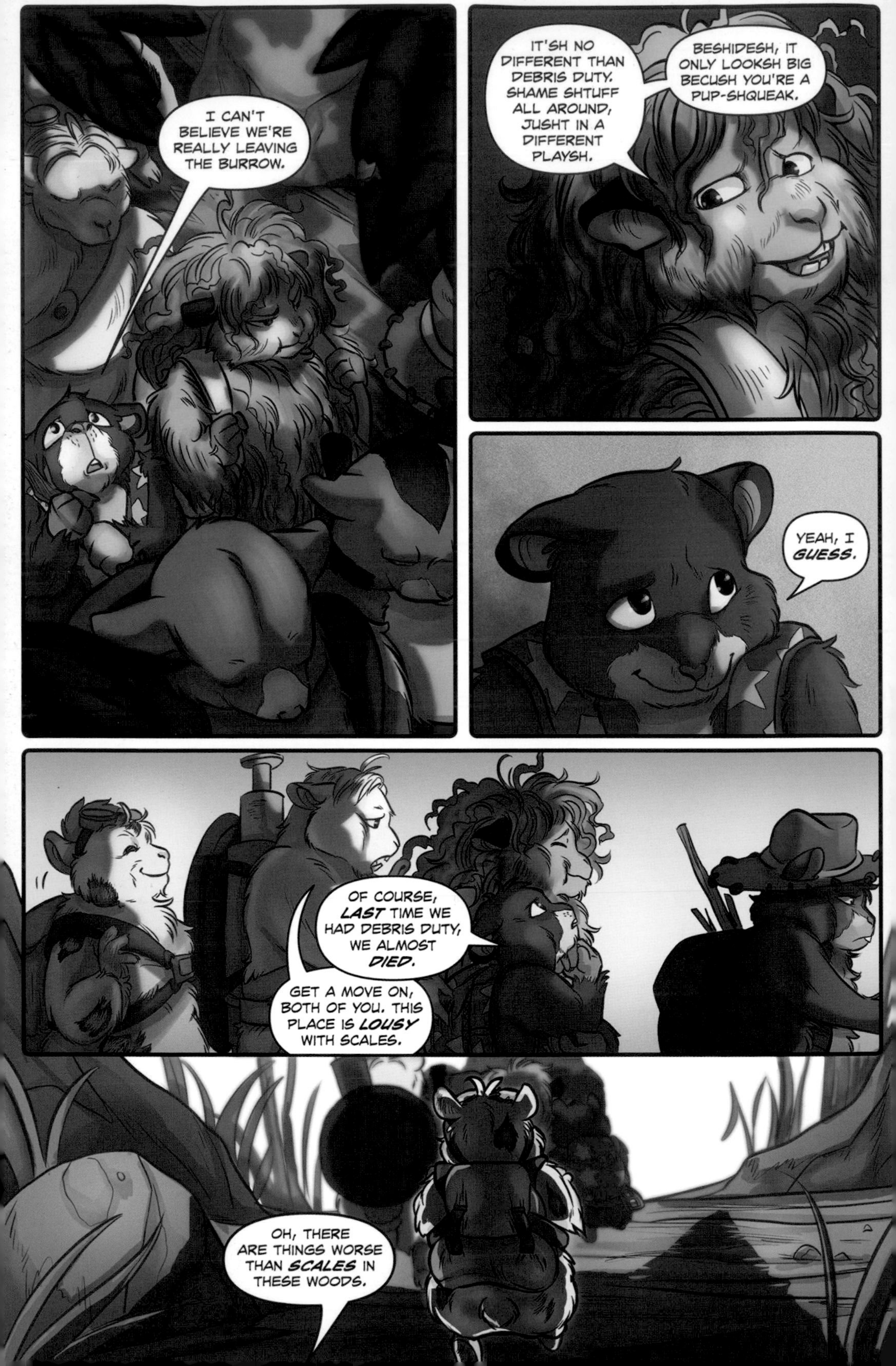

I CAN'T BELIEVE WE'RE REALLY LEAVING THE BURROW.
IT'SH NO DIFFERENT THAN DEBRIS DUTY. SHAME SHTUFF ALL AROUND, JUSHT IN A DIFFERENT PLAYSH.
BESHIDESH, IT ONLY LOOKSH BIG BECUSH YOU'RE A PUP-SHQUEAK.
YEAH, I *GUESS*.
OF COURSE, *LAST* TIME WE HAD DEBRIS DUTY, WE ALMOST *DIED*.
GET A MOVE ON, BOTH OF YOU. THIS PLACE IS *LOUSY* WITH SCALES.
OH, THERE ARE THINGS WORSE THAN *SCALES* IN THESE WOODS.

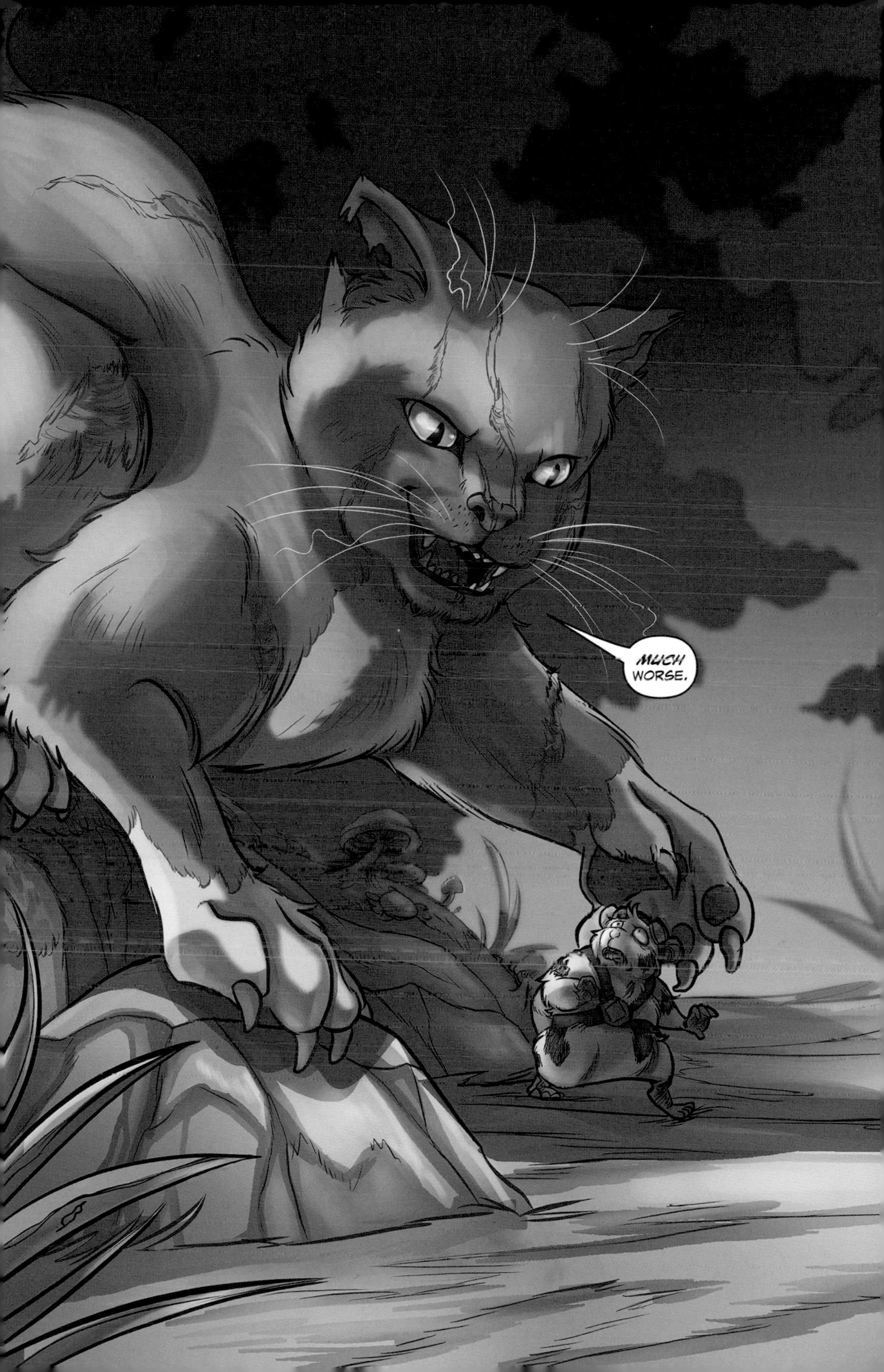
MUCH WORSE.

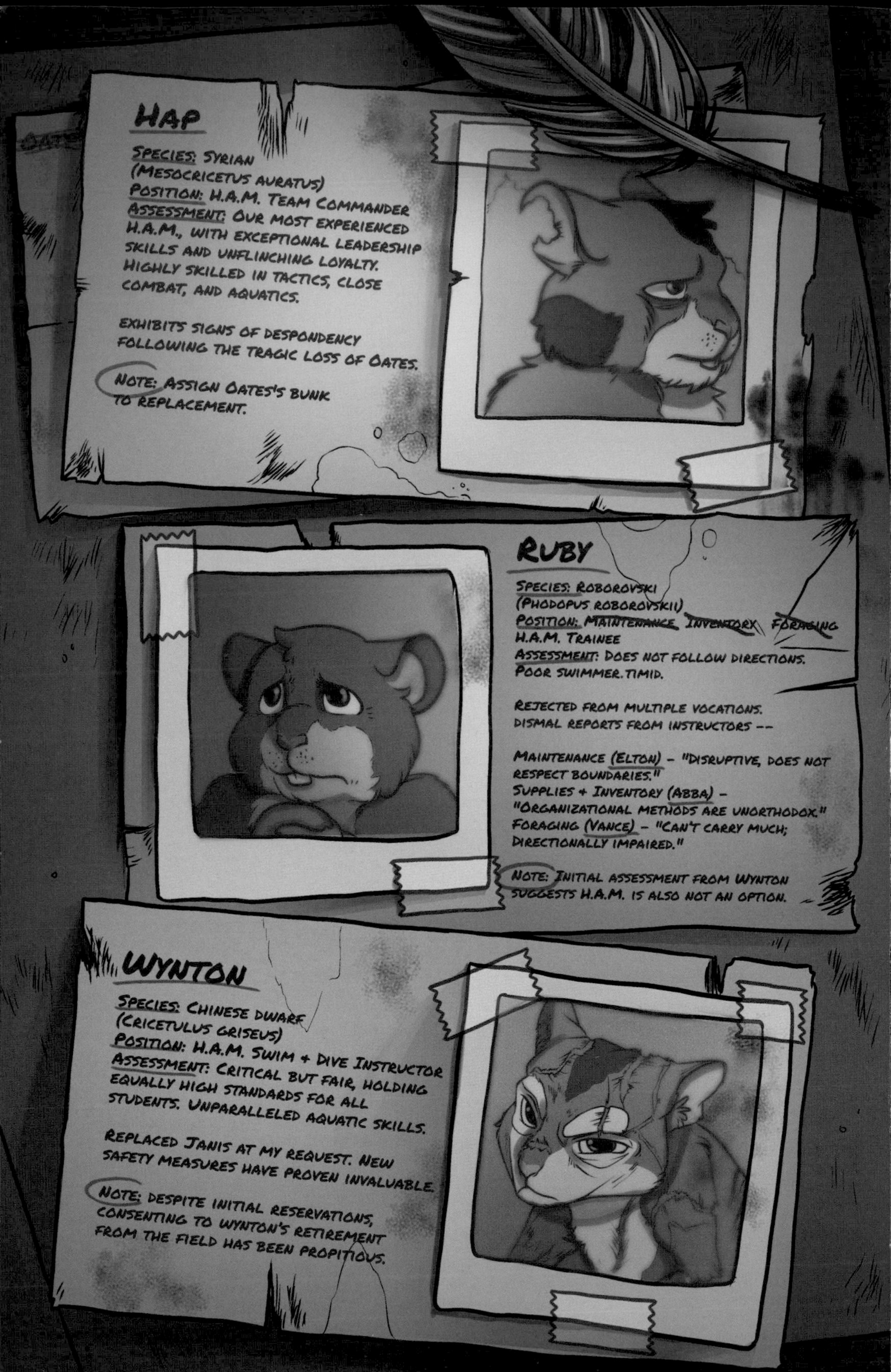
Hap
Species: Syrian (Mesocricetus auratus)
Position: H.A.M. Team Commander
Assessment: Our most experienced H.A.M., with exceptional leadership skills and unflinching loyalty. Highly skilled in tactics, close combat, and aquatics.
Exhibits signs of despondency following the tragic loss of Oates.
Note: Assign Oates's bunk to replacement.
Ruby
Species: Roborovski (Phodopus roborovskii)
Position: Maintenance Inventory Foraging H.A.M. Trainee
Assessment: Does not follow directions. Poor swimmer. timid.
Rejected from multiple vocations. dismal reports from instructors --
Maintenance (Elton) - "Disruptive, does not respect boundaries."
Supplies + Inventory (Abba) - "Organizational methods are unorthodox."
Foraging (Vance) - "Can't carry much; directionally impaired."
Note: Initial assessment from Wynton suggests H.A.M. is also not an option.
Wynton
Species: Chinese dwarf (Cricetulus griseus)
Position: H.A.M. Swim + Dive Instructor
Assessment: Critical but fair, holding equally high standards for all students. Unparalleled aquatic skills.
Replaced Janis at my request. New safety measures have proven invaluable.
Note: despite initial reservations, consenting to Wynton's retirement from the field has been propitious.

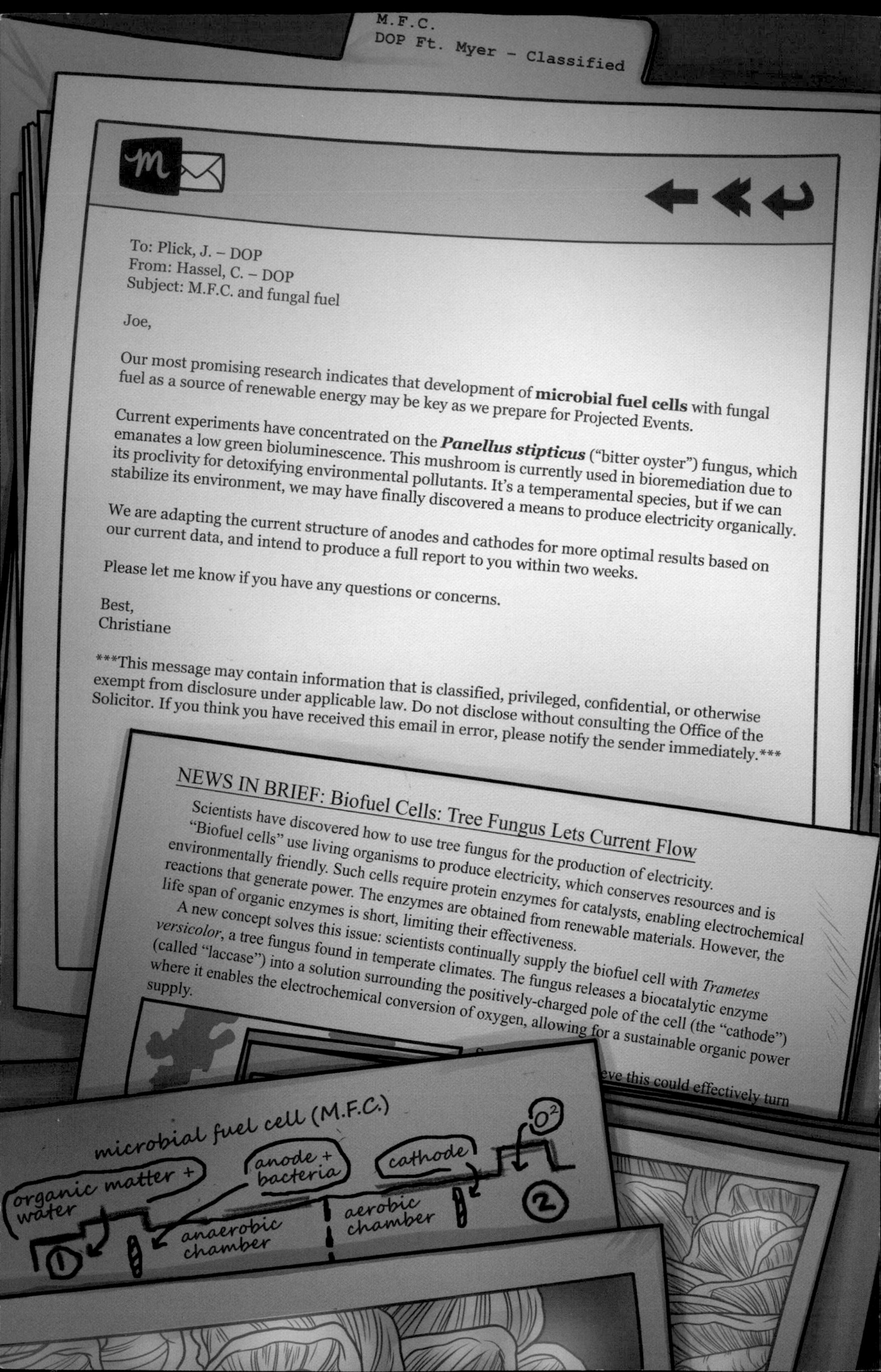
M.F.C.
DOP Ft. Myer - Classified
To: Plick, J. – DOP
From: Hassel, C. – DOP
Subject: M.F.C. and fungal fuel
Joe,
Our most promising research indicates that development of **microbial fuel cells** with fungal fuel as a source of renewable energy may be key as we prepare for Projected Events.
Current experiments have concentrated on the ***Panellus stipticus*** ("bitter oyster") fungus, which emanates a low green bioluminescence. This mushroom is currently used in bioremediation due to its proclivity for detoxifying environmental pollutants. It's a temperamental species, but if we can stabilize its environment, we may have finally discovered a means to produce electricity organically.
We are adapting the current structure of anodes and cathodes for more optimal results based on our current data, and intend to produce a full report to you within two weeks.
Please let me know if you have any questions or concerns.
Best,
Christiane
This message may contain information that is classified, privileged, confidential, or otherwise exempt from disclosure under applicable law. Do not disclose without consulting the Office of the Solicitor. If you think you have received this email in error, please notify the sender immediately.
NEWS IN BRIEF: Biofuel Cells: Tree Fungus Lets Current Flow
Scientists have discovered how to use tree fungus for the production of electricity. "Biofuel cells" use living organisms to produce electricity, which conserves resources and is environmentally friendly. Such cells require protein enzymes for catalysts, enabling electrochemical reactions that generate power. The enzymes are obtained from renewable materials. However, the life span of organic enzymes is short, limiting their effectiveness.
A new concept solves this issue: scientists continually supply the biofuel cell with *Trametes versicolor*, a tree fungus found in temperate climates. The fungus releases a biocatalytic enzyme (called "laccase") into a solution surrounding the positively-charged pole of the cell (the "cathode") where it enables the electrochemical conversion of oxygen, allowing for a sustainable organic power supply.
this could effectively turn
microbial fuel cell (M.F.C.)
organic matter + water
anode + bacteria
cathode
O2
1
2
anaerobic chamber
aerobic chamber

CHAPTER TWO

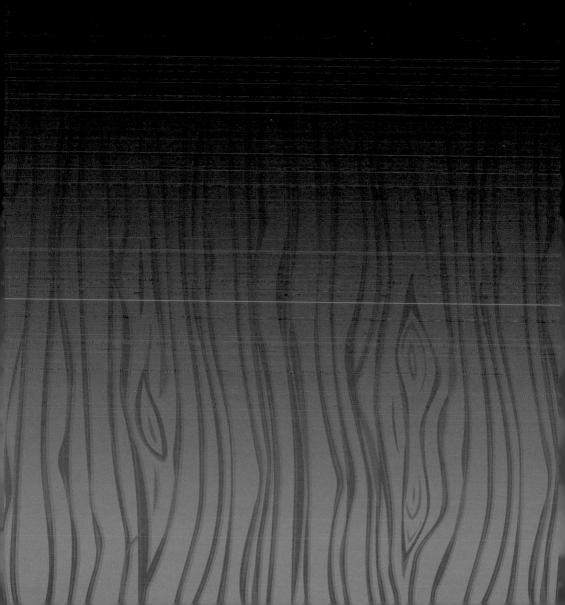

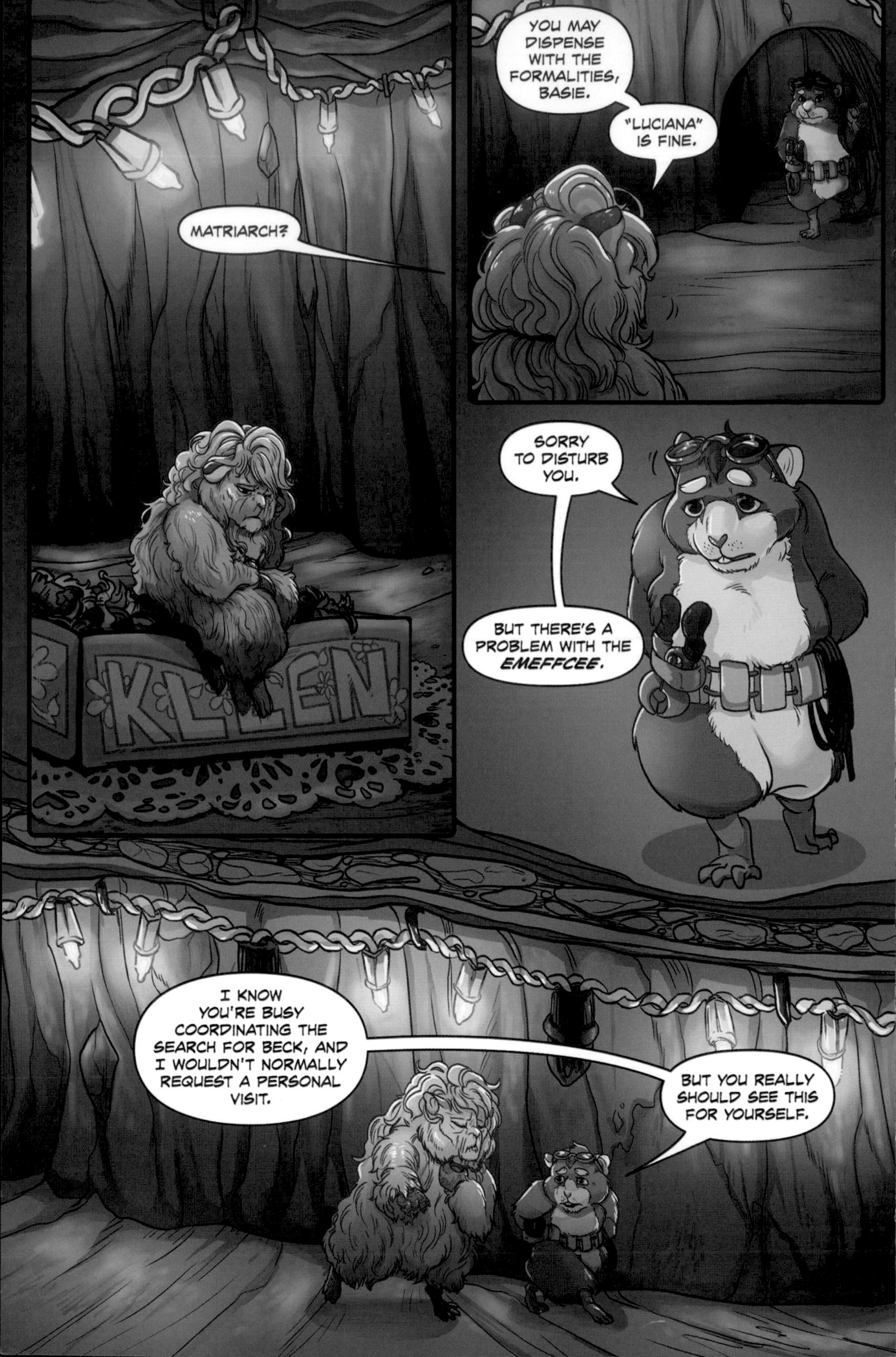
MATRIARCH?
YOU MAY DISPENSE WITH THE FORMALITIES, BASIE.
"LUCIANA" IS FINE.
KLEEN
SORRY TO DISTURB YOU.
BUT THERE'S A PROBLEM WITH THE *EMEFFCEE*.
I KNOW YOU'RE BUSY COORDINATING THE SEARCH FOR BECK, AND I WOULDN'T NORMALLY REQUEST A PERSONAL VISIT.
BUT YOU REALLY SHOULD SEE THIS FOR YOURSELF.

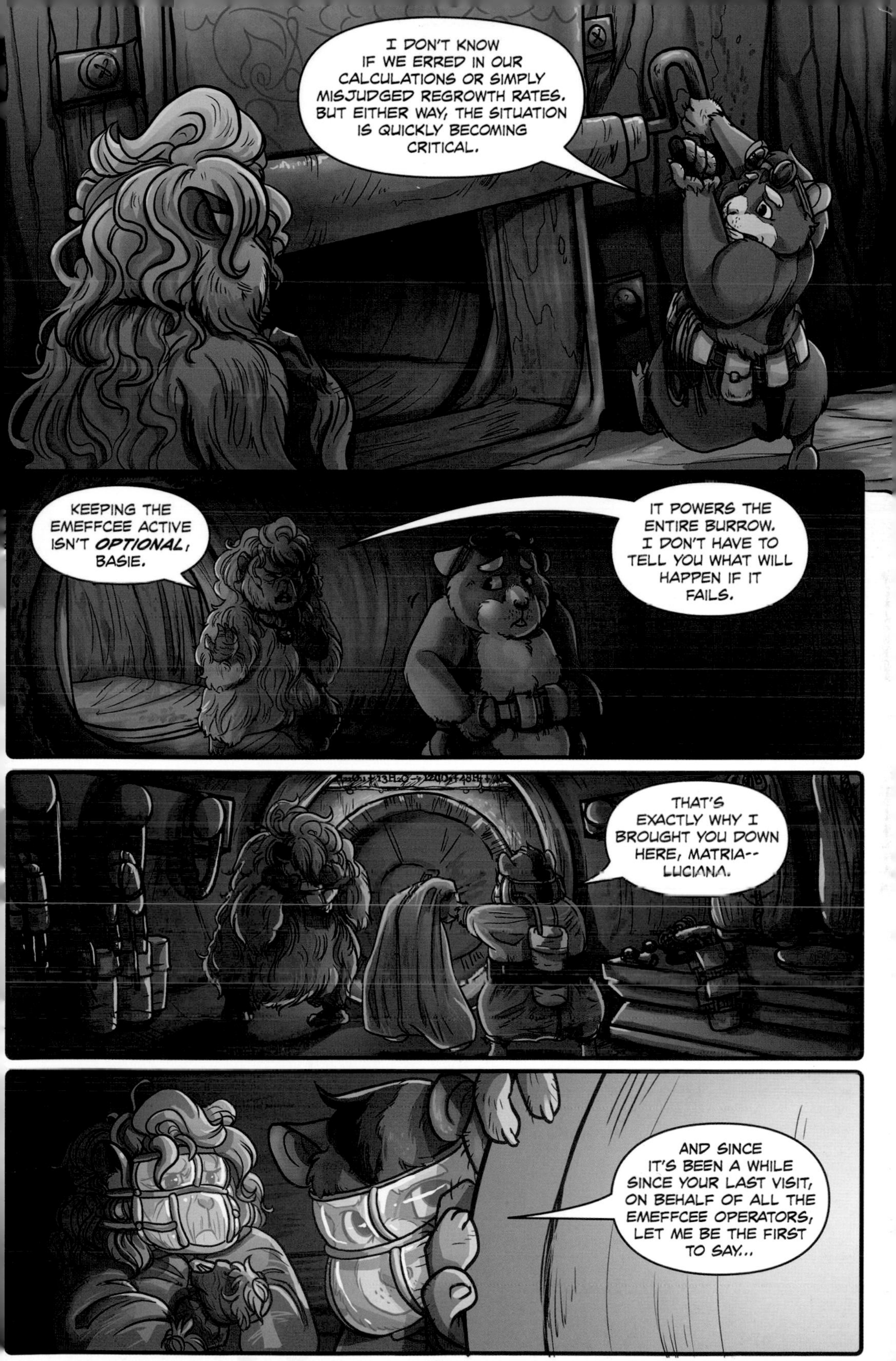
I DON'T KNOW IF WE ERRED IN OUR CALCULATIONS OR SIMPLY MISJUDGED REGROWTH RATES. BUT EITHER WAY, THE SITUATION IS QUICKLY BECOMING CRITICAL.
KEEPING THE EMEFFCEE ACTIVE ISN'T *OPTIONAL*, BASIE.
IT POWERS THE ENTIRE BURROW. I DON'T HAVE TO TELL YOU WHAT WILL HAPPEN IF IT FAILS.
THAT'S EXACTLY WHY I BROUGHT YOU DOWN HERE, MATRIA-- LUCIANA.
AND SINCE IT'S BEEN A WHILE SINCE YOUR LAST VISIT, ON BEHALF OF ALL THE EMEFFCEE OPERATORS, LET ME BE THE FIRST TO SAY...

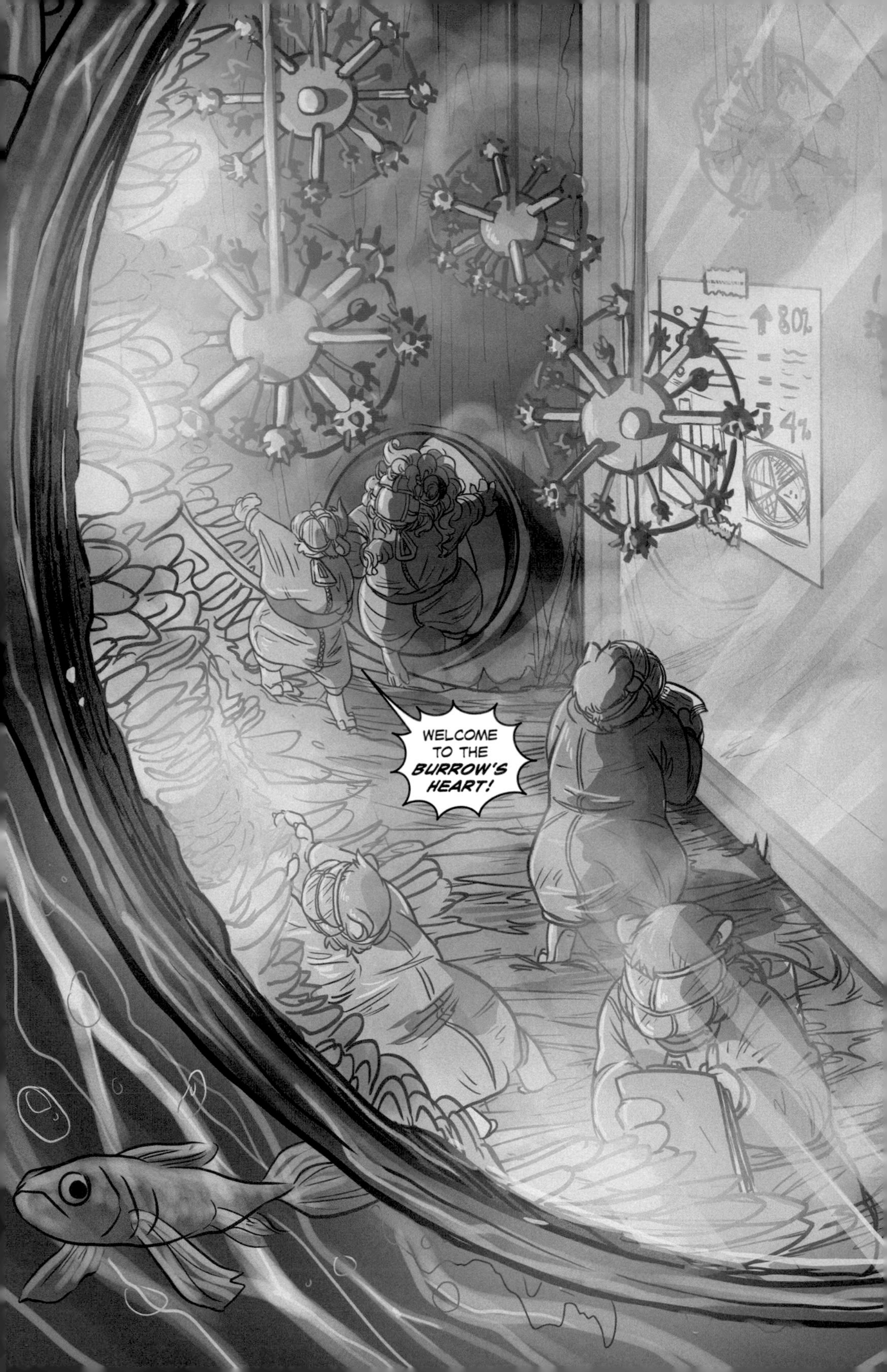
80%
4%
WELCOME TO THE BURROW'S HEART!

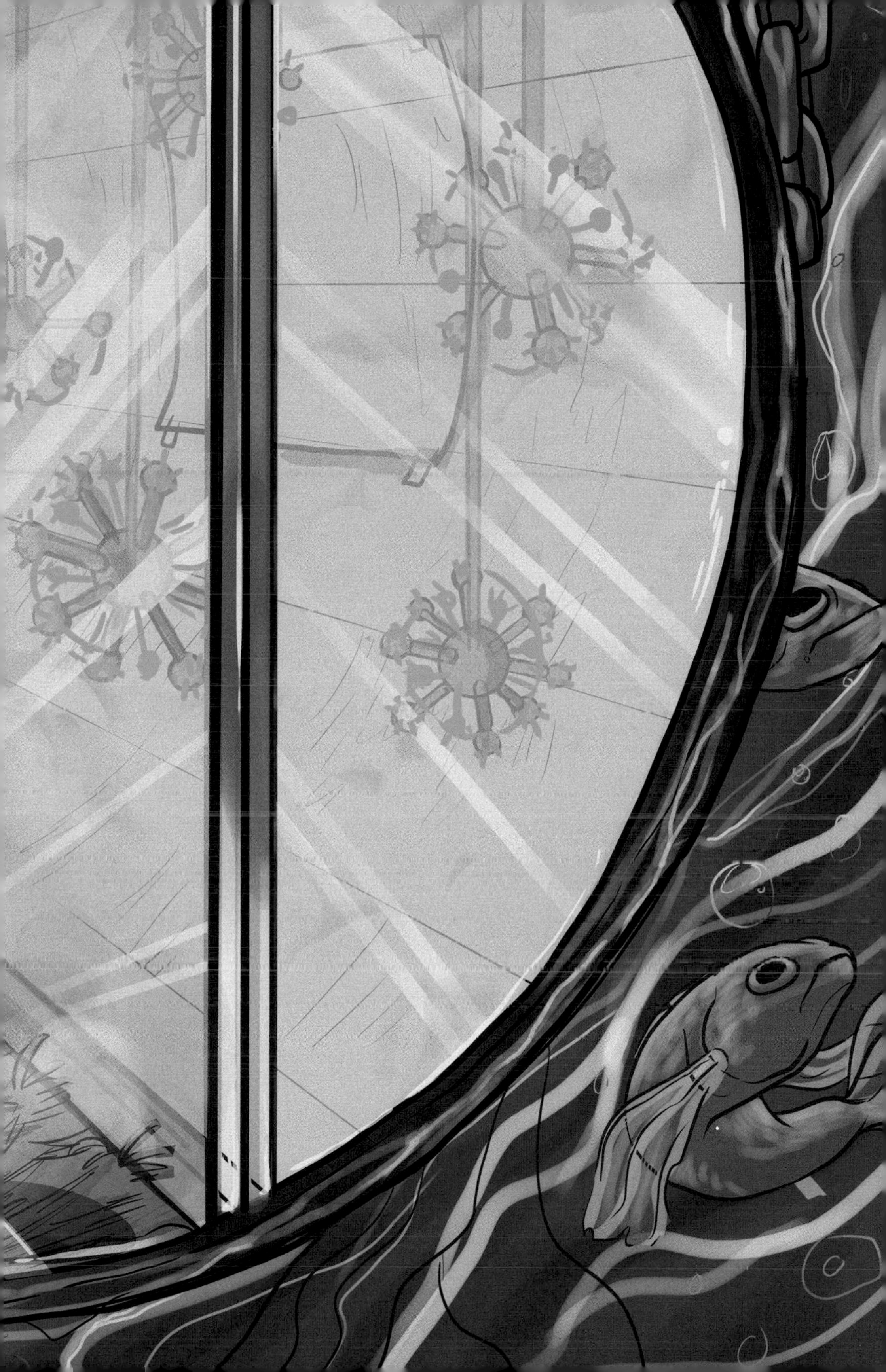

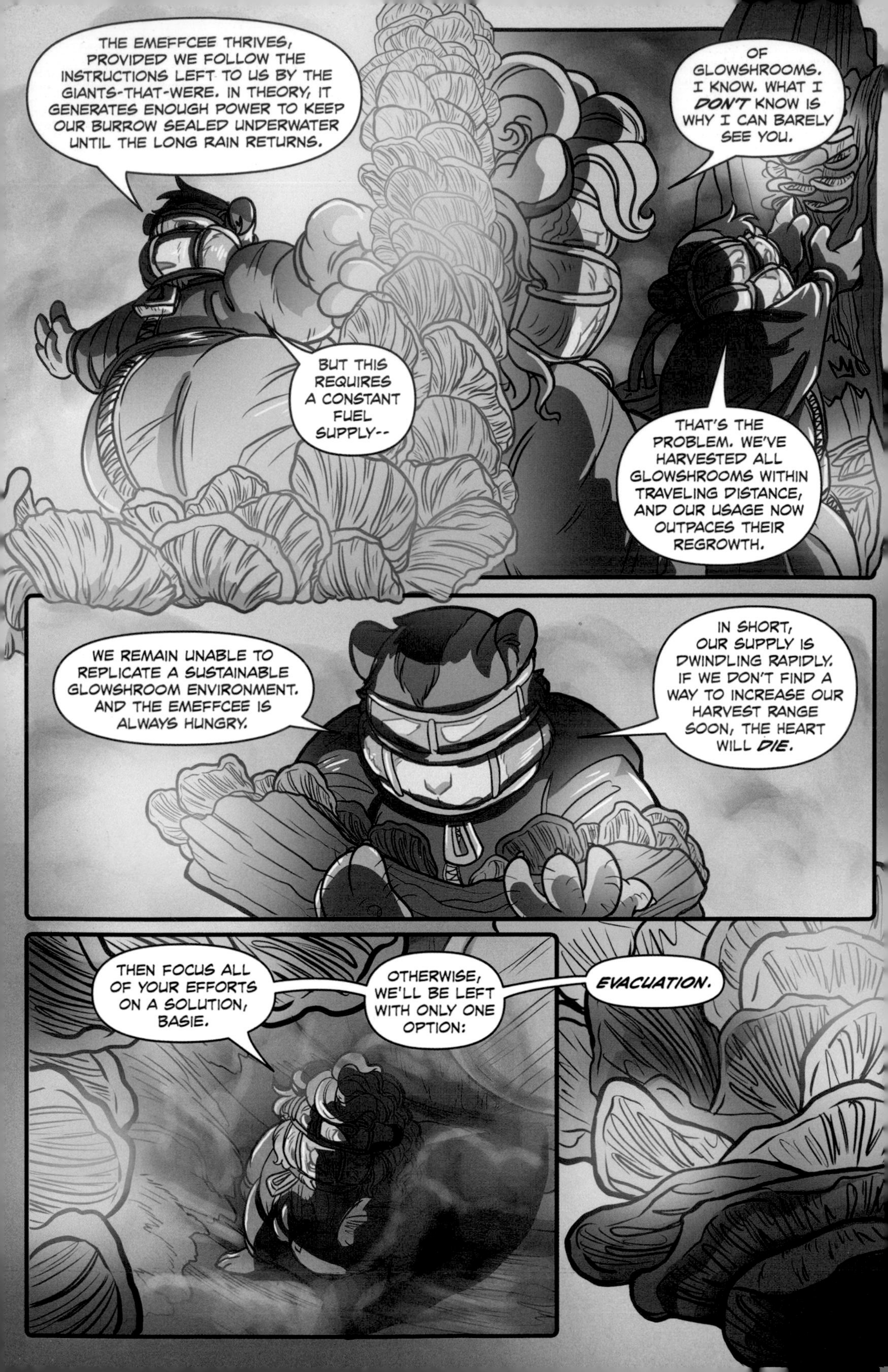
THE EMEFFCEE THRIVES, PROVIDED WE FOLLOW THE INSTRUCTIONS LEFT TO US BY THE GIANTS-THAT-WERE. IN THEORY, IT GENERATES ENOUGH POWER TO KEEP OUR BURROW SEALED UNDERWATER UNTIL THE LONG RAIN RETURNS.
BUT THIS REQUIRES A CONSTANT FUEL SUPPLY--
OF GLOWSHROOMS. I KNOW. WHAT I *DON'T* KNOW IS WHY I CAN BARELY SEE YOU.
THAT'S THE PROBLEM. WE'VE HARVESTED ALL GLOWSHROOMS WITHIN TRAVELING DISTANCE, AND OUR USAGE NOW OUTPACES THEIR REGROWTH.
WE REMAIN UNABLE TO REPLICATE A SUSTAINABLE GLOWSHROOM ENVIRONMENT. AND THE EMEFFCEE IS ALWAYS HUNGRY.
IN SHORT, OUR SUPPLY IS DWINDLING RAPIDLY. IF WE DON'T FIND A WAY TO INCREASE OUR HARVEST RANGE SOON, THE HEART WILL *DIE.*
THEN FOCUS ALL OF YOUR EFFORTS ON A SOLUTION, BASIE.
OTHERWISE, WE'LL BE LEFT WITH ONLY ONE OPTION:
EVACUATION.

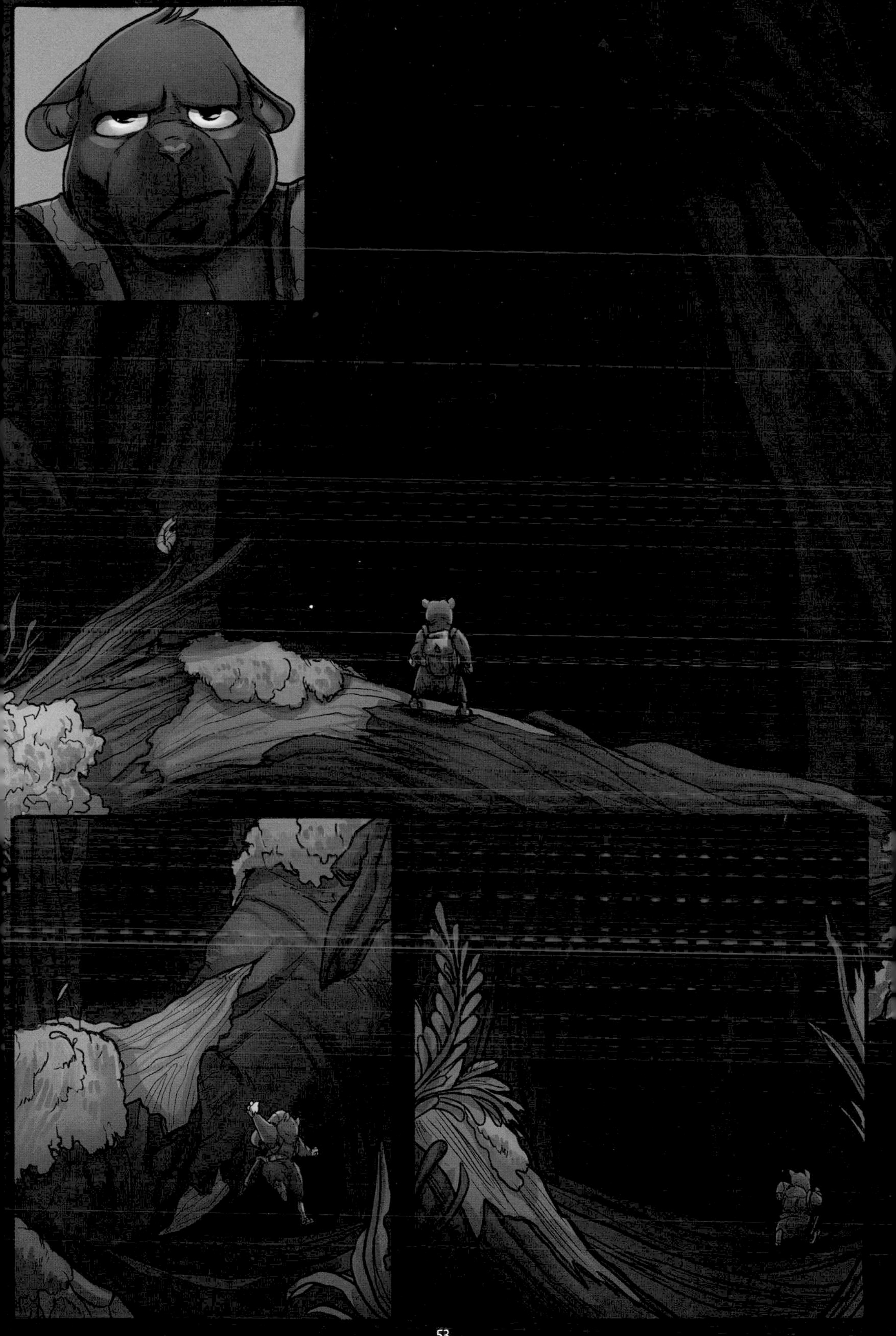

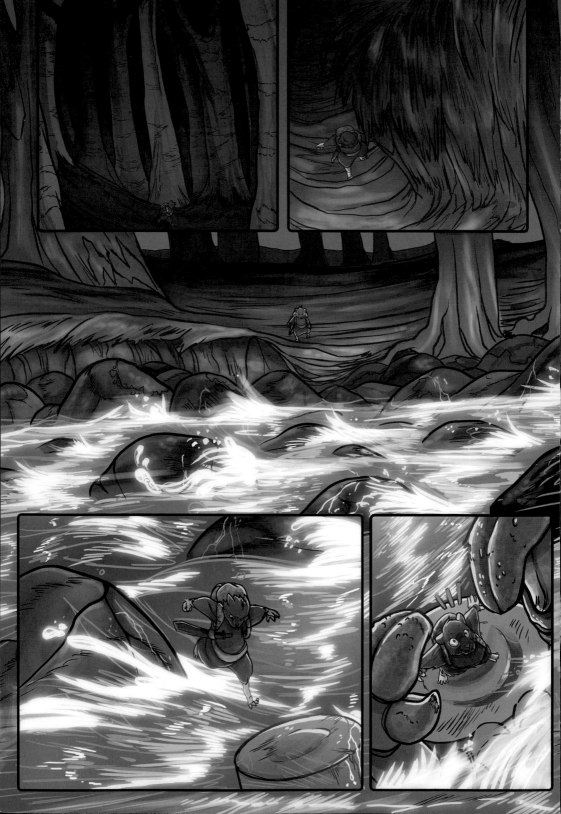

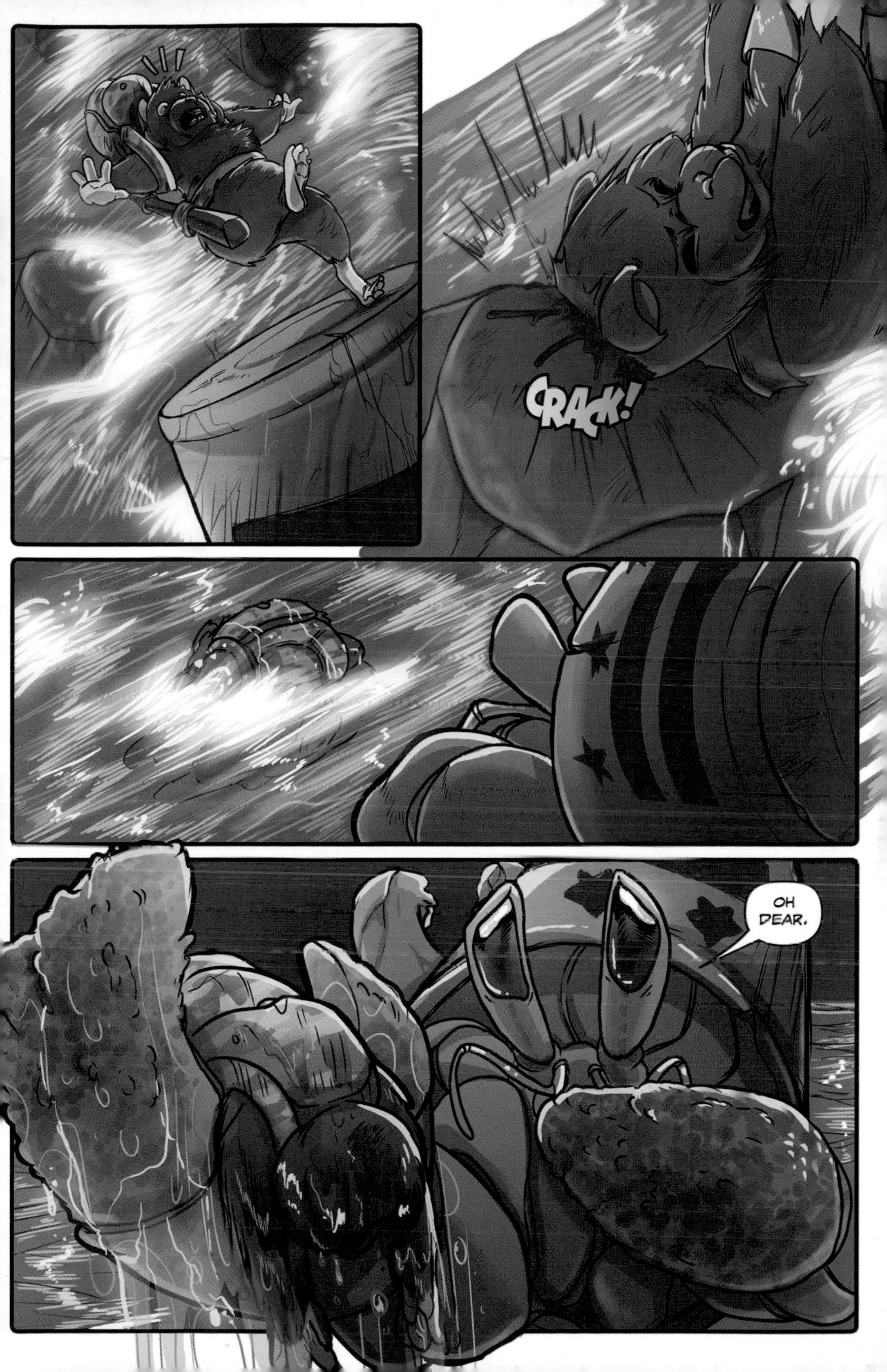
CRACK!
OH DEAR.

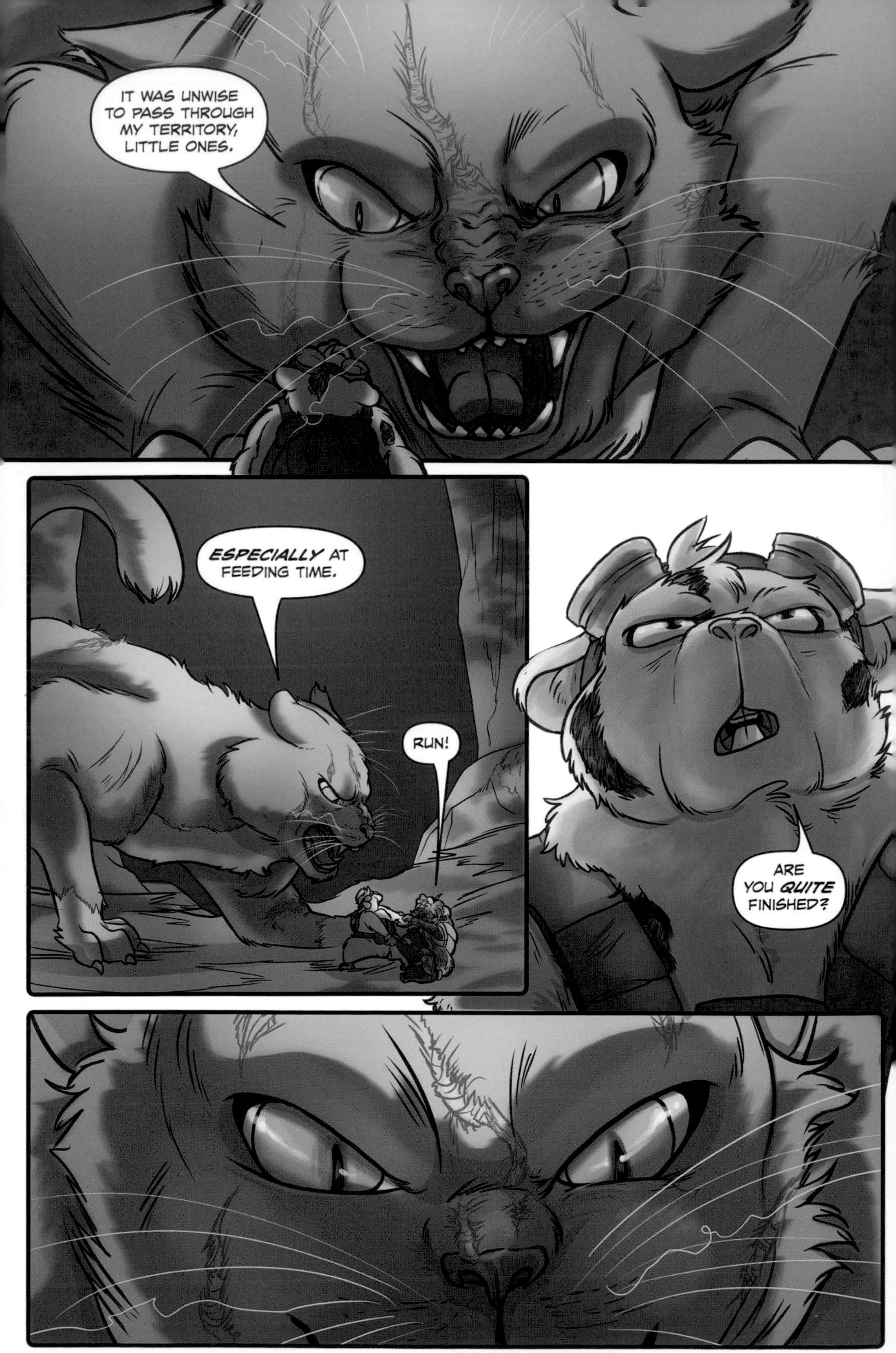
IT WAS UNWISE TO PASS THROUGH MY TERRITORY, LITTLE ONES.
ESPECIALLY AT FEEDING TIME.
RUN!
ARE YOU QUITE FINISHED?

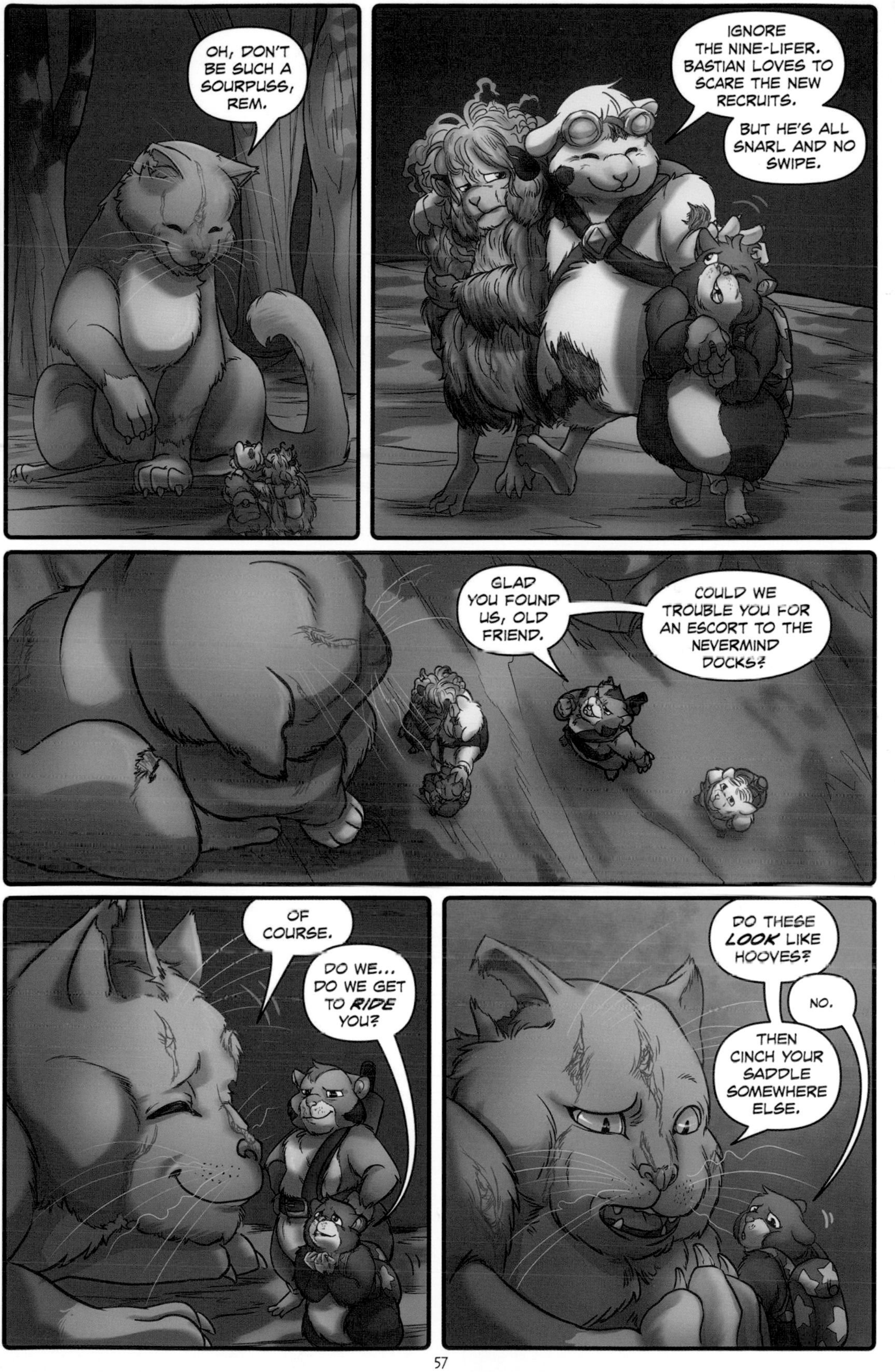
OH, DON'T BE SUCH A SOURPUSS, REM.
IGNORE THE NINE-LIFER. BASTIAN LOVES TO SCARE THE NEW RECRUITS.
BUT HE'S ALL SNARL AND NO SWIPE.
GLAD YOU FOUND US, OLD FRIEND.
COULD WE TROUBLE YOU FOR AN ESCORT TO THE NEVERMIND DOCKS?
OF COURSE.
DO WE... DO WE GET TO *RIDE* YOU?
DO THESE *LOOK* LIKE HOOVES?
NO.
THEN CINCH YOUR SADDLE SOMEWHERE ELSE.

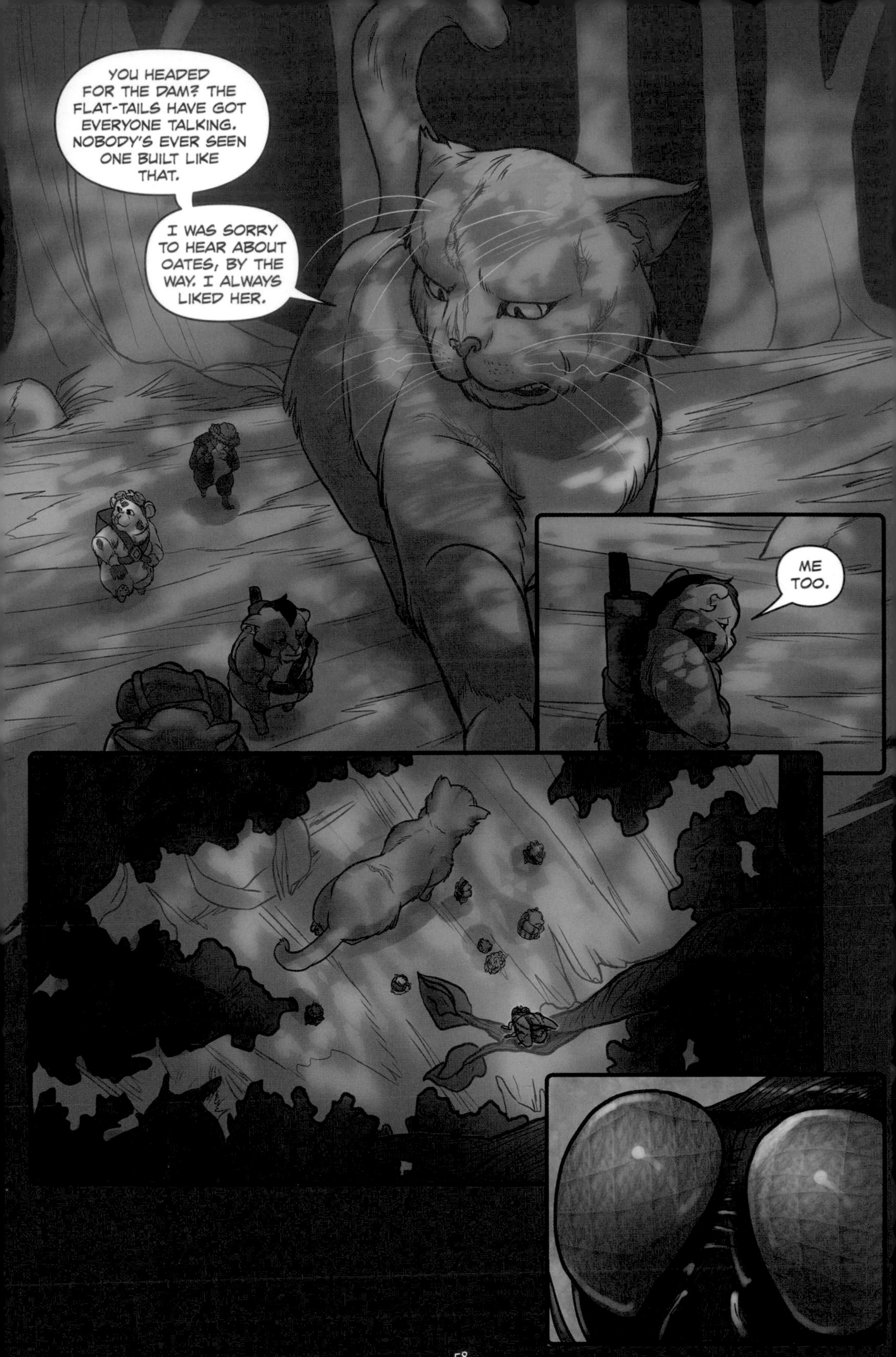
YOU HEADED FOR THE DAM? THE FLAT-TAILS HAVE GOT EVERYONE TALKING. NOBODY'S EVER SEEN ONE BUILT LIKE THAT.
I WAS SORRY TO HEAR ABOUT OATES, BY THE WAY. I ALWAYS LIKED HER.
ME TOO.

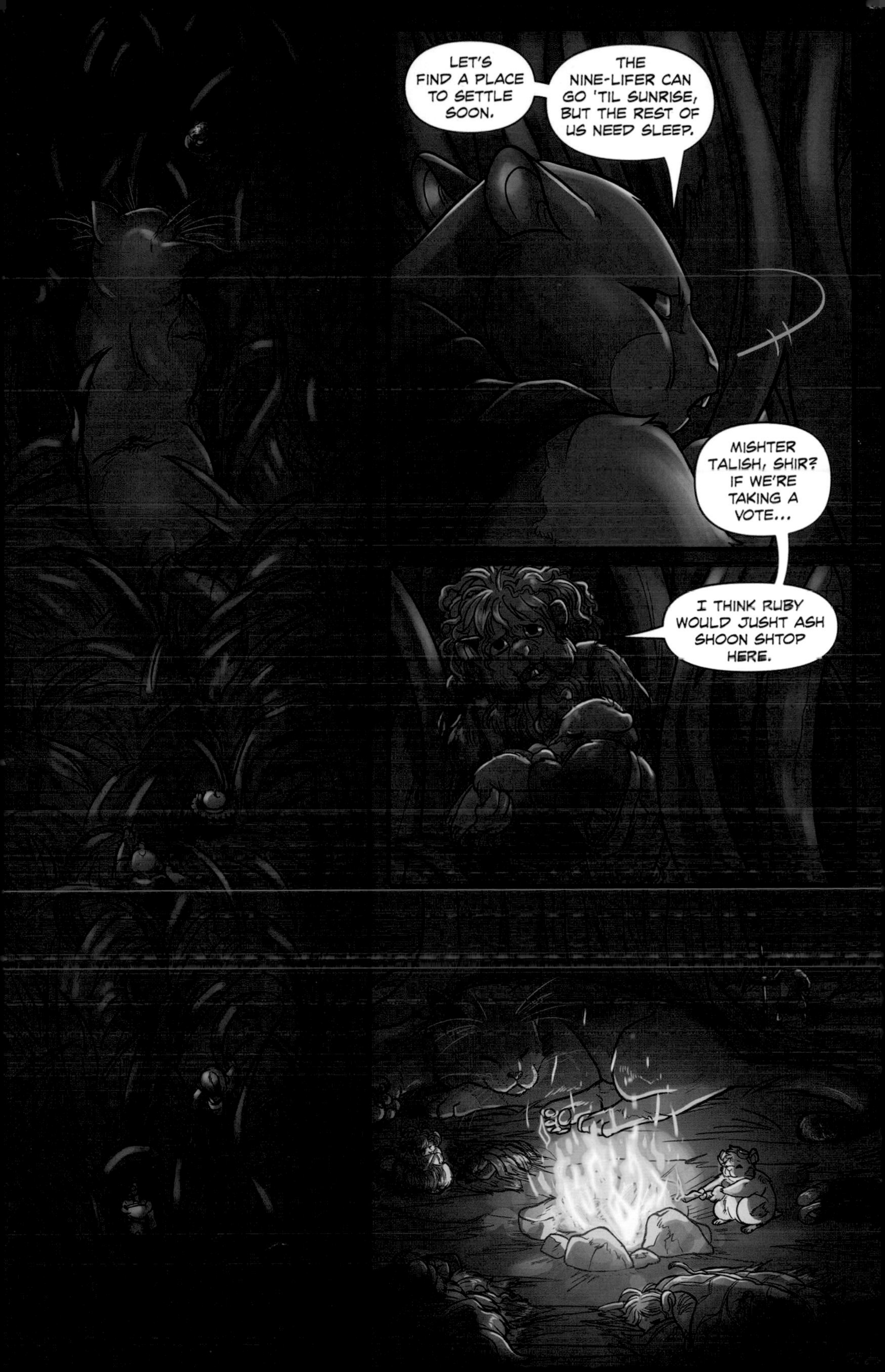
LET'S FIND A PLACE TO SETTLE SOON.
THE NINE-LIFER CAN GO 'TIL SUNRISE, BUT THE REST OF US NEED SLEEP.
MISHTER TALISH, SHIR? IF WE'RE TAKING A VOTE...
I THINK RUBY WOULD JUSHT ASH SHOON SHTOP HERE.

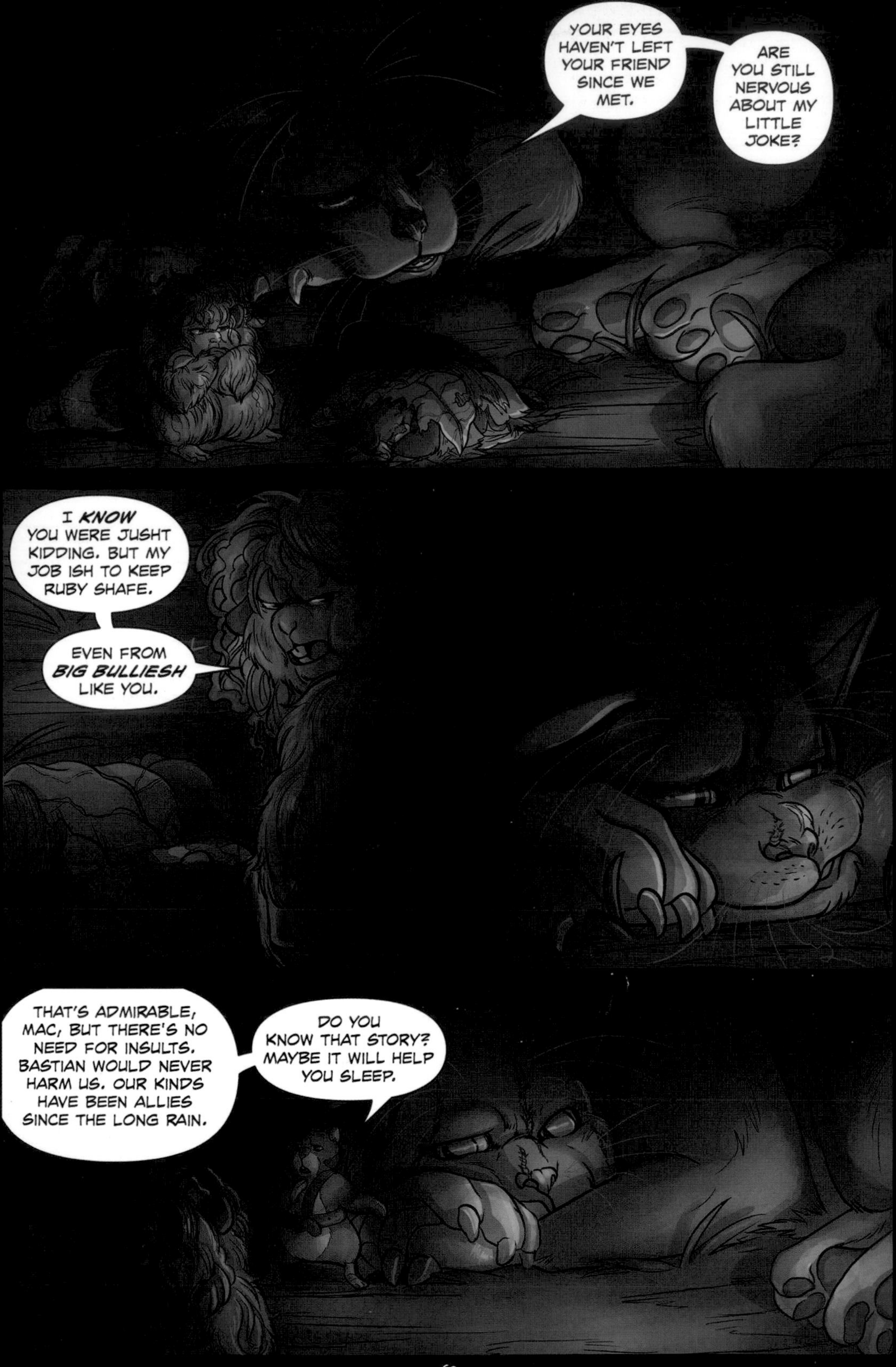

YOUR EYES HAVEN'T LEFT YOUR FRIEND SINCE WE MET.
ARE YOU STILL NERVOUS ABOUT MY LITTLE JOKE?
I KNOW YOU WERE JUSHT KIDDING. BUT MY JOB ISH TO KEEP RUBY SHAFE.
EVEN FROM BIG BULLIESH LIKE YOU.
THAT'S ADMIRABLE, MAC, BUT THERE'S NO NEED FOR INSULTS. BASTIAN WOULD NEVER HARM US. OUR KINDS HAVE BEEN ALLIES SINCE THE LONG RAIN.
DO YOU KNOW THAT STORY? MAYBE IT WILL HELP YOU SLEEP.

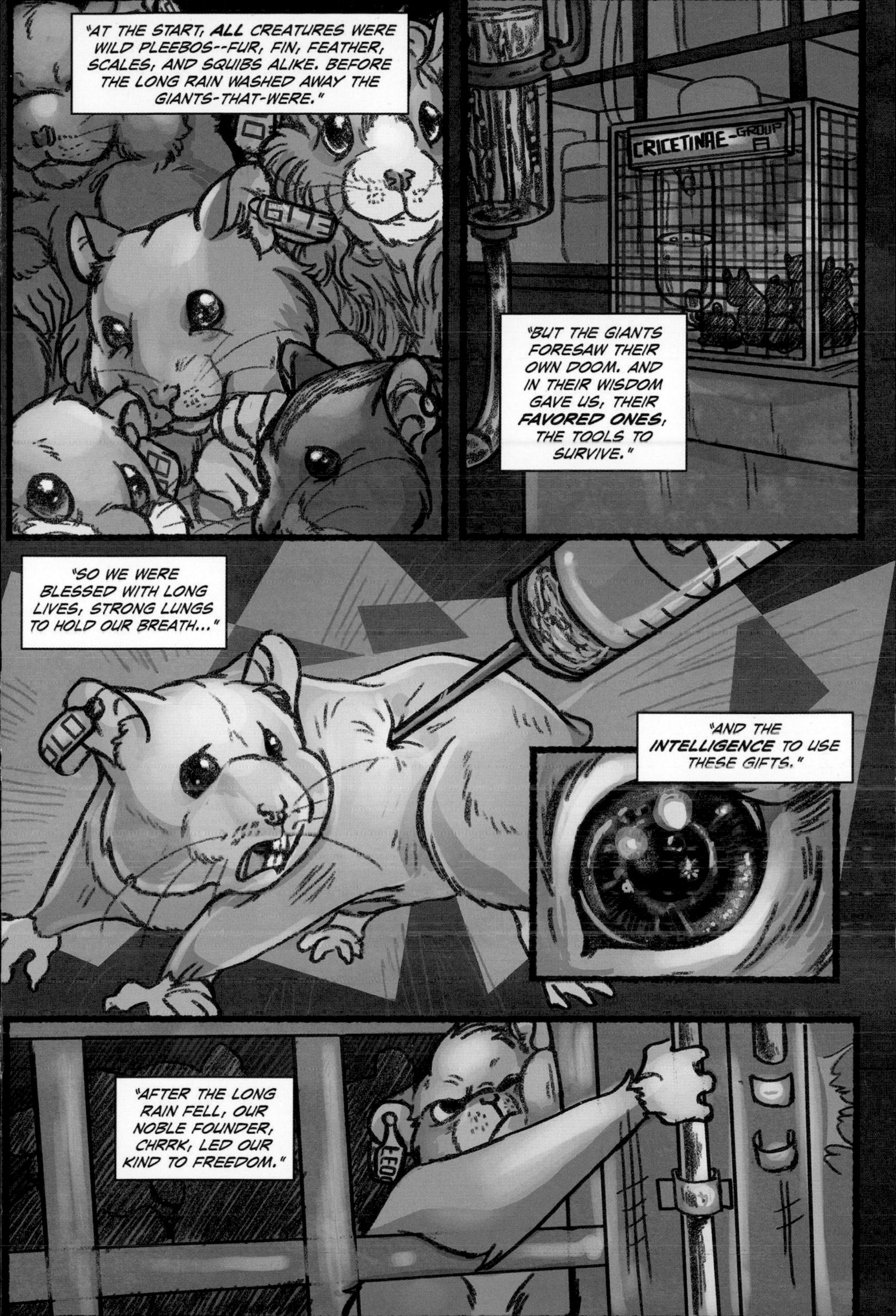
"AT THE START, ALL CREATURES WERE WILD PLEEBOS--FUR, FIN, FEATHER, SCALES, AND SQUIBS ALIKE. BEFORE THE LONG RAIN WASHED AWAY THE GIANTS-THAT-WERE."
CRICETINAE-GROUP
"BUT THE GIANTS FORESAW THEIR OWN DOOM. AND IN THEIR WISDOM GAVE US, THEIR FAVORED ONES, THE TOOLS TO SURVIVE."
"SO WE WERE BLESSED WITH LONG LIVES, STRONG LUNGS TO HOLD OUR BREATH..."
"AND THE INTELLIGENCE TO USE THESE GIFTS."
"AFTER THE LONG RAIN FELL, OUR NOBLE FOUNDER, CHRRK, LED OUR KIND TO FREEDOM."

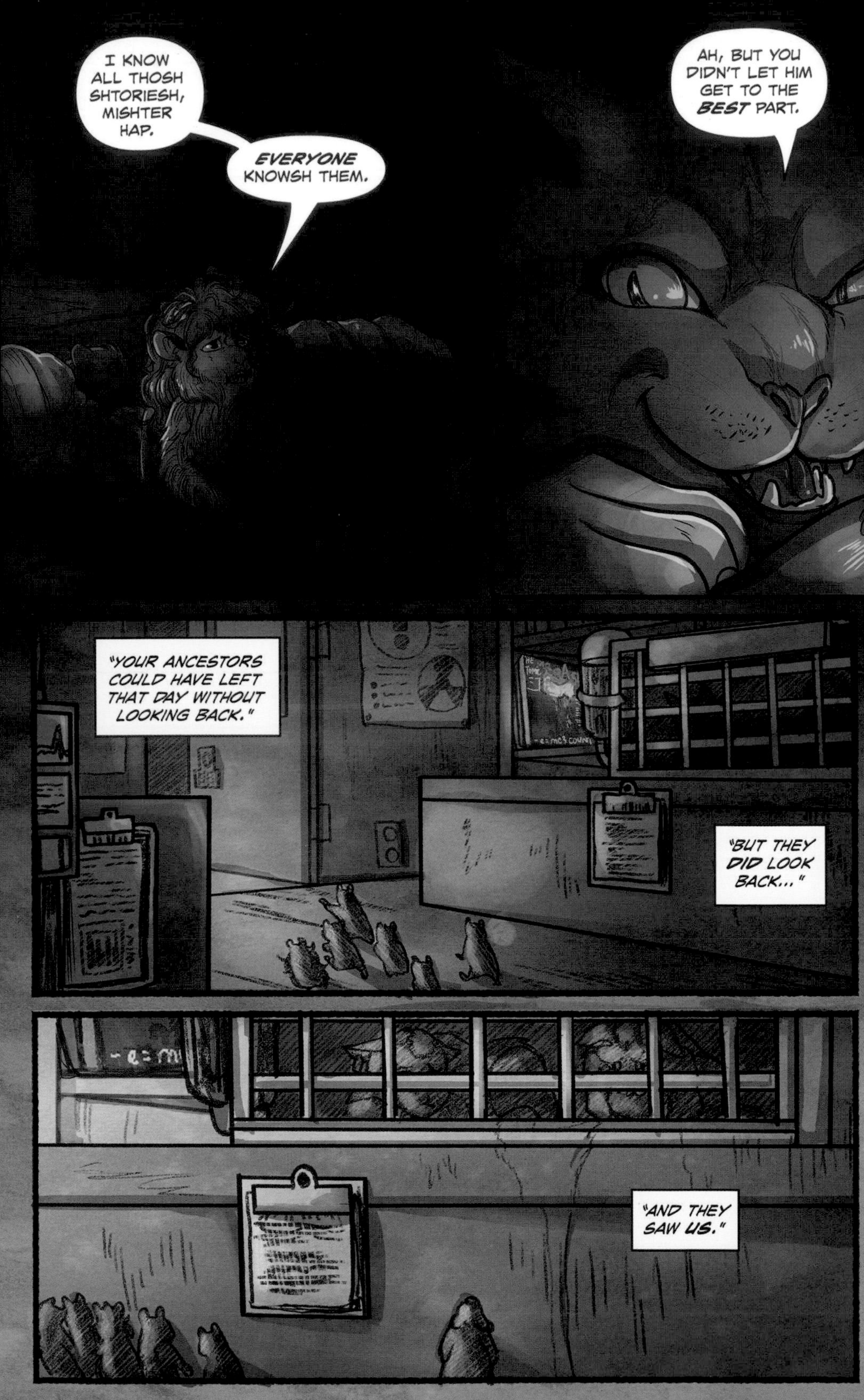
I KNOW ALL THOSH SHTORIESH, MISHTER HAP.
EVERYONE KNOWSH THEM.
AH, BUT YOU DIDN'T LET HIM GET TO THE BEST PART.
"YOUR ANCESTORS COULD HAVE LEFT THAT DAY WITHOUT LOOKING BACK."
"BUT THEY DID LOOK BACK..."
"AND THEY SAW US."

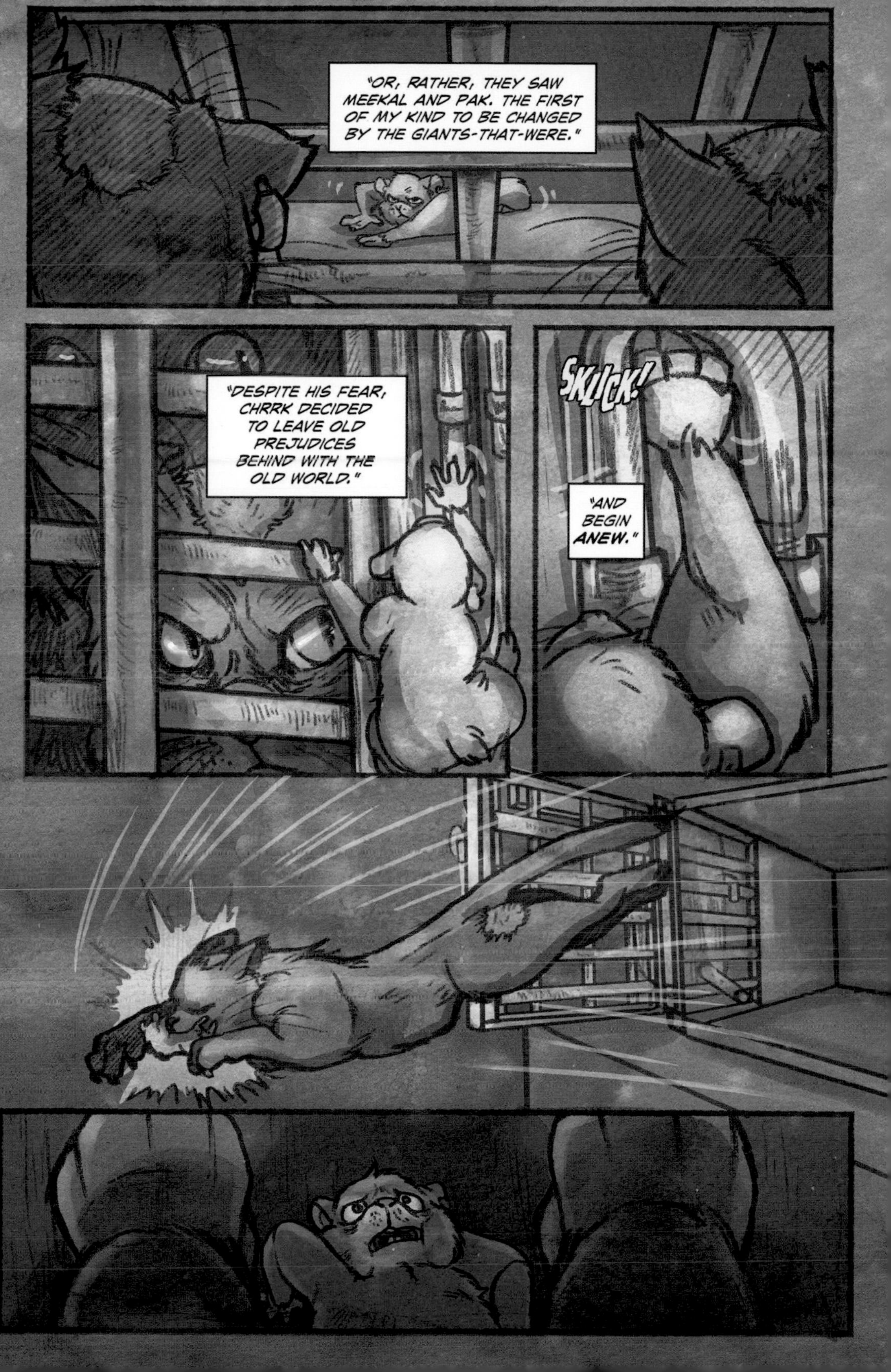
"OR, RATHER, THEY SAW MEEKAL AND PAK. THE FIRST OF MY KIND TO BE CHANGED BY THE GIANTS-THAT-WERE."
"DESPITE HIS FEAR, CHRRK DECIDED TO LEAVE OLD PREJUDICES BEHIND WITH THE OLD WORLD."
SKLICK!
"AND BEGIN ANEW."

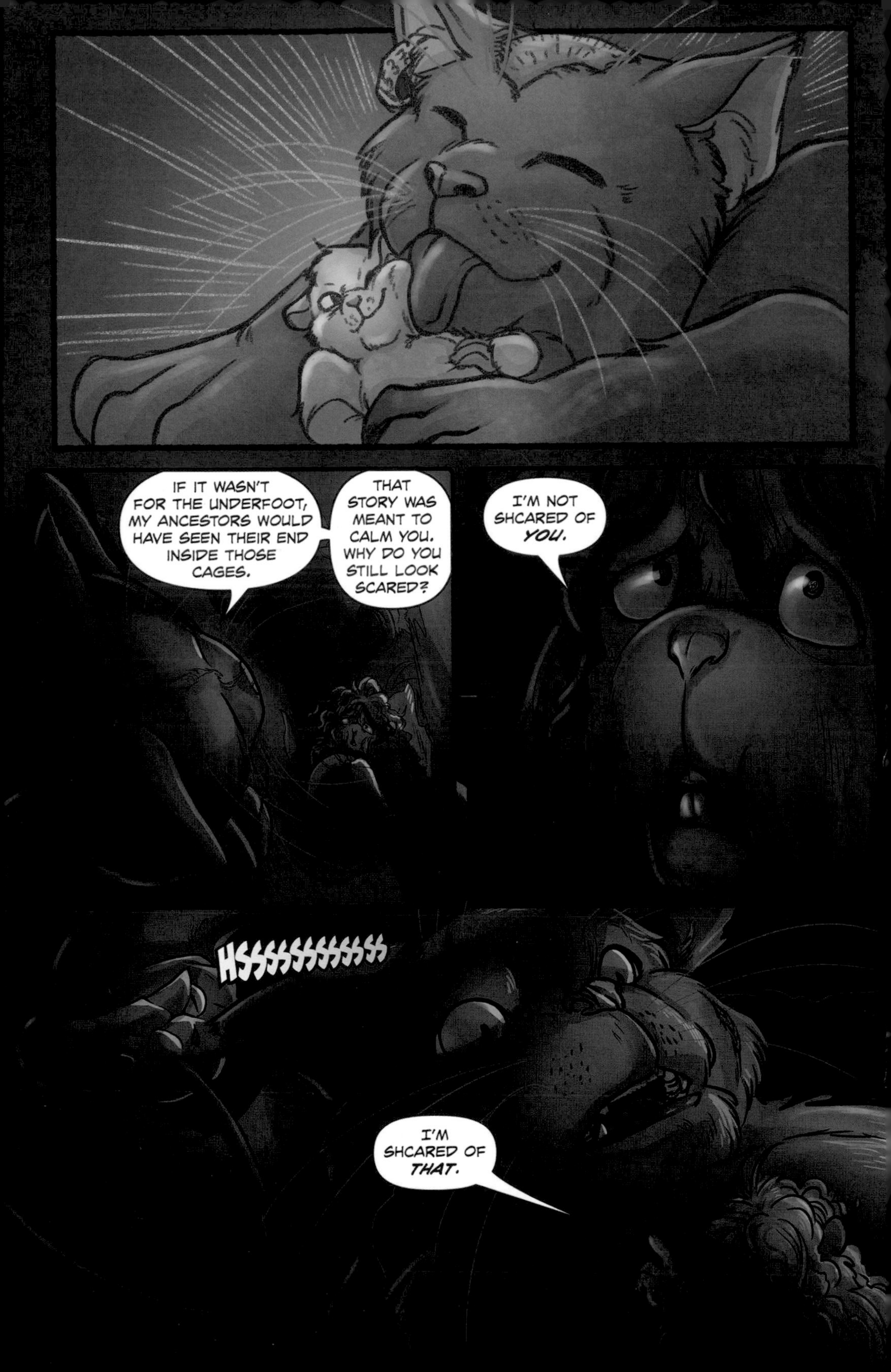
IF IT WASN'T FOR THE UNDERFOOT, MY ANCESTORS WOULD HAVE SEEN THEIR END INSIDE THOSE CAGES.
THAT STORY WAS MEANT TO CALM YOU. WHY DO YOU STILL LOOK SCARED?
I'M NOT SHCARED OF *YOU*.
HSSSSSSSSSSSS
I'M SHCARED OF *THAT*.

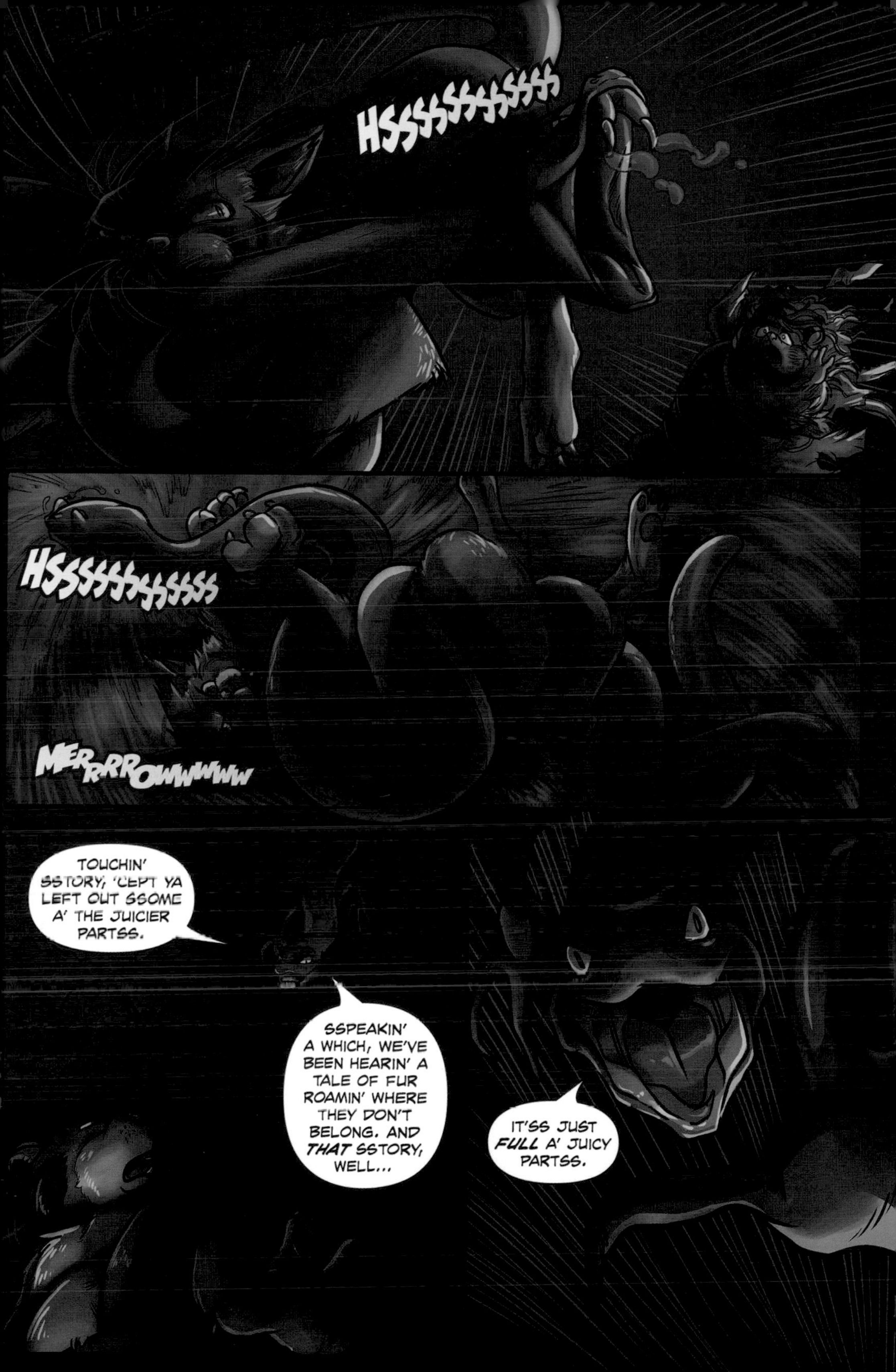
HSSSSSSSSSSSS
HSSSSSSSSSSSS
MERRRROWWWWW
TOUCHIN' SSTORY, 'CEPT YA LEFT OUT SSOME A' THE JUICIER PARTSS.
SSPEAKIN' A WHICH, WE'VE BEEN HEARIN' A TALE OF FUR ROAMIN' WHERE THEY DON'T BELONG. AND *THAT* SSTORY, WELL...
IT'SS JUST *FULL* A' JUICY PARTSS.

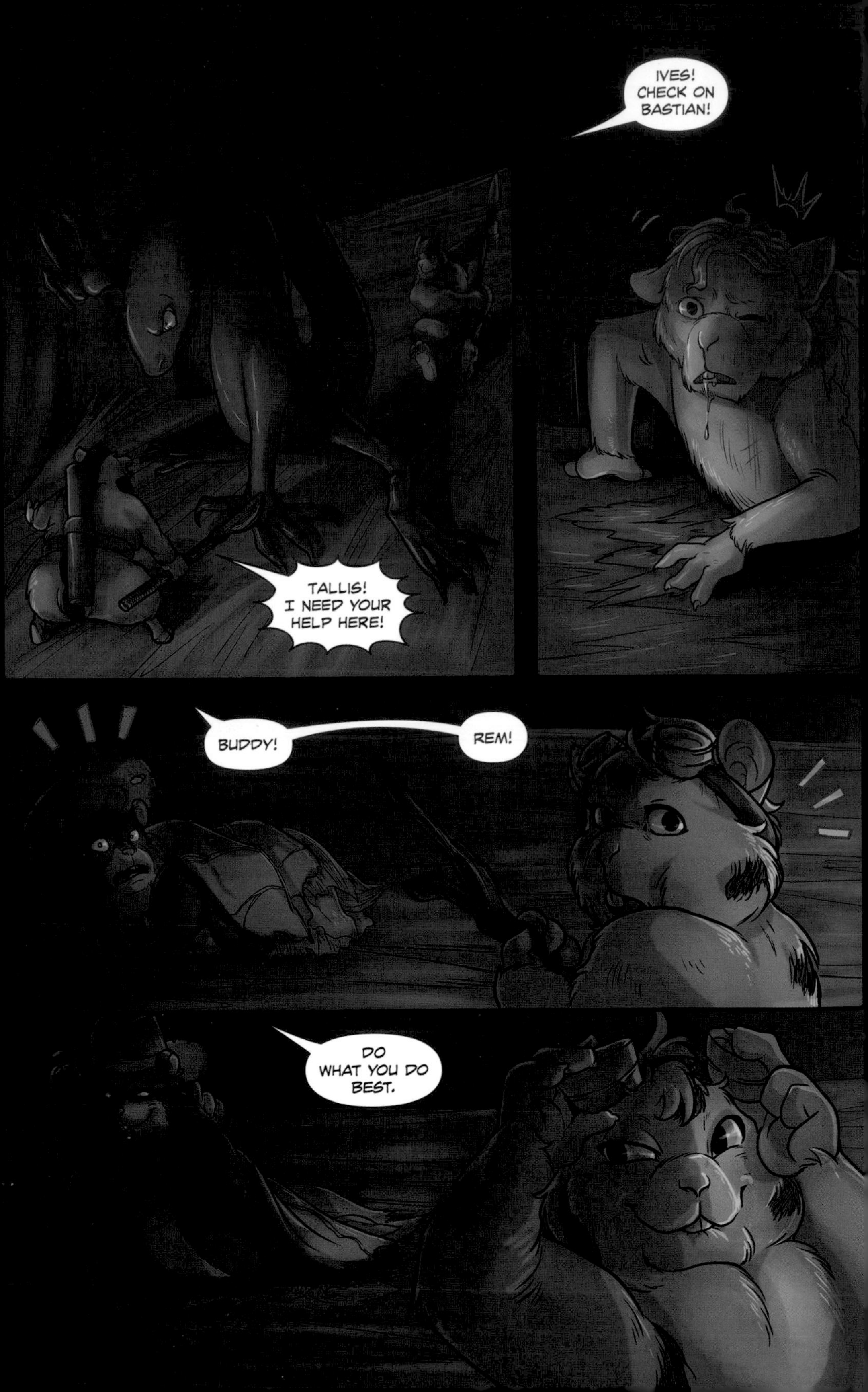
IVES! CHECK ON BASTIAN!
TALLIS! I NEED YOUR HELP HERE!
BUDDY!
REM!
DO WHAT YOU DO BEST.

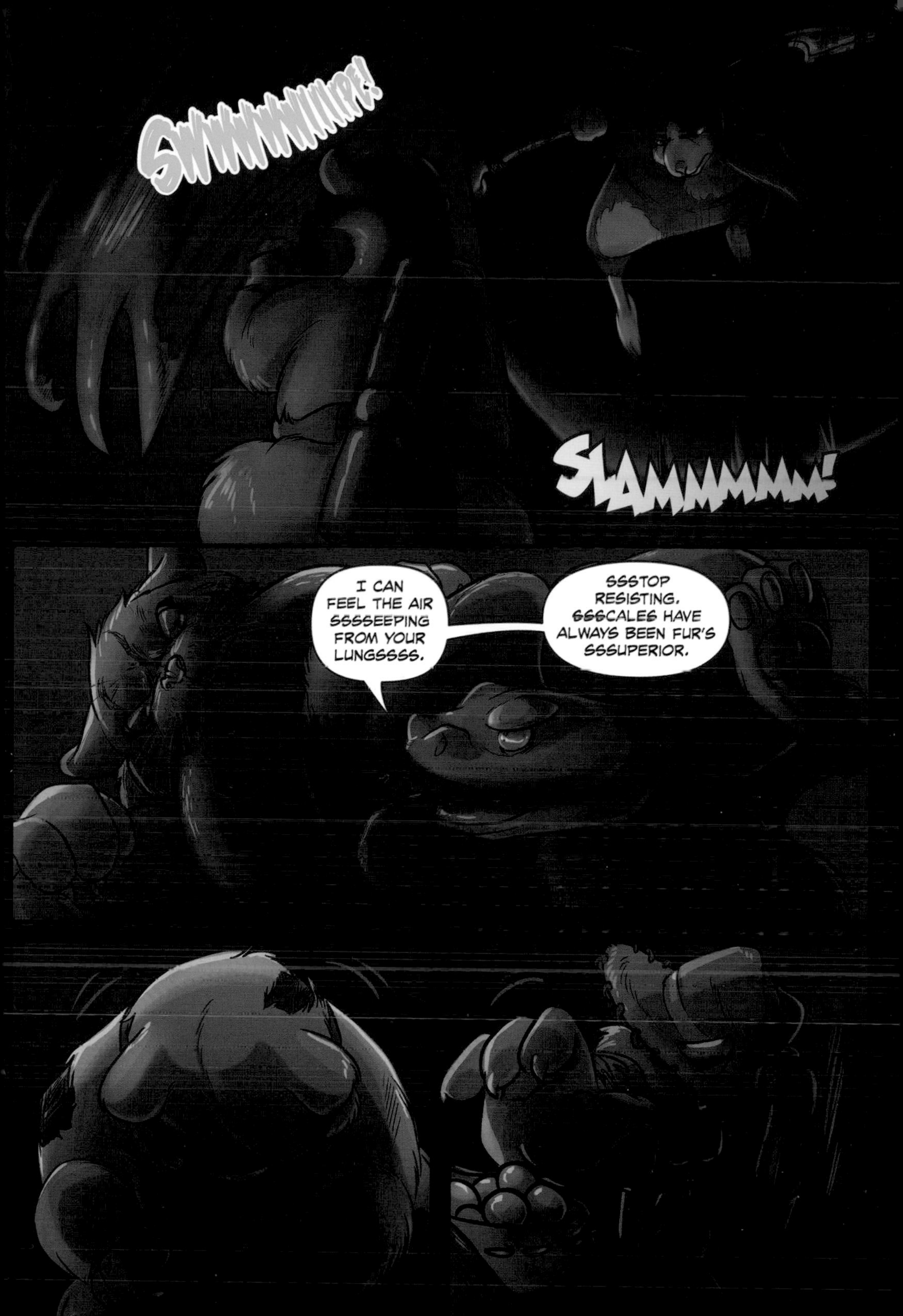
SWIIIIIIIIIPE!
SLAMMMMMM!
I CAN FEEL THE AIR SSSSEEPING FROM YOUR LUNGSSSS.
SSSTOP RESISTING. SSSCALES HAVE ALWAYS BEEN FUR'S SSSUPERIOR.

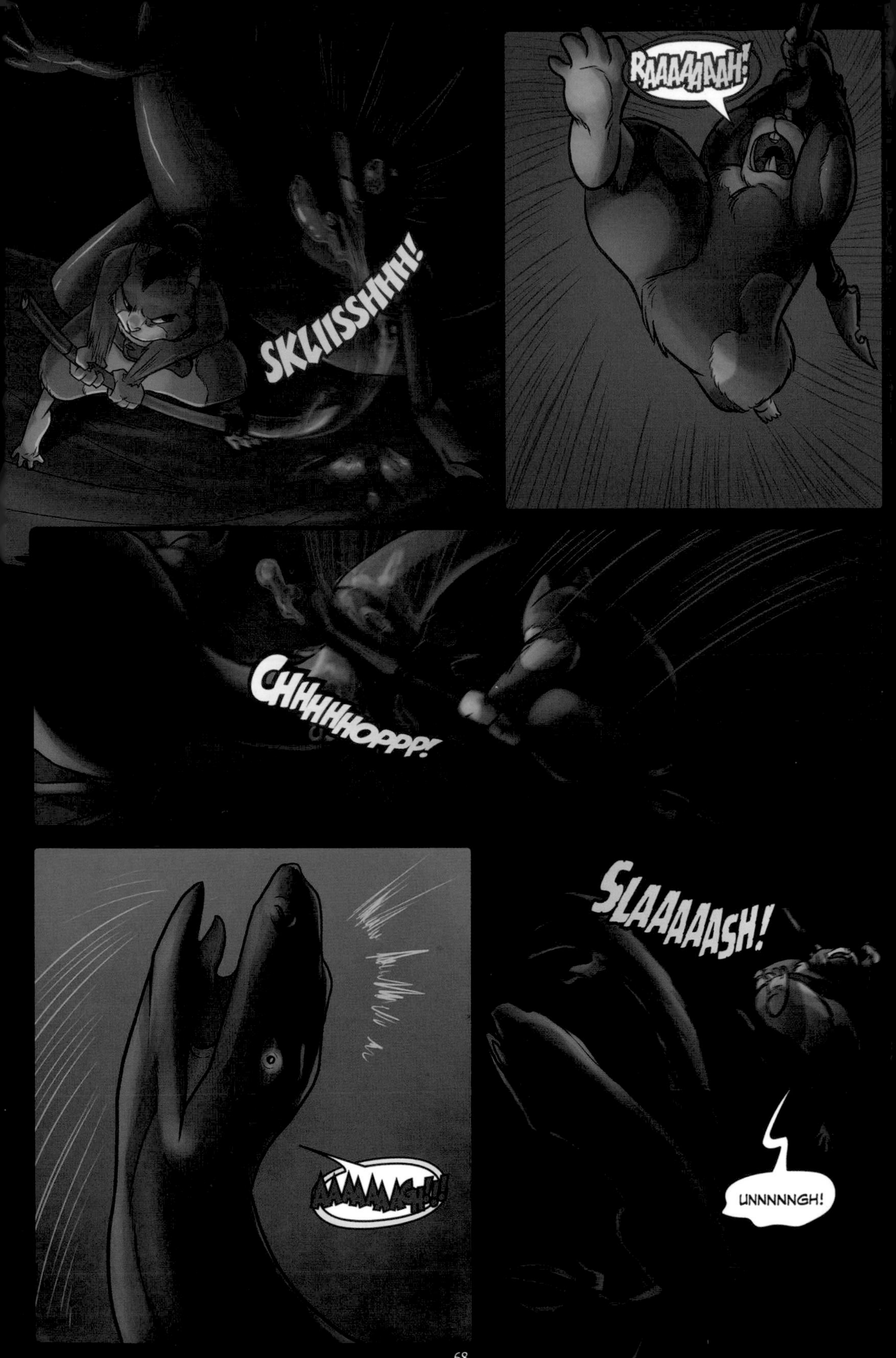
SKLIISSHHH!
RAAAAAAAH!
CHHHHHOPPP!
AAAAAAAGH!!!
SLAAAAAASH!
UNNNNNGH!

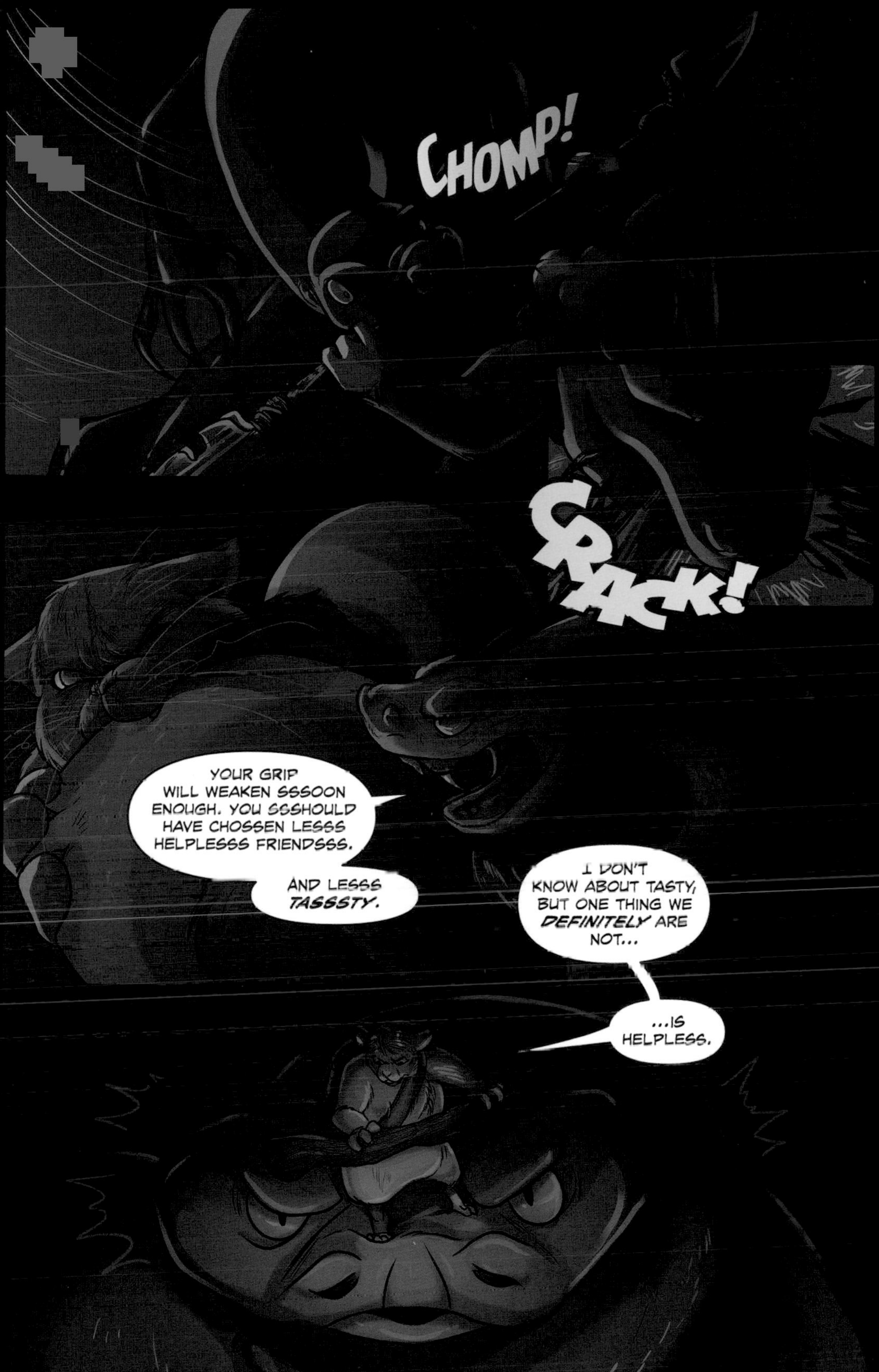
CHOMP!
CRACK!
YOUR GRIP WILL WEAKEN SSSOON ENOUGH. YOU SSSHOULD HAVE CHOSSEN LESSS HELPLESSS FRIENDSSS.
AND LESSS TASSSTY.
I DON'T KNOW ABOUT TASTY, BUT ONE THING WE DEFINITELY ARE NOT...
...IS HELPLESS.

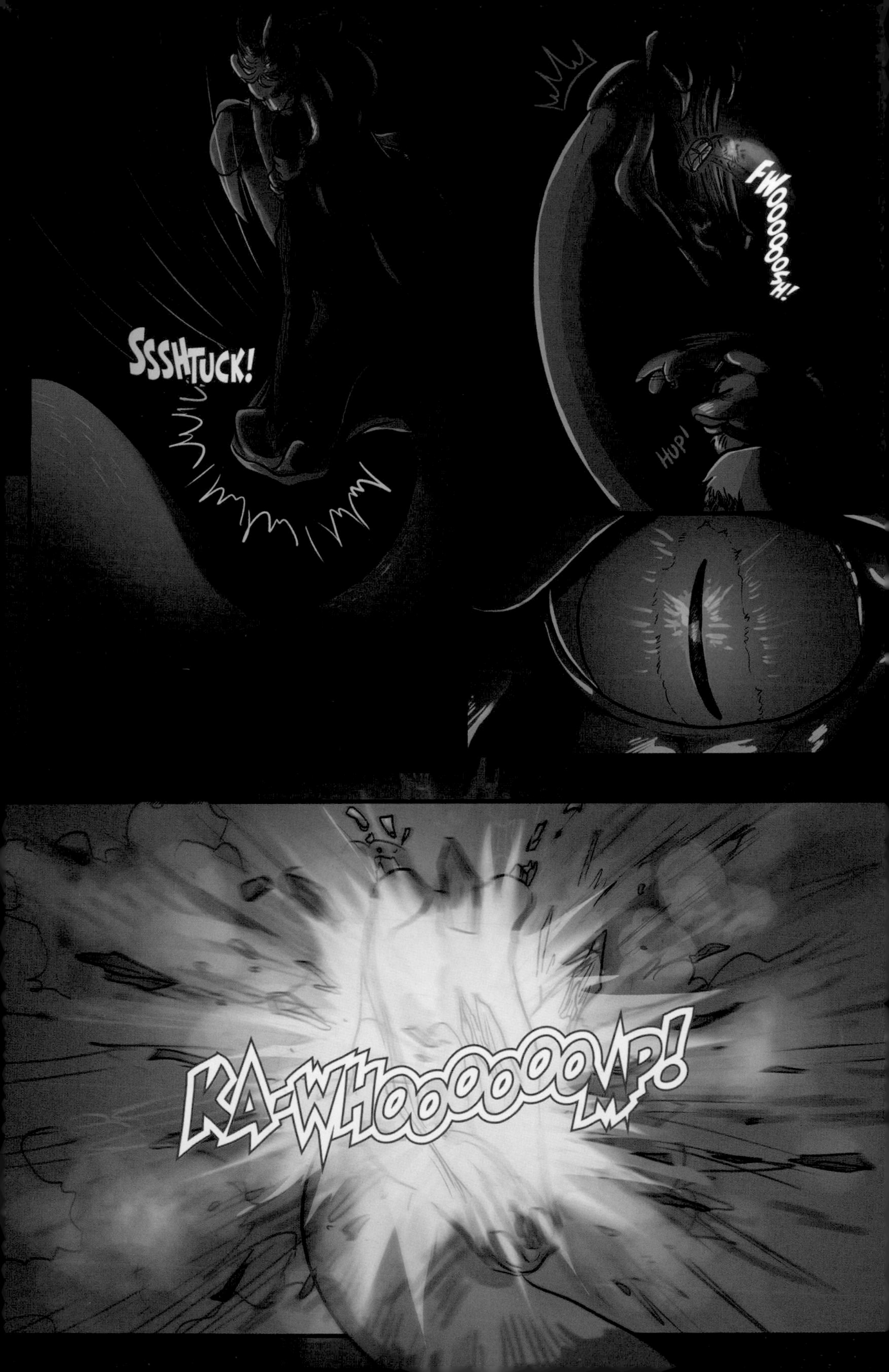
SSSHTUCK!
FWOOOOOSH!
HUP!
KA-WHOOOOOOOMP!

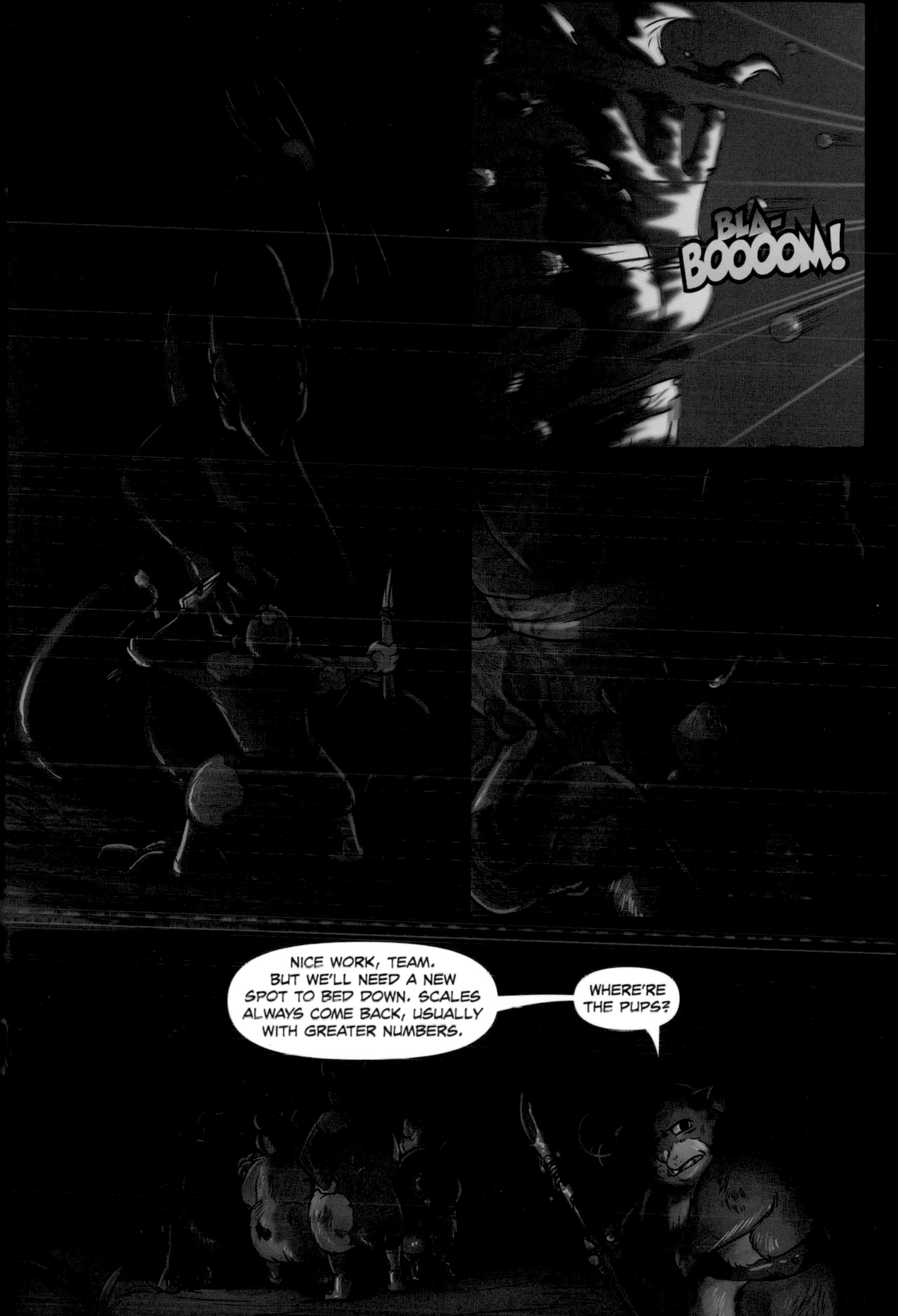
BLA-BOOOOM!
NICE WORK, TEAM. BUT WE'LL NEED A NEW SPOT TO BED DOWN. SCALES ALWAYS COME BACK, USUALLY WITH GREATER NUMBERS.
WHERE'RE THE PUPS?

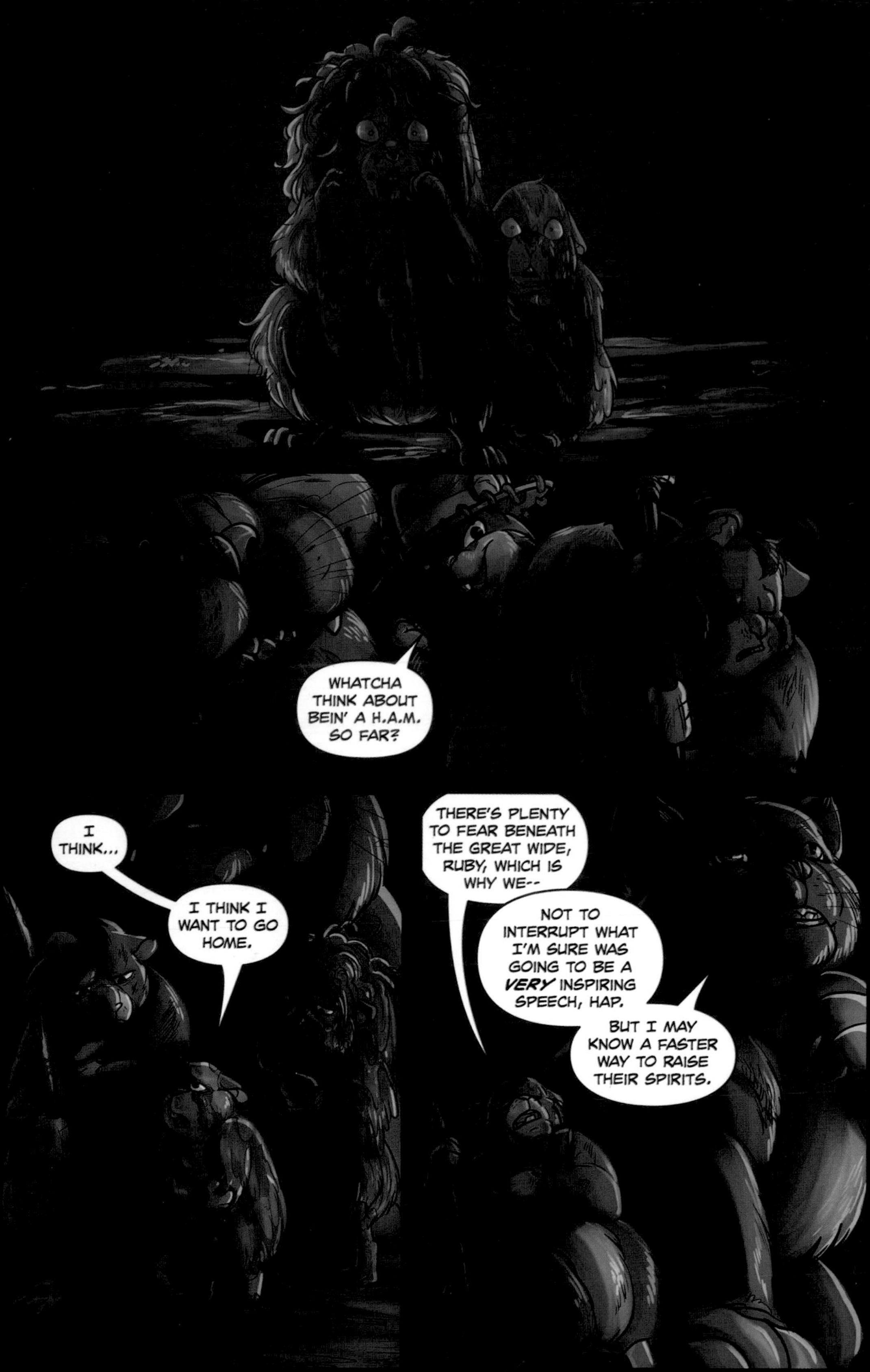
WHATCHA THINK ABOUT BEIN' A H.A.M. SO FAR?
I THINK...
I THINK I WANT TO GO HOME.
THERE'S PLENTY TO FEAR BENEATH THE GREAT WIDE, RUBY, WHICH IS WHY WE--
NOT TO INTERRUPT WHAT I'M SURE WAS GOING TO BE A *VERY* INSPIRING SPEECH, HAP.
BUT I MAY KNOW A FASTER WAY TO RAISE THEIR SPIRITS.

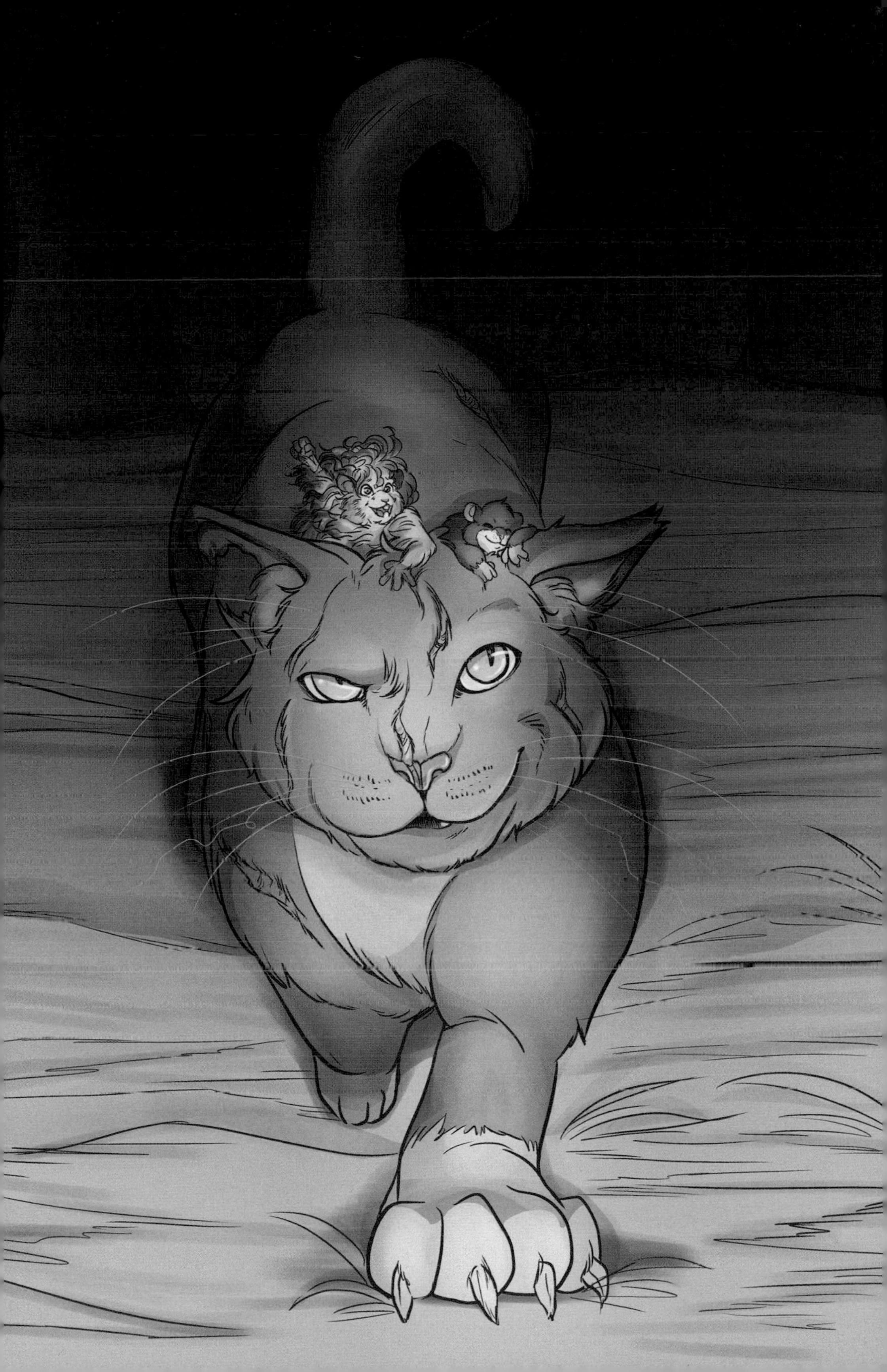

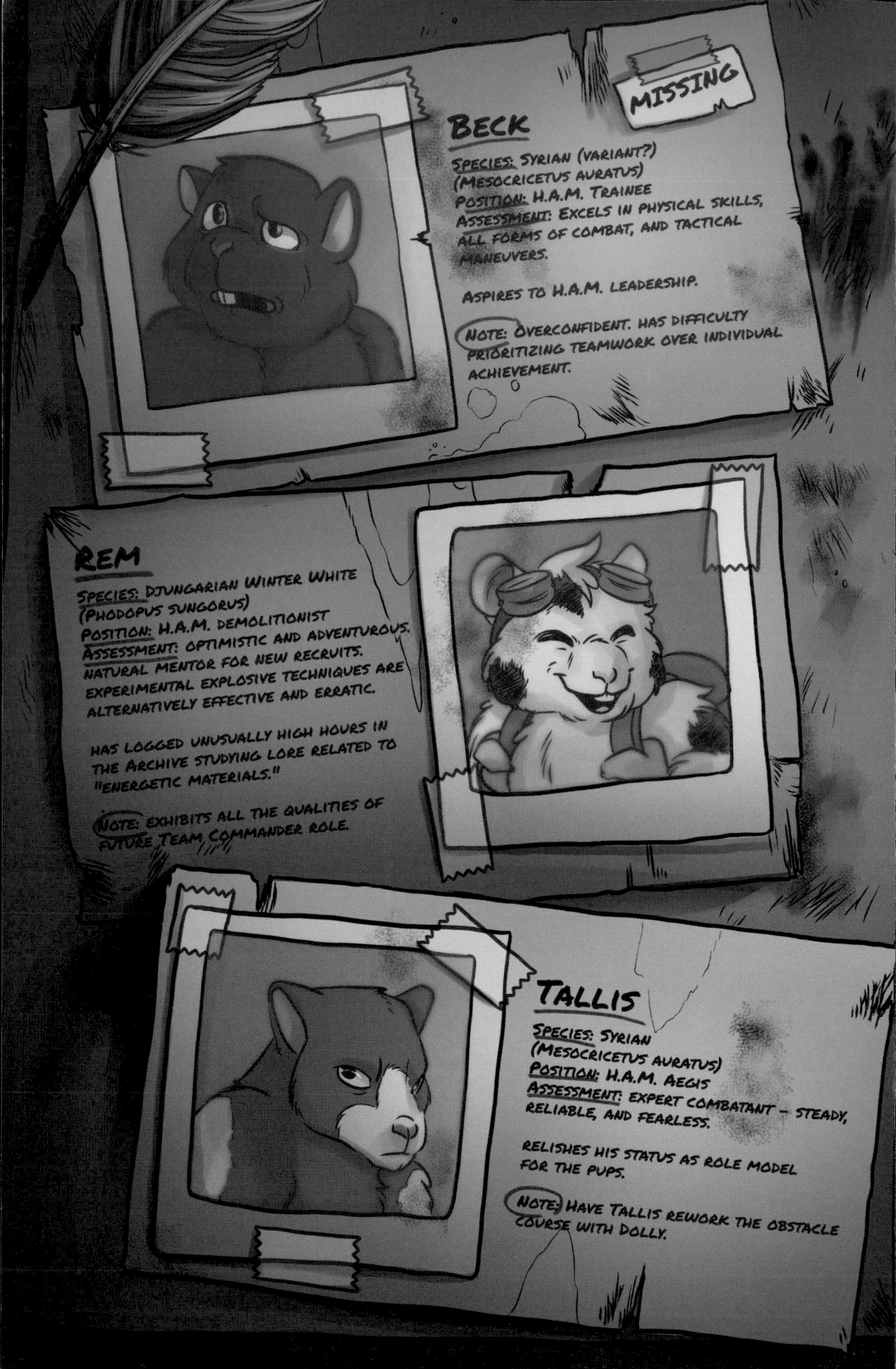
MISSING
BECK
SPECIES: SYRIAN (VARIANT?)
(MESOCRICETUS AURATUS)
POSITION: H.A.M. TRAINEE
ASSESSMENT: EXCELS IN PHYSICAL SKILLS, ALL FORMS OF COMBAT, AND TACTICAL MANEUVERS.
ASPIRES TO H.A.M. LEADERSHIP.
NOTE: OVERCONFIDENT. HAS DIFFICULTY PRIORITIZING TEAMWORK OVER INDIVIDUAL ACHIEVEMENT.
REM
SPECIES: DJUNGARIAN WINTER WHITE
(PHODOPUS SUNGORUS)
POSITION: H.A.M. DEMOLITIONIST
ASSESSMENT: OPTIMISTIC AND ADVENTUROUS. NATURAL MENTOR FOR NEW RECRUITS. EXPERIMENTAL EXPLOSIVE TECHNIQUES ARE ALTERNATIVELY EFFECTIVE AND ERRATIC.
HAS LOGGED UNUSUALLY HIGH HOURS IN THE ARCHIVE STUDYING LORE RELATED TO "ENERGETIC MATERIALS."
NOTE: EXHIBITS ALL THE QUALITIES OF FUTURE TEAM COMMANDER ROLE.
TALLIS
SPECIES: SYRIAN
(MESOCRICETUS AURATUS)
POSITION: H.A.M. AEGIS
ASSESSMENT: EXPERT COMBATANT – STEADY, RELIABLE, AND FEARLESS.
RELISHES HIS STATUS AS ROLE MODEL FOR THE PUPS.
NOTE: HAVE TALLIS REWORK THE OBSTACLE COURSE WITH DOLLY.

Magnetic Lock Lab
Update and Refit
DOP Ft. Myer - Classified

To: Coulter, C. - DOP
From: Reeves, S. - DOJ
Subject: OMG have you seen this?

Hey Chris,

I'm sure you're buried trying to coordinate the lab upgrade, but Dee sent this my way and I know how much you love weird architecture, so I had to share. Some Victorian swindler named Whitaker Wright got rich selling junk mining bonds in the 1880s. He desperately wanted to fit in with the high-class English society, so he used his money to build a mansion on a 9,000 acre estate--and added a ballroom beneath an artificial lake. Apparently, you could watch fish through the glass ceiling! Whitaker died in prison, but his underwater inferiority complex remains watertight to this day. You've got to see the pictures. They're wild.

So forget the new patio -- I'm thinking your next home improvement project should be a man-cave under the swimming pool.

See you at happy hour Thurs.
Steve

100 Wonders: The Underwater Ballroom.pdf

This message may contain information that is classified, privileged, confidential, or otherwise exempt from disclosure under applicable law. Do not disclose without consulting ... egal Counsel. If you think you have received this email in ... .

Interior Electromagnetic Locks

Note: Only "fail safe" maglocks meet federal safety regulations for allowing manual control of exits during business hours. Unlike "fail secure" locks, which remain locked when power is lost, "fail safe" devices demagnetize during outages, allowing personnel to leave the building.

Battery backup is recommended to compensate for the fail safe electromagnetic locks in buildings with higher security requirements.

Lab Security Upgrade Report due 7/2
Cross-check budget requirements

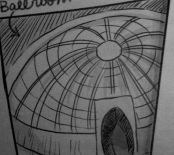

Whitaker's underwater Ballroom

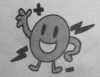

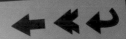

Mitch's Maglocks
Serving the D.C. Area Since 1999

How does it work?

When electricity passes through the electromagnet, it excites the electror creating a magnetic field that attracts the magnet to the metal plating on the opposite side. Single door electromagnetic locks can typically withstand up to 1200 lbs. of force and use less energy than a single light bulb to maintain.

At Mitch's Mag...

CHAPTER THREE

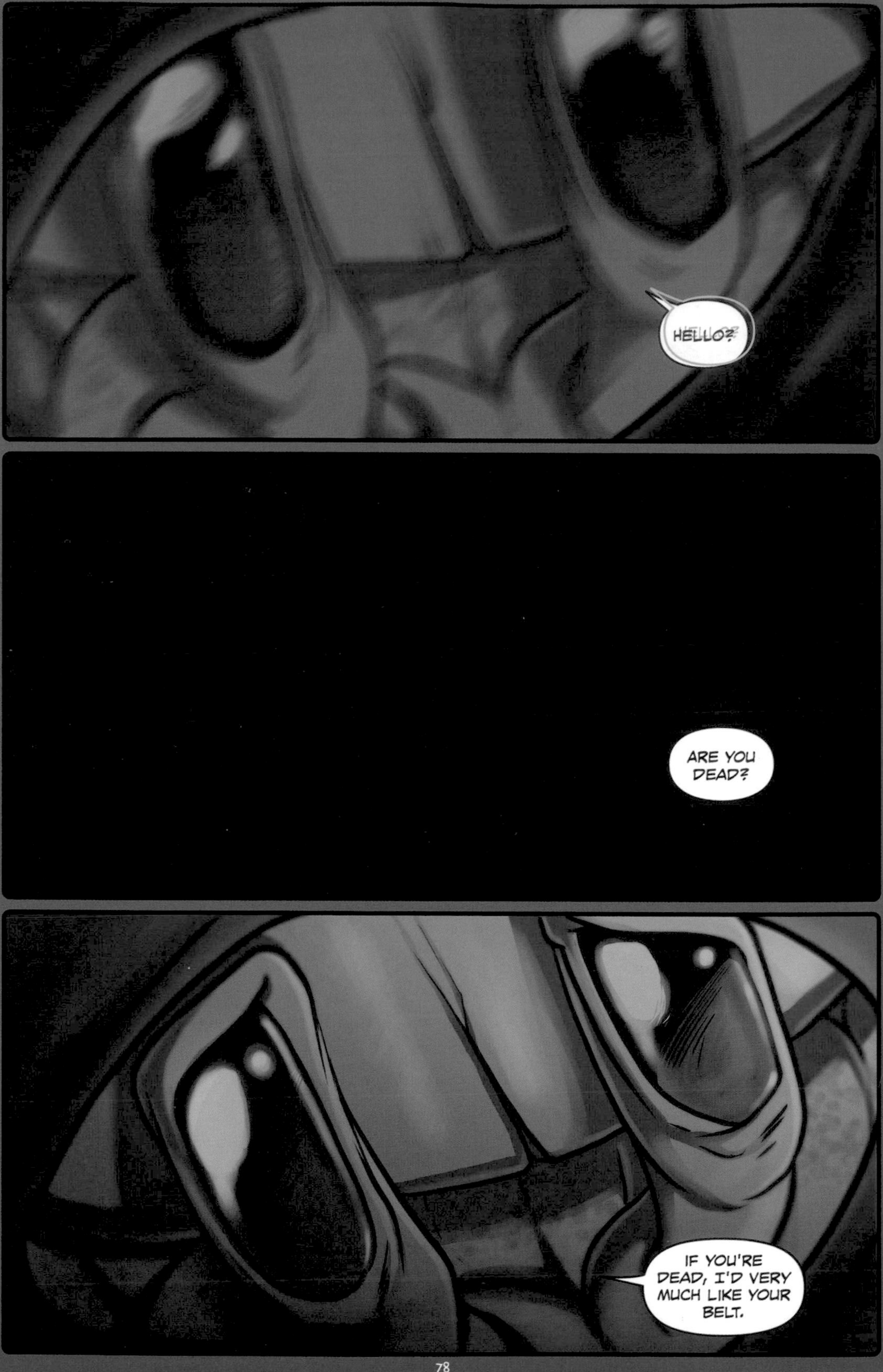
HELLO?
ARE YOU DEAD?
IF YOU'RE DEAD, I'D VERY MUCH LIKE YOUR BELT.

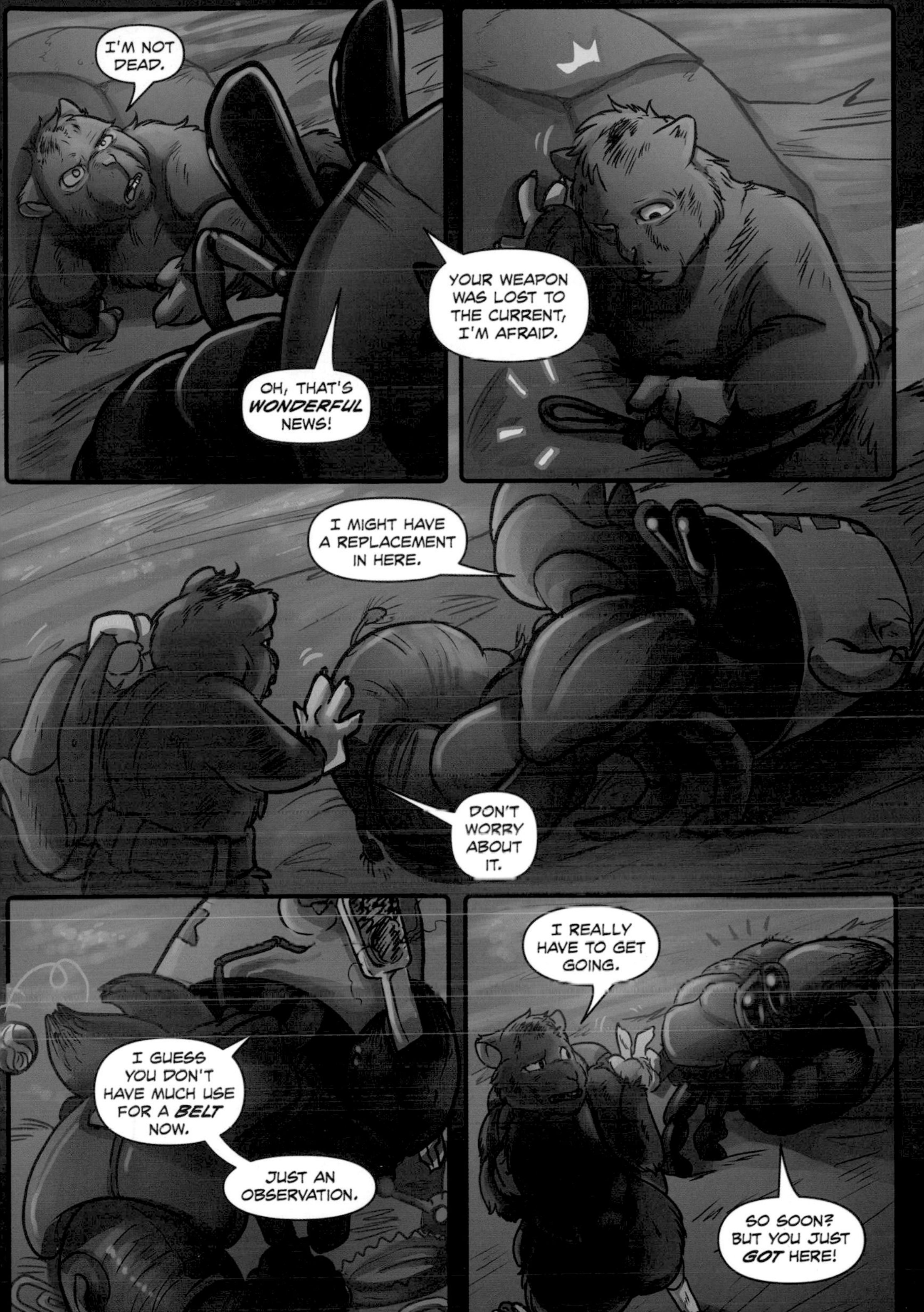
I'M NOT DEAD.
OH, THAT'S WONDERFUL NEWS!
YOUR WEAPON WAS LOST TO THE CURRENT, I'M AFRAID.
I MIGHT HAVE A REPLACEMENT IN HERE.
DON'T WORRY ABOUT IT.
I GUESS YOU DON'T HAVE MUCH USE FOR A BELT NOW.
JUST AN OBSERVATION.
I REALLY HAVE TO GET GOING.
SO SOON? BUT YOU JUST GOT HERE!

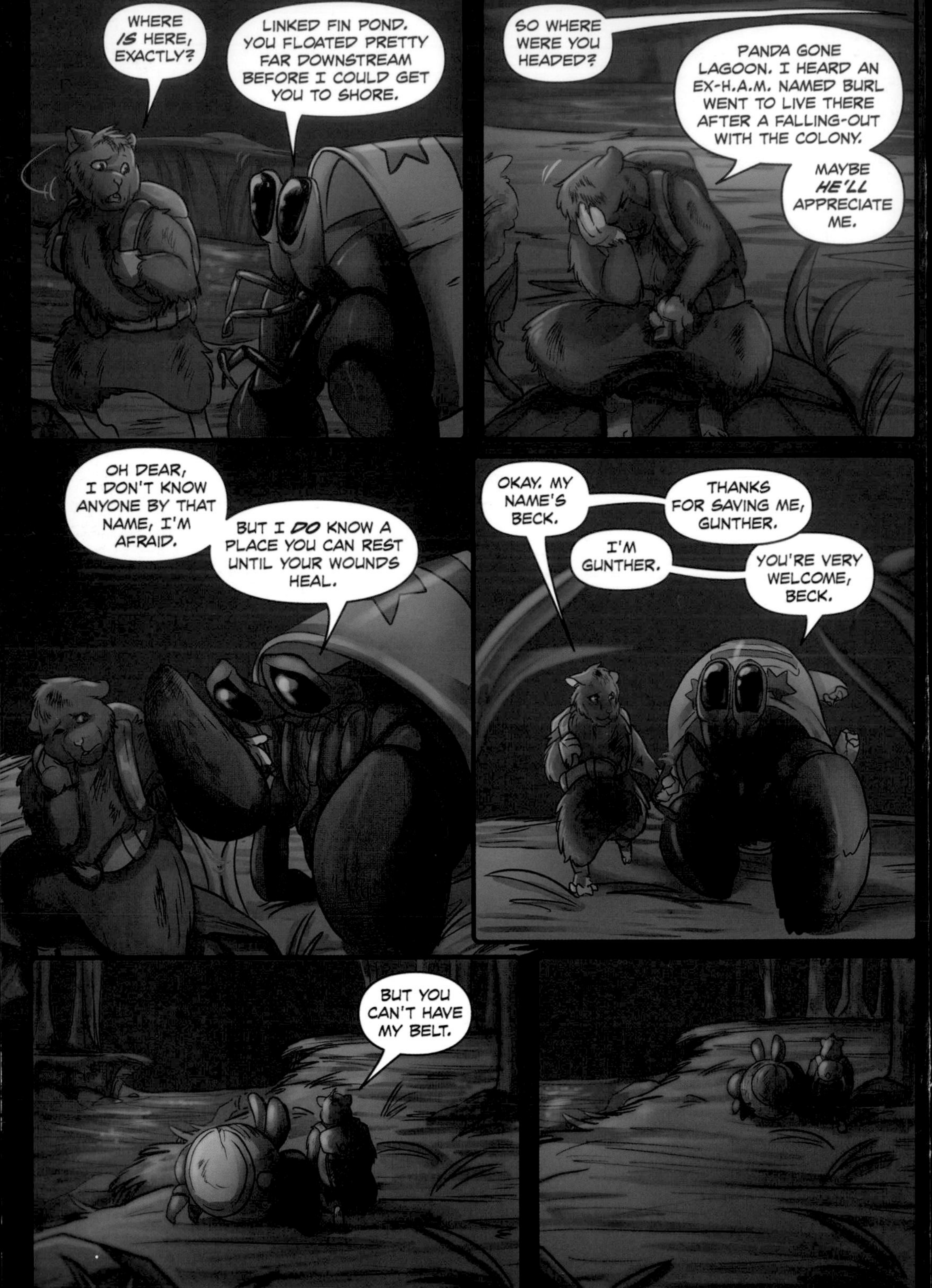
WHERE *IS* HERE, EXACTLY?
LINKED FIN POND. YOU FLOATED PRETTY FAR DOWNSTREAM BEFORE I COULD GET YOU TO SHORE.
SO WHERE WERE YOU HEADED?
PANDA GONE LAGOON. I HEARD AN EX-H.A.M. NAMED BURL WENT TO LIVE THERE AFTER A FALLING-OUT WITH THE COLONY.
MAYBE *HE'LL* APPRECIATE ME.
OH DEAR, I DON'T KNOW ANYONE BY THAT NAME, I'M AFRAID.
BUT I *DO* KNOW A PLACE YOU CAN REST UNTIL YOUR WOUNDS HEAL.
OKAY. MY NAME'S BECK.
I'M GUNTHER.
THANKS FOR SAVING ME, GUNTHER.
YOU'RE VERY WELCOME, BECK.
BUT YOU CAN'T HAVE MY BELT.

I THOUGHT YOU SAID YOU COULD KEEP UP!

I THOUGHT YOU'D GIVE ME A HEAD START!

YOU KNOW THE MISSION'S *OVER*, RIGHT?

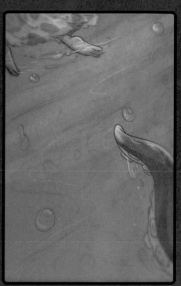

MAYBE I JUST WANTED TO GET YOU AWAY FROM THE OTHERS.

HAVE YOU ALL TO MYSELF FOR A BIT.

HAP!

OATES!

OATES!

HAP!

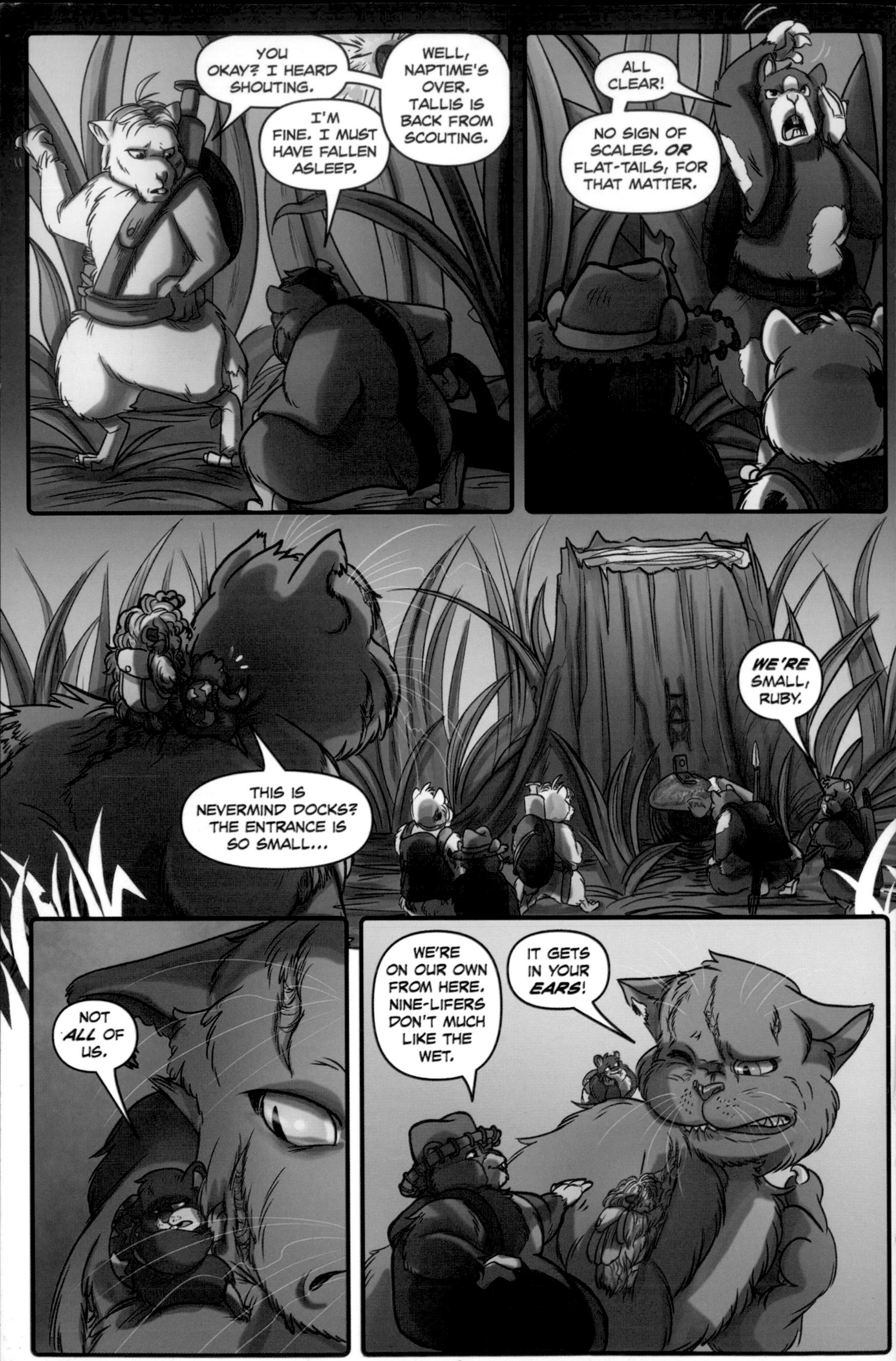
YOU OKAY? I HEARD SHOUTING.
WELL, NAPTIME'S OVER. TALLIS IS BACK FROM SCOUTING.
I'M FINE. I MUST HAVE FALLEN ASLEEP.
ALL CLEAR!
NO SIGN OF SCALES. *OR* FLAT-TAILS, FOR THAT MATTER.
THIS IS NEVERMIND DOCKS? THE ENTRANCE IS SO SMALL...
WE'RE SMALL, RUBY.
NOT *ALL* OF US.
WE'RE ON OUR OWN FROM HERE. NINE-LIFERS DON'T MUCH LIKE THE WET.
IT GETS IN YOUR *EARS*!

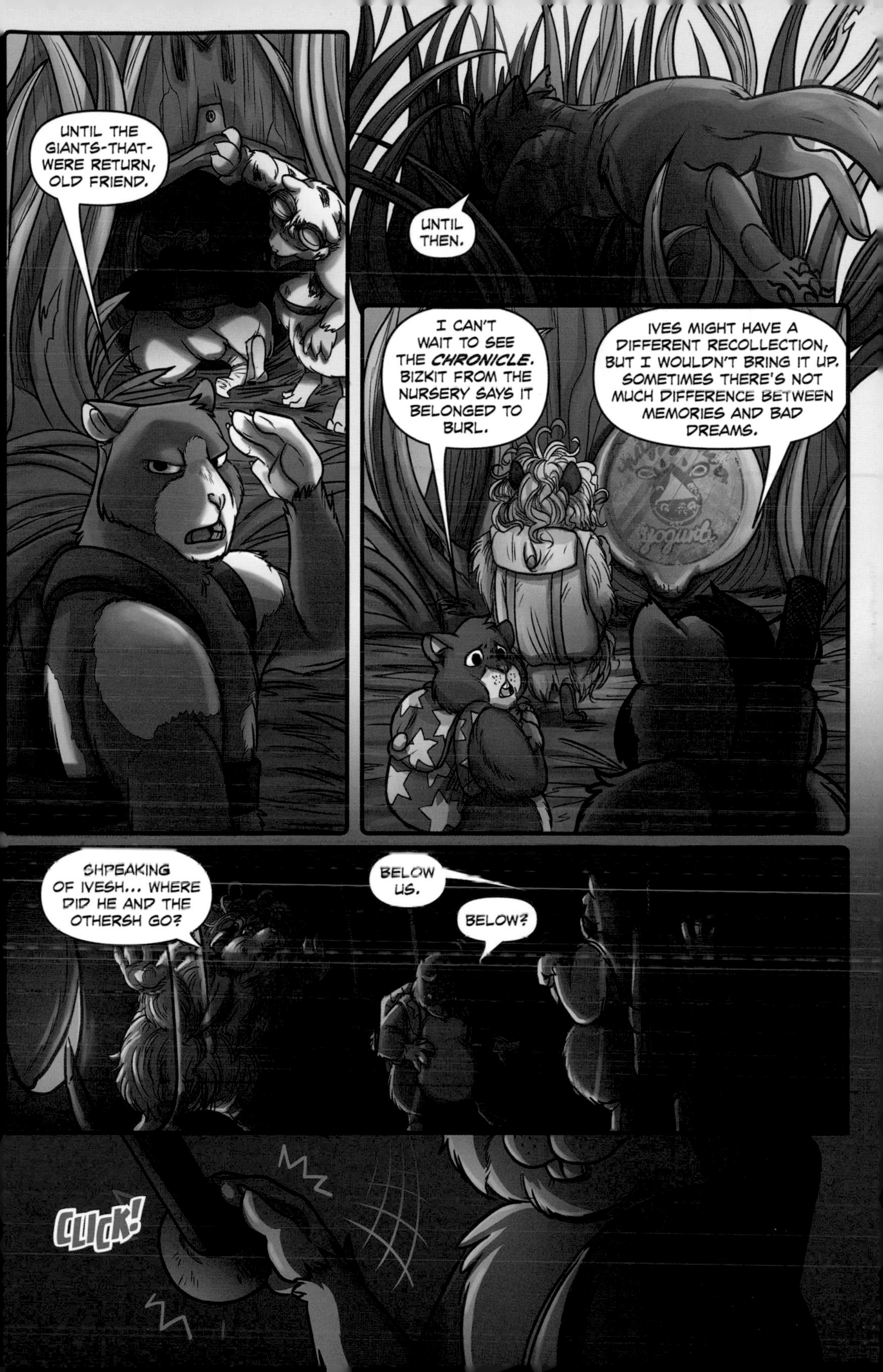
UNTIL THE GIANTS-THAT-WERE RETURN, OLD FRIEND.
UNTIL THEN.
I CAN'T WAIT TO SEE THE *CHRONICLE.* BIZKIT FROM THE NURSERY SAYS IT BELONGED TO BURL.
IVES MIGHT HAVE A DIFFERENT RECOLLECTION, BUT I WOULDN'T BRING IT UP. SOMETIMES THERE'S NOT MUCH DIFFERENCE BETWEEN MEMORIES AND BAD DREAMS.
yogurt
SHPEAKING OF IVESH... WHERE DID HE AND THE OTHERSH GO?
BELOW US.
BELOW?
CLICK!

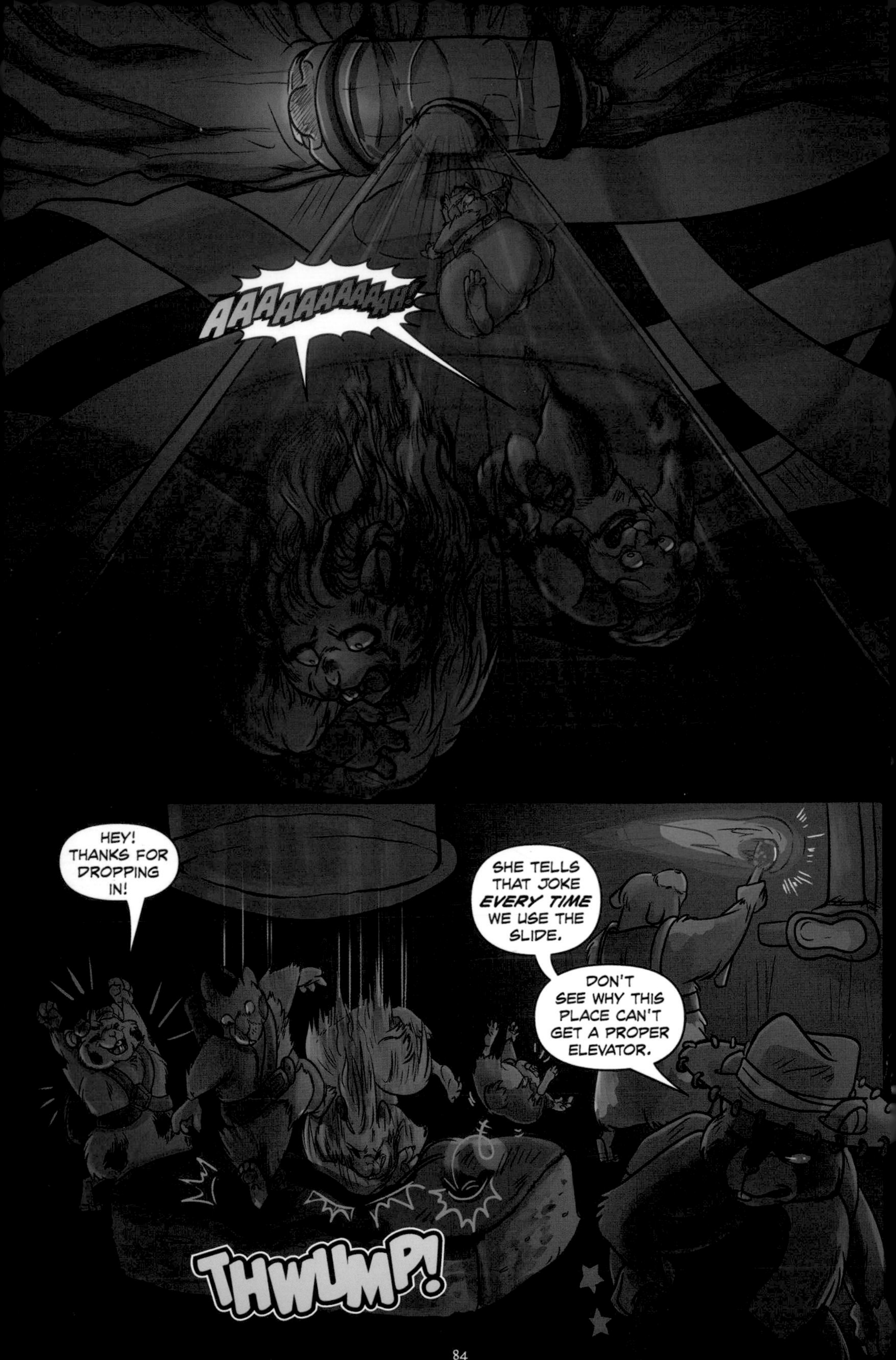
AAAAAAAAAH!
HEY! THANKS FOR DROPPING IN!
SHE TELLS THAT JOKE *EVERY TIME* WE USE THE SLIDE.
DON'T SEE WHY THIS PLACE CAN'T GET A PROPER ELEVATOR.
THWUMP!

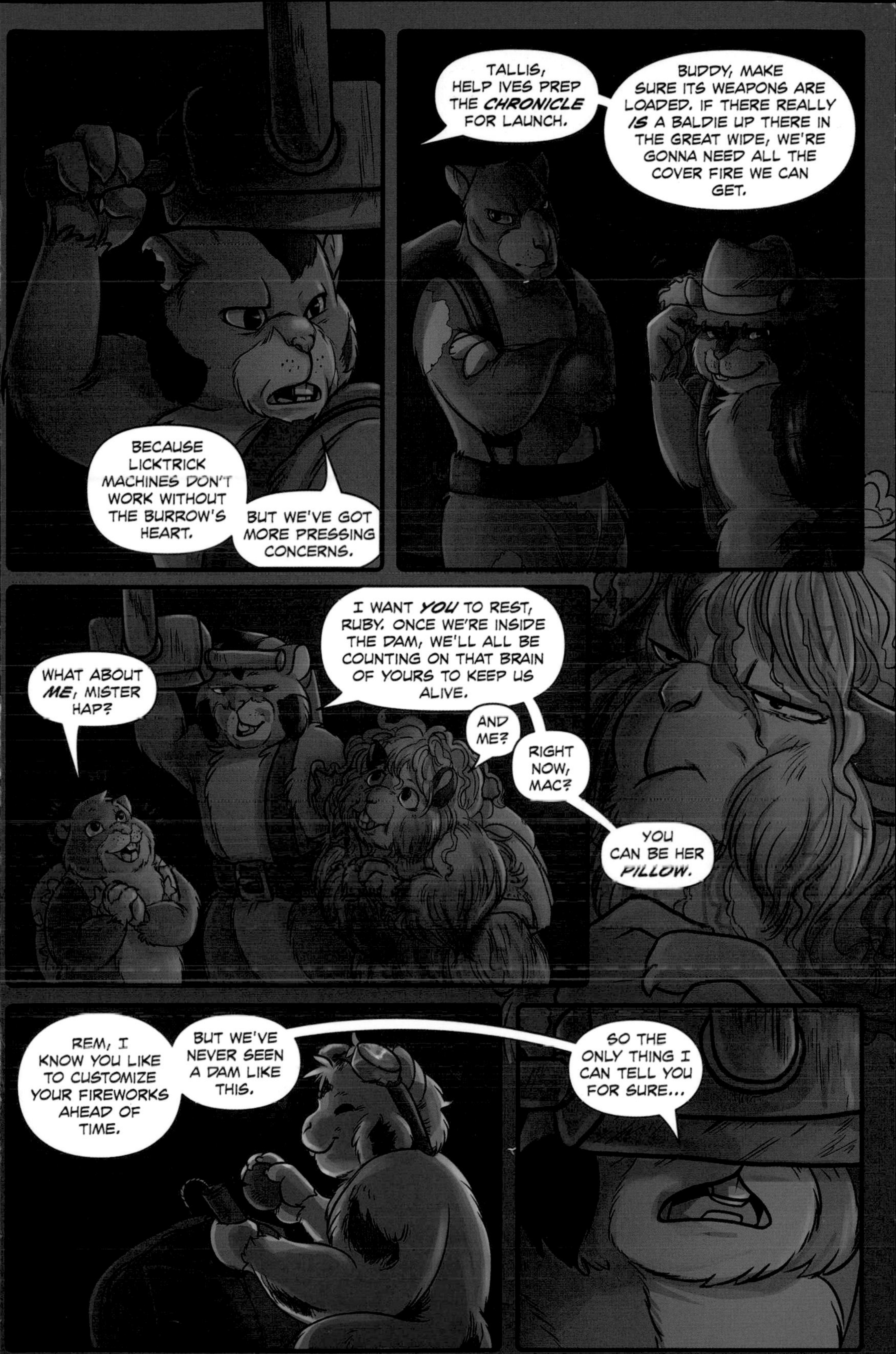
BECAUSE LICKTRICK MACHINES DON'T WORK WITHOUT THE BURROW'S HEART.
BUT WE'VE GOT MORE PRESSING CONCERNS.
TALLIS, HELP IVES PREP THE *CHRONICLE* FOR LAUNCH.
BUDDY, MAKE SURE ITS WEAPONS ARE LOADED. IF THERE REALLY *IS* A BALDIE UP THERE IN THE GREAT WIDE, WE'RE GONNA NEED ALL THE COVER FIRE WE CAN GET.
WHAT ABOUT *ME*, MISTER HAP?
I WANT *YOU* TO REST, RUBY. ONCE WE'RE INSIDE THE DAM, WE'LL ALL BE COUNTING ON THAT BRAIN OF YOURS TO KEEP US ALIVE.
AND ME?
RIGHT NOW, MAC?
YOU CAN BE HER *PILLOW*.
REM, I KNOW YOU LIKE TO CUSTOMIZE YOUR FIREWORKS AHEAD OF TIME.
BUT WE'VE NEVER SEEN A DAM LIKE THIS.
SO THE ONLY THING I CAN TELL YOU FOR SURE...

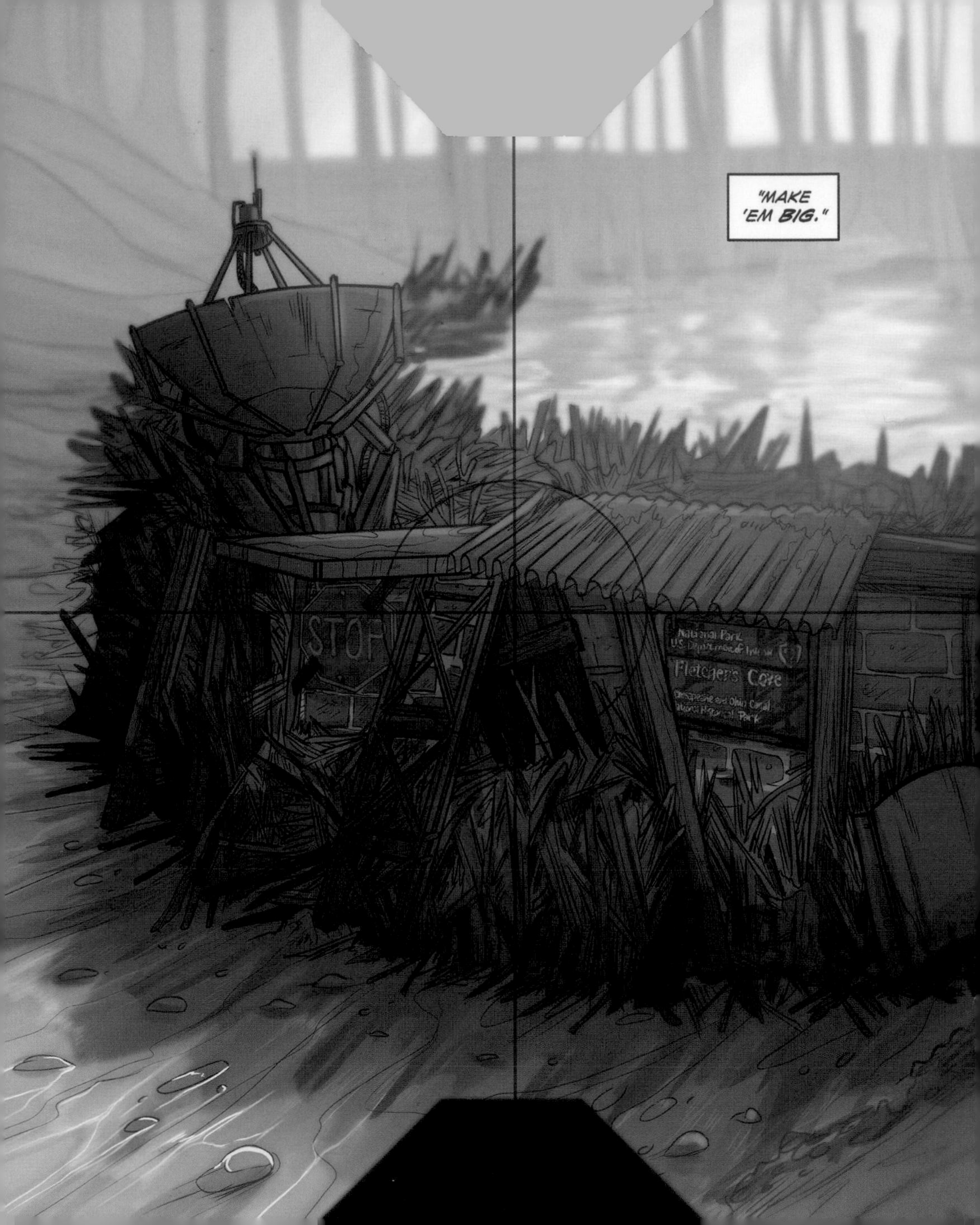
"MAKE 'EM BIG."
STOP
National Park
Fletcher's Cove
Park

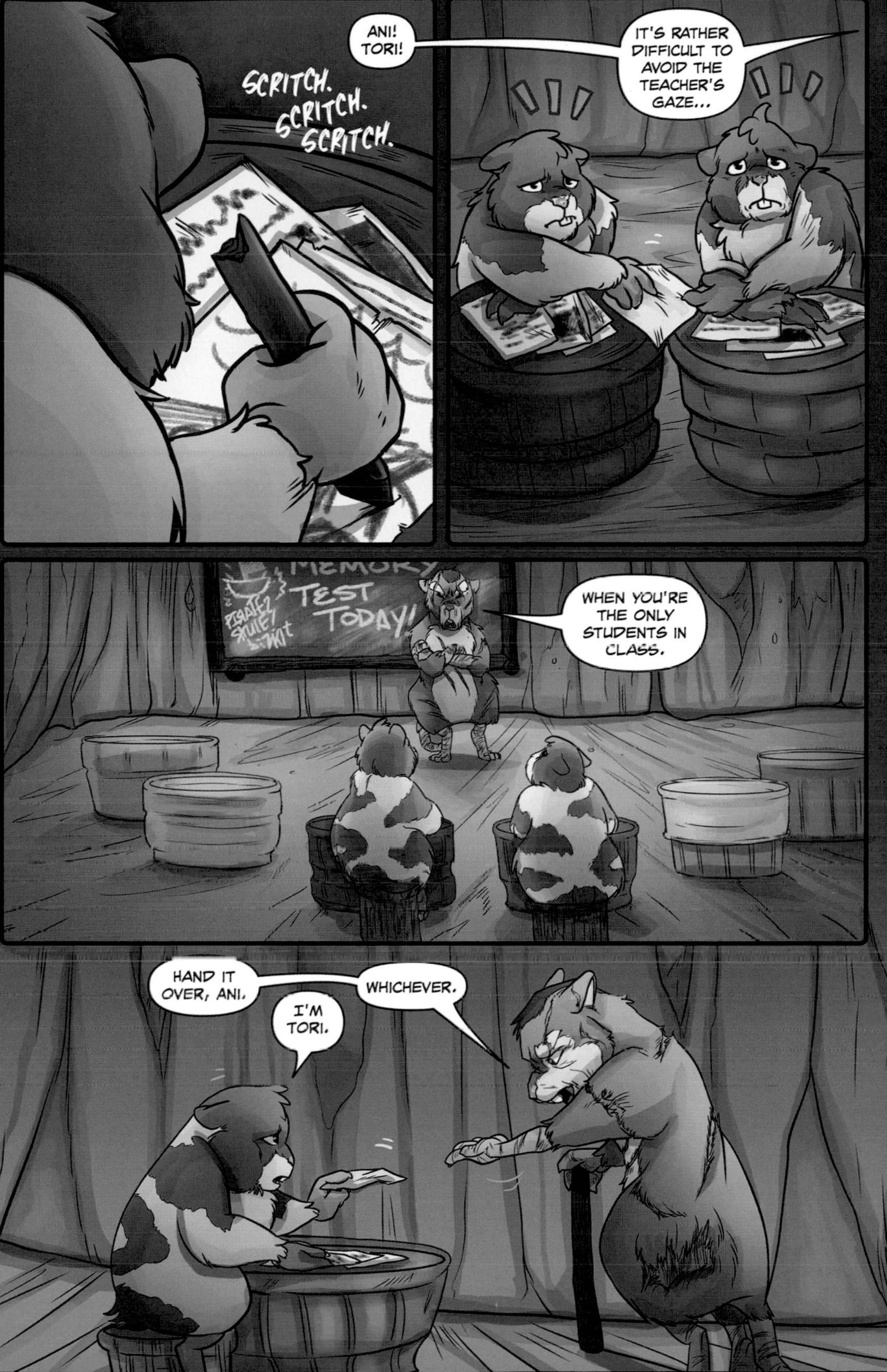
SCRITCH. SCRITCH. SCRITCH.
ANI! TORI!
IT'S RATHER DIFFICULT TO AVOID THE TEACHER'S GAZE...
MEMORY TEST TODAY!
WHEN YOU'RE THE ONLY STUDENTS IN CLASS.
HAND IT OVER, ANI.
I'M TORI.
WHICHEVER.

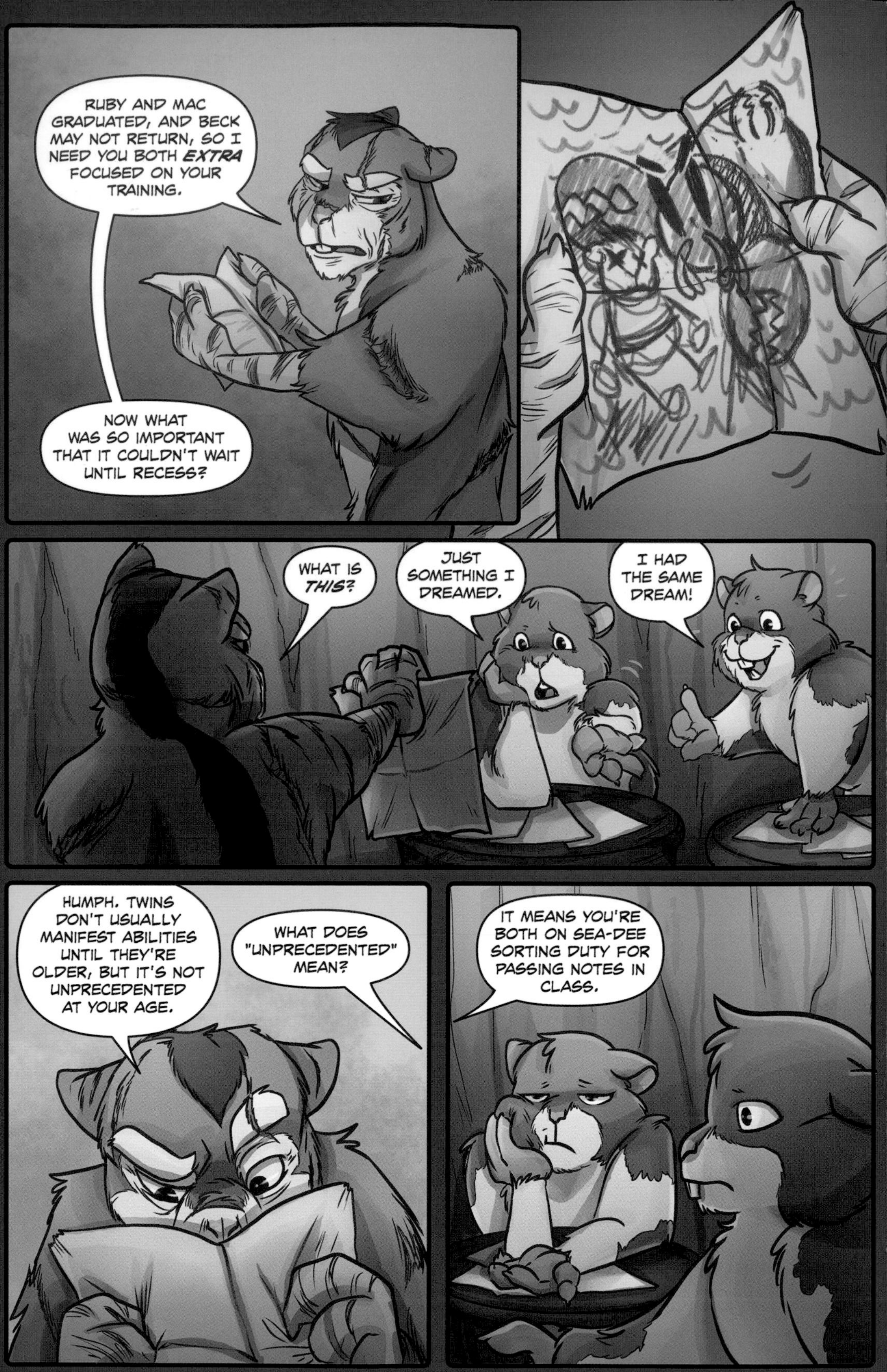
RUBY AND MAC GRADUATED, AND BECK MAY NOT RETURN, SO I NEED YOU BOTH EXTRA FOCUSED ON YOUR TRAINING.
NOW WHAT WAS SO IMPORTANT THAT IT COULDN'T WAIT UNTIL RECESS?
WHAT IS THIS?
JUST SOMETHING I DREAMED.
I HAD THE SAME DREAM!
HUMPH. TWINS DON'T USUALLY MANIFEST ABILITIES UNTIL THEY'RE OLDER, BUT IT'S NOT UNPRECEDENTED AT YOUR AGE.
WHAT DOES "UNPRECEDENTED" MEAN?
IT MEANS YOU'RE BOTH ON SEA-DEE SORTING DUTY FOR PASSING NOTES IN CLASS.

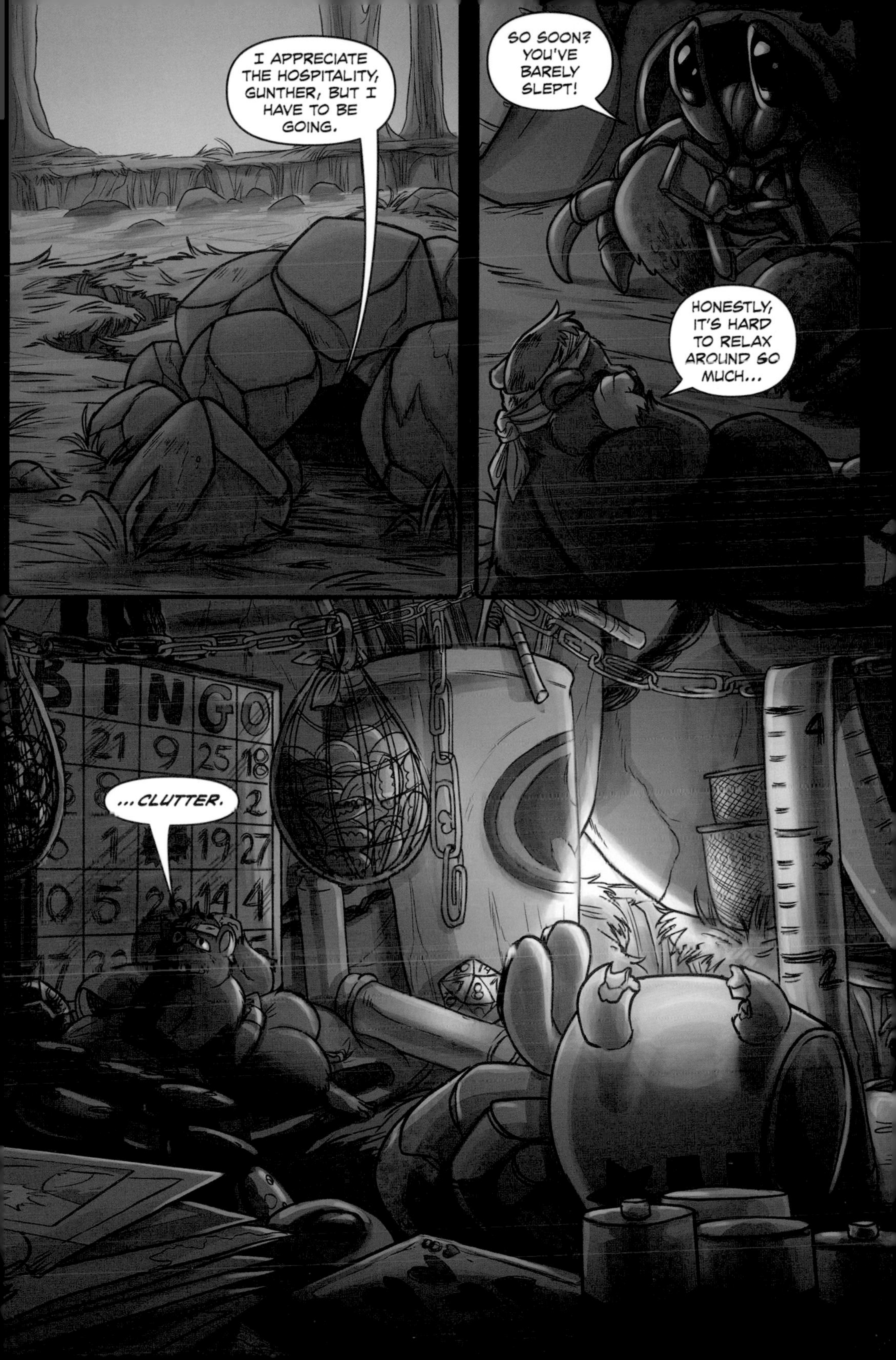
I APPRECIATE THE HOSPITALITY, GUNTHER, BUT I HAVE TO BE GOING.
SO SOON? YOU'VE BARELY SLEPT!
HONESTLY, IT'S HARD TO RELAX AROUND SO MUCH...
...CLUTTER.

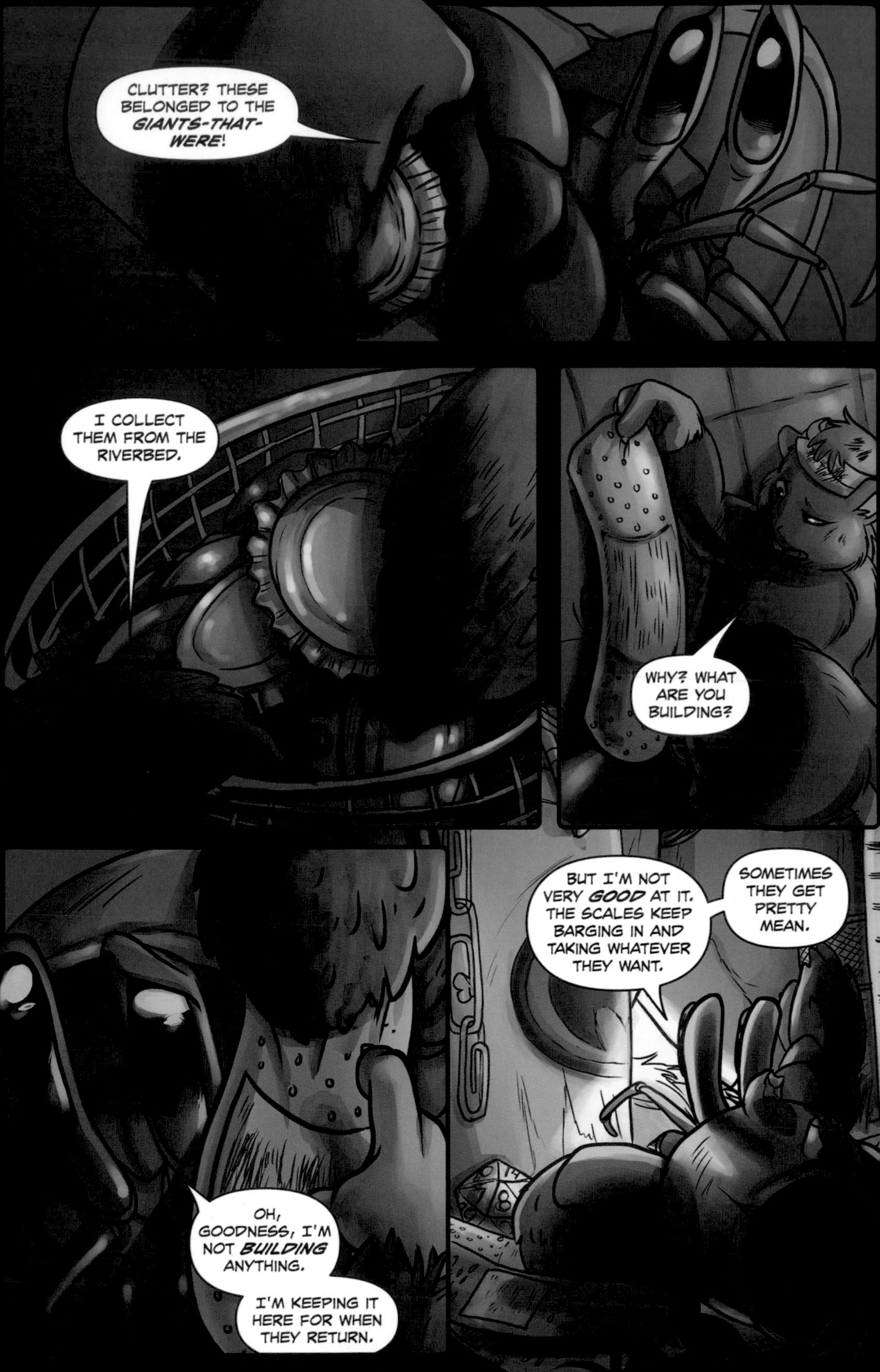
CLUTTER? THESE BELONGED TO THE *GIANTS-THAT-WERE*!
I COLLECT THEM FROM THE RIVERBED.
WHY? WHAT ARE YOU BUILDING?
OH, GOODNESS, I'M NOT *BUILDING* ANYTHING.
I'M KEEPING IT HERE FOR WHEN THEY RETURN.
BUT I'M NOT VERY *GOOD* AT IT. THE SCALES KEEP BARGING IN AND TAKING WHATEVER THEY WANT.
SOMETIMES THEY GET PRETTY MEAN.

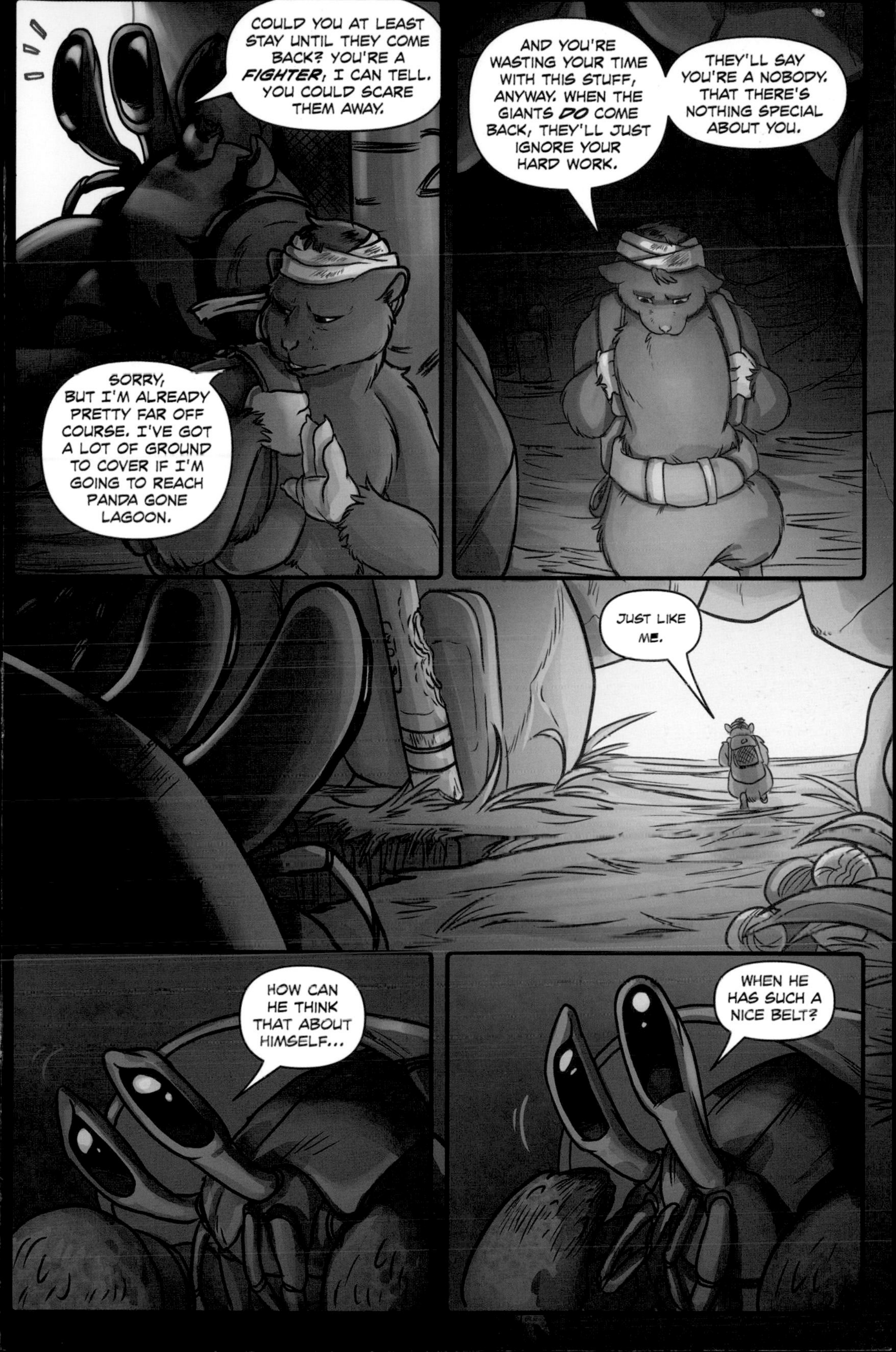
COULD YOU AT LEAST STAY UNTIL THEY COME BACK? YOU'RE A FIGHTER; I CAN TELL. YOU COULD SCARE THEM AWAY.
SORRY, BUT I'M ALREADY PRETTY FAR OFF COURSE. I'VE GOT A LOT OF GROUND TO COVER IF I'M GOING TO REACH PANDA GONE LAGOON.
AND YOU'RE WASTING YOUR TIME WITH THIS STUFF, ANYWAY. WHEN THE GIANTS DO COME BACK, THEY'LL JUST IGNORE YOUR HARD WORK.
THEY'LL SAY YOU'RE A NOBODY. THAT THERE'S NOTHING SPECIAL ABOUT YOU.
JUST LIKE ME.
HOW CAN HE THINK THAT ABOUT HIMSELF...
WHEN HE HAS SUCH A NICE BELT?

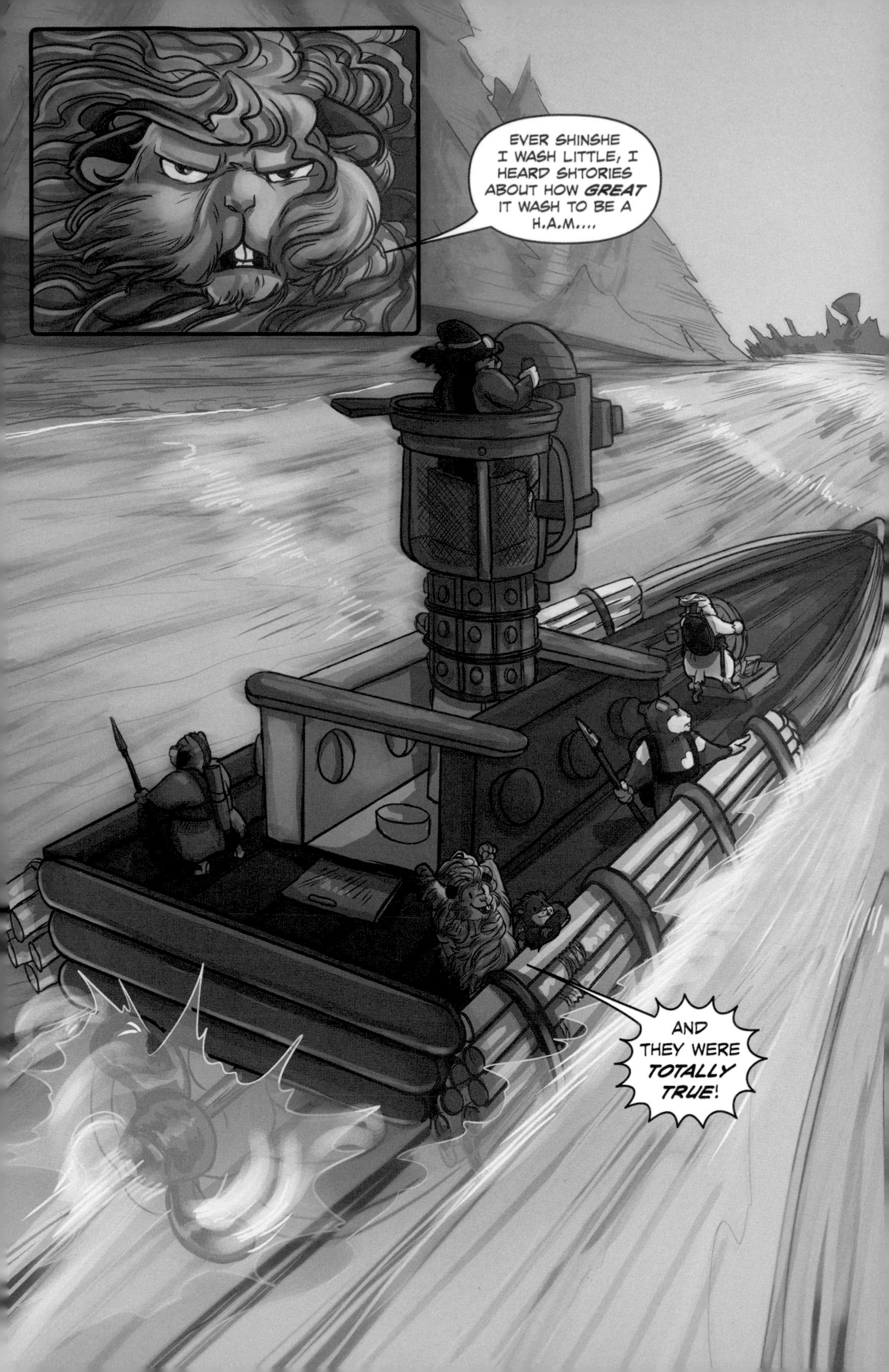
EVER SHINSHE I WASH LITTLE, I HEARD SHTORIES ABOUT HOW *GREAT* IT WASH TO BE A H.A.M....
AND THEY WERE *TOTALLY TRUE*!

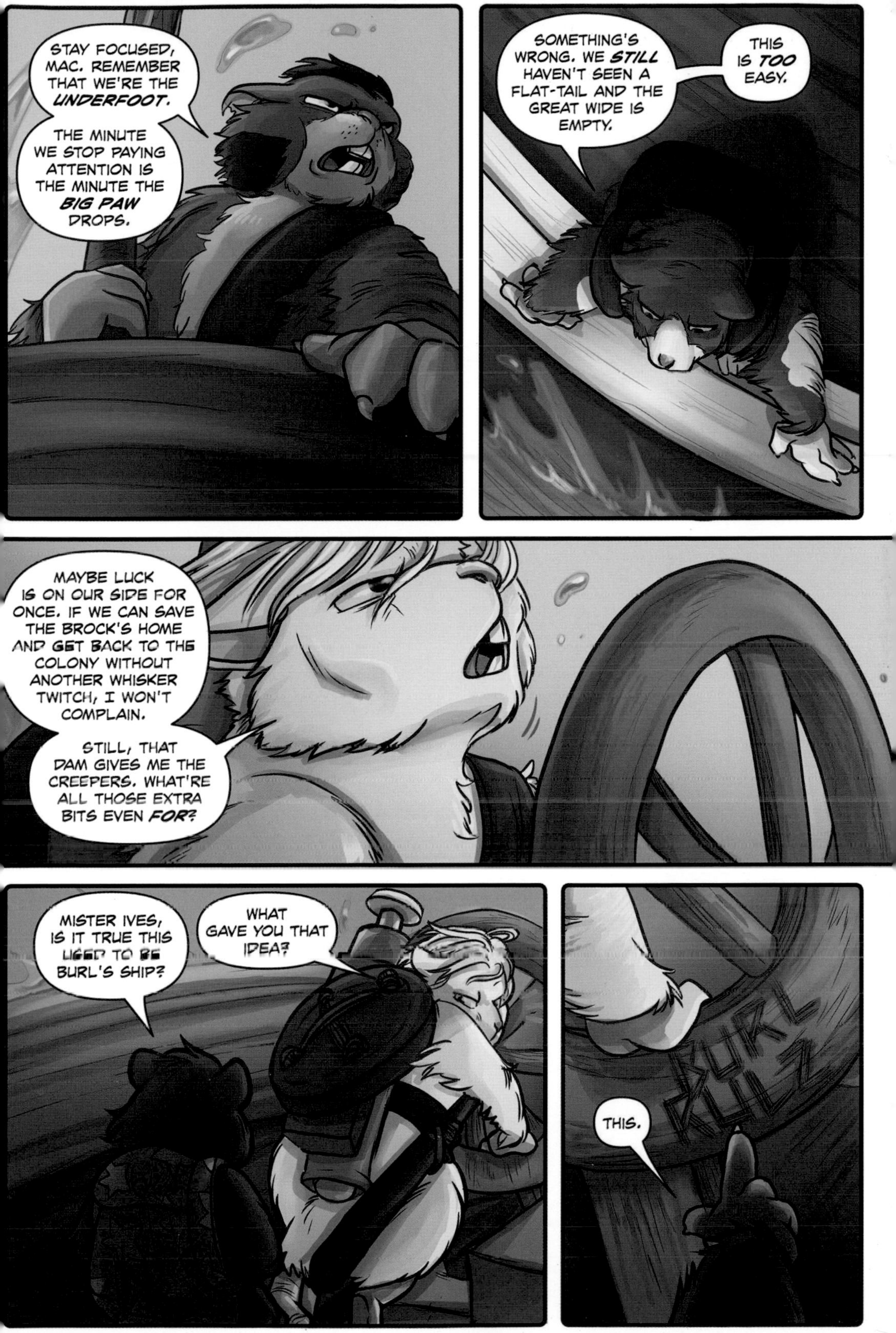

STAY FOCUSED, MAC. REMEMBER THAT WE'RE THE UNDERFOOT.
THE MINUTE WE STOP PAYING ATTENTION IS THE MINUTE THE BIG PAW DROPS.
SOMETHING'S WRONG. WE STILL HAVEN'T SEEN A FLAT-TAIL AND THE GREAT WIDE IS EMPTY.
THIS IS TOO EASY.
MAYBE LUCK IS ON OUR SIDE FOR ONCE. IF WE CAN SAVE THE BROCK'S HOME AND GET BACK TO THE COLONY WITHOUT ANOTHER WHISKER TWITCH, I WON'T COMPLAIN.
STILL, THAT DAM GIVES ME THE CREEPERS. WHAT'RE ALL THOSE EXTRA BITS EVEN FOR?
MISTER IVES, IS IT TRUE THIS USED TO BE BURL'S SHIP?
WHAT GAVE YOU THAT IDEA?
BURL RULZ
THIS.

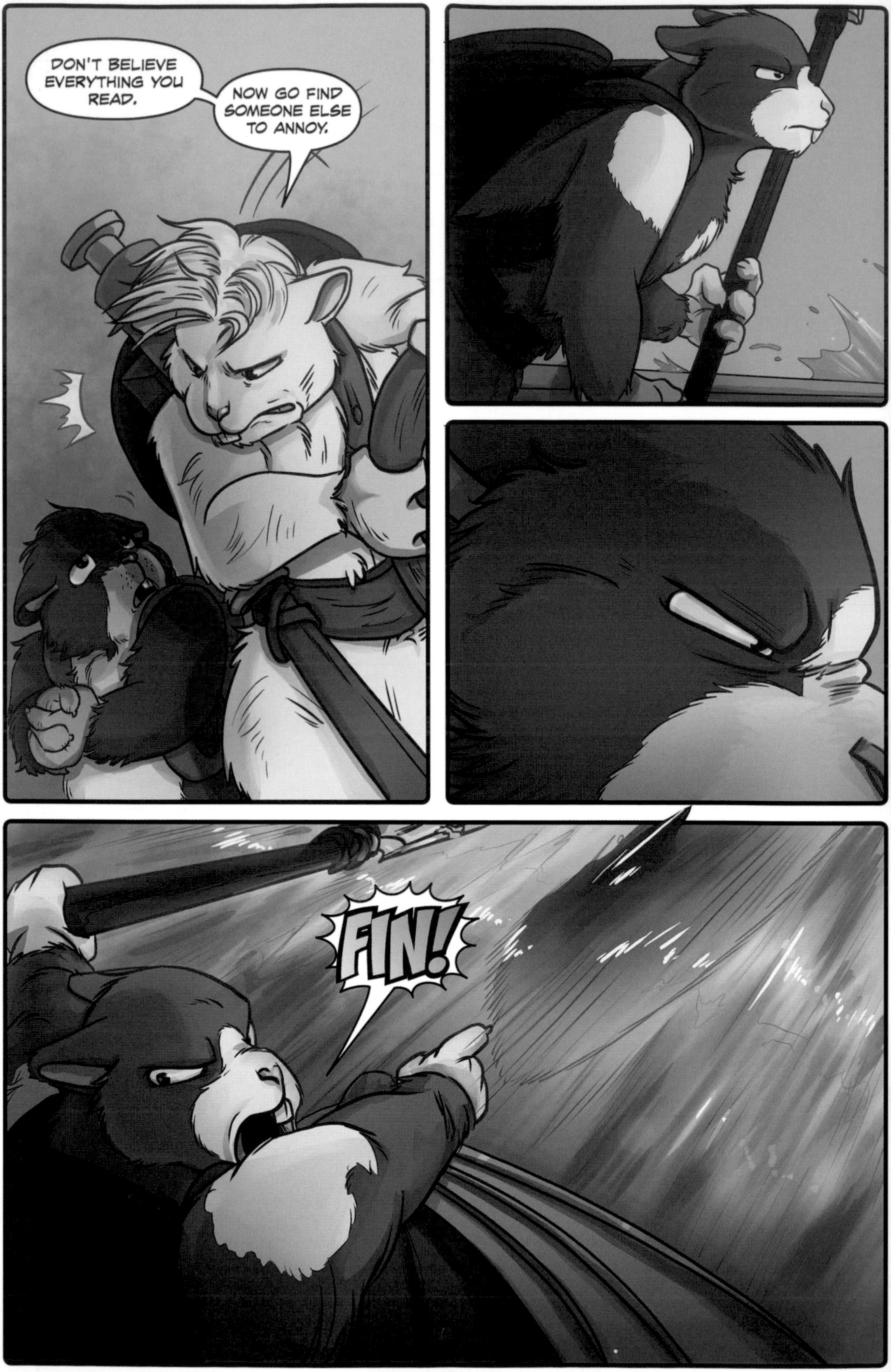
DON'T BELIEVE EVERYTHING YOU READ.
NOW GO FIND SOMEONE ELSE TO ANNOY.
FIN!

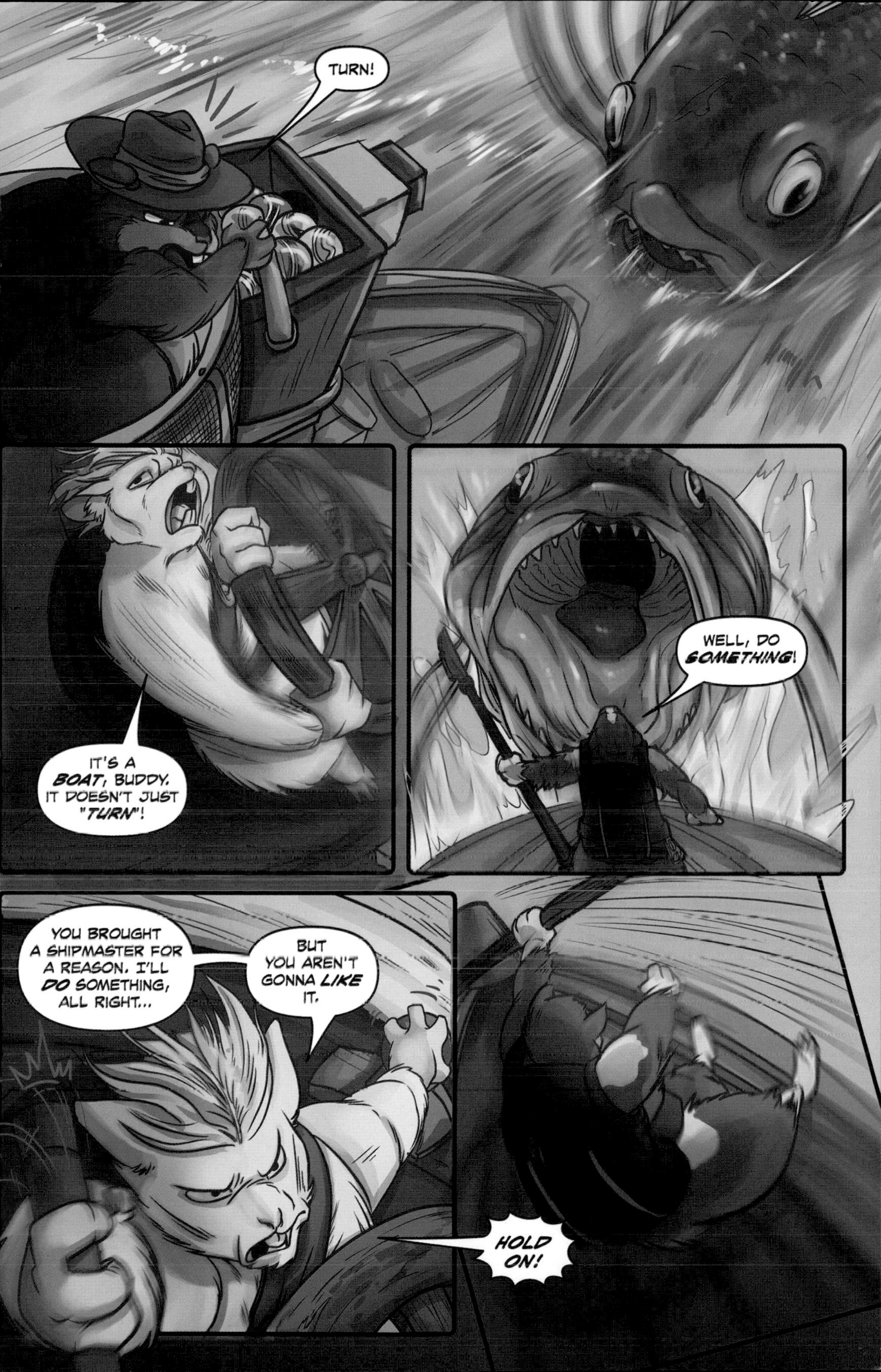
TURN!
IT'S A BOAT, BUDDY. IT DOESN'T JUST "TURN"!
WELL, DO SOMETHING!
YOU BROUGHT A SHIPMASTER FOR A REASON. I'LL DO SOMETHING, ALL RIGHT...
BUT YOU AREN'T GONNA LIKE IT.
HOLD ON!

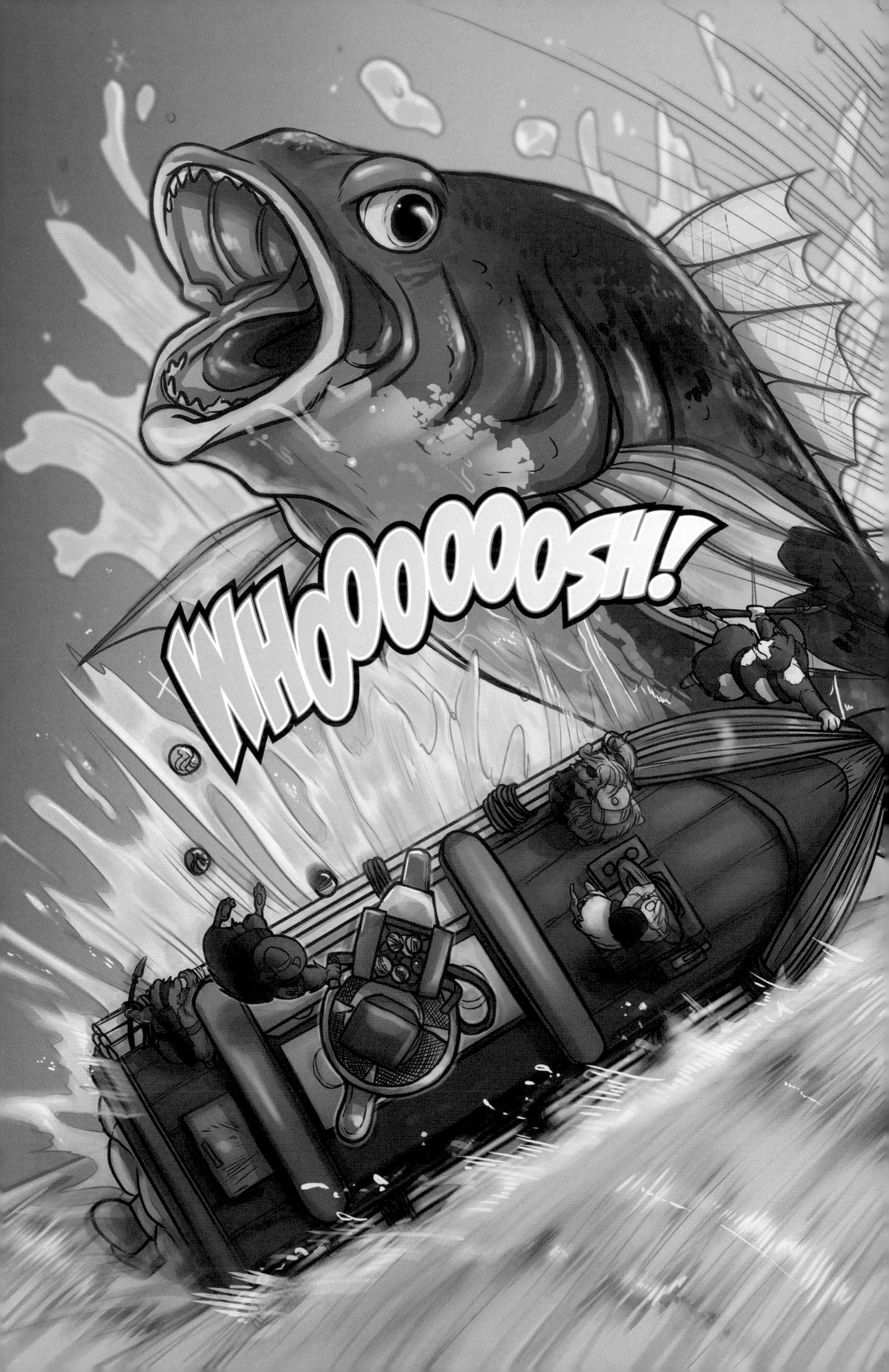
WHOOOOOOSH!

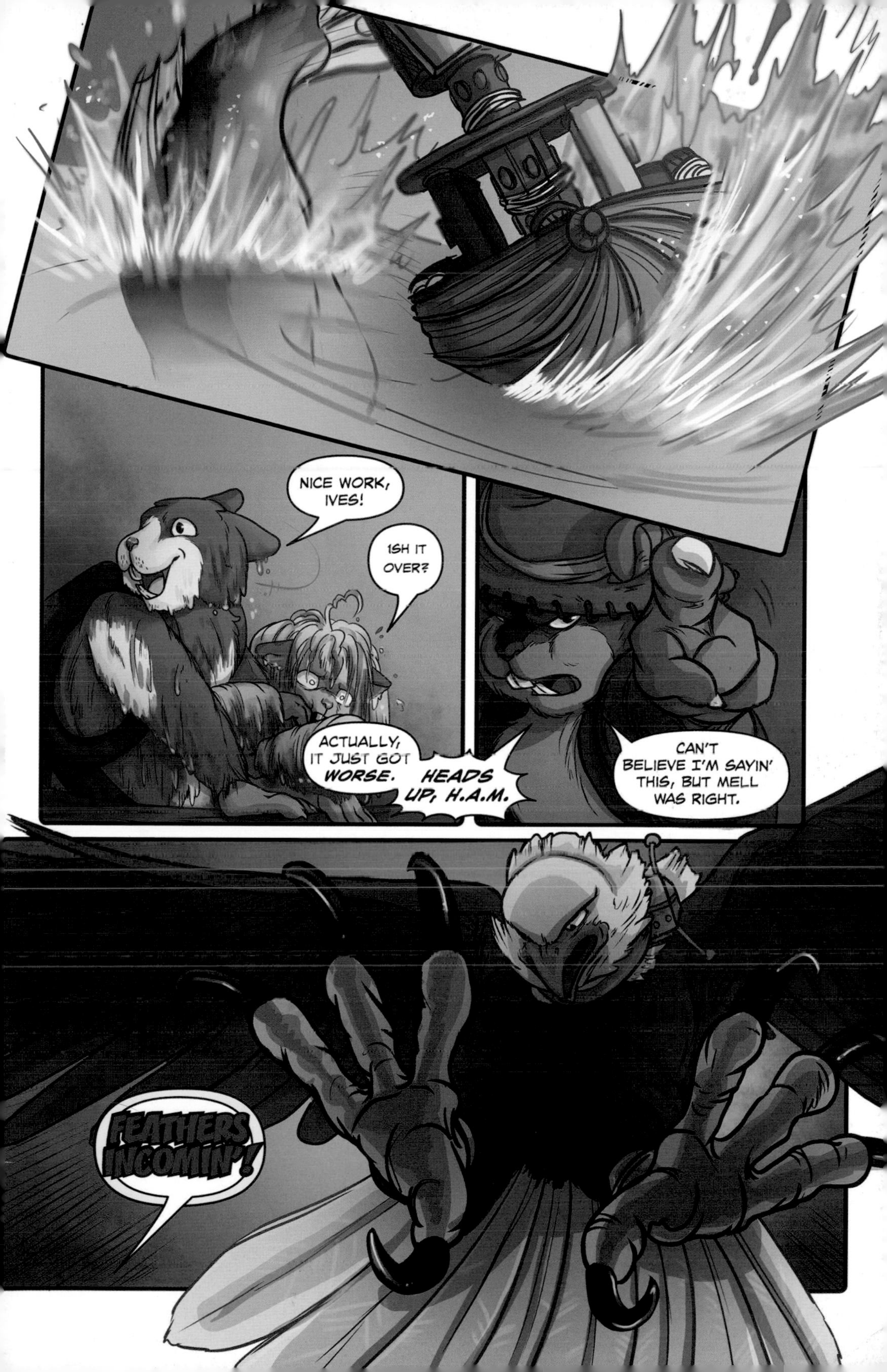
NICE WORK, IVES!
ISH IT OVER?
ACTUALLY, IT JUST GOT WORSE.
HEADS UP, H.A.M.
CAN'T BELIEVE I'M SAYIN' THIS, BUT MELL WAS RIGHT.
FEATHERS INCOMIN'!

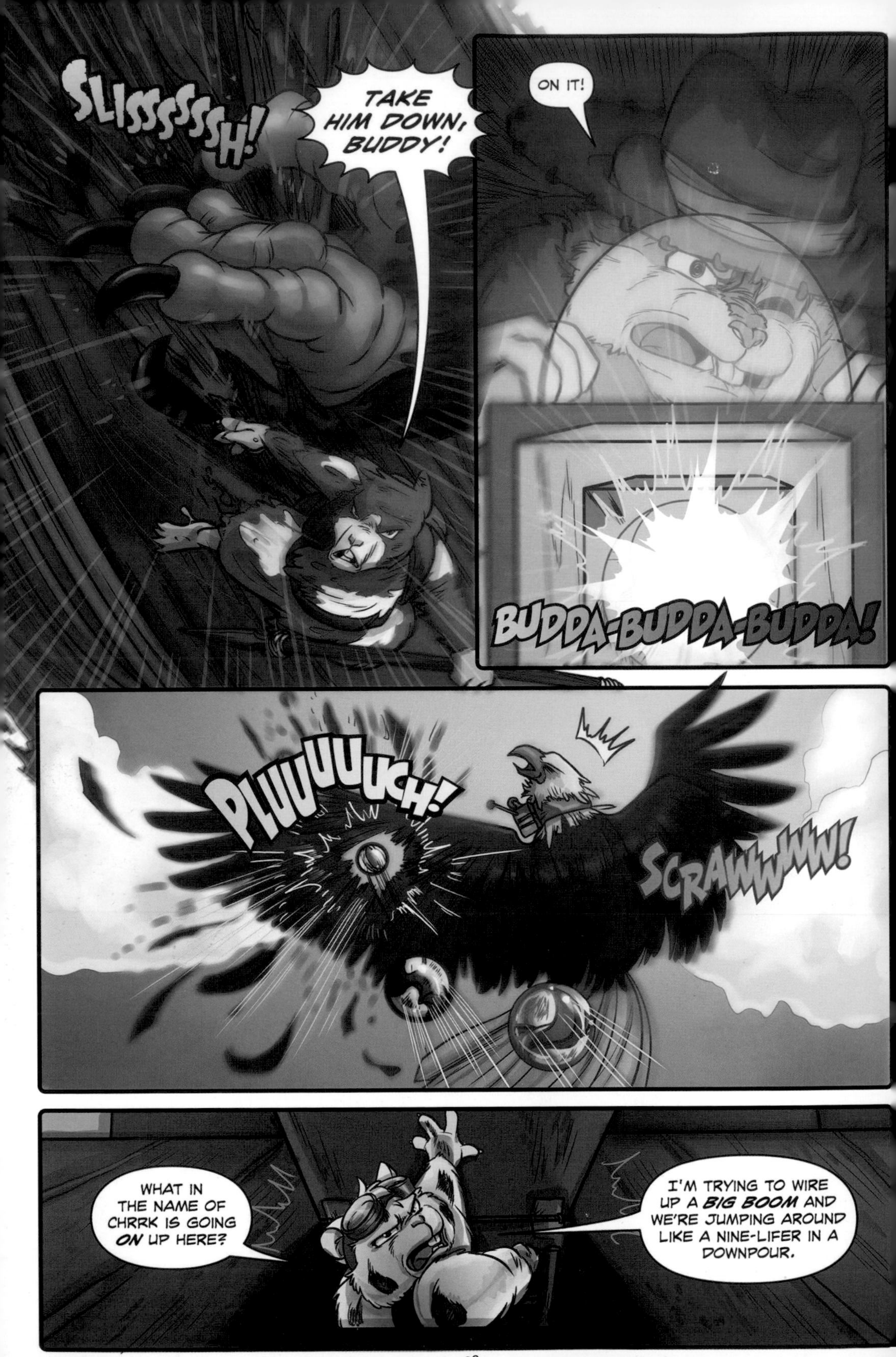
SLISSSSSSH!
TAKE HIM DOWN, BUDDY!
ON IT!
BUDDA-BUDDA-BUDDA!
PLUUUUUCH!
SCRAWWWW!
WHAT IN THE NAME OF CHRRK IS GOING ON UP HERE?
I'M TRYING TO WIRE UP A BIG BOOM AND WE'RE JUMPING AROUND LIKE A NINE-LIFER IN A DOWNPOUR.

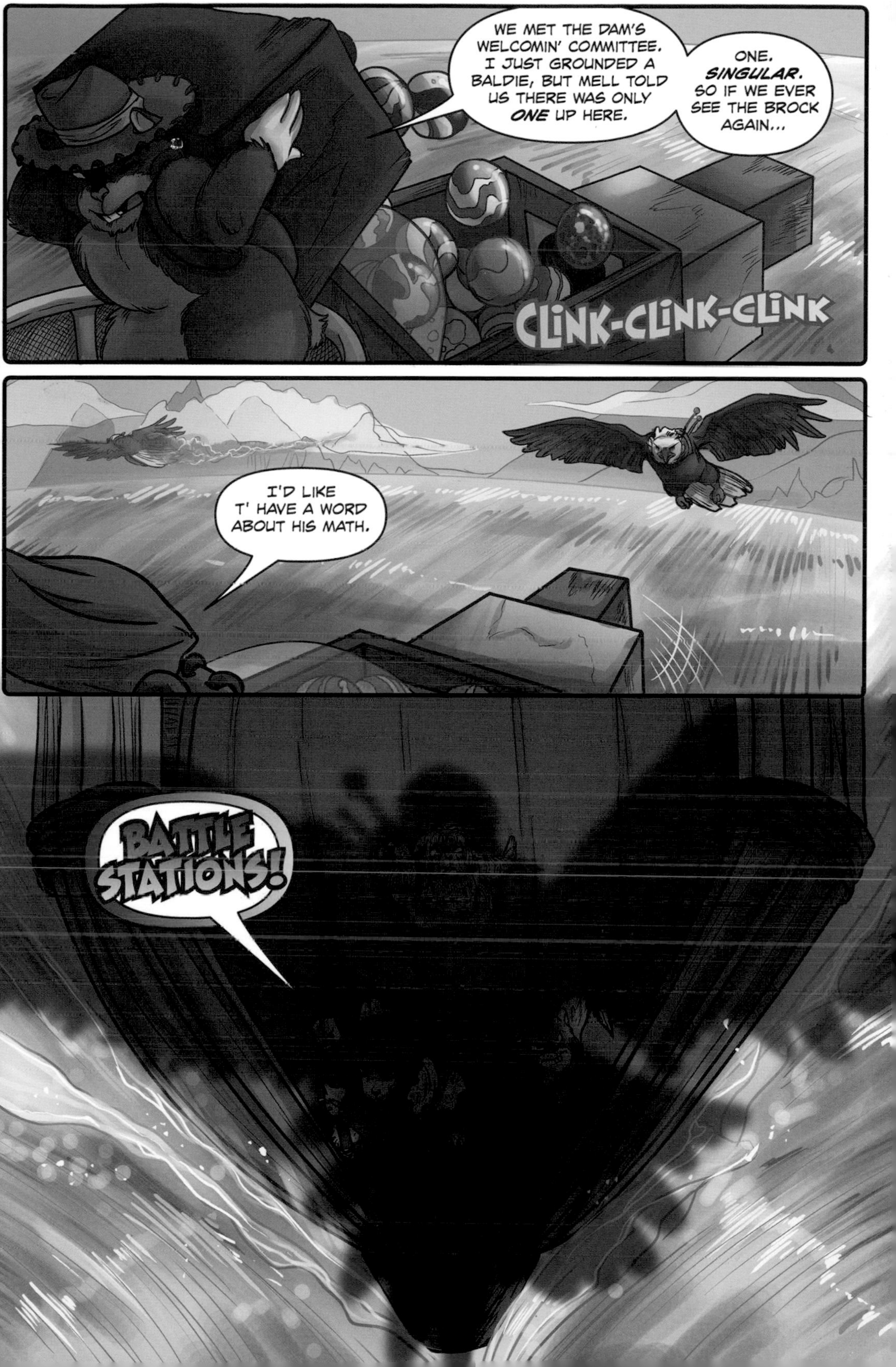

WE MET THE DAM'S WELCOMIN' COMMITTEE. I JUST GROUNDED A BALDIE, BUT MELL TOLD US THERE WAS ONLY *ONE* UP HERE.
ONE. *SINGULAR.* SO IF WE EVER SEE THE BROCK AGAIN...
CLINK-CLINK-CLINK
I'D LIKE T' HAVE A WORD ABOUT HIS MATH.
BATTLE STATIONS!

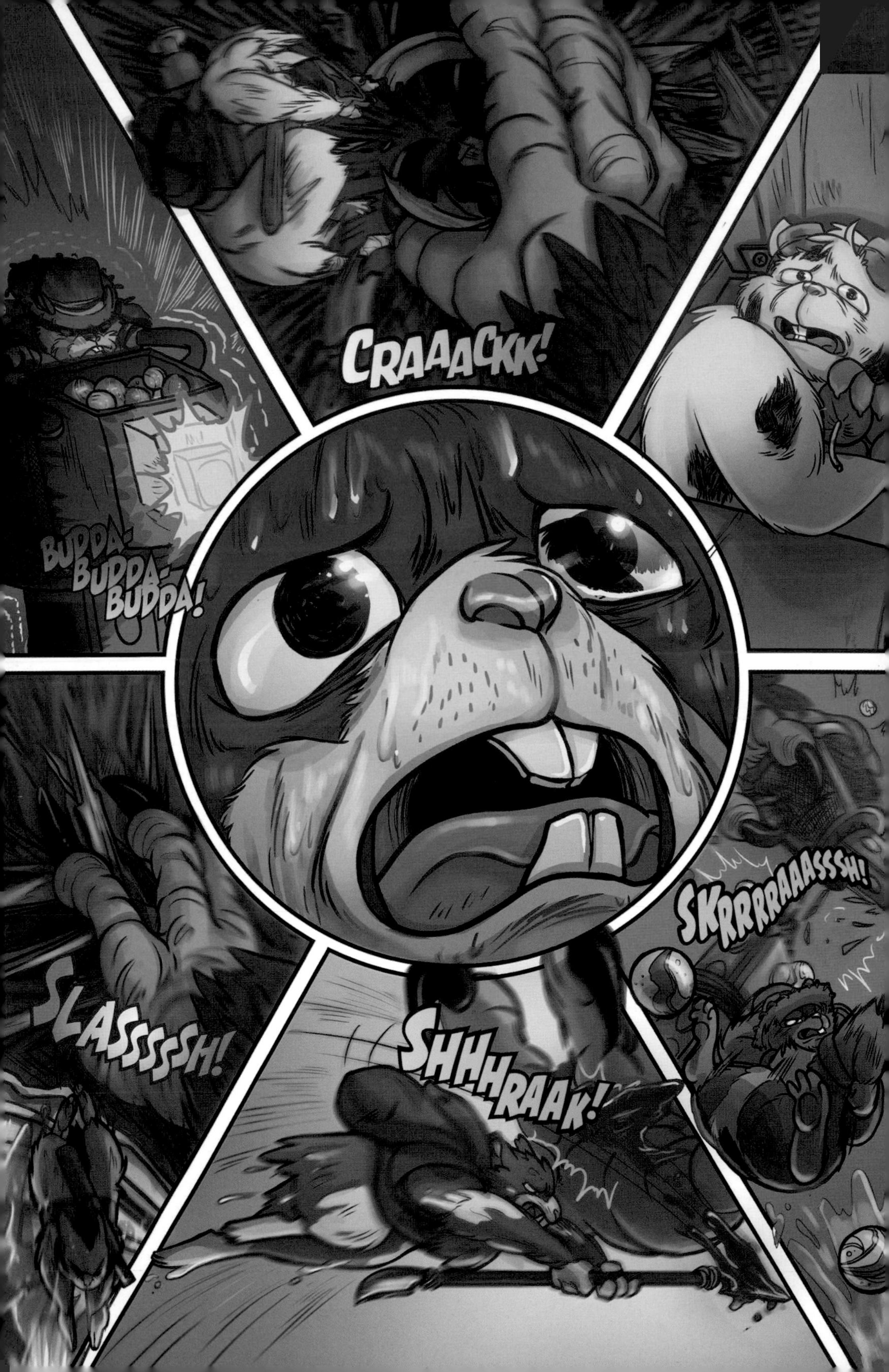
CRAAACKK!
BUDDA-BUDDA-BUDDA!
SKRRRRAAASSSH!
SLASSSSSH!
SHHHRAAK!

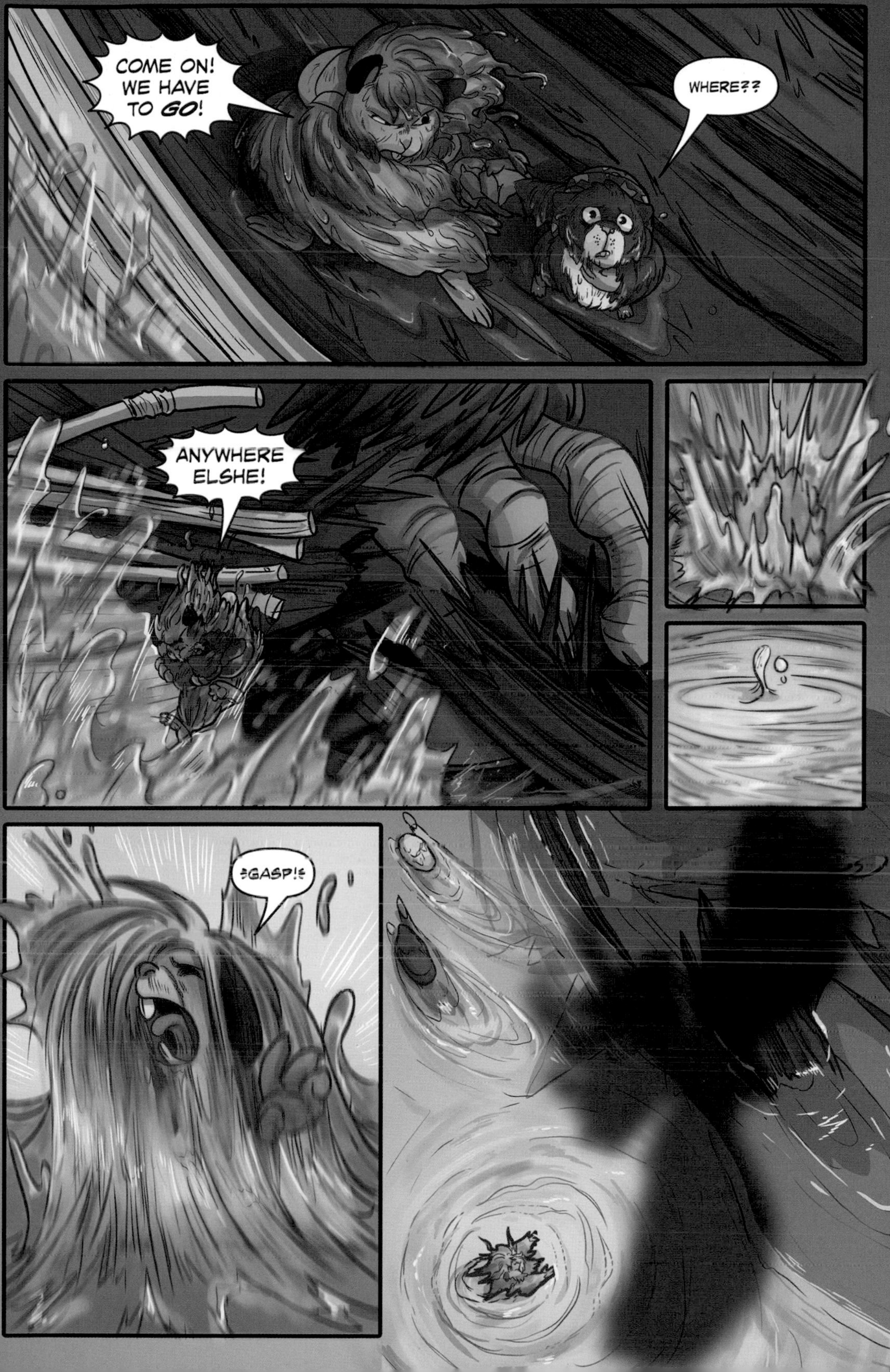
COME ON! WE HAVE TO GO!
WHERE??
ANYWHERE ELSHE!
GASP!

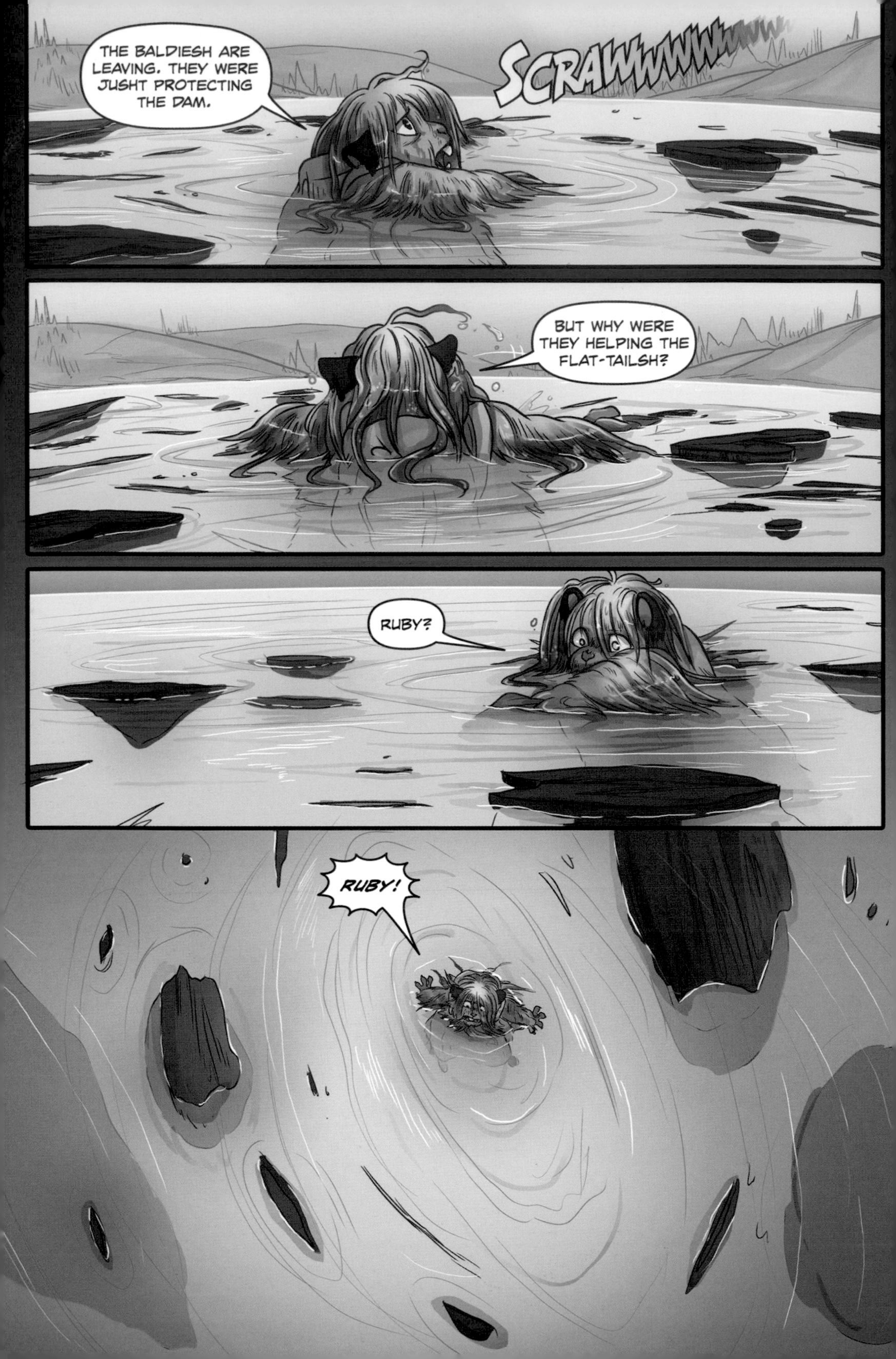
THE BALDIESH ARE LEAVING. THEY WERE JUSHT PROTECTING THE DAM.
SCRAWWWWWWWW
BUT WHY WERE THEY HELPING THE FLAT-TAILSH?
RUBY?
RUBY!

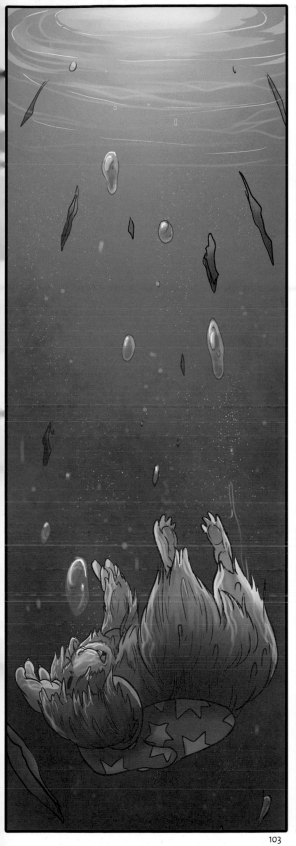

≠GASP!≠

≠GASP!≠

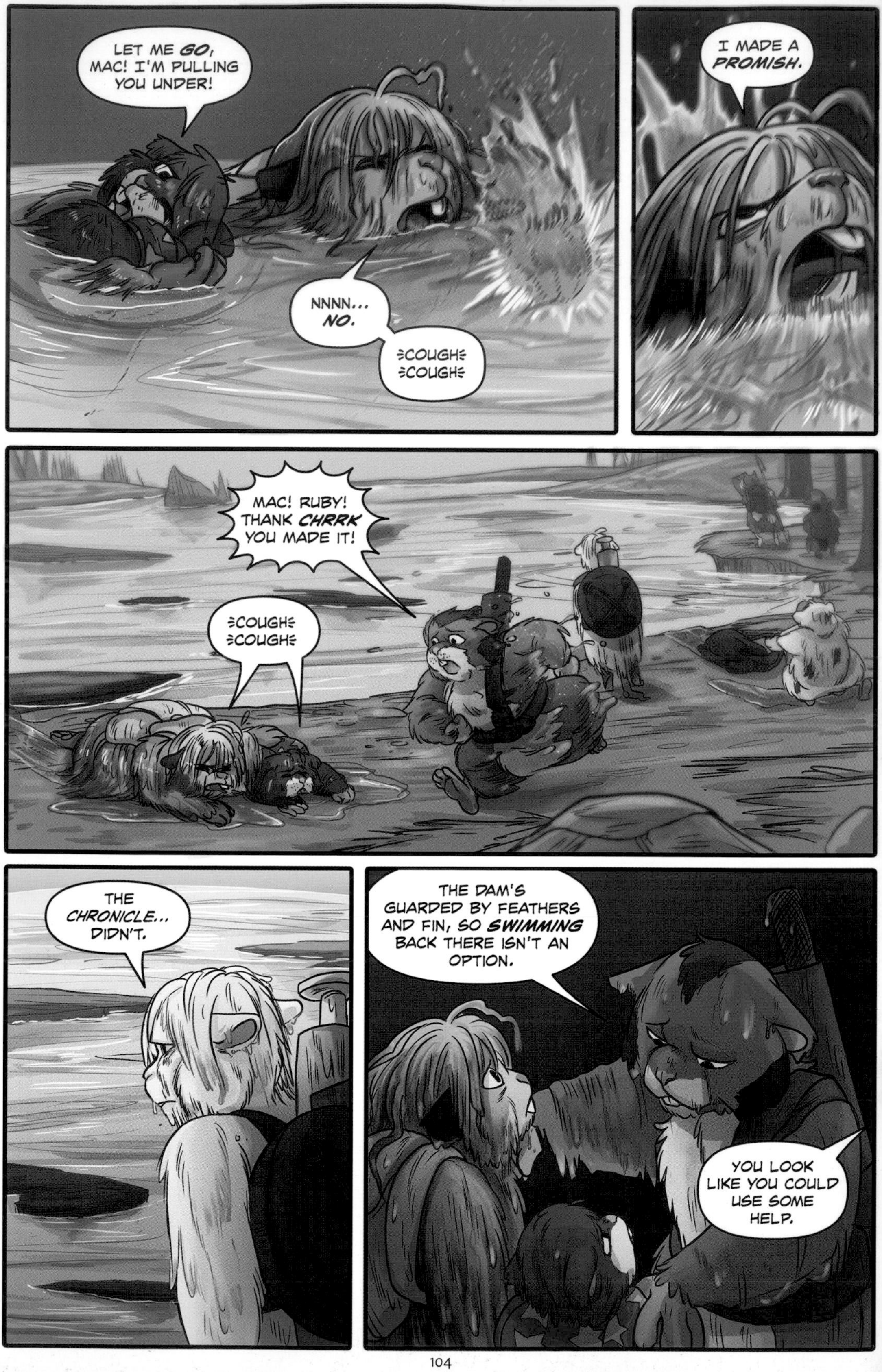
LET ME GO, MAC! I'M PULLING YOU UNDER!
NNNN... NO.
≈COUGH≈ ≈COUGH≈
I MADE A PROMISH.
MAC! RUBY! THANK CHRRK YOU MADE IT!
≈COUGH≈ ≈COUGH≈
THE CHRONICLE... DIDN'T.
THE DAM'S GUARDED BY FEATHERS AND FIN, SO SWIMMING BACK THERE ISN'T AN OPTION.
YOU LOOK LIKE YOU COULD USE SOME HELP.

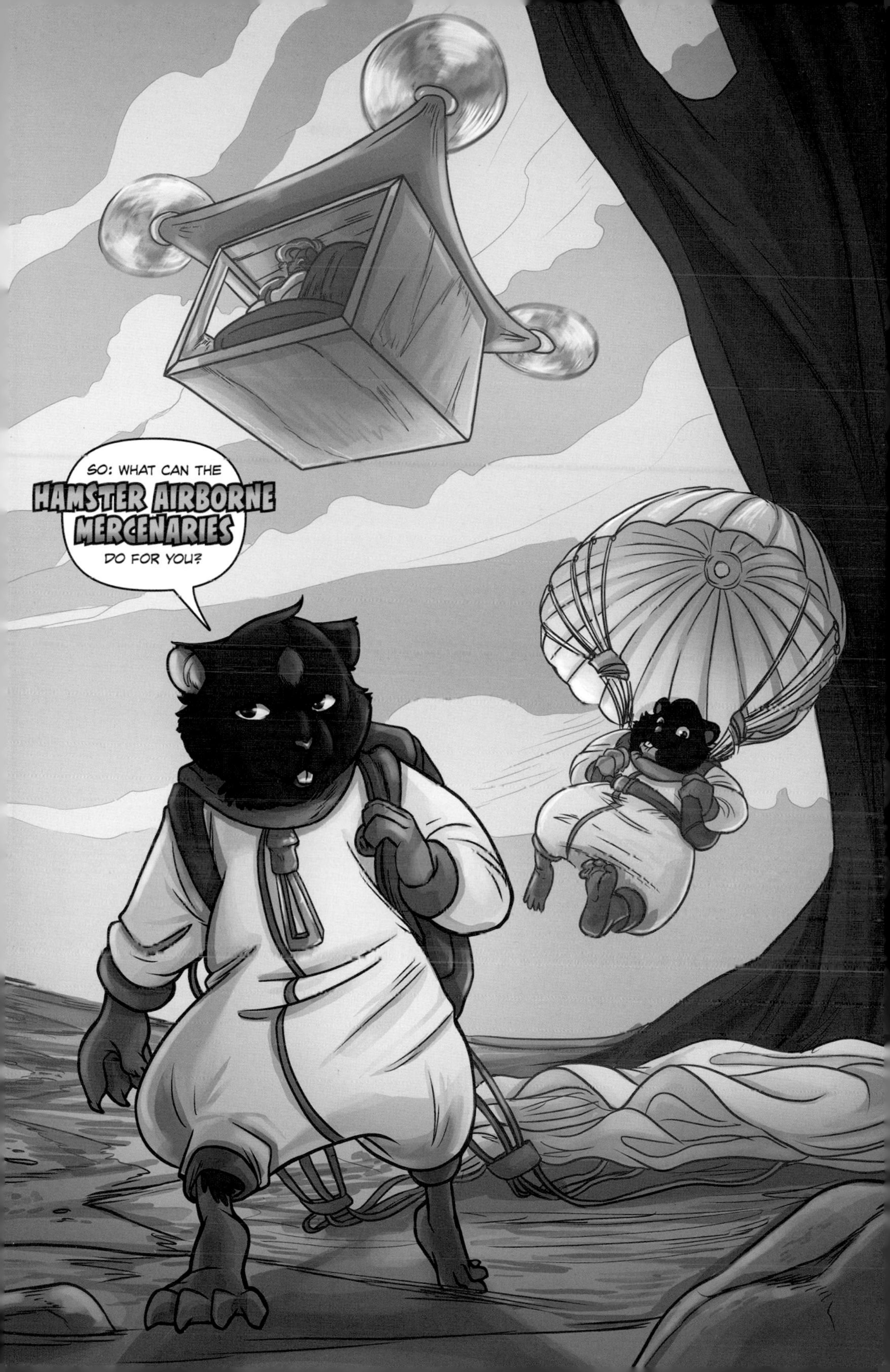
SO: WHAT CAN THE HAMSTER AIRBORNE MERCENARIES DO FOR YOU?

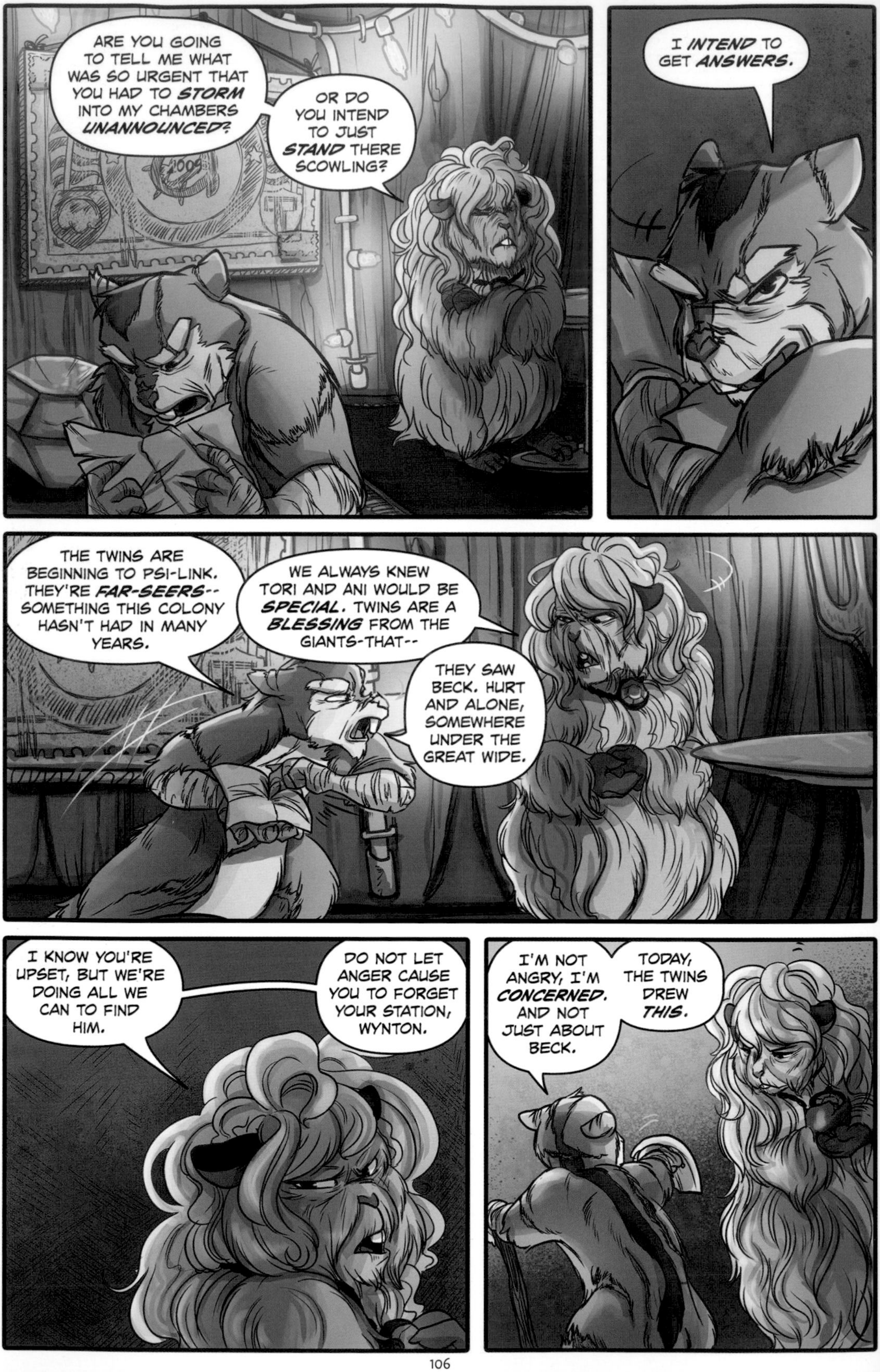
ARE YOU GOING TO TELL ME WHAT WAS SO URGENT THAT YOU HAD TO STORM INTO MY CHAMBERS UNANNOUNCED?
OR DO YOU INTEND TO JUST STAND THERE SCOWLING?
I INTEND TO GET ANSWERS.
THE TWINS ARE BEGINNING TO PSI-LINK. THEY'RE FAR-SEERS-- SOMETHING THIS COLONY HASN'T HAD IN MANY YEARS.
WE ALWAYS KNEW TORI AND ANI WOULD BE SPECIAL. TWINS ARE A BLESSING FROM THE GIANTS-THAT--
THEY SAW BECK. HURT AND ALONE, SOMEWHERE UNDER THE GREAT WIDE.
I KNOW YOU'RE UPSET, BUT WE'RE DOING ALL WE CAN TO FIND HIM.
DO NOT LET ANGER CAUSE YOU TO FORGET YOUR STATION, WYNTON.
I'M NOT ANGRY, I'M CONCERNED. AND NOT JUST ABOUT BECK.
TODAY, THE TWINS DREW THIS.

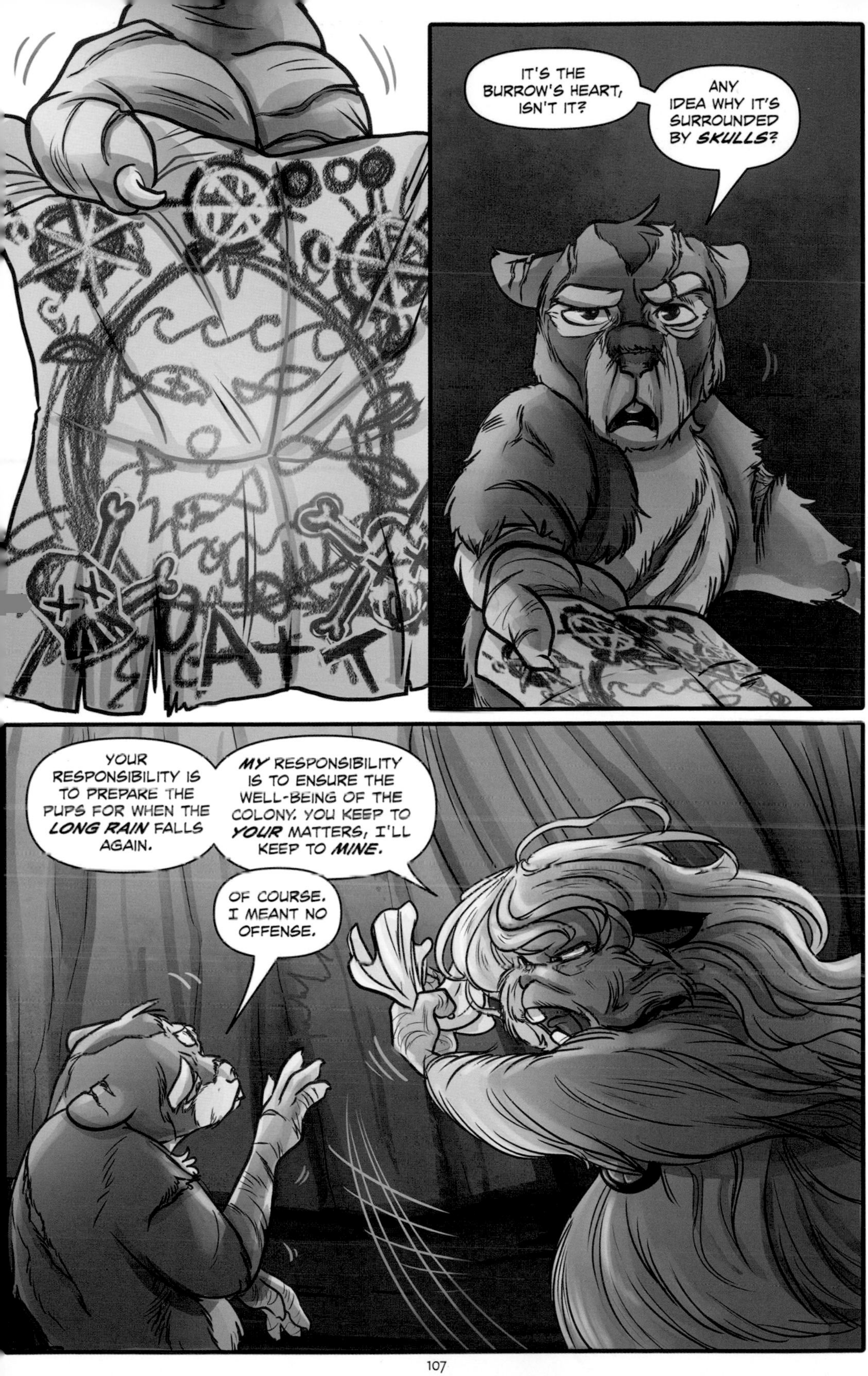
IT'S THE BURROW'S HEART, ISN'T IT?
ANY IDEA WHY IT'S SURROUNDED BY ***SKULLS***?
YOUR RESPONSIBILITY IS TO PREPARE THE PUPS FOR WHEN THE ***LONG RAIN*** FALLS AGAIN.
MY RESPONSIBILITY IS TO ENSURE THE WELL-BEING OF THE COLONY. YOU KEEP TO ***YOUR*** MATTERS, I'LL KEEP TO ***MINE.***
OF COURSE. I MEANT NO OFFENSE.

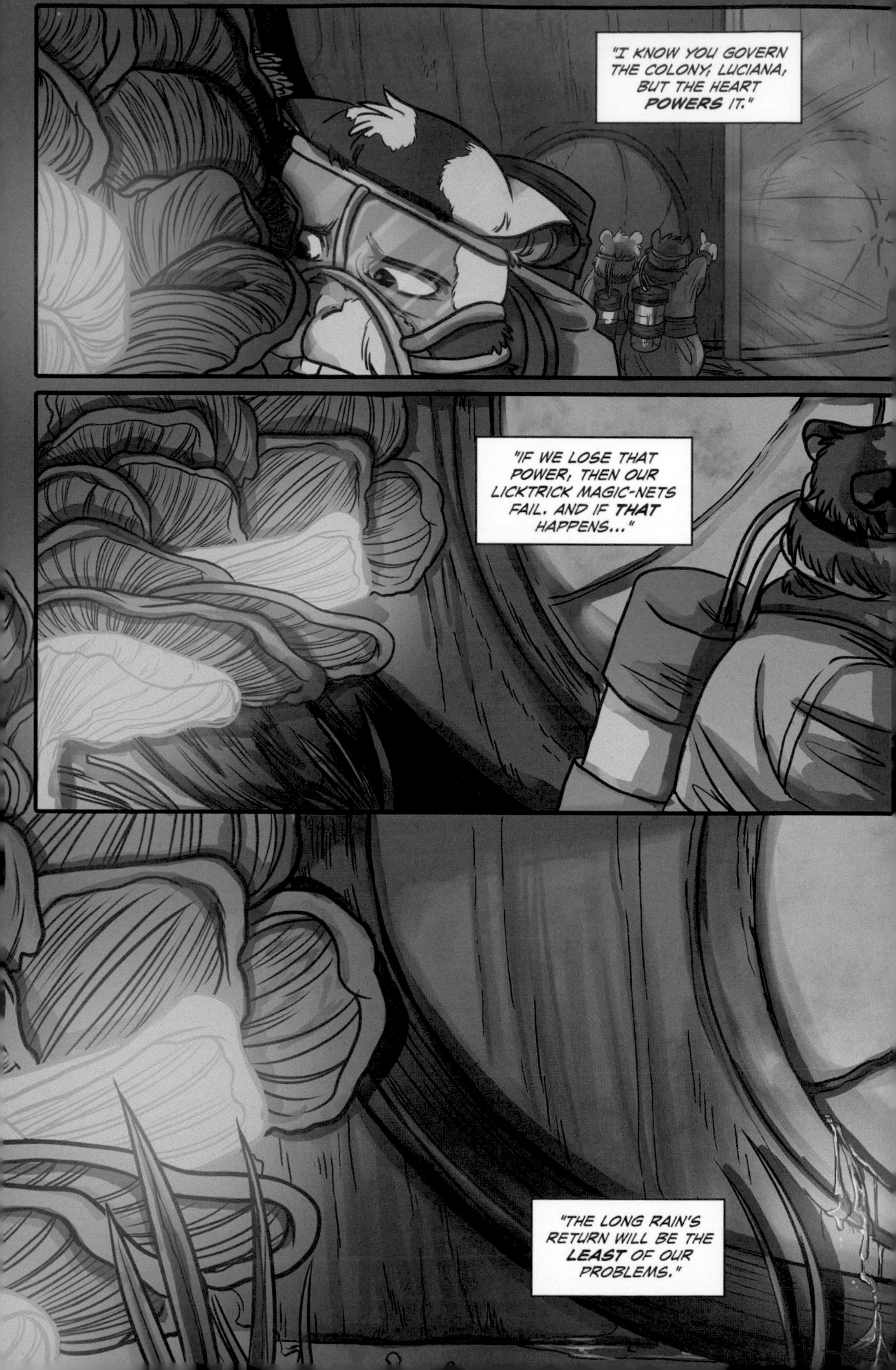
"I KNOW YOU GOVERN THE COLONY, LUCIANA, BUT THE HEART **POWERS** IT."
"IF WE LOSE THAT POWER, THEN OUR LICKTRICK MAGIC-NETS FAIL. AND IF **THAT** HAPPENS..."
"THE LONG RAIN'S RETURN WILL BE THE **LEAST** OF OUR PROBLEMS."

Buddy

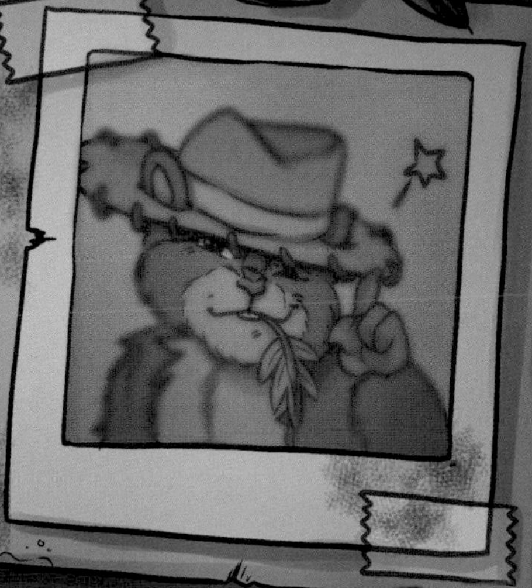

Species: Campbell's dwarf (Phodopus campbelli)
Position: H.A.M. Sharpshooter
Assessment: Tough and cocky, with the skill to back it up. Her attachment to that tacky toy cowboy hat is unfortunate.

Note: Need to find another H.A.M. with comparable marksmanship to stoke her competitive spirit.

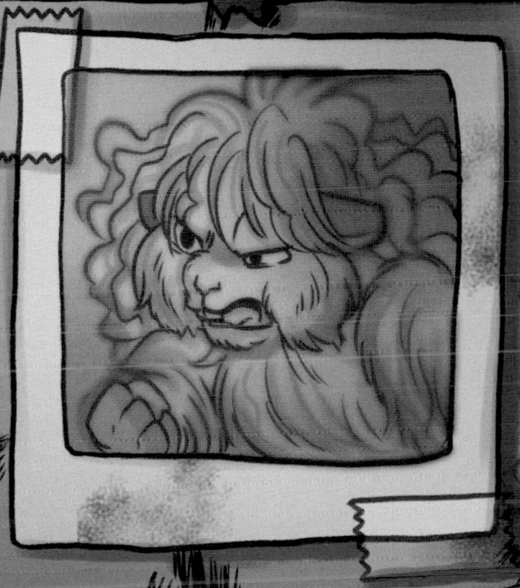

Mac

Species: Syrian – Teddy Bear (Mesocricetus auratus)
Position: ~~H.A.M. Trainee~~
H.A.M. special guard (provisional)
Assessment: Teachers report she is physically skilled but awkward and "prickly."

Note: exhibits difficulty making friends, neglects grooming, and refuses to speak properly.

Note: I despair of her behavior and don't know where she inherited such traits.

Note: after current mission, consider transfer to burrow maintenance.

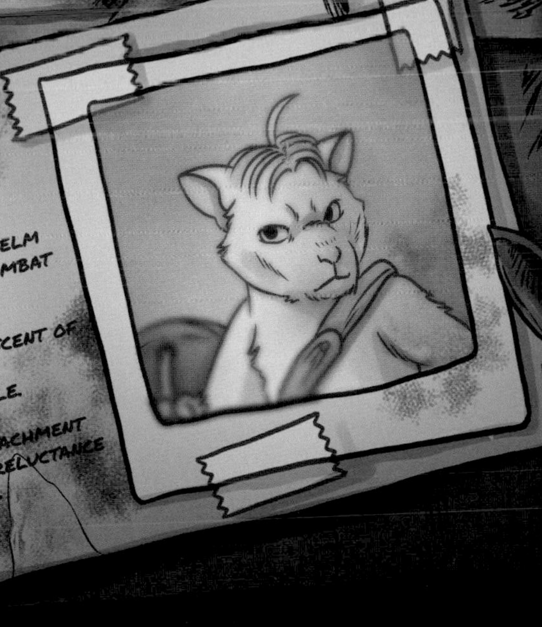

Ives

Species: Chinese dwarf – albino (Cricetulus griseus)
Position: H.A.M. Shipmaster
Assessment: unparalleled at the helm of watercraft. excels in melee combat and aquatics.

Ives's skill set is highly reminiscent of [redacted] His temperament is, [redacted] fortunately, much more reliable.

Note: exhibits a possessive attachment to the chronicle, despite his reluctance to actually board the vessel.

DOP – Essential Functions
DOP Ft. Myer – Classified

Predictive Modeling –
Natural & Man-made Hazards
DOP Ft. Myer – Classified

Anthropogenic Climate Change

Ron -- Elimination of climate change information in the public arena and self-serving denial in the political lexicon have severely slowed our funding and preparations. DOP continues to play catch-up in attempts to prepare for Projected Events.

Less dire, Wenndi has discovered an ancillary use for those "bitter oysters" by mixing them with vinegar to create invisible ink. So check your stationary for inappropriate limericks before using.

The current global warming trend is recognized with near unanimous scientific consensus by geologists and climatologists, who directly attribute the temperature increase to modern era human activity. Evidence suggests that this increase is occurring roughly ten times faster than the average rate of ice age recovery warming, an unprecedented acceleration. Carbon dioxide, released by humans into the atmosphere, traps heat on the planet's surface, which has caused an approximately 1.62°F temperature increase since the late nineteenth century. Even this minor variation dramatically affects weather patterns, melts Antarctic ice caps, and causes sea levels to rise.

Unless d... has a un... should ...

Certain... unrelat... suggest... unfortu...

Solutio... could o... Earth ... entropy... researc...

NEWS IN BRIEF: Near-Earth Asteroid Detected

Sixty-six million years ago, an asteroid the size of a small city collided with Earth and wiped out seventy-five percent of all life. The sulfur vaporized by the impact blocked the sun for decades, dropping worldwide temperatures by 50°F.

More recently, we've had a few close scares (at least by astronomy standards). The relative danger that an asteroid poses to life on Earth is measured by the Torino Impact Hazard Scale. In 2004, it was believed that there was a 2.7% chance that the 1000'-wide asteroid *99942 Apophis* (a Level 4 on the Torino scale) would strike the Earth by 2029, although those odds have since dropped to zero. On average, it is expected that at least one Level 4 asteroid will impact the Earth every 80,000 years.

Athough there... including...

VIROLOGY TODAY: Scientists Condemn Creation of Deadly Airborne Flu Virus

Scientists have artificially recreated the deadly 1918 Spanish flu strain by using "reverse genetics" to combine existing virus fragments, but mutated the result to make it airborne. Researchers claim the experiments are crucial for understanding the health risk posed by viruses currently circulating in wild birds, but critics condemned the studies as reckless. Many fear that this heightens the risk of a global pandemic.

Most airborne viruses are passed from person to person by contact with respiratory droplets generated when a person coughs or sneezes. Respiratory droplets can be propelled into the eyes, nose, or mouth over short distances. Safety precautions would include...

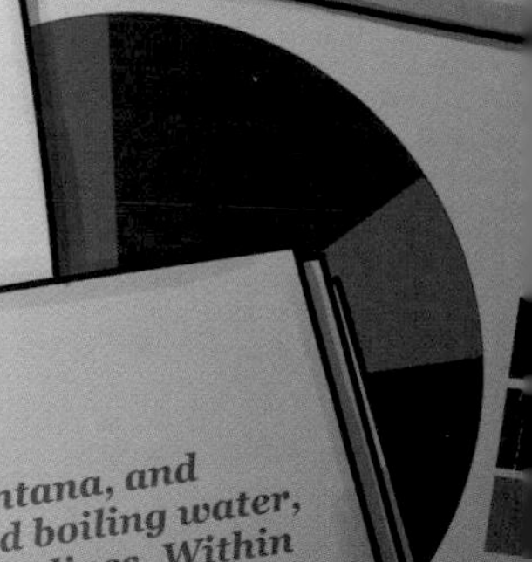

Yellowstone Plateau

The Yellowstone Plateau, located in the states of Wyoming, Montana, and Idaho, is centered on an active volcanic system with pressurized boiling water, subterranean molten rock (magma), and a variety of active fault lines. Within the next few decades, significant earthquakes and hydrothermal explosions are certain to occur.

The culprit is a "supervolcano" beneath the surface, which is expcted to release over 240 cubic miles of debris directly into the atmosphere when it finally erupts. The resulting fallout will devastate the landscape for thousands of miles in every direction. In fact, much of the Amerian midwest would become buried in over three feet of ash.

...full extent of environmental repercussions are incalculable, although a ...s been developed by the Department of Preparedness. ...tamination of water supplies and a reduction ...breathing.

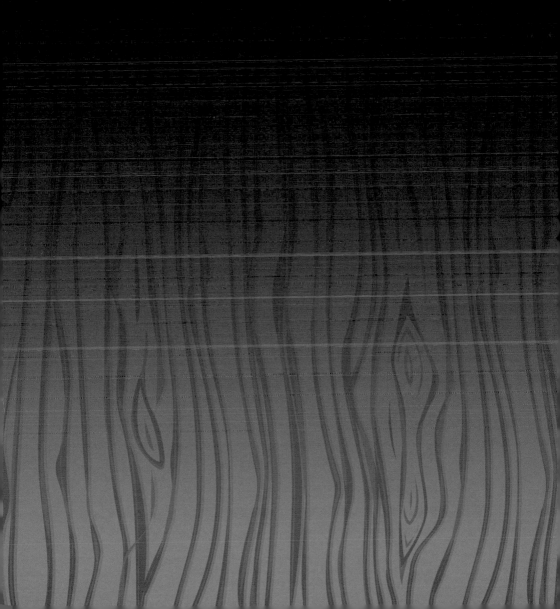

CHAPTER FOUR

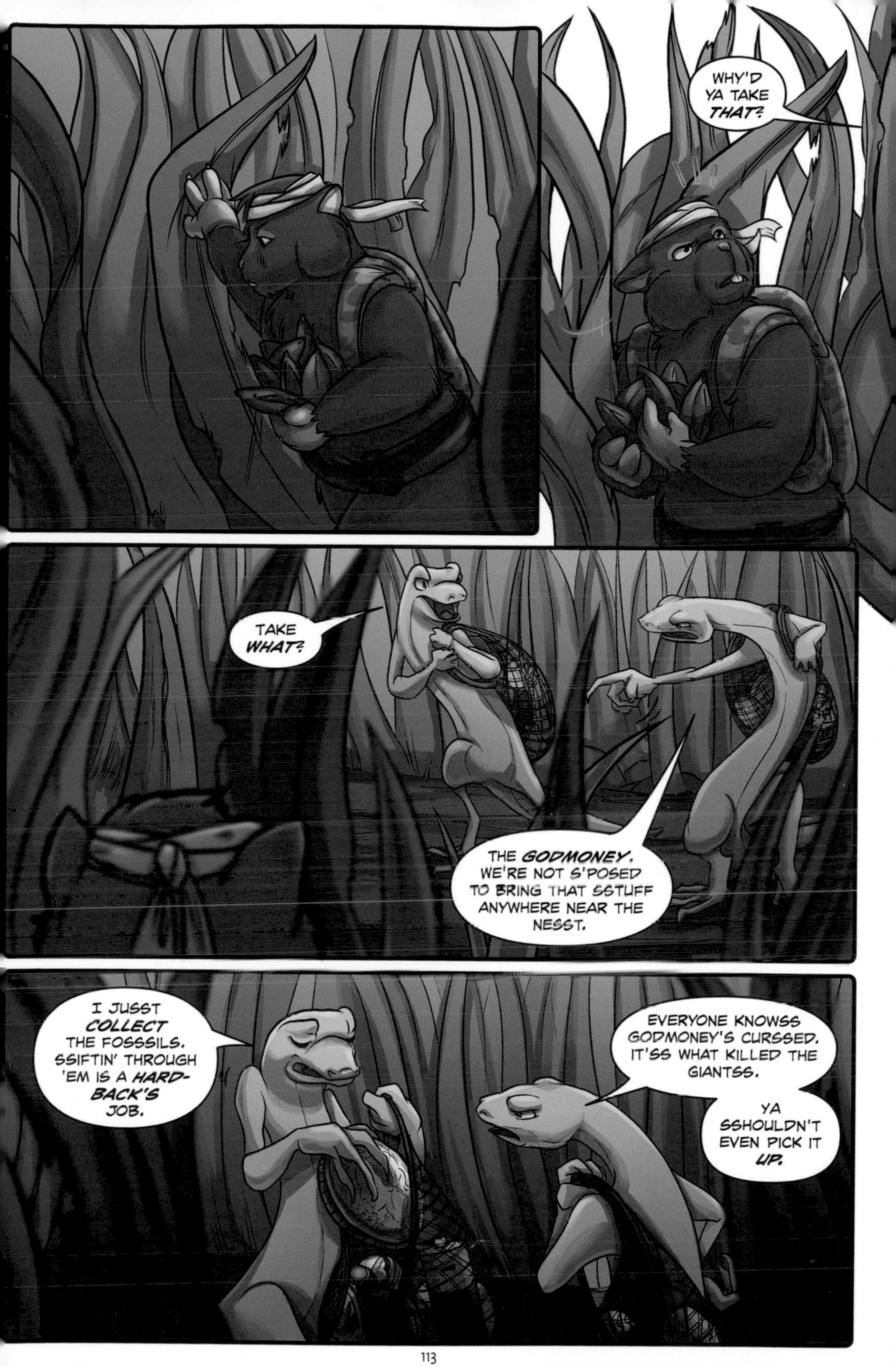
WHY'D YA TAKE *THAT?*
TAKE *WHAT?*
THE *GODMONEY*. WE'RE NOT S'POSED TO BRING THAT SSTUFF ANYWHERE NEAR THE NESST.
I JUSST *COLLECT* THE FOSSSILS. SSIFTIN' THROUGH 'EM IS A *HARD-BACK'S* JOB.
EVERYONE KNOWSS GODMONEY'S CURSSED. IT'SS WHAT KILLED THE GIANTSS.
YA SSHOULDN'T EVEN PICK IT *UP*.

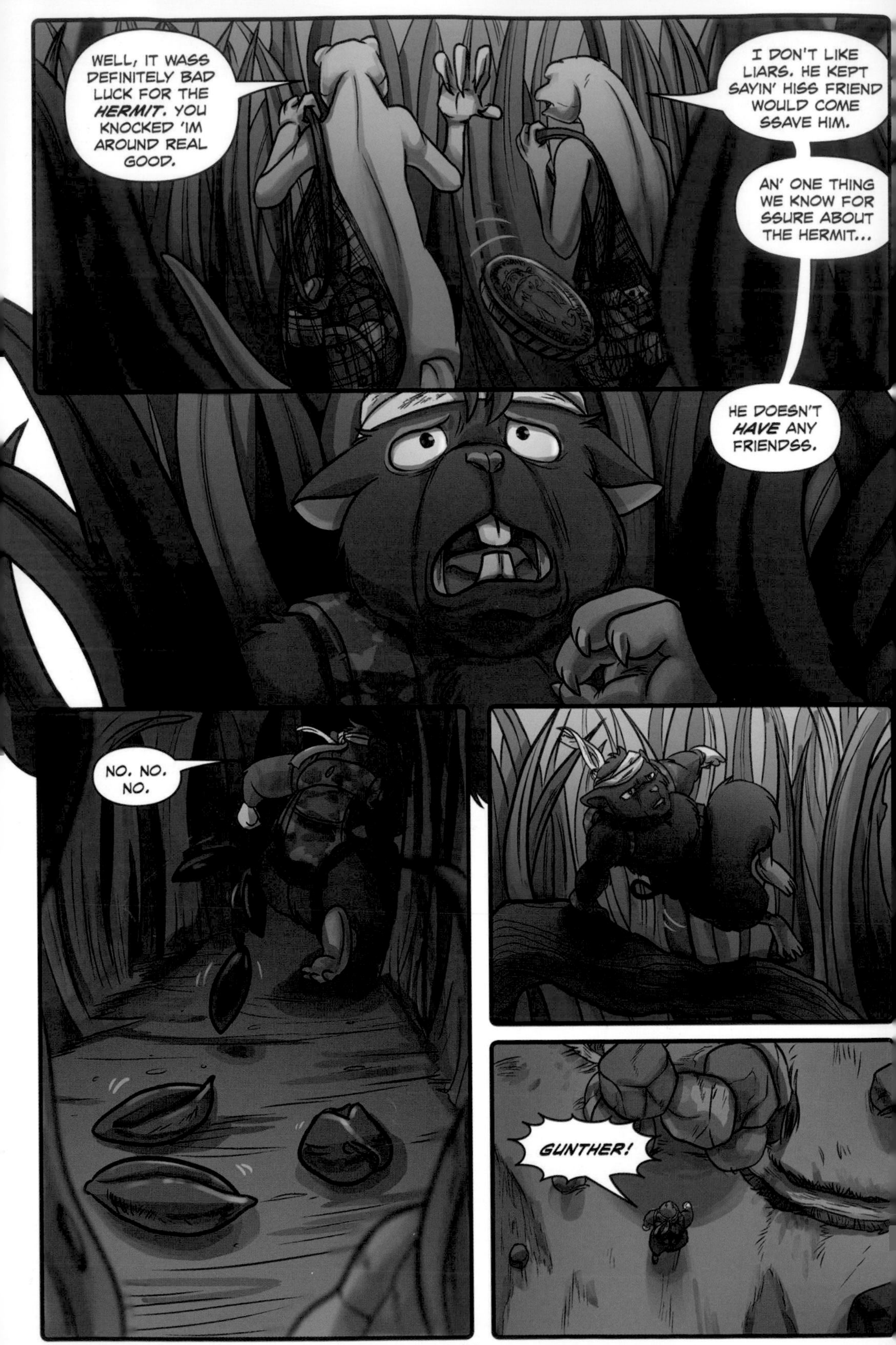
WELL, IT WASS DEFINITELY BAD LUCK FOR THE *HERMIT*. YOU KNOCKED 'IM AROUND REAL GOOD.
I DON'T LIKE LIARS. HE KEPT SAYIN' HISS FRIEND WOULD COME SSAVE HIM.
AN' ONE THING WE KNOW FOR SSURE ABOUT THE HERMIT...
HE DOESN'T *HAVE* ANY FRIENDSS.
NO. NO. NO.
GUNTHER!

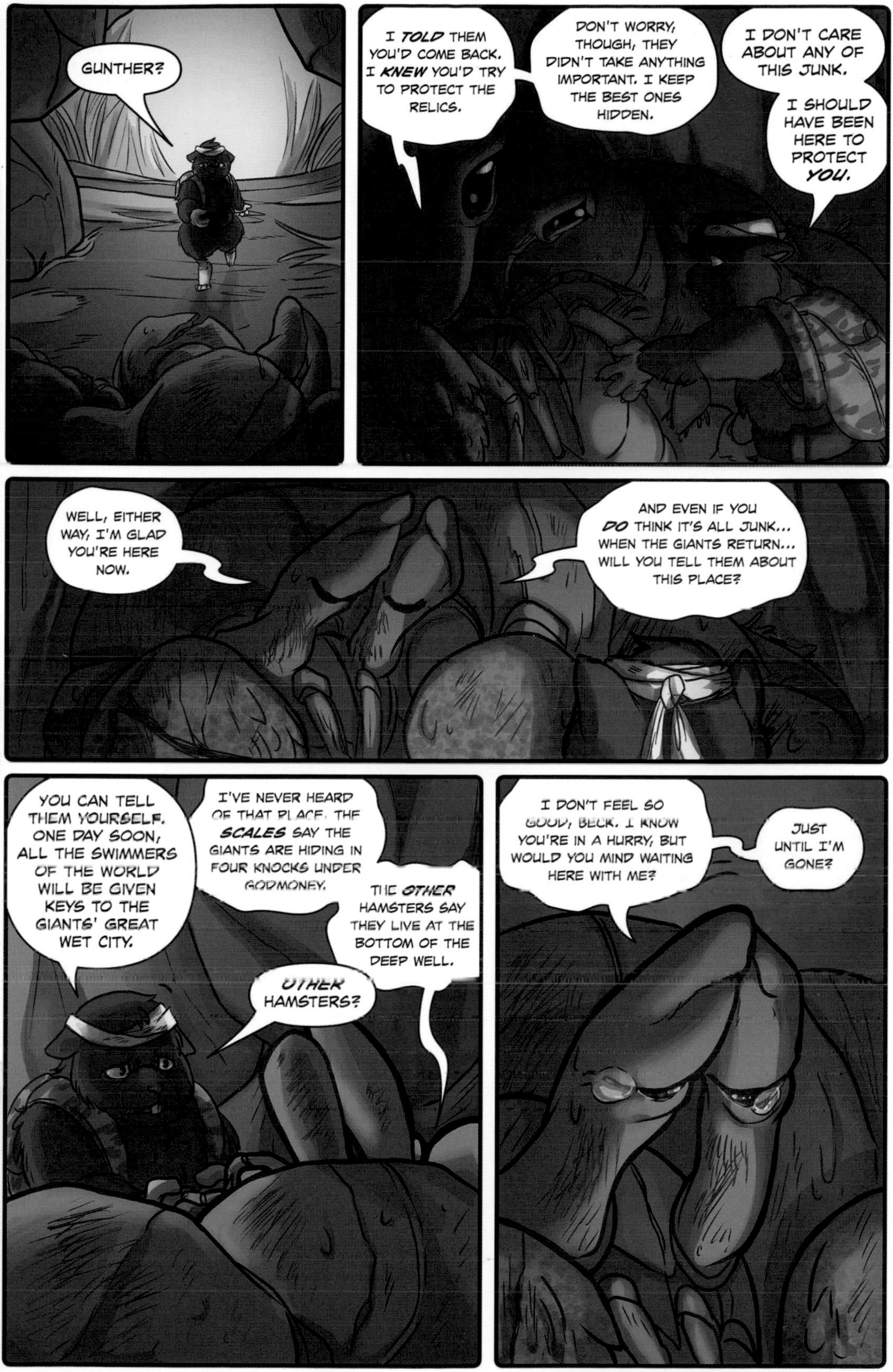
GUNTHER?
I *TOLD* THEM YOU'D COME BACK. I *KNEW* YOU'D TRY TO PROTECT THE RELICS.
DON'T WORRY, THOUGH, THEY DIDN'T TAKE ANYTHING IMPORTANT. I KEEP THE BEST ONES HIDDEN.
I DON'T CARE ABOUT ANY OF THIS JUNK.
I SHOULD HAVE BEEN HERE TO PROTECT *YOU.*
WELL, EITHER WAY, I'M GLAD YOU'RE HERE NOW.
AND EVEN IF YOU *DO* THINK IT'S ALL JUNK... WHEN THE GIANTS RETURN... WILL YOU TELL THEM ABOUT THIS PLACE?
YOU CAN TELL THEM YOURSELF. ONE DAY SOON, ALL THE SWIMMERS OF THE WORLD WILL BE GIVEN KEYS TO THE GIANTS' GREAT WET CITY.
I'VE NEVER HEARD OF THAT PLACE. THE *SCALES* SAY THE GIANTS ARE HIDING IN FOUR KNOCKS UNDER GODMONEY.
THE *OTHER* HAMSTERS SAY THEY LIVE AT THE BOTTOM OF THE DEEP WELL.
OTHER HAMSTERS?
I DON'T FEEL SO GOOD, BECK. I KNOW YOU'RE IN A HURRY, BUT WOULD YOU MIND WAITING HERE WITH ME?
JUST UNTIL I'M GONE?

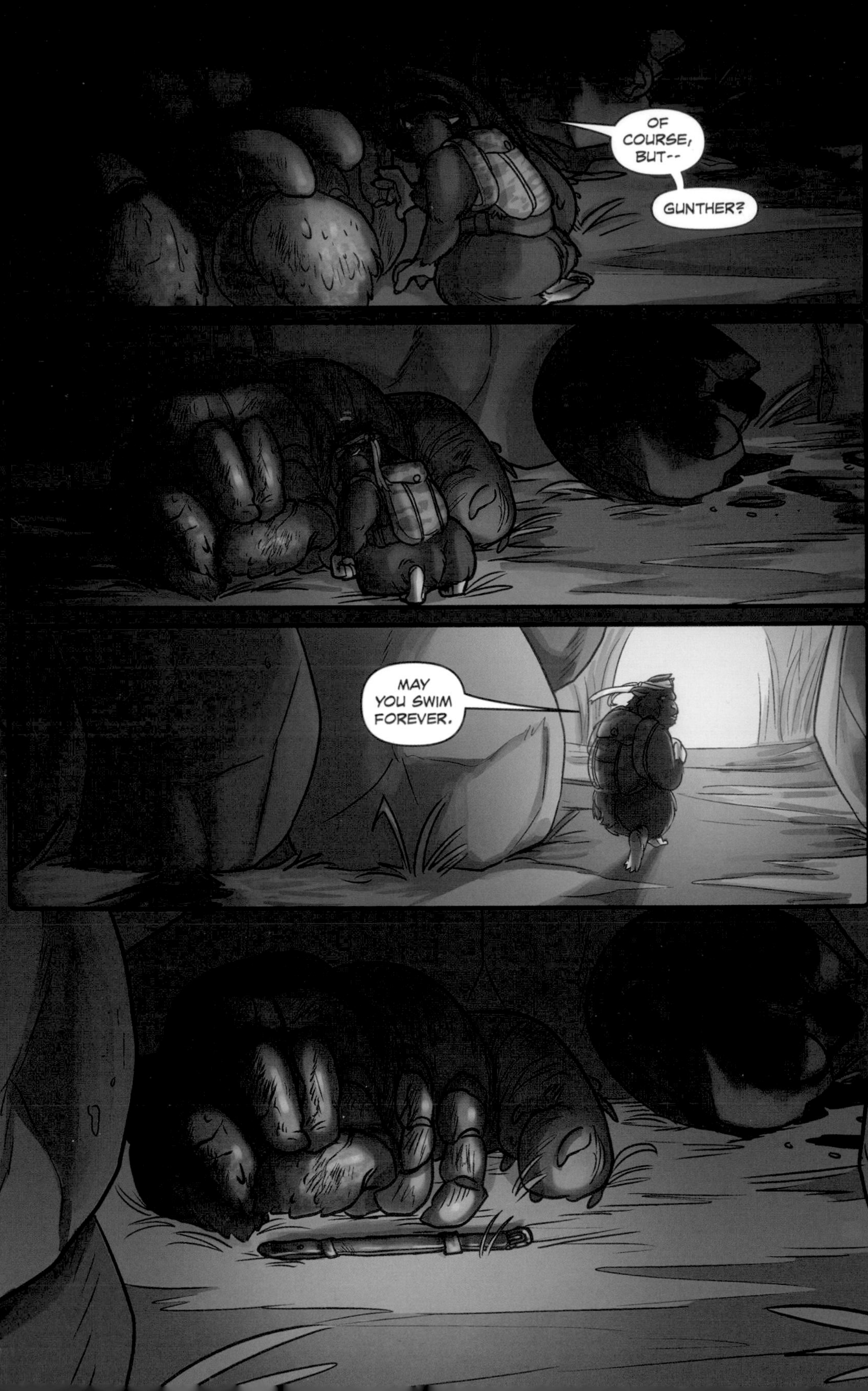
OF COURSE, BUT--
GUNTHER?
MAY YOU SWIM FOREVER.

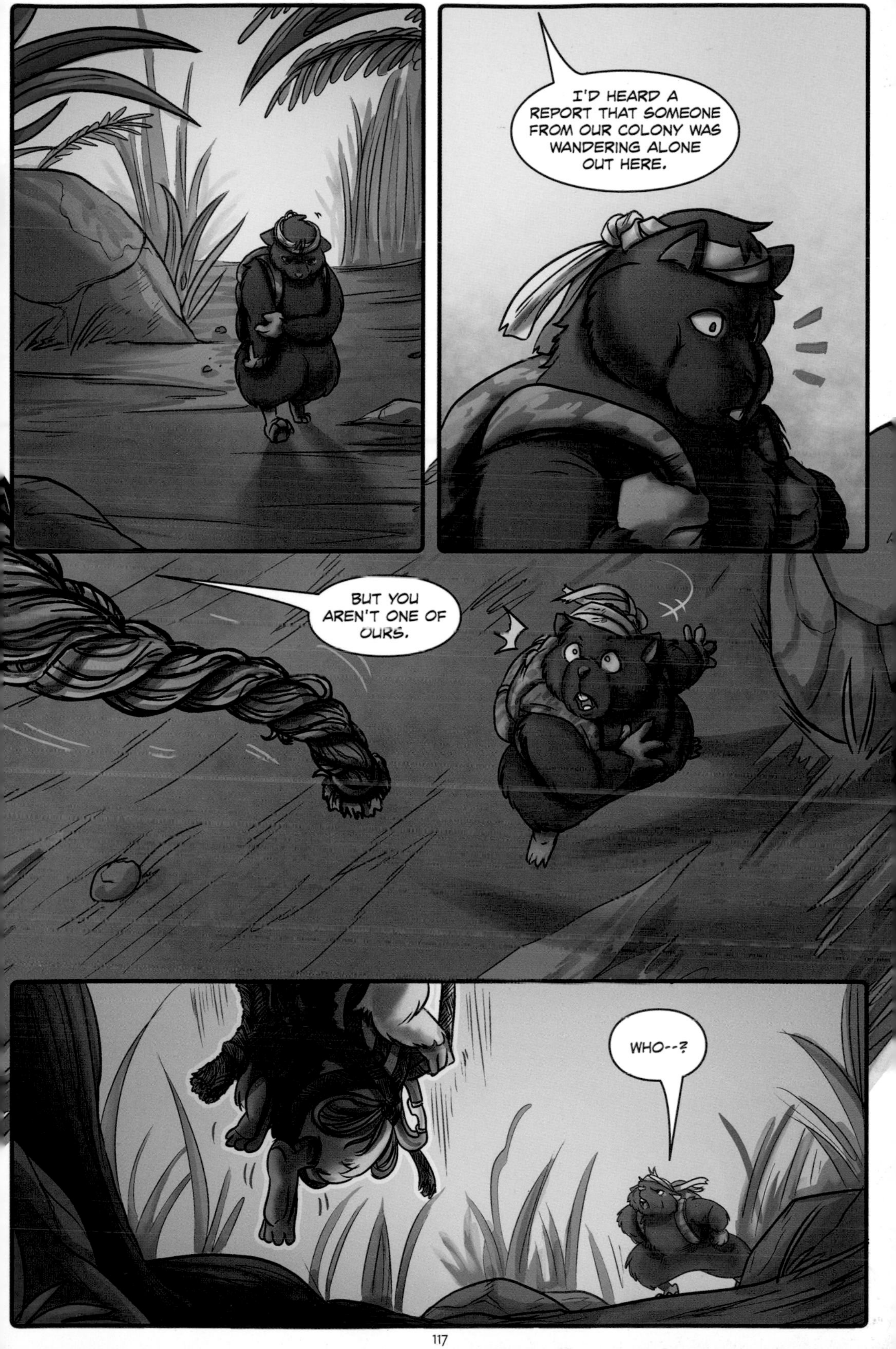
I'D HEARD A REPORT THAT SOMEONE FROM OUR COLONY WAS WANDERING ALONE OUT HERE.
BUT YOU AREN'T ONE OF OURS.
WHO--?

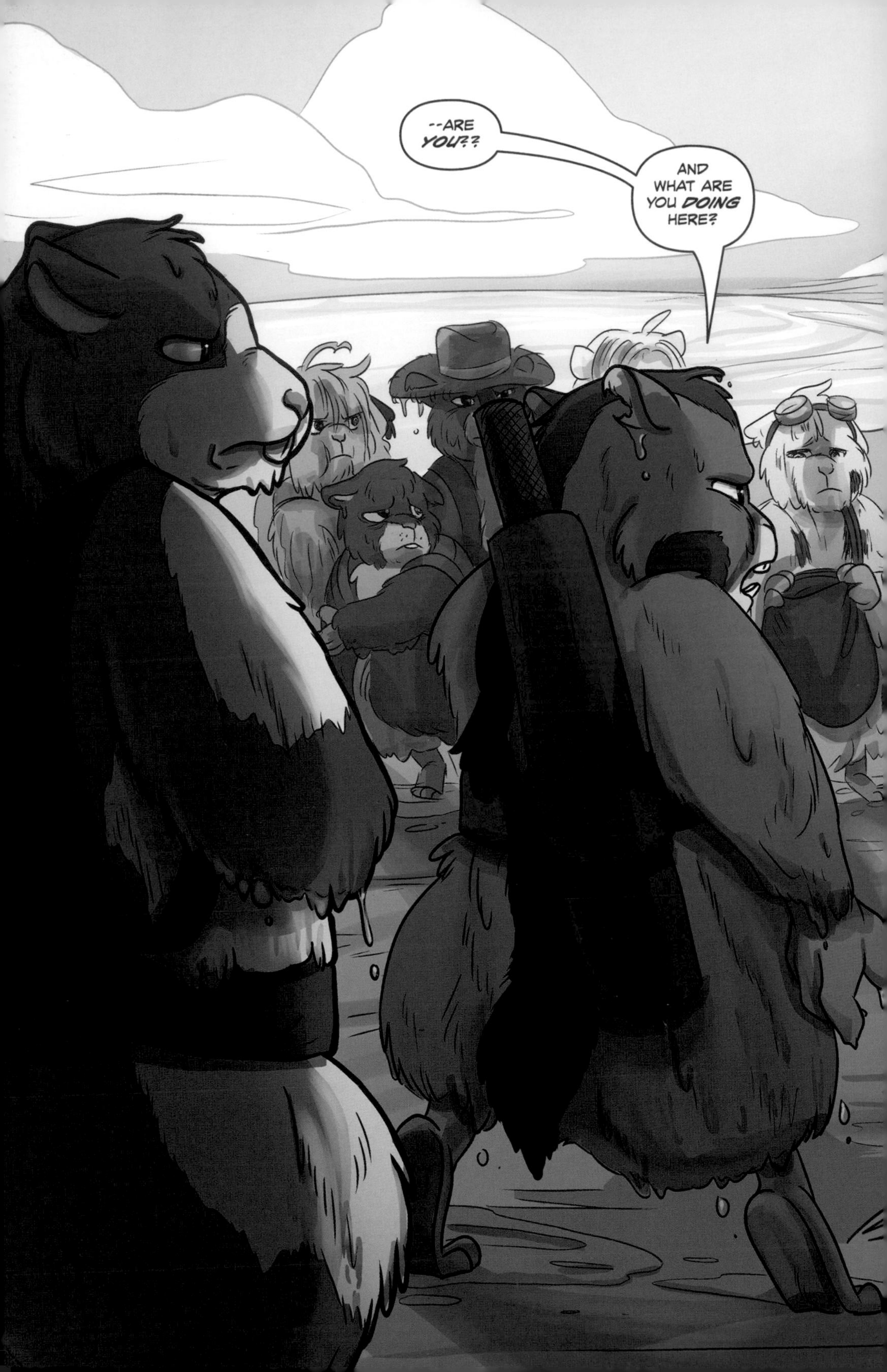
--ARE *YOU*??
AND WHAT ARE YOU *DOING* HERE?

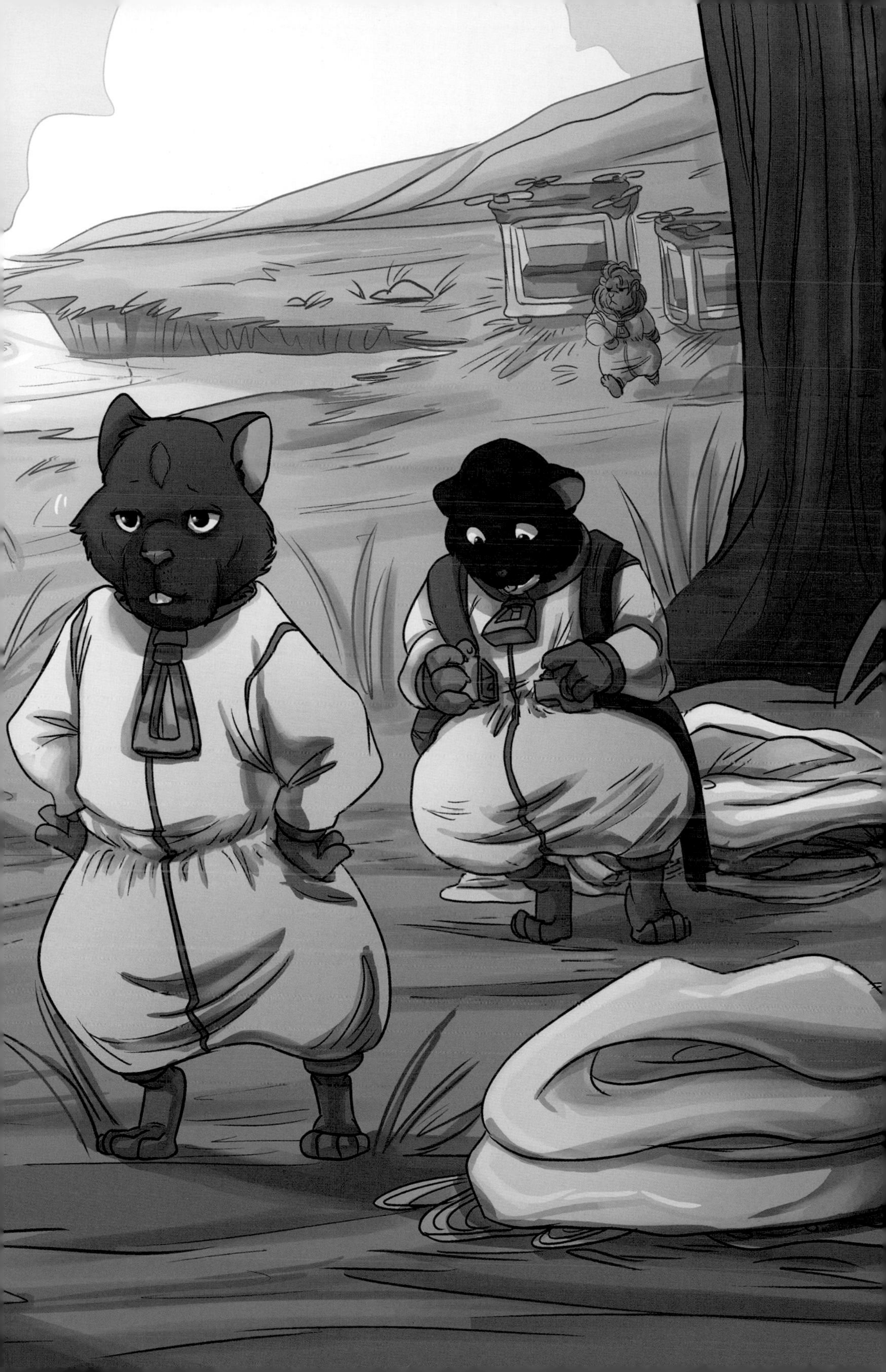

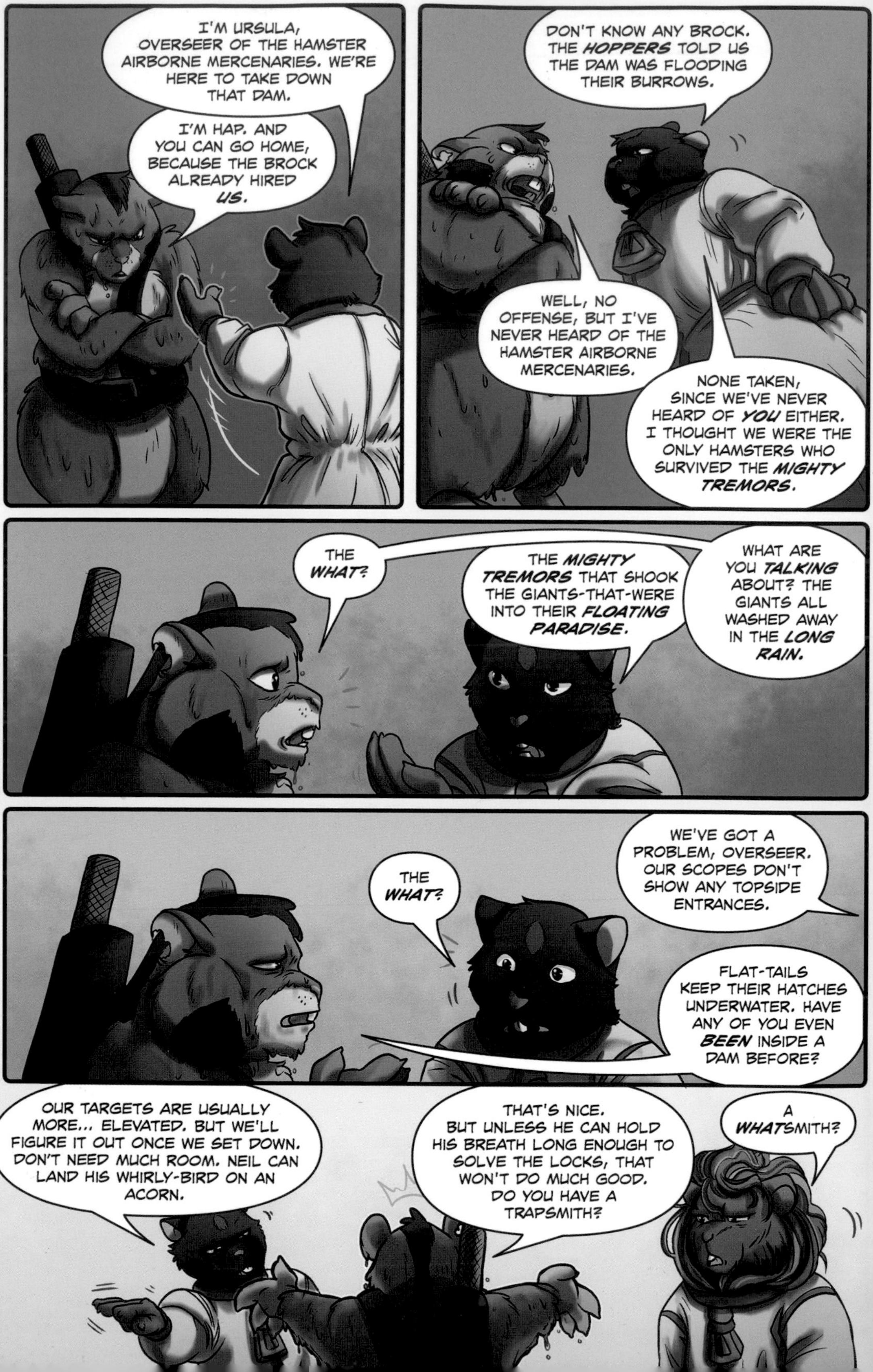
I'M URSULA, OVERSEER OF THE HAMSTER AIRBORNE MERCENARIES. WE'RE HERE TO TAKE DOWN THAT DAM.
I'M HAP. AND YOU CAN GO HOME, BECAUSE THE BROCK ALREADY HIRED *US*.
DON'T KNOW ANY BROCK. THE *HOPPERS* TOLD US THE DAM WAS FLOODING THEIR BURROWS.
WELL, NO OFFENSE, BUT I'VE NEVER HEARD OF THE HAMSTER AIRBORNE MERCENARIES.
NONE TAKEN, SINCE WE'VE NEVER HEARD OF *YOU* EITHER. I THOUGHT WE WERE THE ONLY HAMSTERS WHO SURVIVED THE *MIGHTY TREMORS*.
THE *WHAT?*
THE *MIGHTY TREMORS* THAT SHOOK THE GIANTS-THAT-WERE INTO THEIR *FLOATING PARADISE*.
WHAT ARE YOU *TALKING* ABOUT? THE GIANTS ALL WASHED AWAY IN THE *LONG RAIN*.
THE *WHAT?*
WE'VE GOT A PROBLEM, OVERSEER. OUR SCOPES DON'T SHOW ANY TOPSIDE ENTRANCES.
FLAT-TAILS KEEP THEIR HATCHES UNDERWATER. HAVE ANY OF YOU EVEN *BEEN* INSIDE A DAM BEFORE?
OUR TARGETS ARE USUALLY MORE... ELEVATED. BUT WE'LL FIGURE IT OUT ONCE WE SET DOWN. DON'T NEED MUCH ROOM. NEIL CAN LAND HIS WHIRLY-BIRD ON AN ACORN.
THAT'S NICE. BUT UNLESS HE CAN HOLD HIS BREATH LONG ENOUGH TO SOLVE THE LOCKS, THAT WON'T DO MUCH GOOD. DO YOU HAVE A TRAPSMITH?
A *WHAT*SMITH?

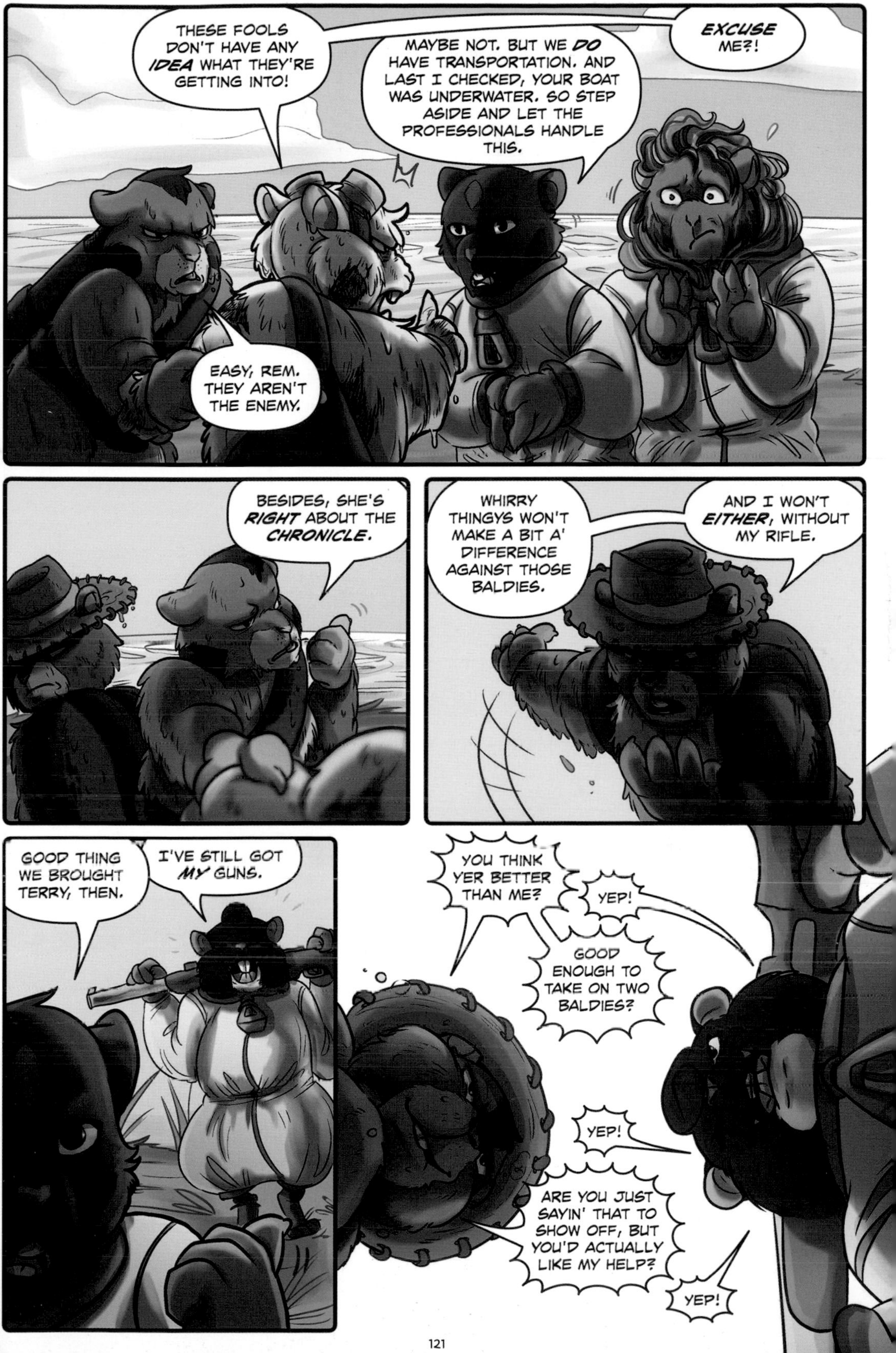
THESE FOOLS DON'T HAVE ANY *IDEA* WHAT THEY'RE GETTING INTO!
MAYBE NOT. BUT WE *DO* HAVE TRANSPORTATION. AND LAST I CHECKED, YOUR BOAT WAS UNDERWATER. SO STEP ASIDE AND LET THE PROFESSIONALS HANDLE THIS.
EXCUSE ME?!
EASY, REM. THEY AREN'T THE ENEMY.
BESIDES, SHE'S *RIGHT* ABOUT THE *CHRONICLE*.
WHIRRY THINGYS WON'T MAKE A BIT A' DIFFERENCE AGAINST THOSE BALDIES.
AND I WON'T *EITHER*, WITHOUT MY RIFLE.
GOOD THING WE BROUGHT TERRY, THEN.
I'VE STILL GOT *MY* GUNS.
YOU THINK YER BETTER THAN ME?
YEP!
GOOD ENOUGH TO TAKE ON TWO BALDIES?
YEP!
ARE YOU JUST SAYIN' THAT TO SHOW OFF, BUT YOU'D ACTUALLY LIKE MY HELP?
YEP!

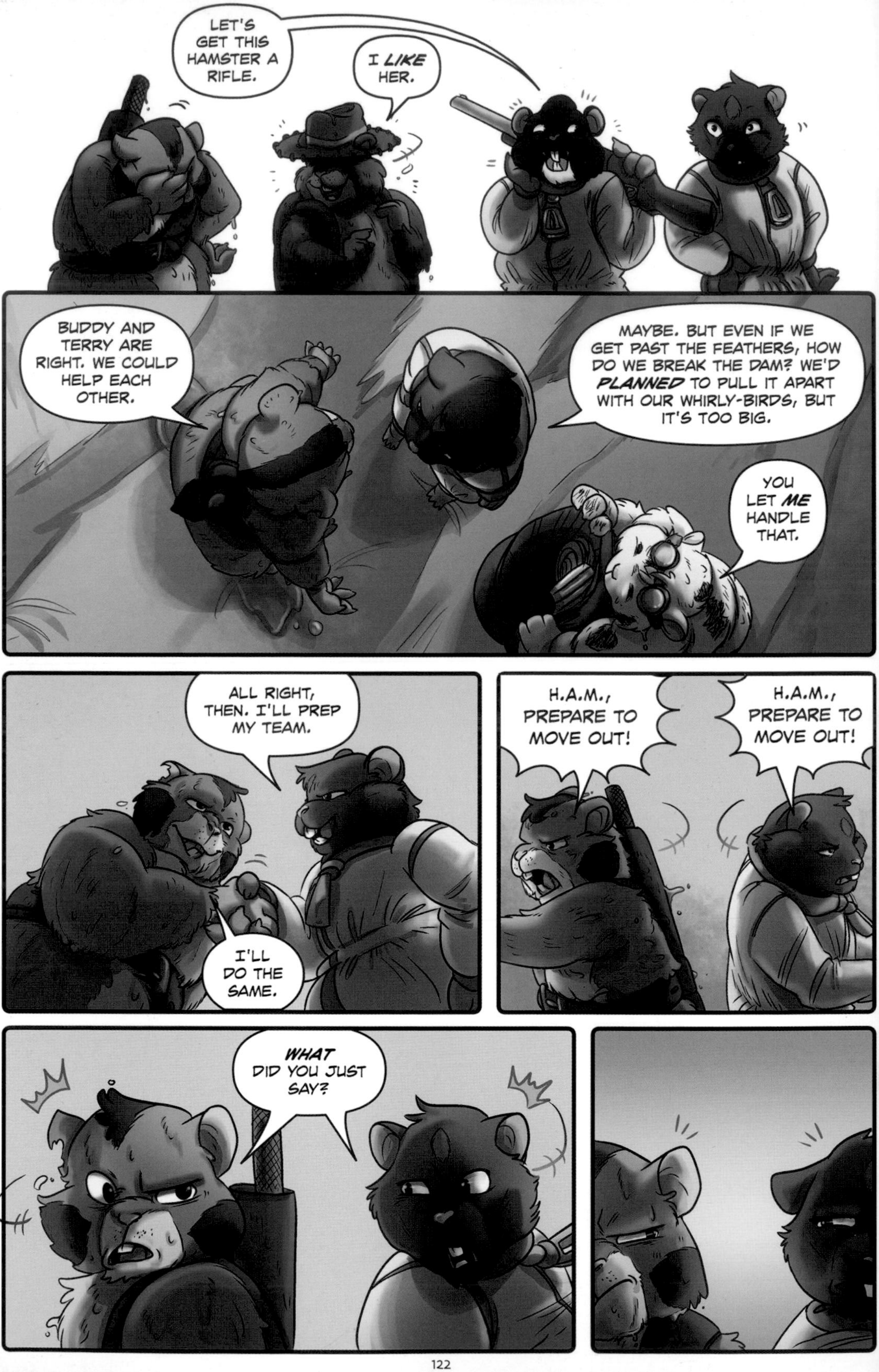
LET'S GET THIS HAMSTER A RIFLE.
I *LIKE* HER.
BUDDY AND TERRY ARE RIGHT. WE COULD HELP EACH OTHER.
MAYBE. BUT EVEN IF WE GET PAST THE FEATHERS, HOW DO WE BREAK THE DAM? WE'D *PLANNED* TO PULL IT APART WITH OUR WHIRLY-BIRDS, BUT IT'S TOO BIG.
YOU LET *ME* HANDLE THAT.
ALL RIGHT, THEN. I'LL PREP MY TEAM.
I'LL DO THE SAME.
H.A.M., PREPARE TO MOVE OUT!
H.A.M., PREPARE TO MOVE OUT!
WHAT DID YOU JUST SAY?

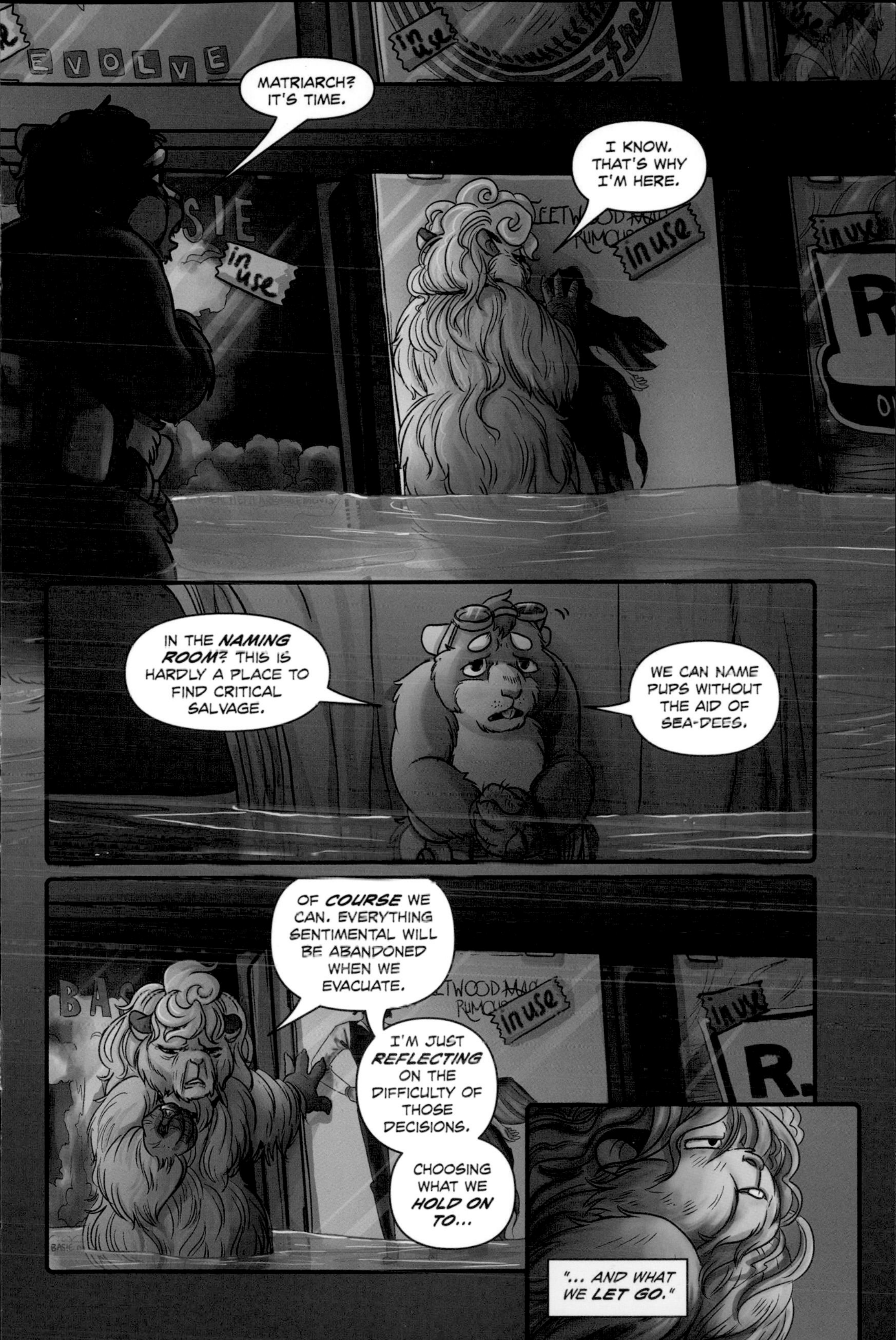
EVOLVE
MATRIARCH? IT'S TIME.
I KNOW. THAT'S WHY I'M HERE.
in use
in use
in use
IN THE *NAMING ROOM*? THIS IS HARDLY A PLACE TO FIND CRITICAL SALVAGE.
WE CAN NAME PUPS WITHOUT THE AID OF SEA-DEES.
OF *COURSE* WE CAN. EVERYTHING SENTIMENTAL WILL BE ABANDONED WHEN WE EVACUATE.
I'M JUST *REFLECTING* ON THE DIFFICULTY OF THOSE DECISIONS.
CHOOSING WHAT WE *HOLD ON TO*...
in use
in use
"... AND WHAT WE *LET GO*."

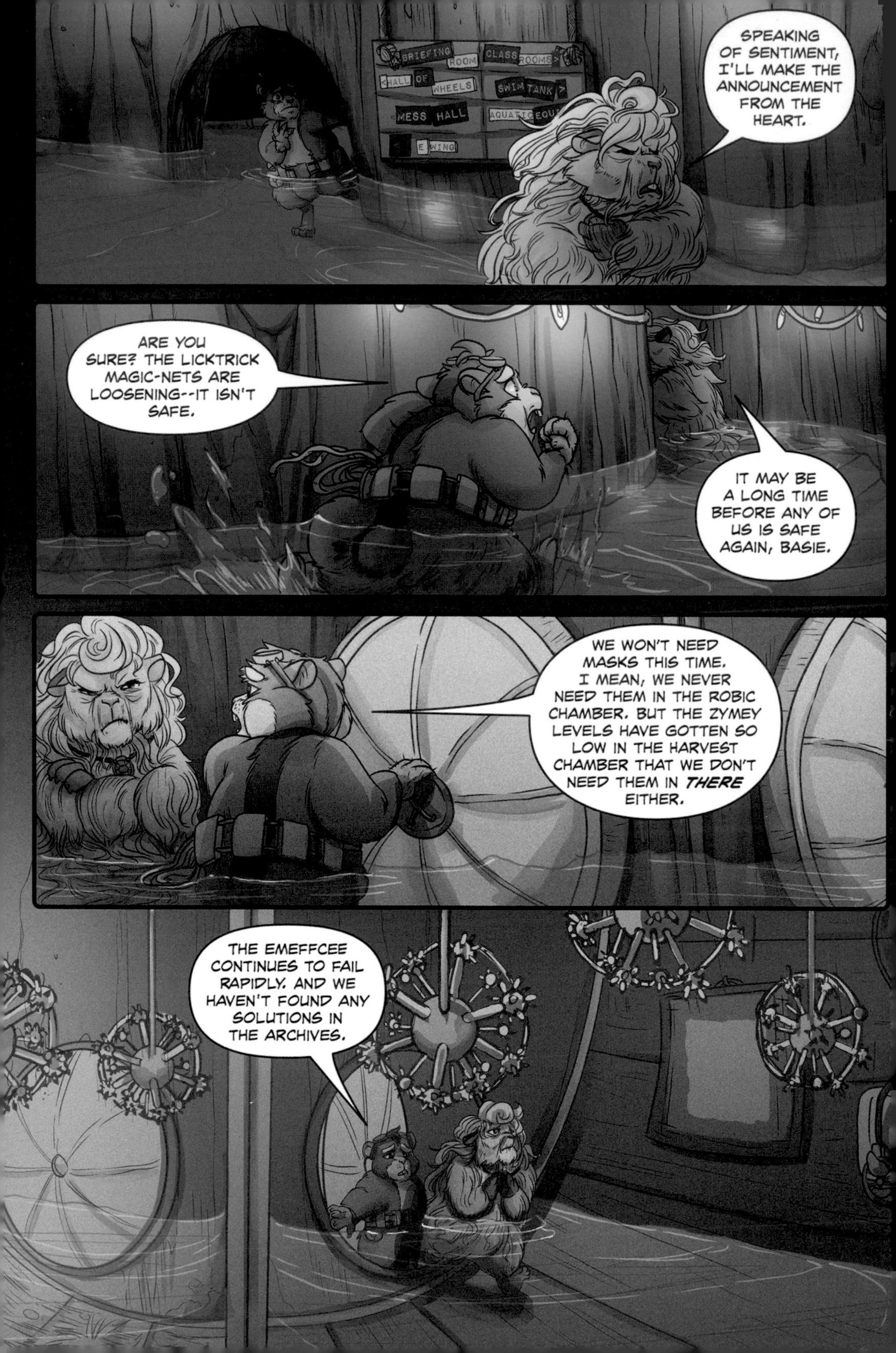
BRIEFING ROOM
CLASSROOMS
HALL OF WHEELS
SWIM TANK
MESS HALL
SPEAKING OF SENTIMENT, I'LL MAKE THE ANNOUNCEMENT FROM THE HEART.
ARE YOU SURE? THE LICKTRICK MAGIC-NETS ARE LOOSENING--IT ISN'T SAFE.
IT MAY BE A LONG TIME BEFORE ANY OF US IS SAFE AGAIN, BASIE.
WE WON'T NEED MASKS THIS TIME. I MEAN, WE NEVER NEED THEM IN THE ROBIC CHAMBER. BUT THE ZYMEY LEVELS HAVE GOTTEN SO LOW IN THE HARVEST CHAMBER THAT WE DON'T NEED THEM IN *THERE* EITHER.
THE EMEFFCEE CONTINUES TO FAIL RAPIDLY. AND WE HAVEN'T FOUND ANY SOLUTIONS IN THE ARCHIVES.

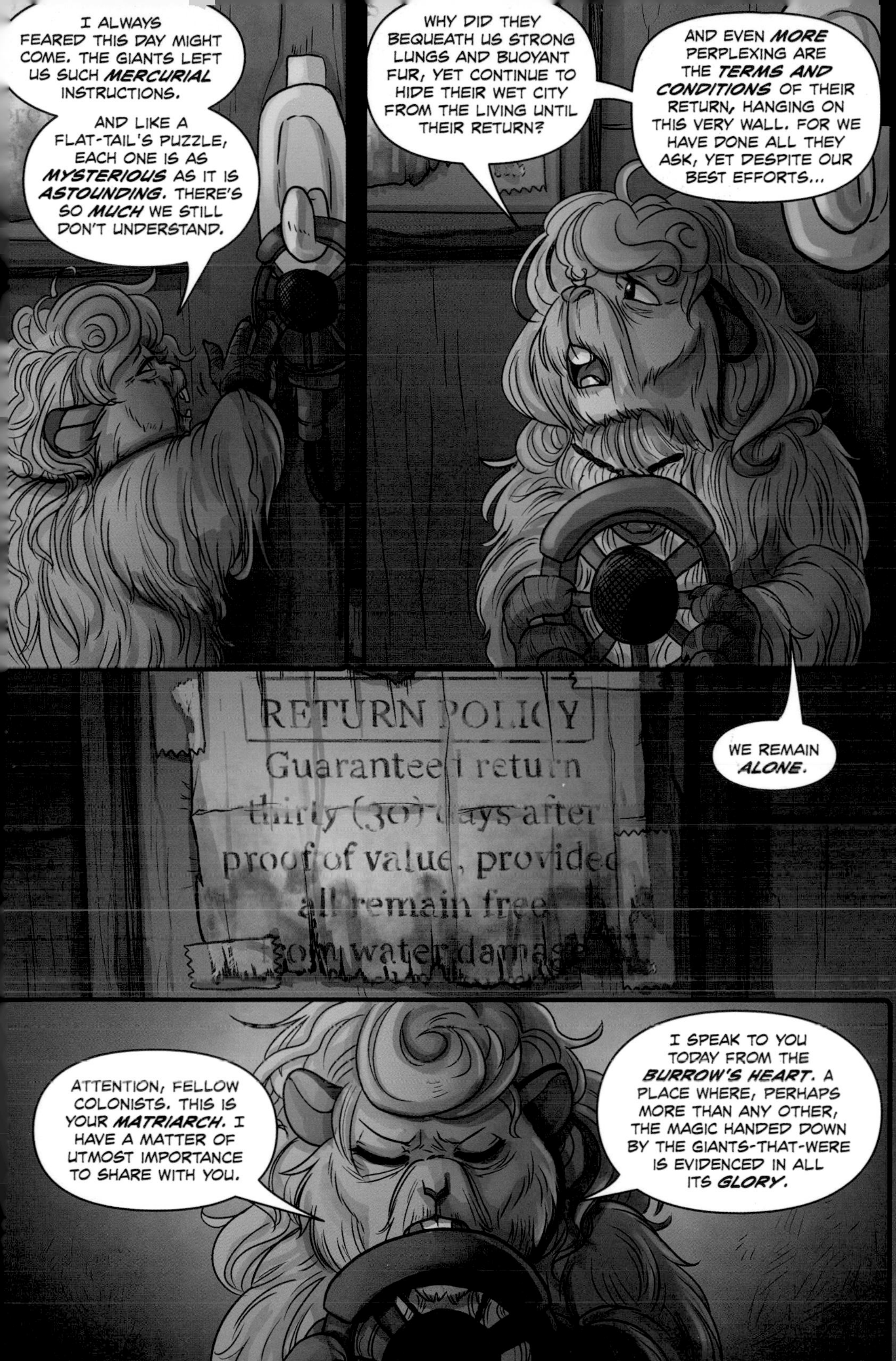
I ALWAYS FEARED THIS DAY MIGHT COME. THE GIANTS LEFT US SUCH MERCURIAL INSTRUCTIONS.
AND LIKE A FLAT-TAIL'S PUZZLE, EACH ONE IS AS MYSTERIOUS AS IT IS ASTOUNDING. THERE'S SO MUCH WE STILL DON'T UNDERSTAND.
WHY DID THEY BEQUEATH US STRONG LUNGS AND BUOYANT FUR, YET CONTINUE TO HIDE THEIR WET CITY FROM THE LIVING UNTIL THEIR RETURN?
AND EVEN MORE PERPLEXING ARE THE TERMS AND CONDITIONS OF THEIR RETURN, HANGING ON THIS VERY WALL. FOR WE HAVE DONE ALL THEY ASK, YET DESPITE OUR BEST EFFORTS...
RETURN POLICY
Guaranteed return
thirty (30) days after
proof of value, provided
all remain free
WE REMAIN ALONE.
ATTENTION, FELLOW COLONISTS. THIS IS YOUR MATRIARCH. I HAVE A MATTER OF UTMOST IMPORTANCE TO SHARE WITH YOU.
I SPEAK TO YOU TODAY FROM THE BURROW'S HEART. A PLACE WHERE, PERHAPS MORE THAN ANY OTHER, THE MAGIC HANDED DOWN BY THE GIANTS-THAT-WERE IS EVIDENCED IN ALL ITS GLORY.

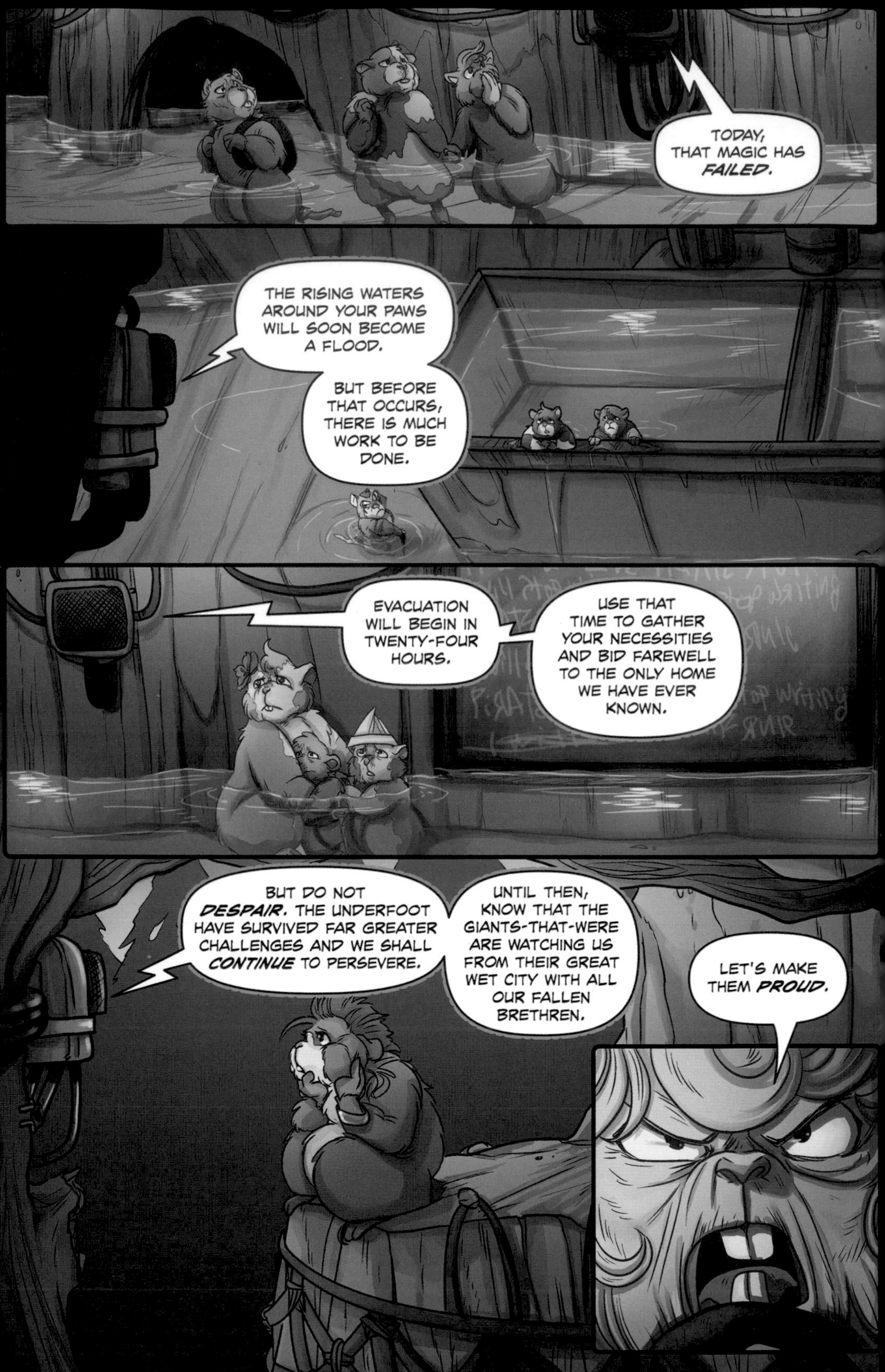
TODAY, THAT MAGIC HAS *FAILED*.
THE RISING WATERS AROUND YOUR PAWS WILL SOON BECOME A FLOOD.
BUT BEFORE THAT OCCURS, THERE IS MUCH WORK TO BE DONE.
EVACUATION WILL BEGIN IN TWENTY-FOUR HOURS.
USE THAT TIME TO GATHER YOUR NECESSITIES AND BID FAREWELL TO THE ONLY HOME WE HAVE EVER KNOWN.
BUT DO NOT *DESPAIR*. THE UNDERFOOT HAVE SURVIVED FAR GREATER CHALLENGES AND WE SHALL *CONTINUE* TO PERSEVERE.
UNTIL THEN, KNOW THAT THE GIANTS-THAT-WERE ARE WATCHING US FROM THEIR GREAT WET CITY WITH ALL OUR FALLEN BRETHREN.
LET'S MAKE THEM *PROUD*.

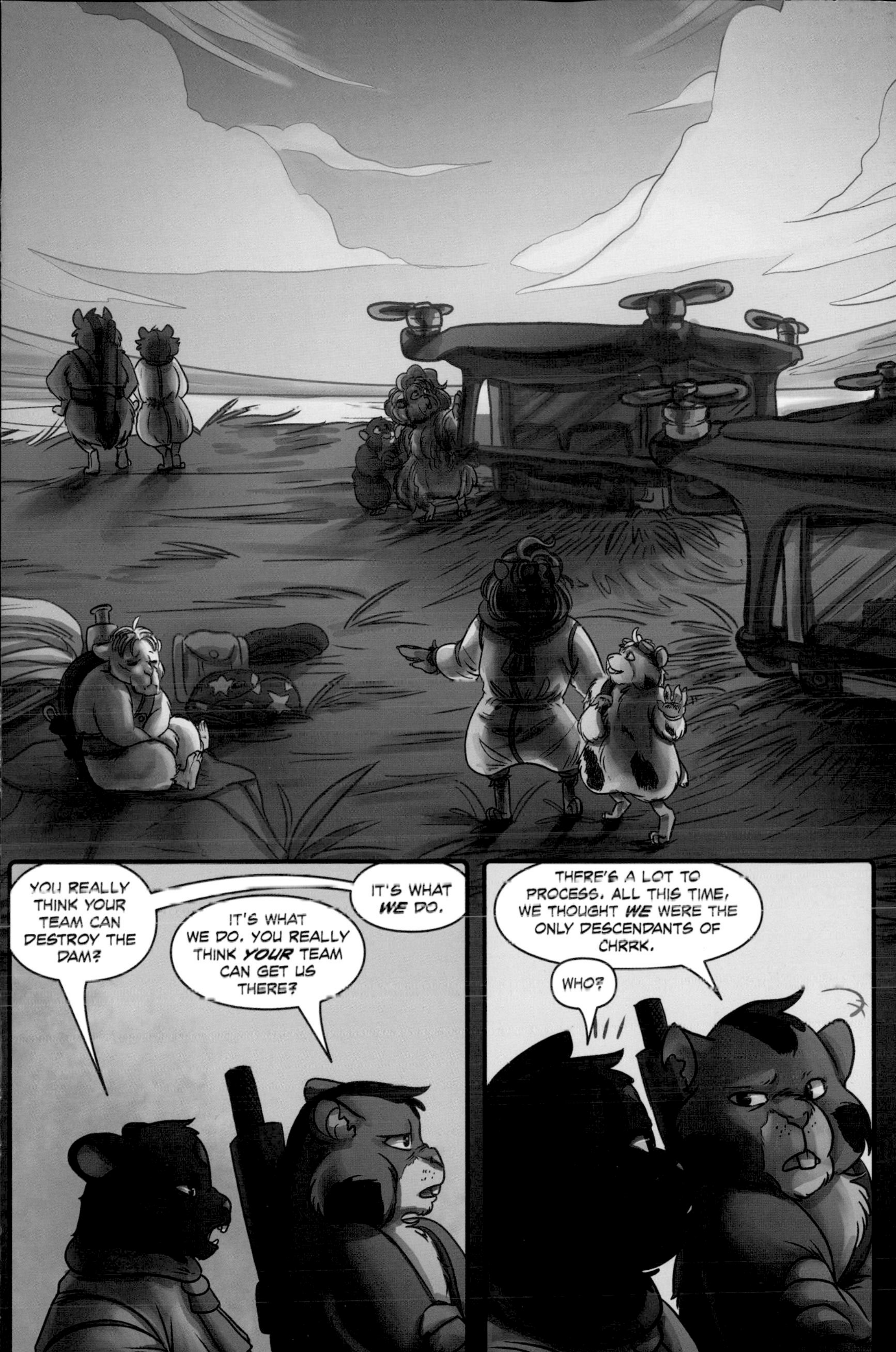
YOU REALLY THINK YOUR TEAM CAN DESTROY THE DAM?
IT'S WHAT WE DO. YOU REALLY THINK YOUR TEAM CAN GET US THERE?
IT'S WHAT WE DO.
THERE'S A LOT TO PROCESS. ALL THIS TIME, WE THOUGHT WE WERE THE ONLY DESCENDANTS OF CHRRK.
WHO?

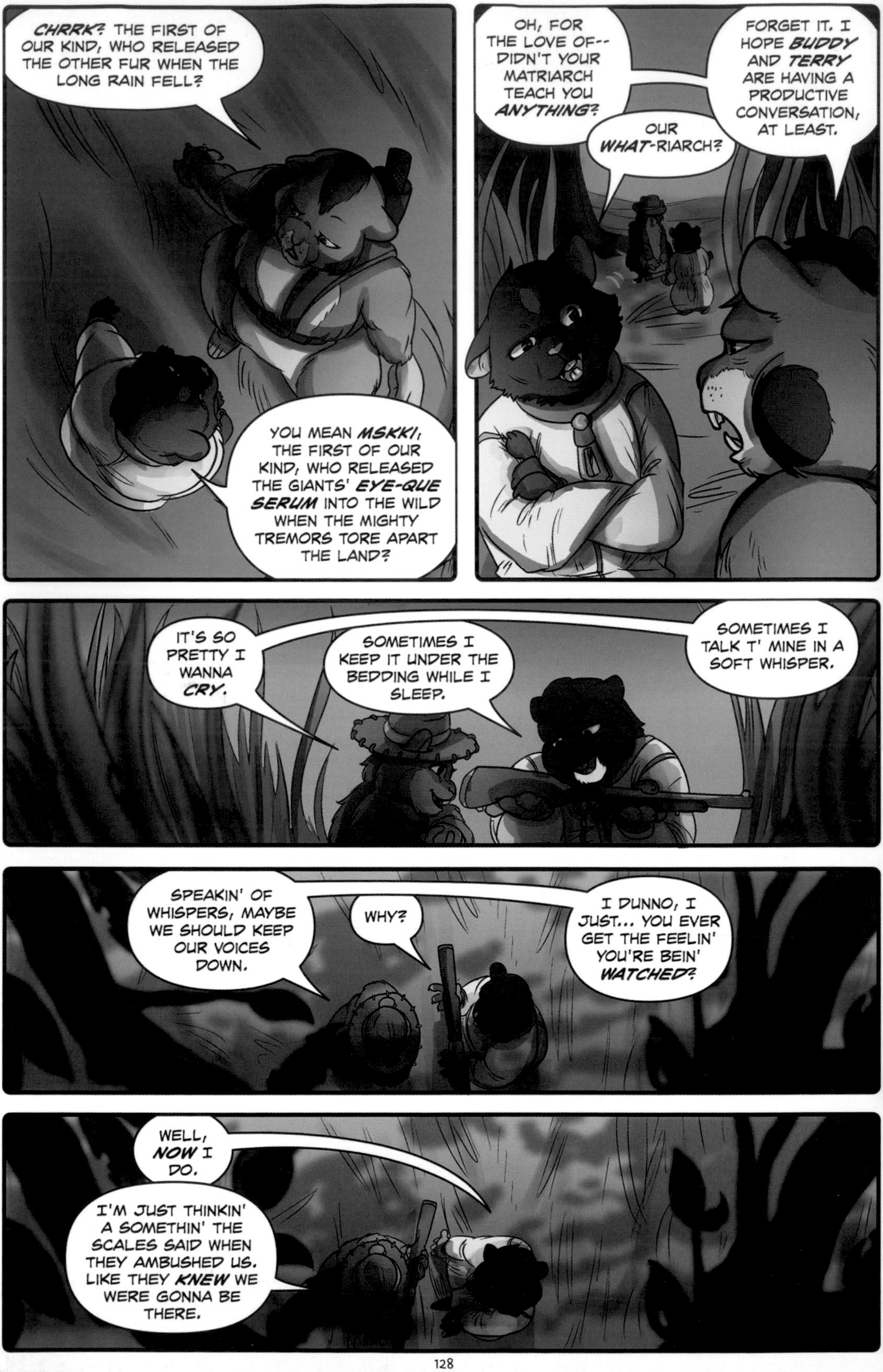
CHRRK? THE FIRST OF OUR KIND, WHO RELEASED THE OTHER FUR WHEN THE LONG RAIN FELL?
YOU MEAN MSKKI, THE FIRST OF OUR KIND, WHO RELEASED THE GIANTS' EYE-QUE SERUM INTO THE WILD WHEN THE MIGHTY TREMORS TORE APART THE LAND?
OH, FOR THE LOVE OF-- DIDN'T YOUR MATRIARCH TEACH YOU ANYTHING?
OUR WHAT-RIARCH?
FORGET IT. I HOPE BUDDY AND TERRY ARE HAVING A PRODUCTIVE CONVERSATION, AT LEAST.
IT'S SO PRETTY I WANNA CRY.
SOMETIMES I KEEP IT UNDER THE BEDDING WHILE I SLEEP.
SOMETIMES I TALK T' MINE IN A SOFT WHISPER.
SPEAKIN' OF WHISPERS, MAYBE WE SHOULD KEEP OUR VOICES DOWN.
WHY?
I DUNNO, I JUST... YOU EVER GET THE FEELIN' YOU'RE BEIN' WATCHED?
WELL, NOW I DO.
I'M JUST THINKIN' A SOMETHIN' THE SCALES SAID WHEN THEY AMBUSHED US. LIKE THEY KNEW WE WERE GONNA BE THERE.

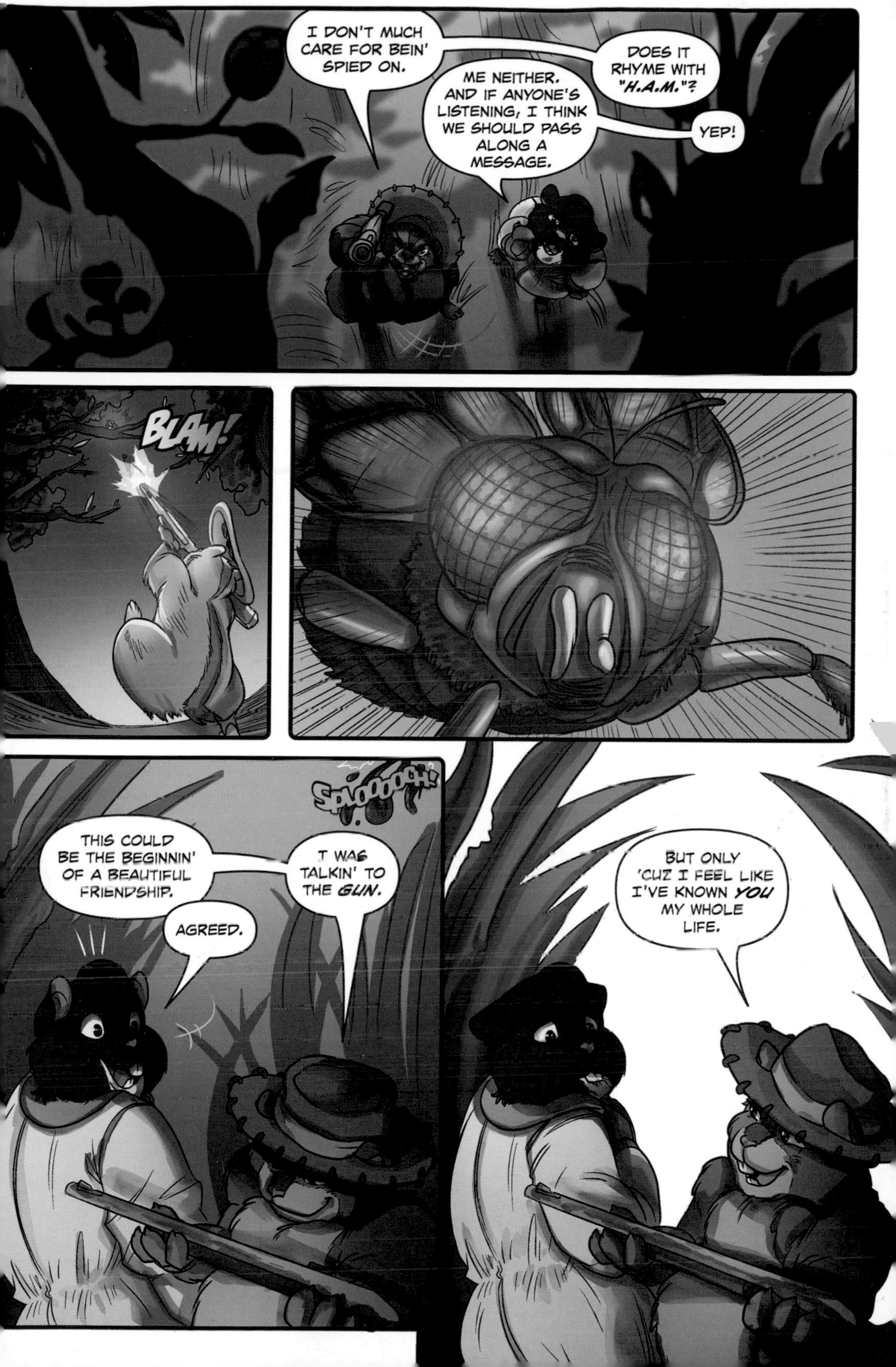

I DON'T MUCH CARE FOR BEIN' SPIED ON.
DOES IT RHYME WITH "H.A.M."?
ME NEITHER. AND IF ANYONE'S LISTENING, I THINK WE SHOULD PASS ALONG A MESSAGE.
YEP!
BLAM!
SPLOOOOOCH!
THIS COULD BE THE BEGINNIN' OF A BEAUTIFUL FRIENDSHIP.
I WAS TALKIN' TO THE GUN.
AGREED.
BUT ONLY 'CUZ I FEEL LIKE I'VE KNOWN YOU MY WHOLE LIFE.

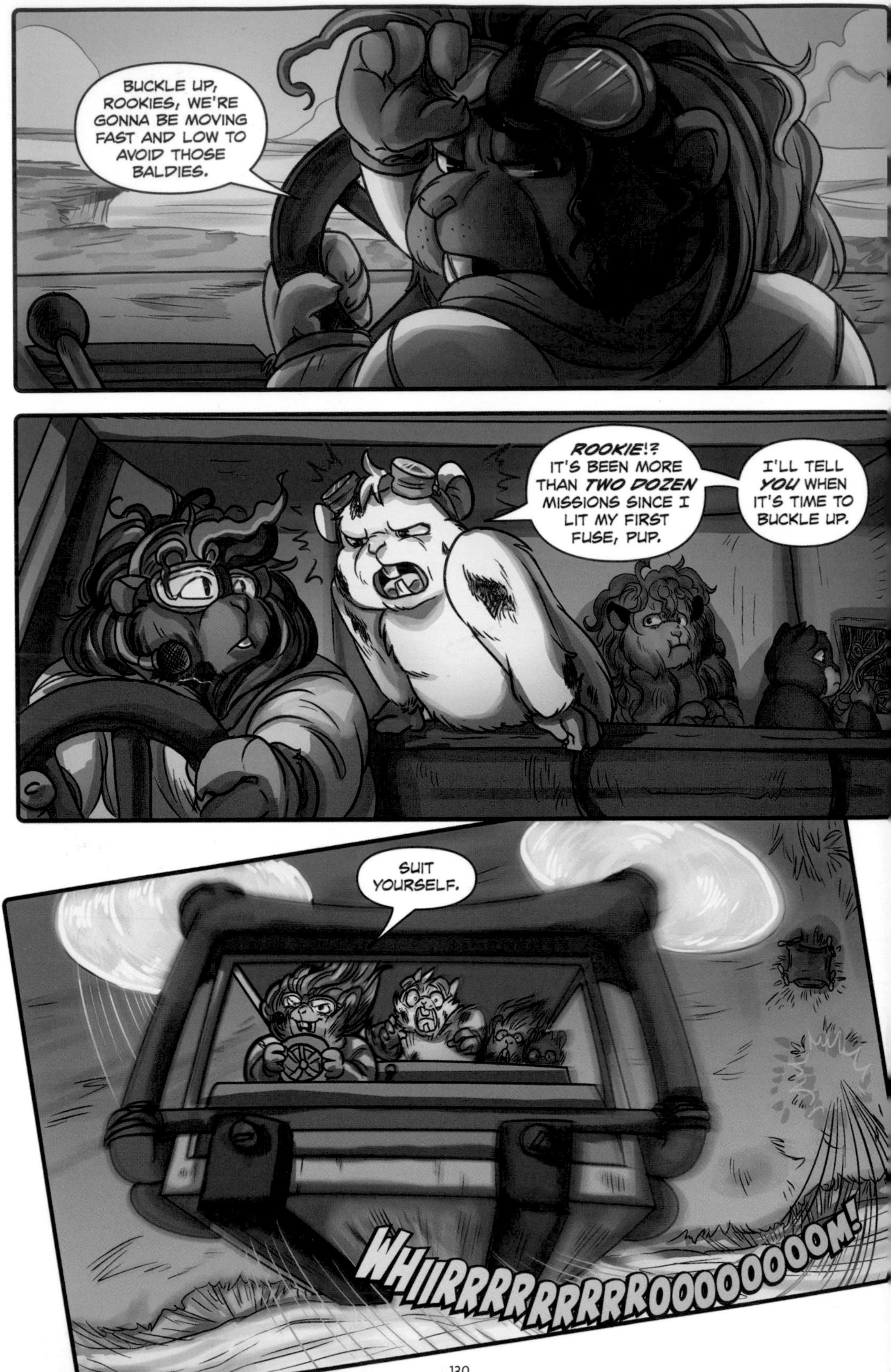
BUCKLE UP, ROOKIES, WE'RE GONNA BE MOVING FAST AND LOW TO AVOID THOSE BALDIES.
ROOKIE!? IT'S BEEN MORE THAN *TWO DOZEN* MISSIONS SINCE I LIT MY FIRST FUSE, PUP.
I'LL TELL *YOU* WHEN IT'S TIME TO BUCKLE UP.
SUIT YOURSELF.
WHIIRRRRRRRRRRROOOOOOOOOM!

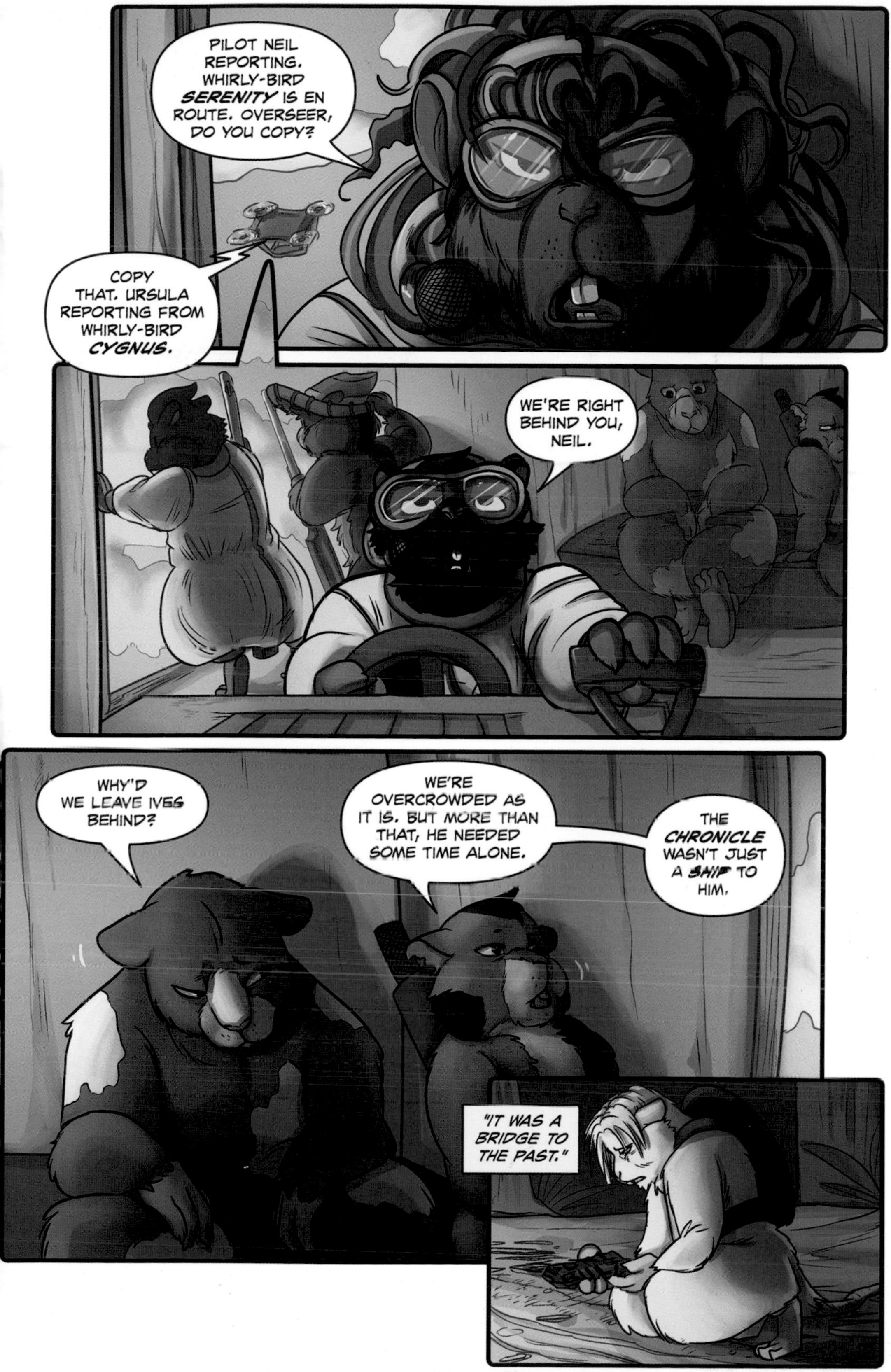
PILOT NEIL REPORTING. WHIRLY-BIRD SERENITY IS EN ROUTE. OVERSEER, DO YOU COPY?
COPY THAT. URSULA REPORTING FROM WHIRLY-BIRD CYGNUS.
WE'RE RIGHT BEHIND YOU, NEIL.
WHY'D WE LEAVE IVES BEHIND?
WE'RE OVERCROWDED AS IT IS. BUT MORE THAN THAT, HE NEEDED SOME TIME ALONE.
THE CHRONICLE WASN'T JUST A SHIP TO HIM.
"IT WAS A BRIDGE TO THE PAST."

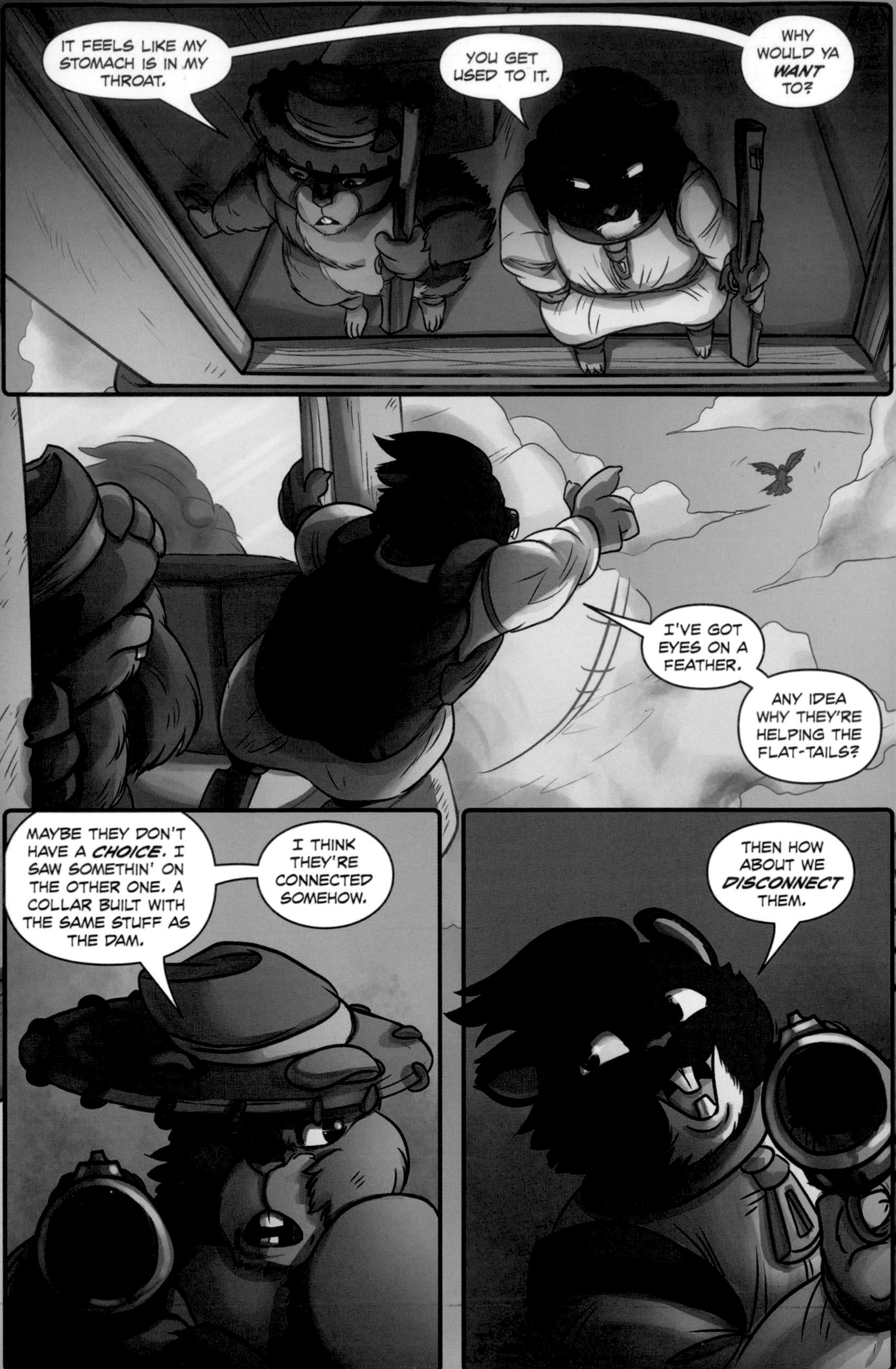

IT FEELS LIKE MY STOMACH IS IN MY THROAT.
YOU GET USED TO IT.
WHY WOULD YA WANT TO?
I'VE GOT EYES ON A FEATHER.
ANY IDEA WHY THEY'RE HELPING THE FLAT-TAILS?
MAYBE THEY DON'T HAVE A CHOICE. I SAW SOMETHIN' ON THE OTHER ONE. A COLLAR BUILT WITH THE SAME STUFF AS THE DAM.
I THINK THEY'RE CONNECTED SOMEHOW.
THEN HOW ABOUT WE DISCONNECT THEM.

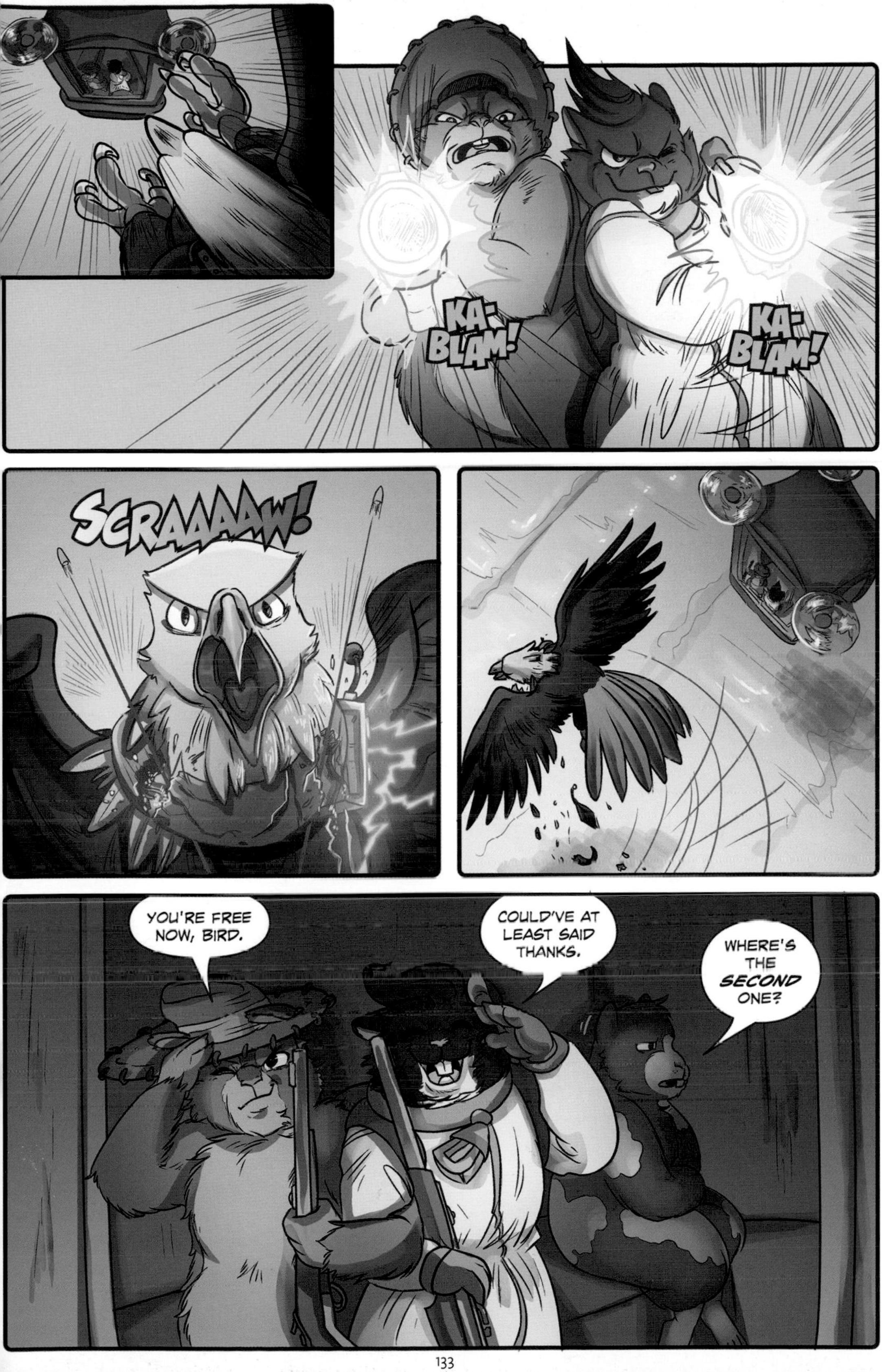
KA-BLAM!
KA-BLAM!
SCRAAAAW!
YOU'RE FREE NOW, BIRD.
COULD'VE AT LEAST SAID THANKS.
WHERE'S THE *SECOND* ONE?

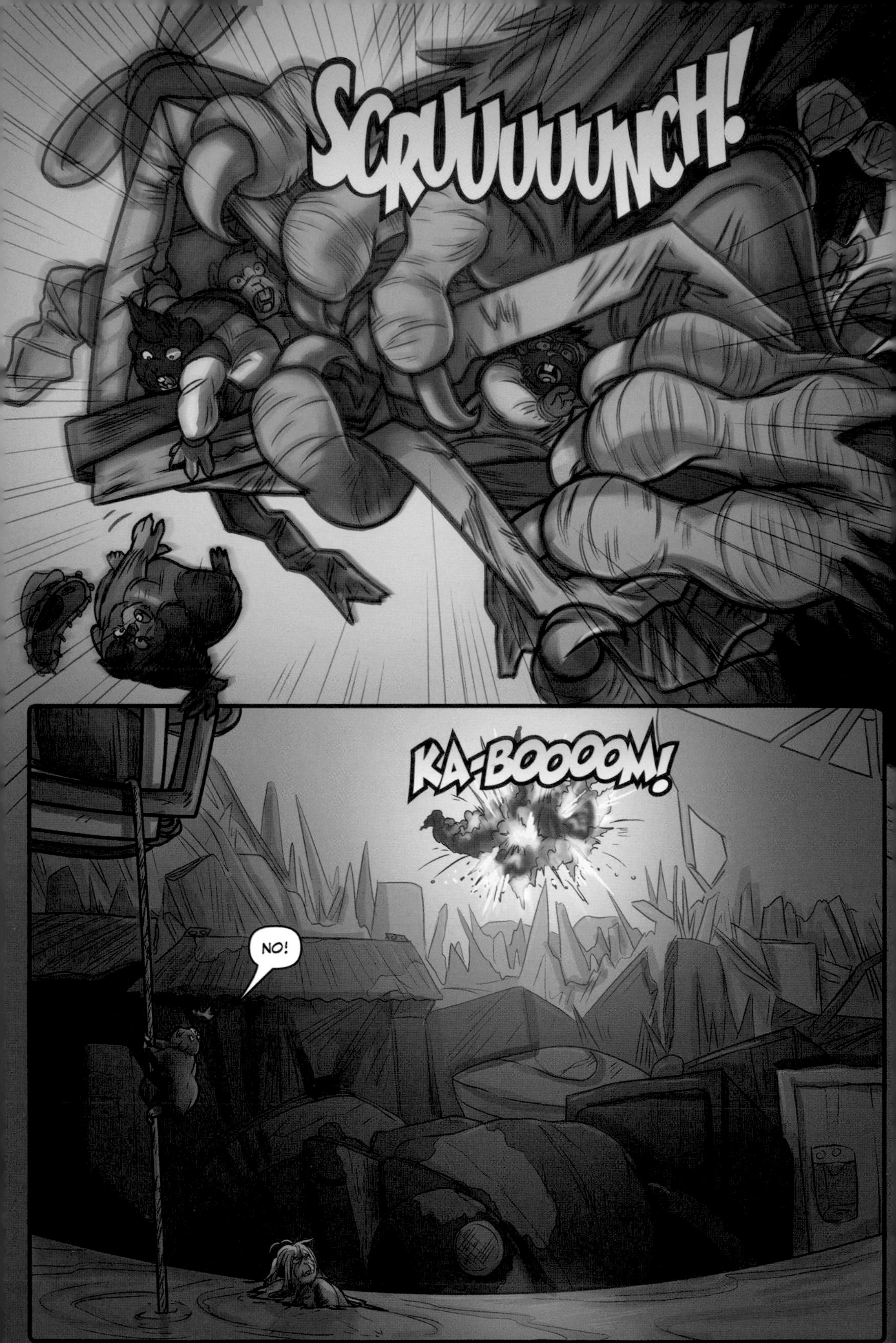
SCRUUUUUNCH!
KA-BOOOOM!
NO!

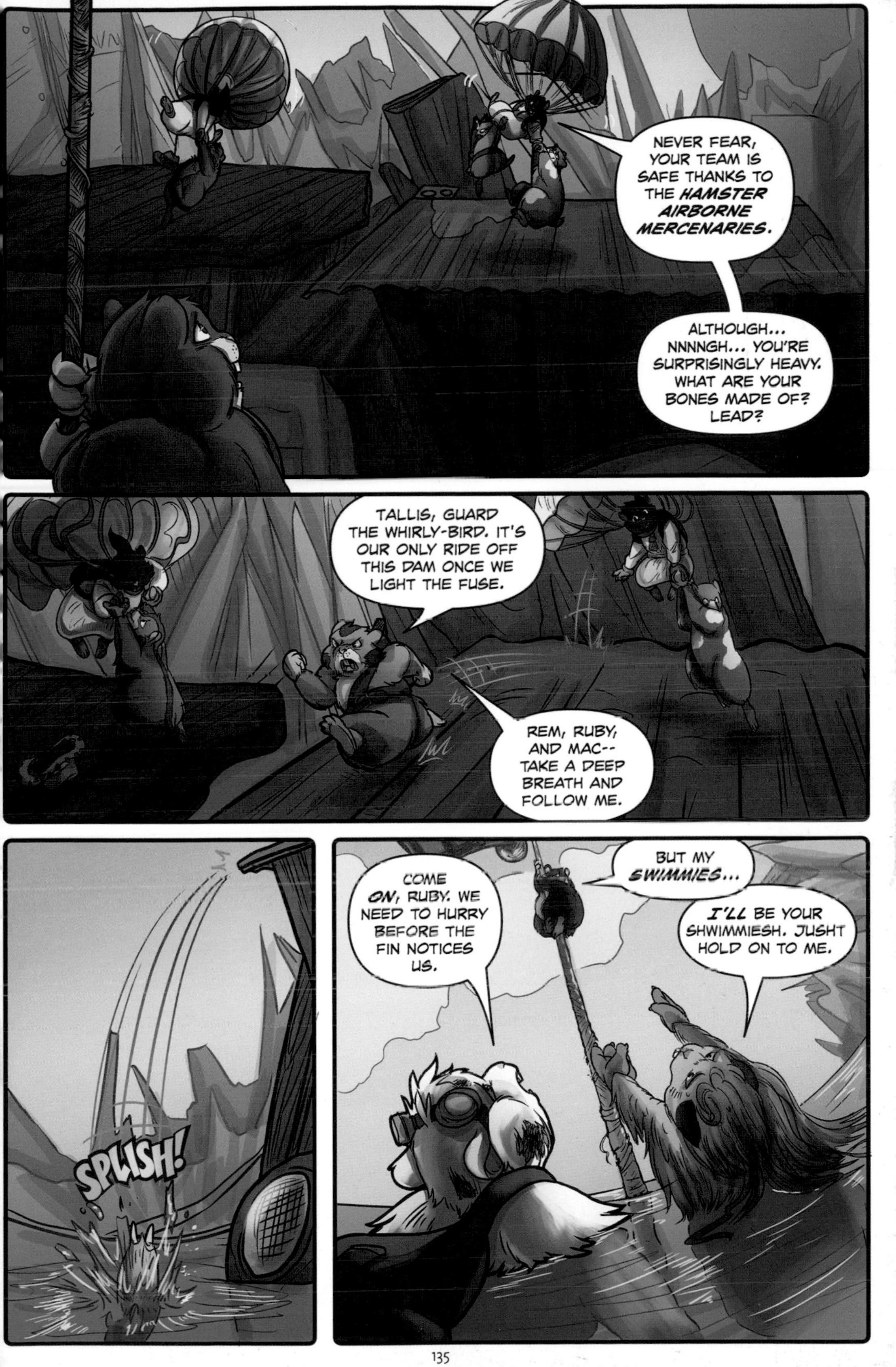
NEVER FEAR, YOUR TEAM IS SAFE THANKS TO THE ***HAMSTER AIRBORNE MERCENARIES.***
ALTHOUGH... NNNNGH... YOU'RE SURPRISINGLY HEAVY. WHAT ARE YOUR BONES MADE OF? LEAD?
TALLIS, GUARD THE WHIRLY-BIRD. IT'S OUR ONLY RIDE OFF THIS DAM ONCE WE LIGHT THE FUSE.
REM, RUBY, AND MAC-- TAKE A DEEP BREATH AND FOLLOW ME.
SPLISH!
COME *ON*, RUBY. WE NEED TO HURRY BEFORE THE FIN NOTICES US.
BUT MY *SWIMMIES...*
I'LL BE YOUR SHWIMMIESH. JUSHT HOLD ON TO ME.

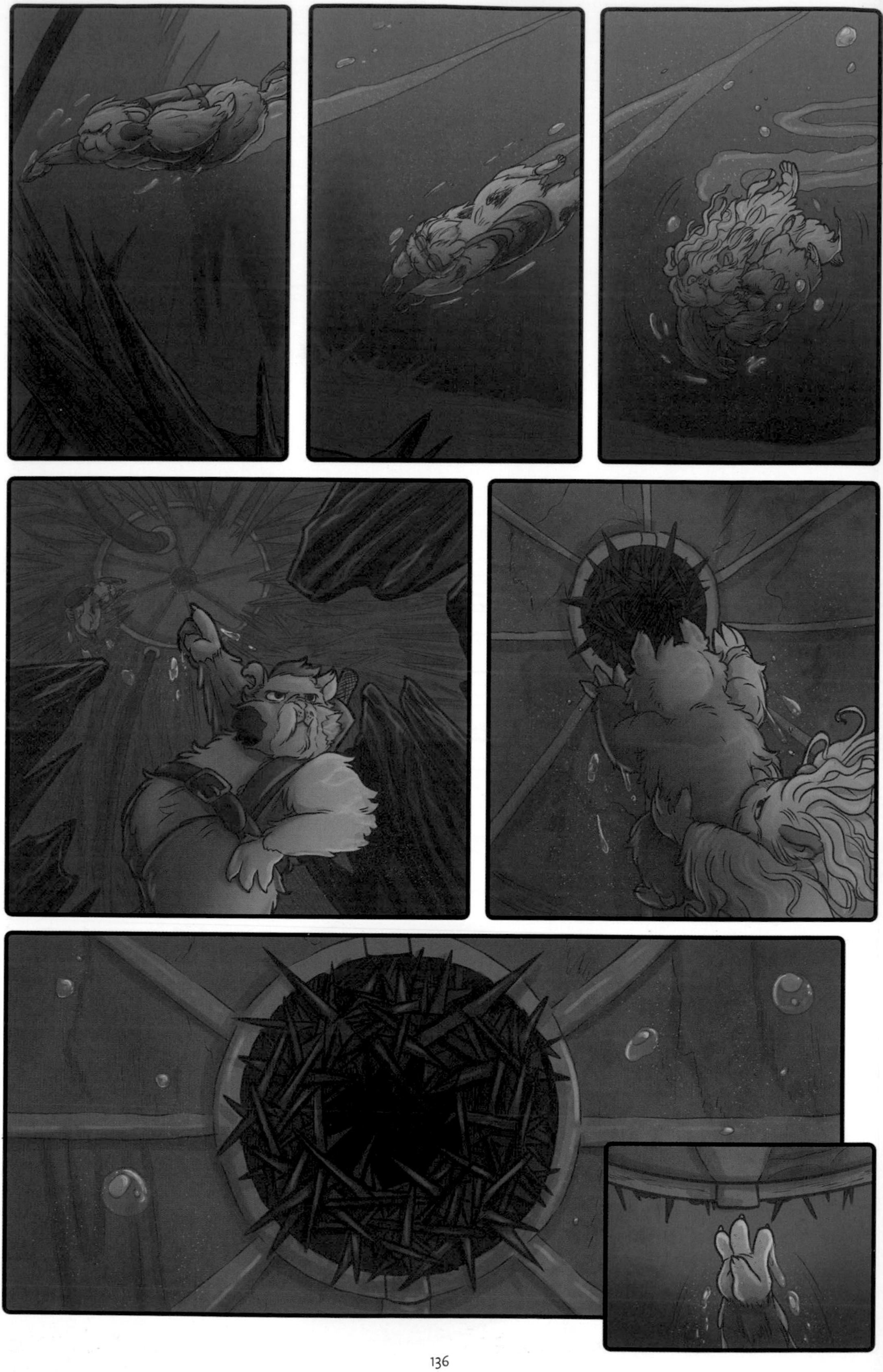

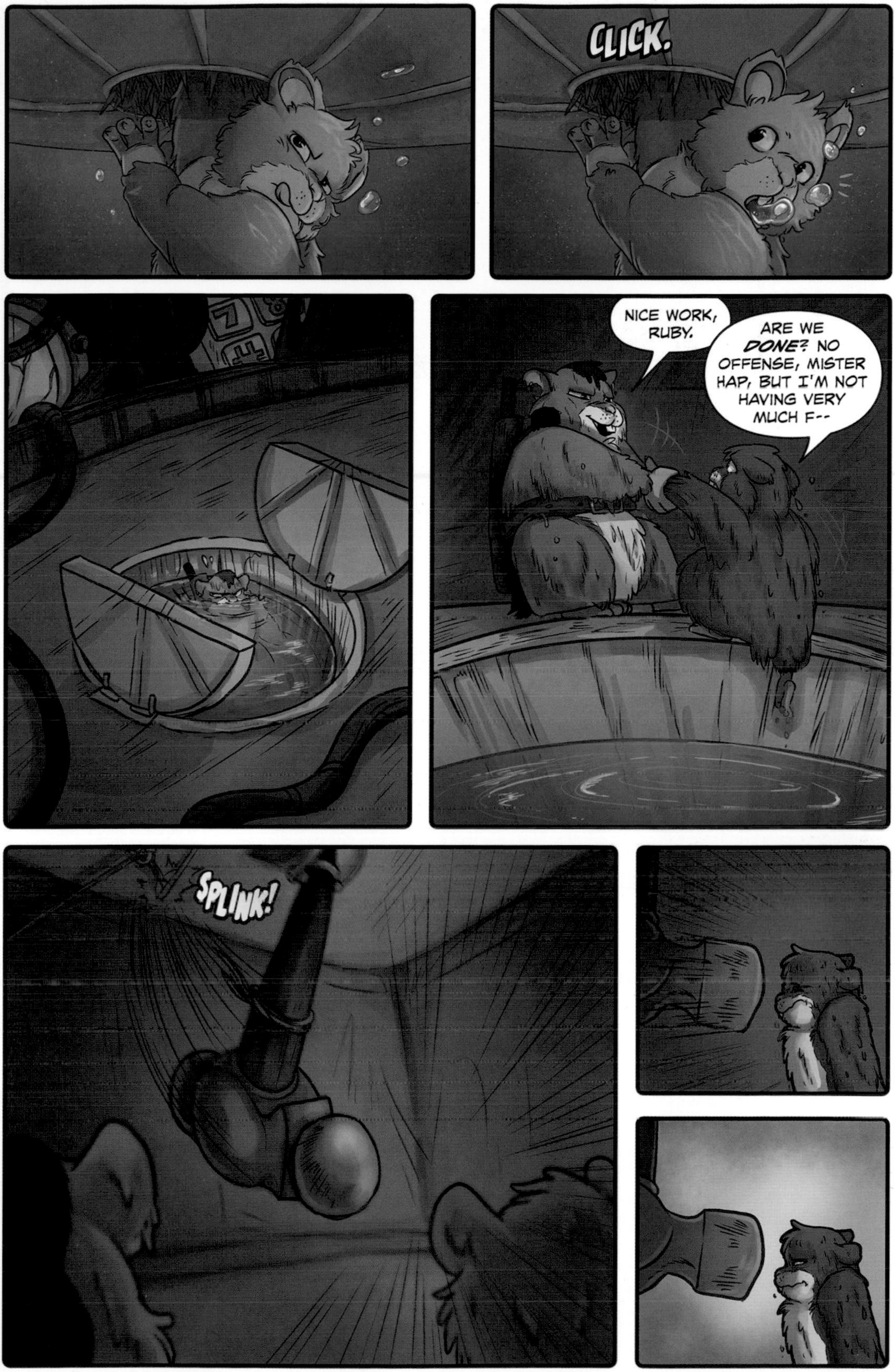
CLICK.
NICE WORK, RUBY.
ARE WE DONE? NO OFFENSE, MISTER HAP, BUT I'M NOT HAVING VERY MUCH F--
SPLINK!

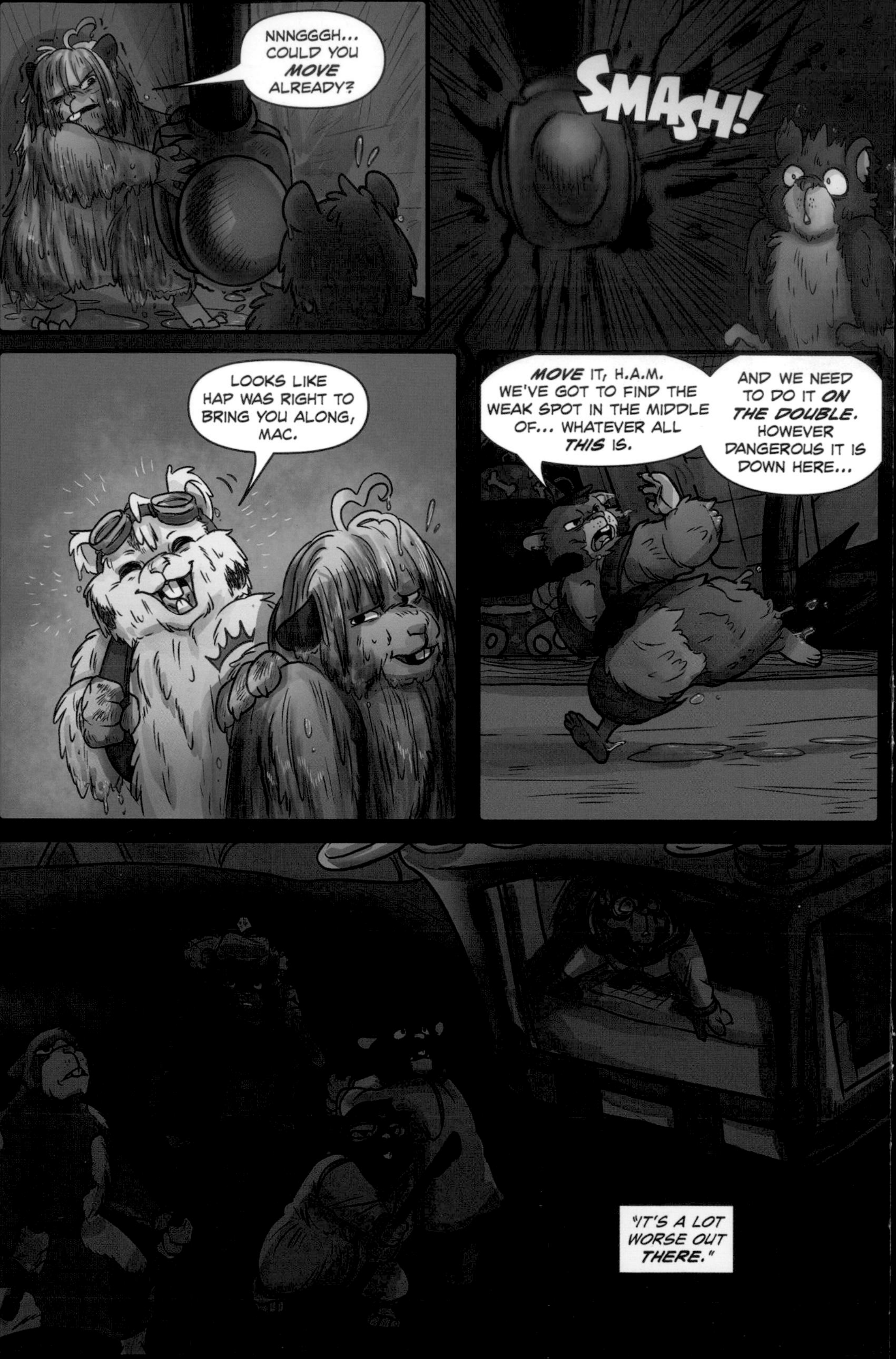

NNNGGGH... COULD YOU *MOVE* ALREADY?
SMASH!
LOOKS LIKE HAP WAS RIGHT TO BRING YOU ALONG, MAC.
MOVE IT, H.A.M. WE'VE GOT TO FIND THE WEAK SPOT IN THE MIDDLE OF... WHATEVER ALL *THIS* IS.
AND WE NEED TO DO IT *ON THE DOUBLE.* HOWEVER DANGEROUS IT IS DOWN HERE...
"IT'S A LOT WORSE OUT *THERE.*"

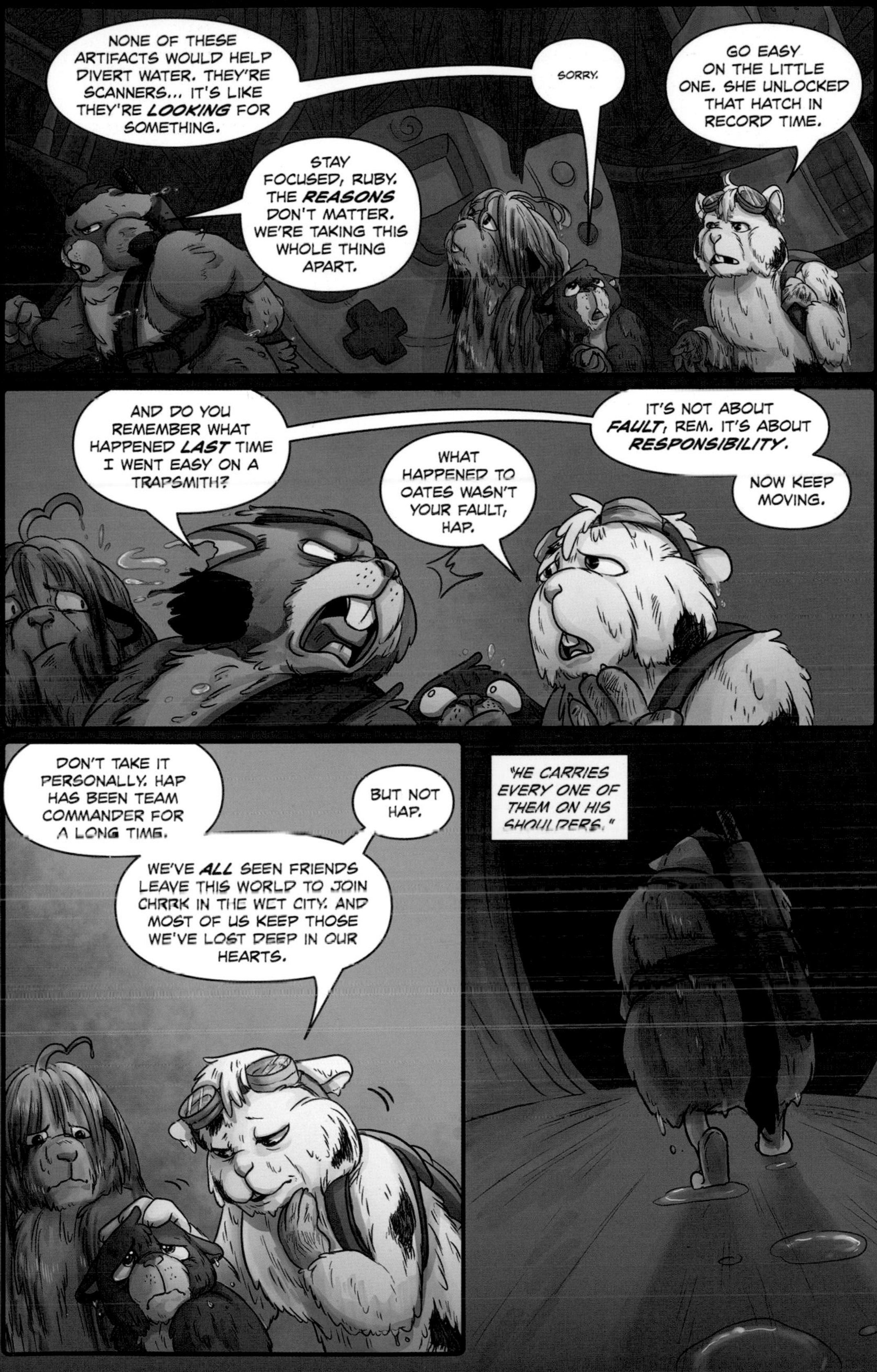
NONE OF THESE ARTIFACTS WOULD HELP DIVERT WATER. THEY'RE SCANNERS... IT'S LIKE THEY'RE *LOOKING* FOR SOMETHING.
STAY FOCUSED, RUBY. THE *REASONS* DON'T MATTER. WE'RE TAKING THIS WHOLE THING APART.
SORRY.
GO EASY ON THE LITTLE ONE. SHE UNLOCKED THAT HATCH IN RECORD TIME.
AND DO YOU REMEMBER WHAT HAPPENED *LAST* TIME I WENT EASY ON A TRAPSMITH?
WHAT HAPPENED TO OATES WASN'T YOUR FAULT, HAP.
IT'S NOT ABOUT *FAULT*, REM. IT'S ABOUT *RESPONSIBILITY*.
NOW KEEP MOVING.
DON'T TAKE IT PERSONALLY. HAP HAS BEEN TEAM COMMANDER FOR A LONG TIME.
BUT NOT HAP.
WE'VE *ALL* SEEN FRIENDS LEAVE THIS WORLD TO JOIN CHRRK IN THE WET CITY. AND MOST OF US KEEP THOSE WE'VE LOST DEEP IN OUR HEARTS.
"HE CARRIES EVERY ONE OF THEM ON HIS SHOULDERS."

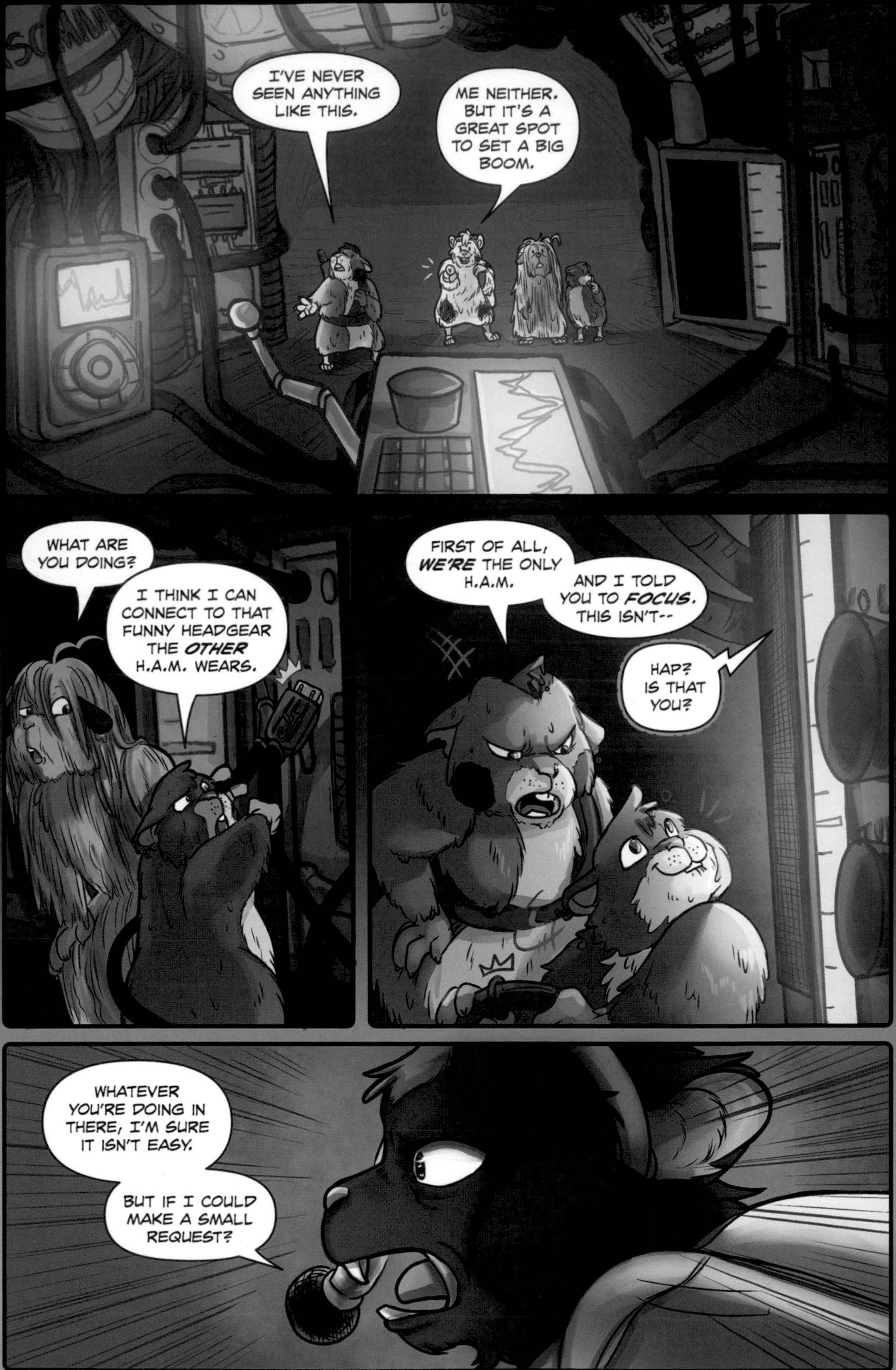
I'VE NEVER SEEN ANYTHING LIKE THIS.
ME NEITHER. BUT IT'S A GREAT SPOT TO SET A BIG BOOM.
WHAT ARE YOU DOING?
I THINK I CAN CONNECT TO THAT FUNNY HEADGEAR THE *OTHER* H.A.M. WEARS.
FIRST OF ALL, ***WE'RE*** THE ONLY H.A.M.
AND I TOLD YOU TO ***FOCUS***. THIS ISN'T--
HAP? IS THAT YOU?
WHATEVER YOU'RE DOING IN THERE, I'M SURE IT ISN'T EASY.
BUT IF I COULD MAKE A SMALL REQUEST?

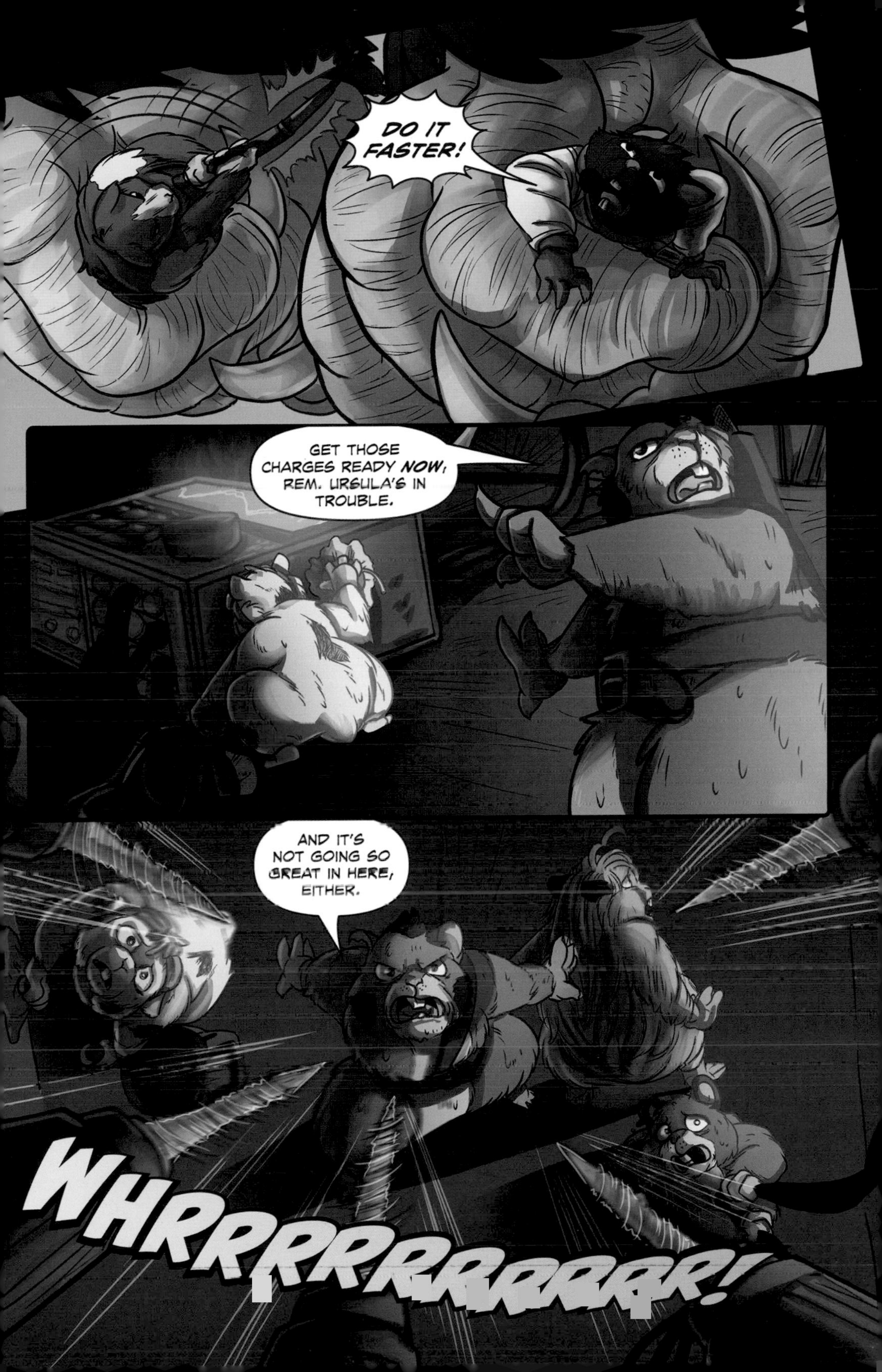
DO IT FASTER!
GET THOSE CHARGES READY *NOW*, REM. URSULA'S IN TROUBLE.
AND IT'S NOT GOING SO GREAT IN HERE, EITHER.
WHRRRRRRRRRR!

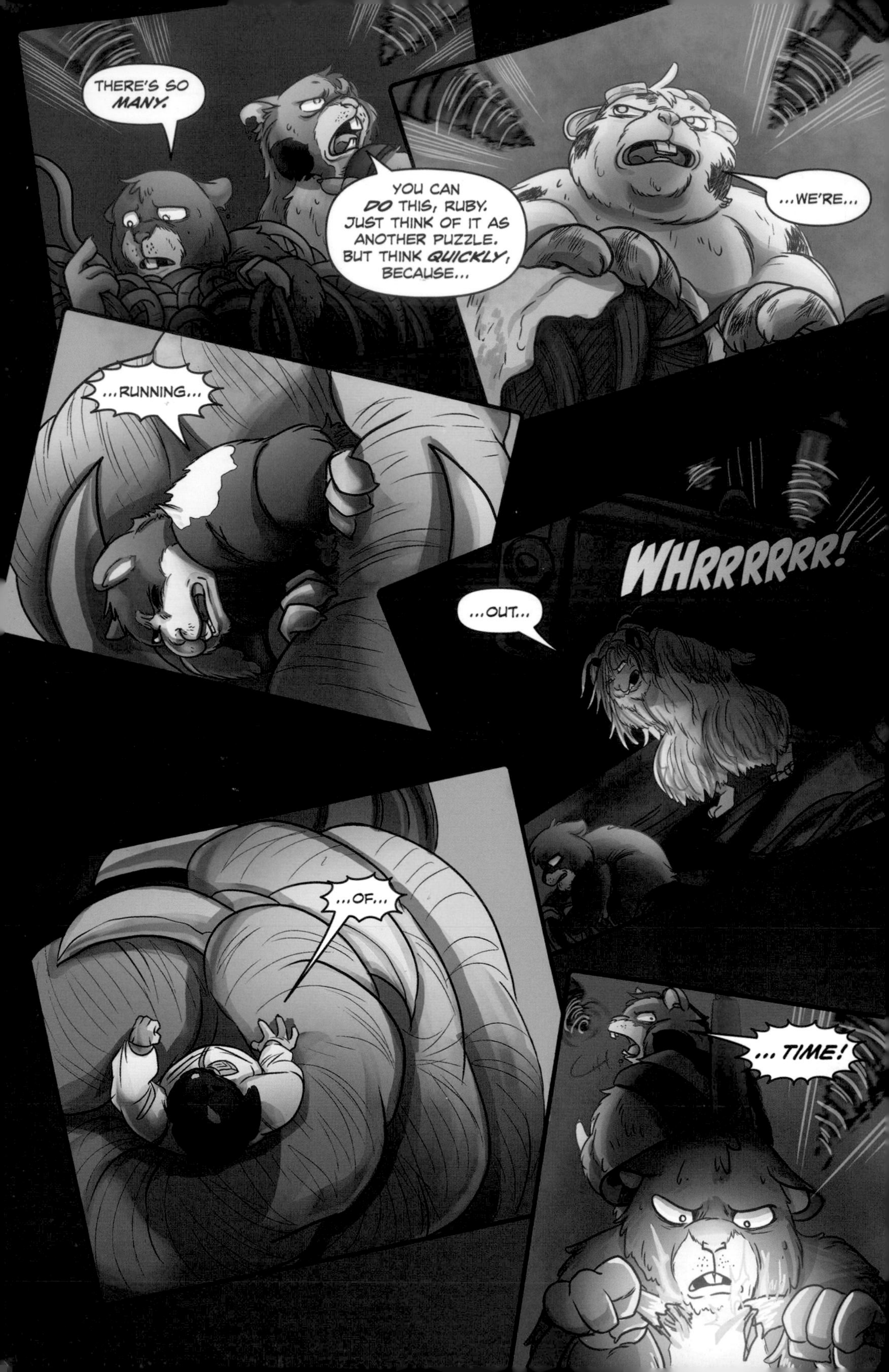
THERE'S SO MANY.
YOU CAN DO THIS, RUBY. JUST THINK OF IT AS ANOTHER PUZZLE. BUT THINK QUICKLY, BECAUSE...
...WE'RE...
...RUNNING...
WHRRRRRR!
...OUT...
...OF...
...TIME!

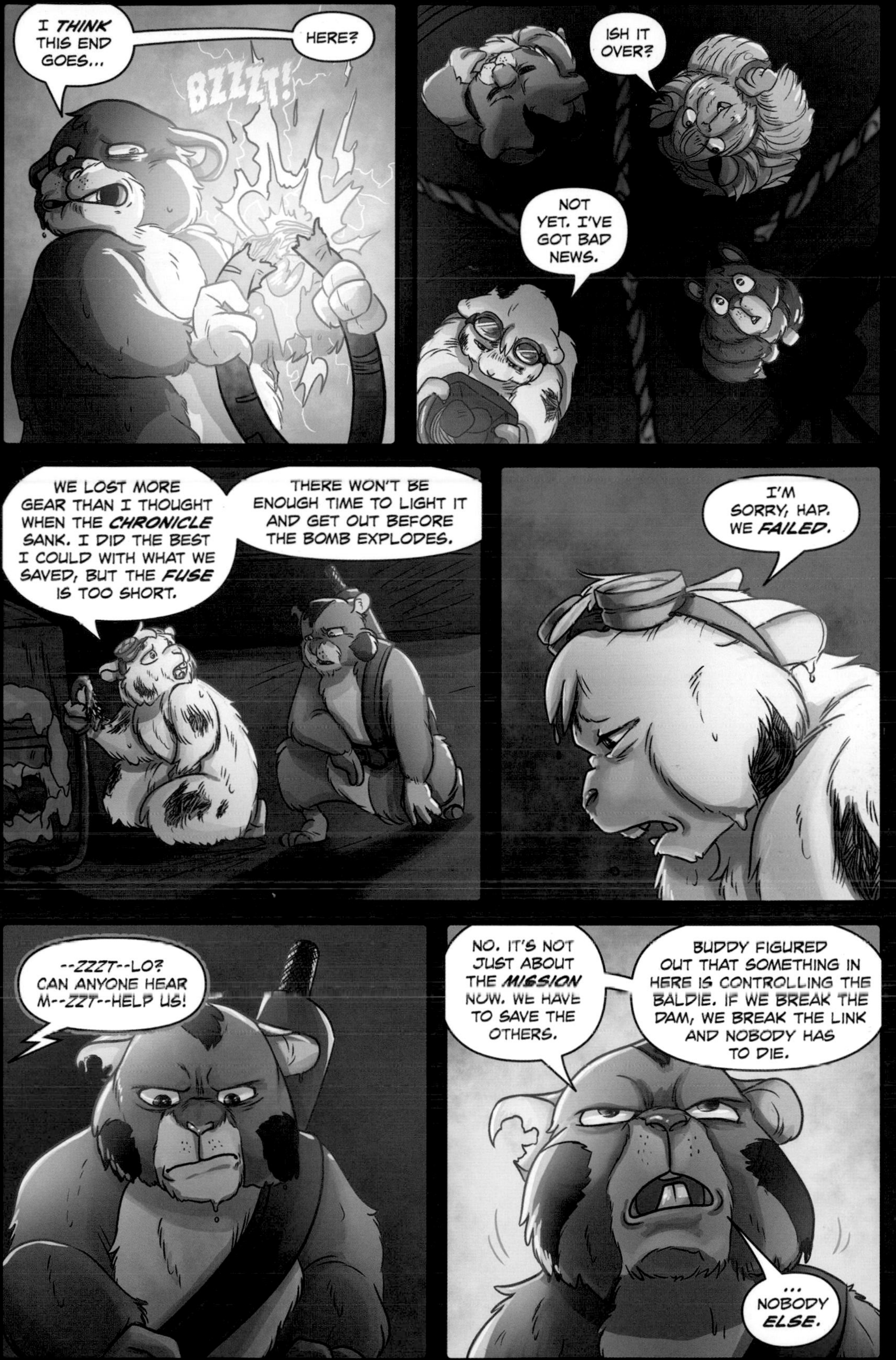
I *THINK* THIS END GOES...
HERE?
BZZZT!
ISH IT OVER?
NOT YET. I'VE GOT BAD NEWS.
WE LOST MORE GEAR THAN I THOUGHT WHEN THE *CHRONICLE* SANK. I DID THE BEST I COULD WITH WHAT WE SAVED, BUT THE *FUSE* IS TOO SHORT.
THERE WON'T BE ENOUGH TIME TO LIGHT IT AND GET OUT BEFORE THE BOMB EXPLODES.
I'M SORRY, HAP. WE *FAILED*.
--*ZZZT*--LO? CAN ANYONE HEAR M--*ZZT*--HELP US!
NO. IT'S NOT JUST ABOUT THE *MISSION* NOW. WE HAVE TO SAVE THE OTHERS.
BUDDY FIGURED OUT THAT SOMETHING IN HERE IS CONTROLLING THE BALDIE. IF WE BREAK THE DAM, WE BREAK THE LINK AND NOBODY HAS TO DIE.
... NOBODY *ELSE*.

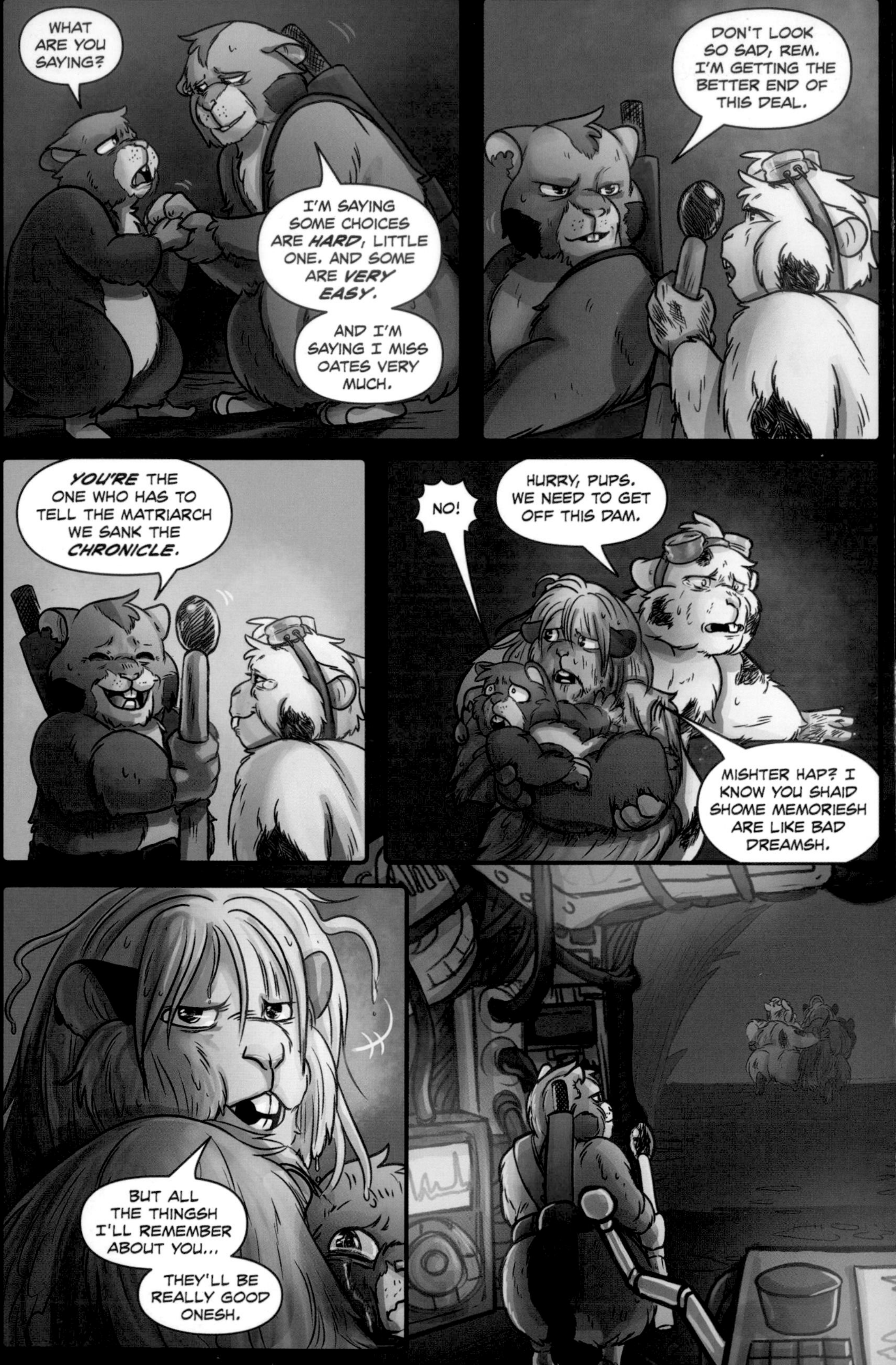
WHAT ARE YOU SAYING?
I'M SAYING SOME CHOICES ARE HARD, LITTLE ONE. AND SOME ARE VERY EASY.
AND I'M SAYING I MISS OATES VERY MUCH.
DON'T LOOK SO SAD, REM. I'M GETTING THE BETTER END OF THIS DEAL.
YOU'RE THE ONE WHO HAS TO TELL THE MATRIARCH WE SANK THE CHRONICLE.
NO!
HURRY, PUPS. WE NEED TO GET OFF THIS DAM.
MISHTER HAP? I KNOW YOU SHAID SHOME MEMORIESH ARE LIKE BAD DREAMSH.
BUT ALL THE THINGSH I'LL REMEMBER ABOUT YOU...
THEY'LL BE REALLY GOOD ONESH.

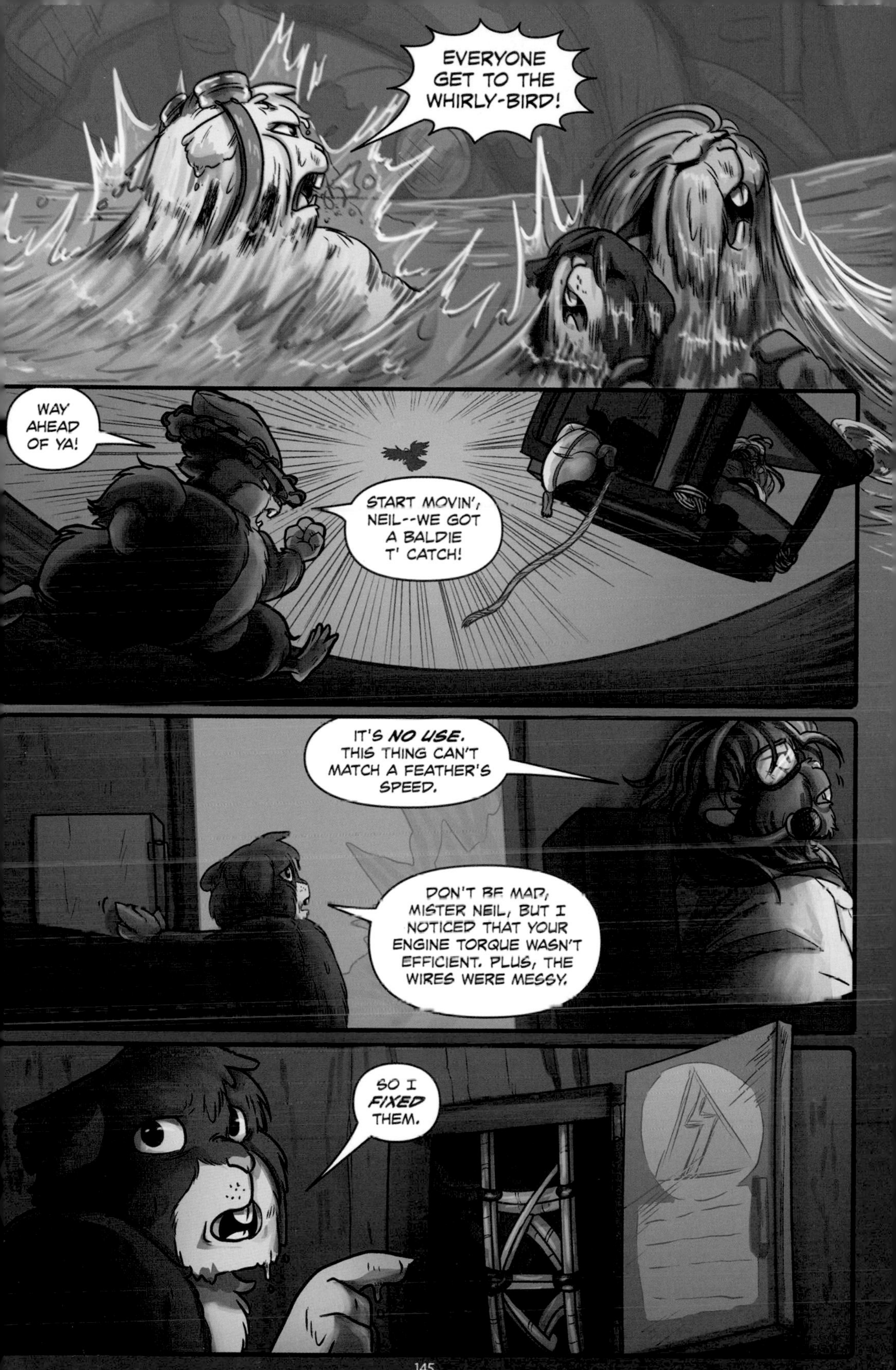
EVERYONE GET TO THE WHIRLY-BIRD!
WAY AHEAD OF YA!
START MOVIN', NEIL--WE GOT A BALDIE T' CATCH!
IT'S *NO USE.* THIS THING CAN'T MATCH A FEATHER'S SPEED.
DON'T BE MAD, MISTER NEIL, BUT I NOTICED THAT YOUR ENGINE TORQUE WASN'T EFFICIENT. PLUS, THE WIRES WERE MESSY.
SO I *FIXED* THEM.

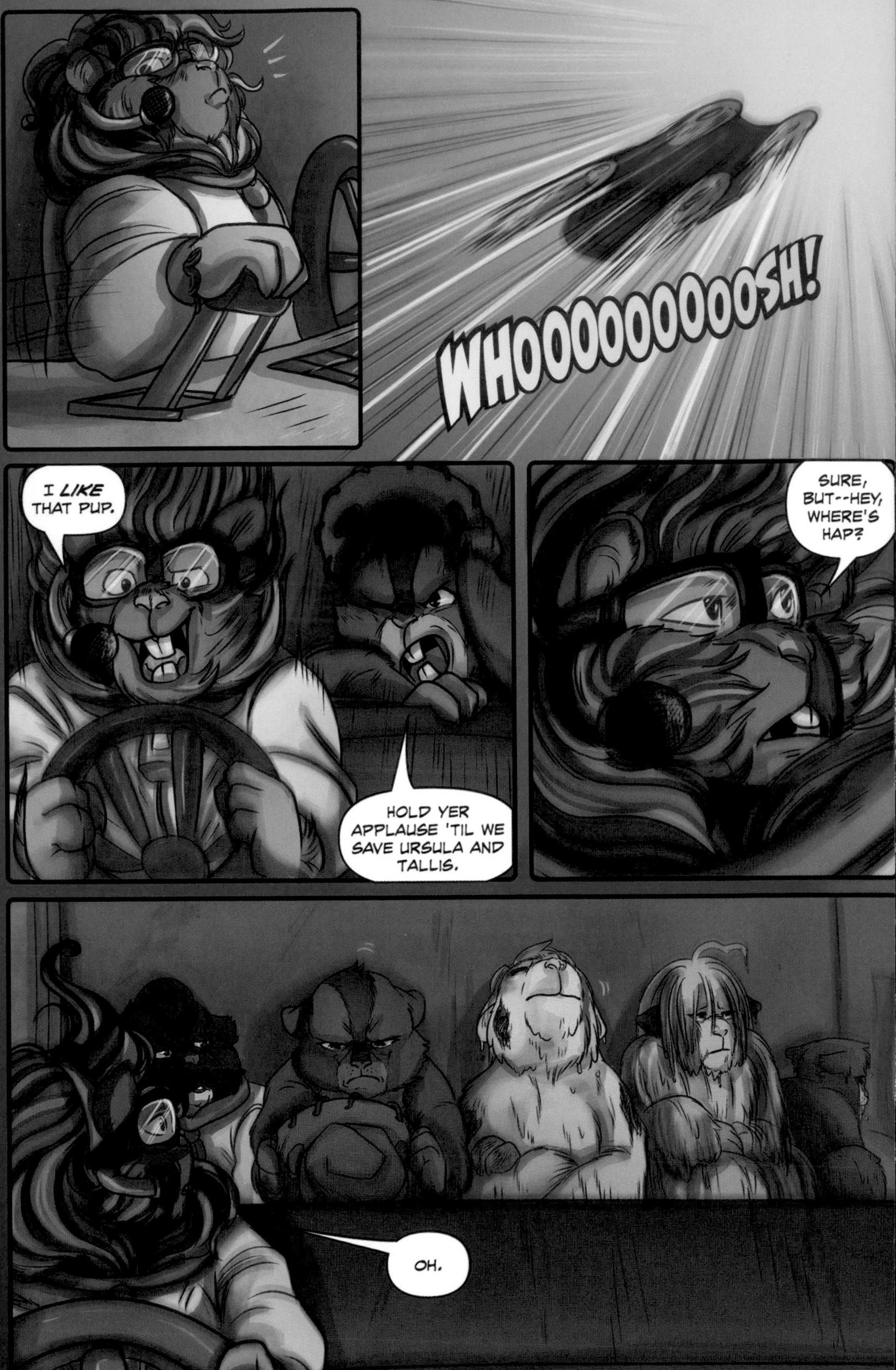
WHOOOOOOOOOSH!
I LIKE THAT PUP.
HOLD YER APPLAUSE 'TIL WE SAVE URSULA AND TALLIS.
SURE, BUT--HEY, WHERE'S HAP?
OH.

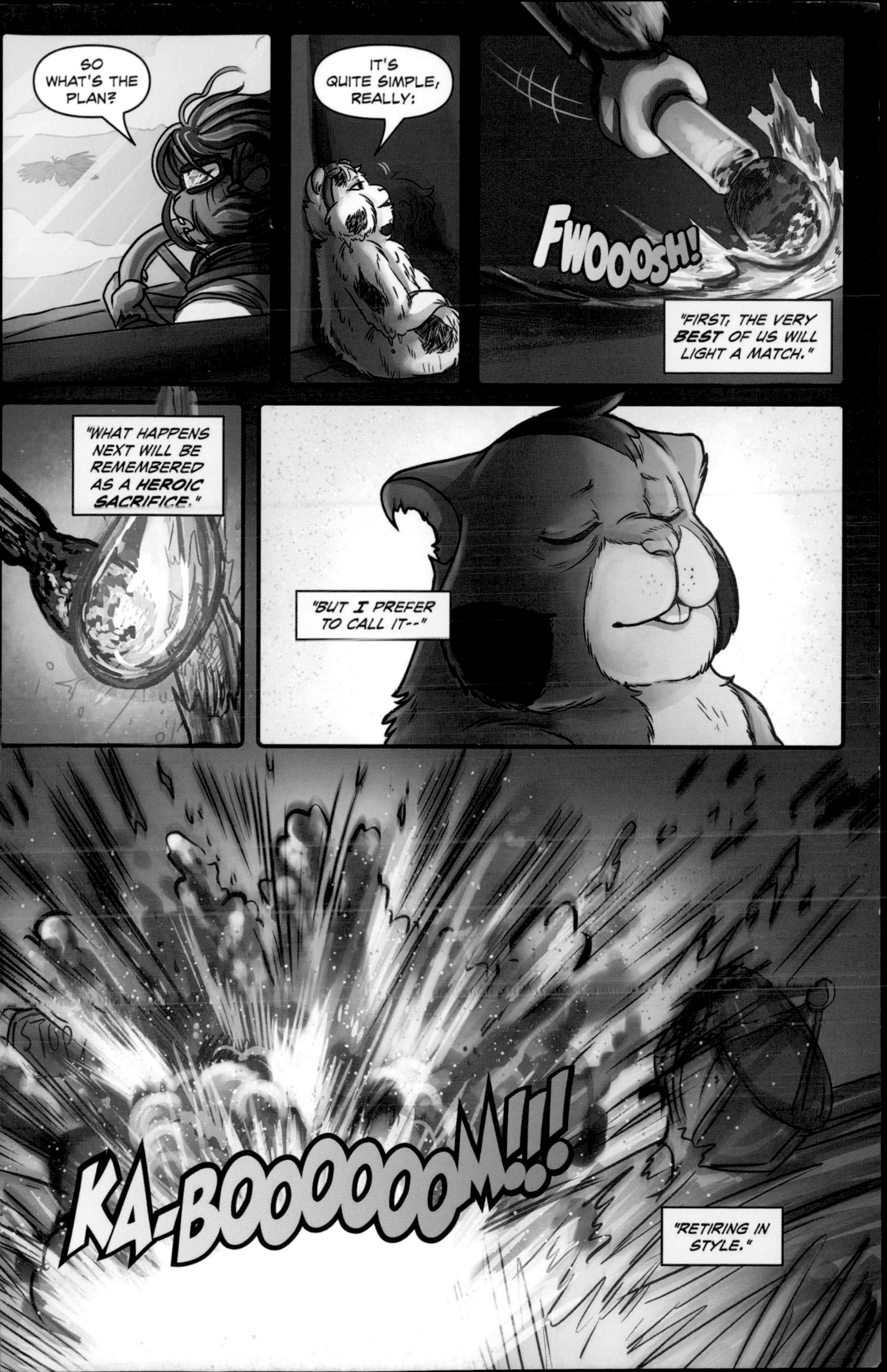
SO WHAT'S THE PLAN?
IT'S QUITE SIMPLE, REALLY:
FWOOOSH!
"FIRST, THE VERY BEST OF US WILL LIGHT A MATCH."
"WHAT HAPPENS NEXT WILL BE REMEMBERED AS A HEROIC SACRIFICE."
"BUT I PREFER TO CALL IT--"
KA-BOOOOOOOM!!!
"RETIRING IN STYLE."

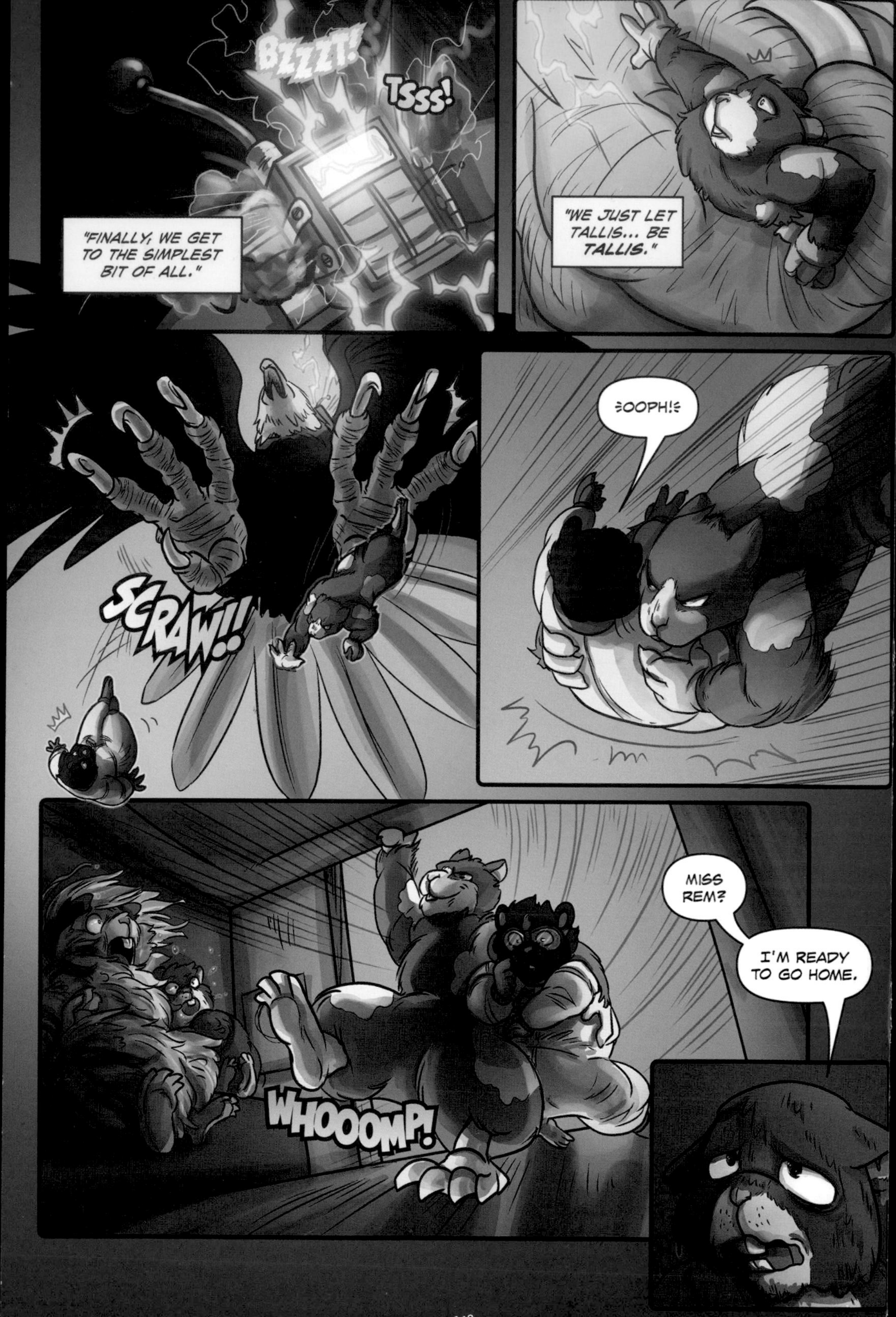
BZZZT!
TSSS!
"FINALLY, WE GET TO THE SIMPLEST BIT OF ALL."
"WE JUST LET TALLIS... BE TALLIS."
SCRAW!!
OOPH!
WHOOOMP!
MISS REM?
I'M READY TO GO HOME.

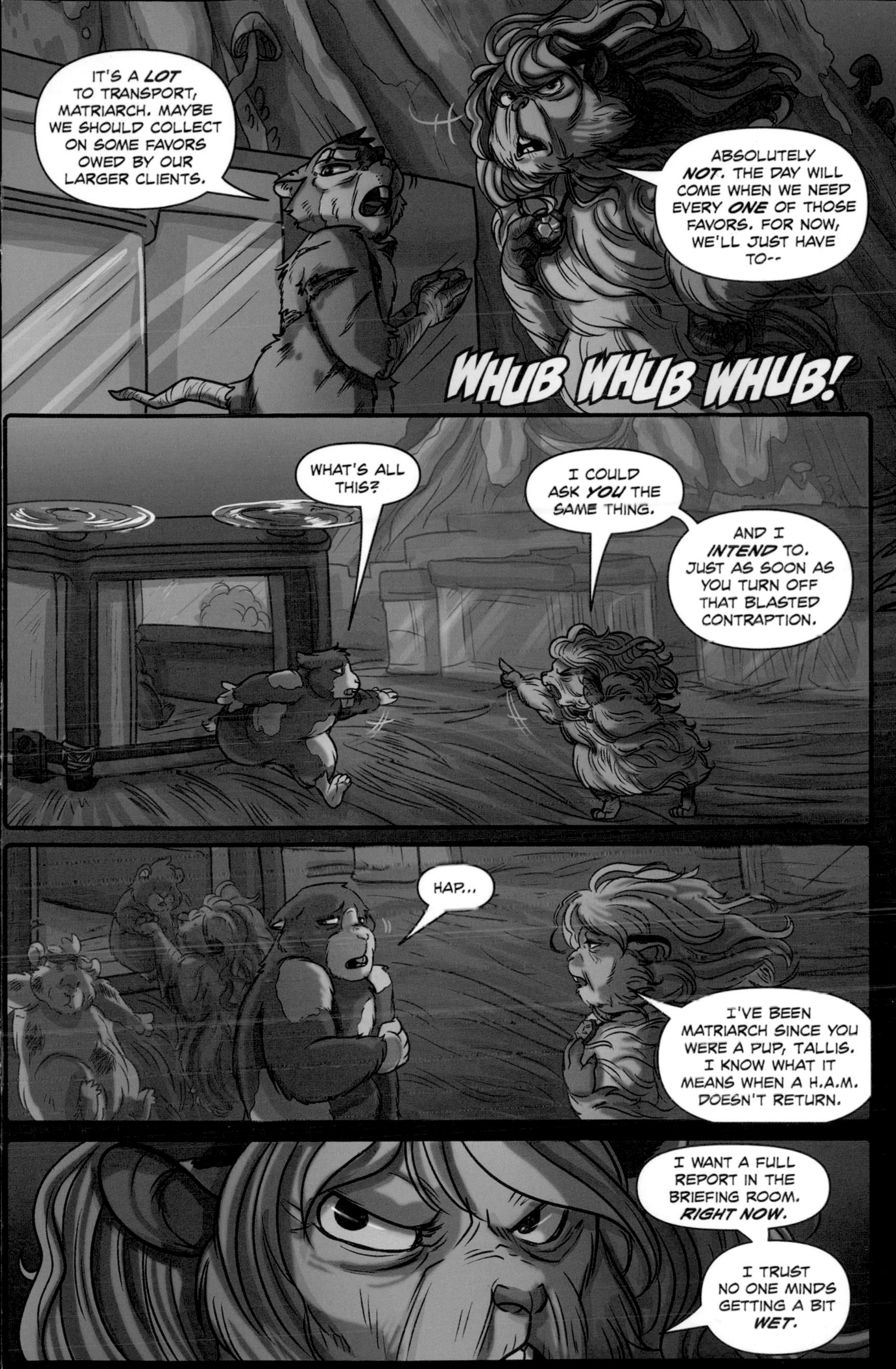
IT'S A LOT TO TRANSPORT, MATRIARCH. MAYBE WE SHOULD COLLECT ON SOME FAVORS OWED BY OUR LARGER CLIENTS.
ABSOLUTELY NOT. THE DAY WILL COME WHEN WE NEED EVERY ONE OF THOSE FAVORS. FOR NOW, WE'LL JUST HAVE TO--
WHUB WHUB WHUB!
WHAT'S ALL THIS?
I COULD ASK YOU THE SAME THING.
AND I INTEND TO. JUST AS SOON AS YOU TURN OFF THAT BLASTED CONTRAPTION.
HAP...
I'VE BEEN MATRIARCH SINCE YOU WERE A PUP, TALLIS. I KNOW WHAT IT MEANS WHEN A H.A.M. DOESN'T RETURN.
I WANT A FULL REPORT IN THE BRIEFING ROOM. RIGHT NOW.
I TRUST NO ONE MINDS GETTING A BIT WET.

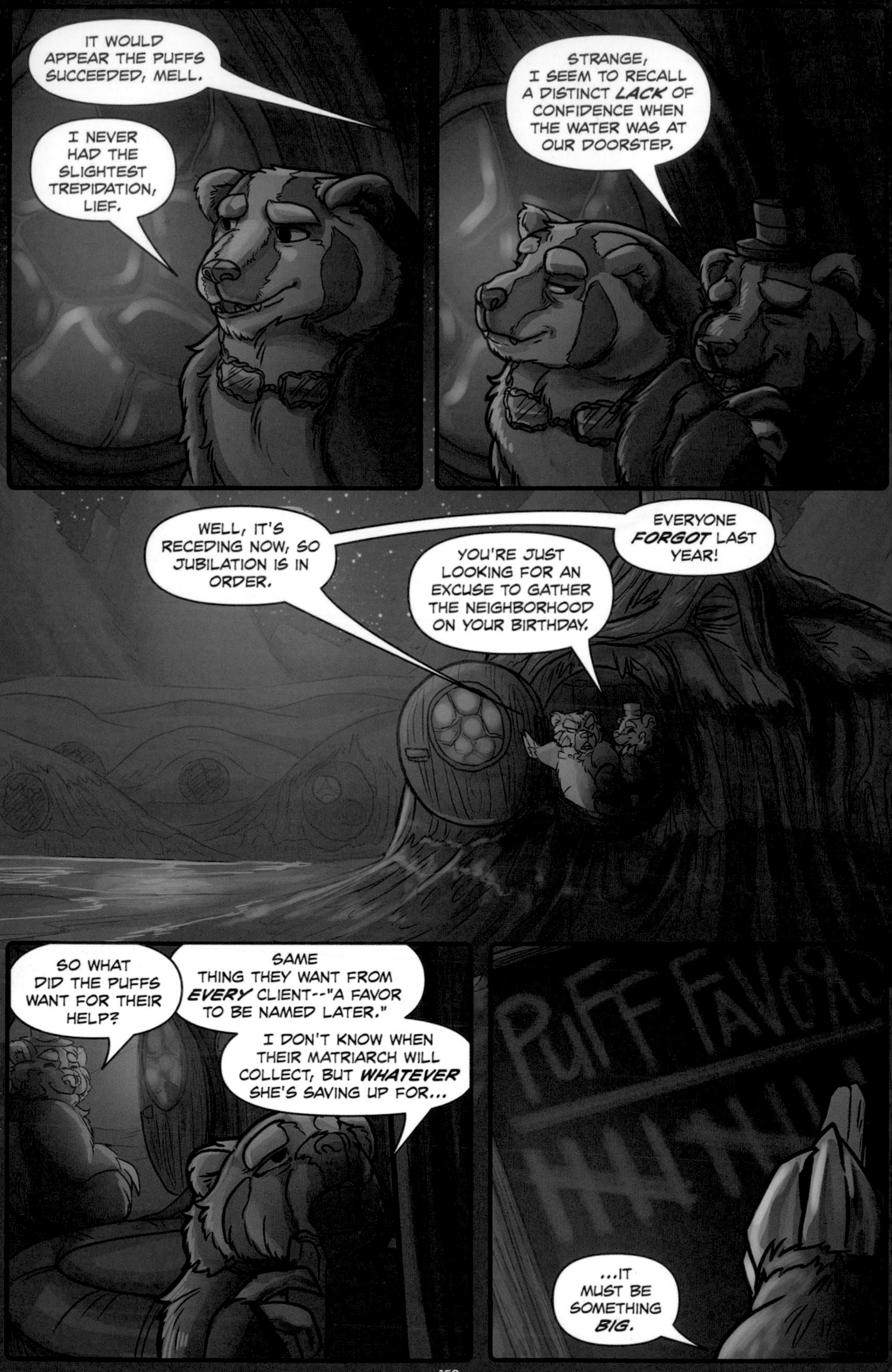
IT WOULD APPEAR THE PUFFS SUCCEEDED, MELL.
I NEVER HAD THE SLIGHTEST TREPIDATION, LIEF.
STRANGE, I SEEM TO RECALL A DISTINCT *LACK* OF CONFIDENCE WHEN THE WATER WAS AT OUR DOORSTEP.
WELL, IT'S RECEDING NOW, SO JUBILATION IS IN ORDER.
YOU'RE JUST LOOKING FOR AN EXCUSE TO GATHER THE NEIGHBORHOOD ON YOUR BIRTHDAY.
EVERYONE *FORGOT* LAST YEAR!
SO WHAT DID THE PUFFS WANT FOR THEIR HELP?
SAME THING THEY WANT FROM *EVERY* CLIENT--"A FAVOR TO BE NAMED LATER."
I DON'T KNOW WHEN THEIR MATRIARCH WILL COLLECT, BUT *WHATEVER* SHE'S SAVING UP FOR...
PUFF FAVOR
...IT MUST BE SOMETHING *BIG*.

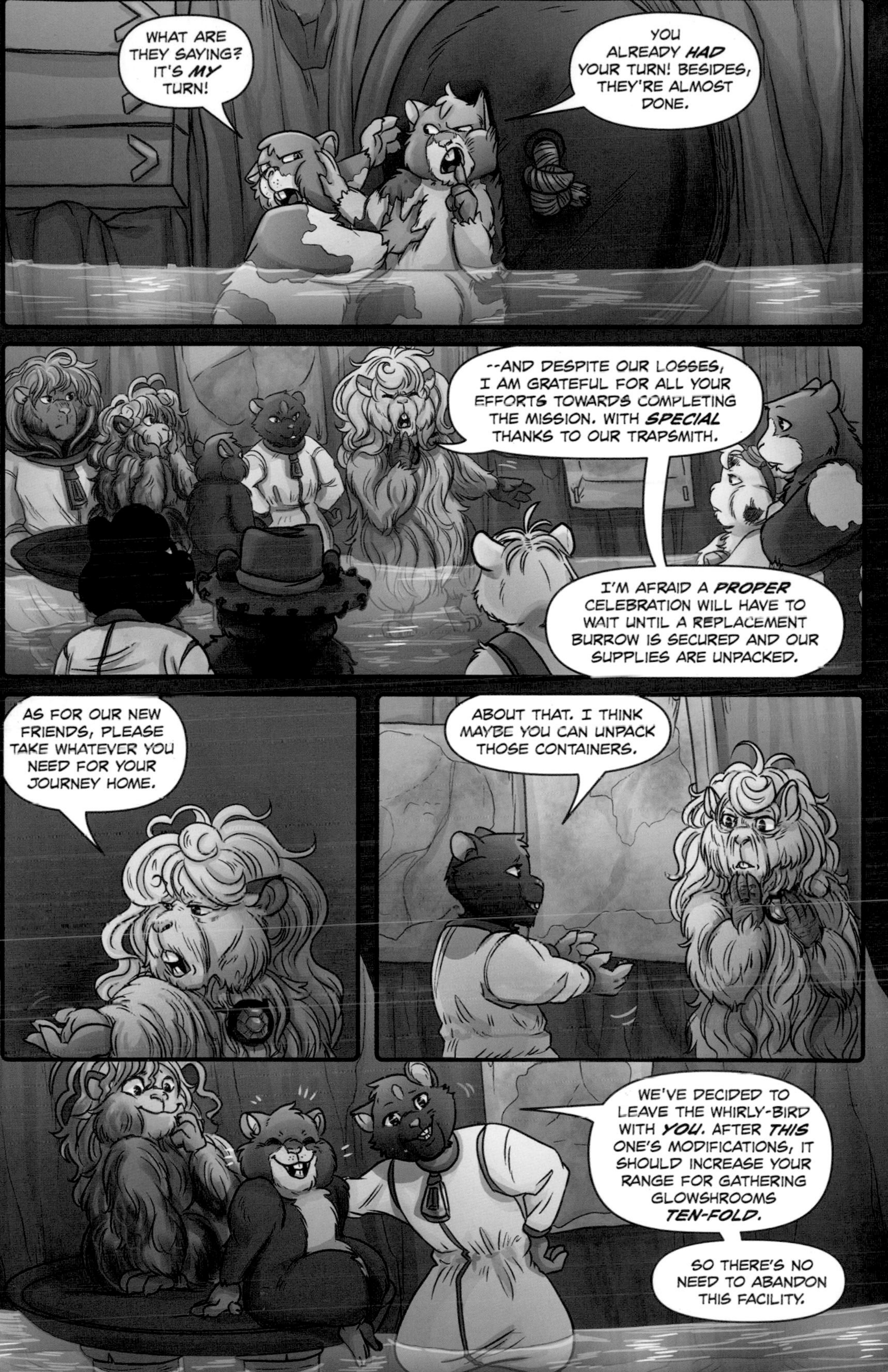
WHAT ARE THEY SAYING? IT'S *MY* TURN!
YOU ALREADY *HAD* YOUR TURN! BESIDES, THEY'RE ALMOST DONE.
--AND DESPITE OUR LOSSES, I AM GRATEFUL FOR ALL YOUR EFFORTS TOWARDS COMPLETING THE MISSION. WITH *SPECIAL* THANKS TO OUR TRAPSMITH.
I'M AFRAID A *PROPER* CELEBRATION WILL HAVE TO WAIT UNTIL A REPLACEMENT BURROW IS SECURED AND OUR SUPPLIES ARE UNPACKED.
AS FOR OUR NEW FRIENDS, PLEASE TAKE WHATEVER YOU NEED FOR YOUR JOURNEY HOME.
ABOUT THAT. I THINK MAYBE YOU CAN UNPACK THOSE CONTAINERS.
WE'VE DECIDED TO LEAVE THE WHIRLY-BIRD WITH *YOU*. AFTER *THIS* ONE'S MODIFICATIONS, IT SHOULD INCREASE YOUR RANGE FOR GATHERING GLOWSHROOMS *TEN-FOLD*.
SO THERE'S NO NEED TO ABANDON THIS FACILITY.

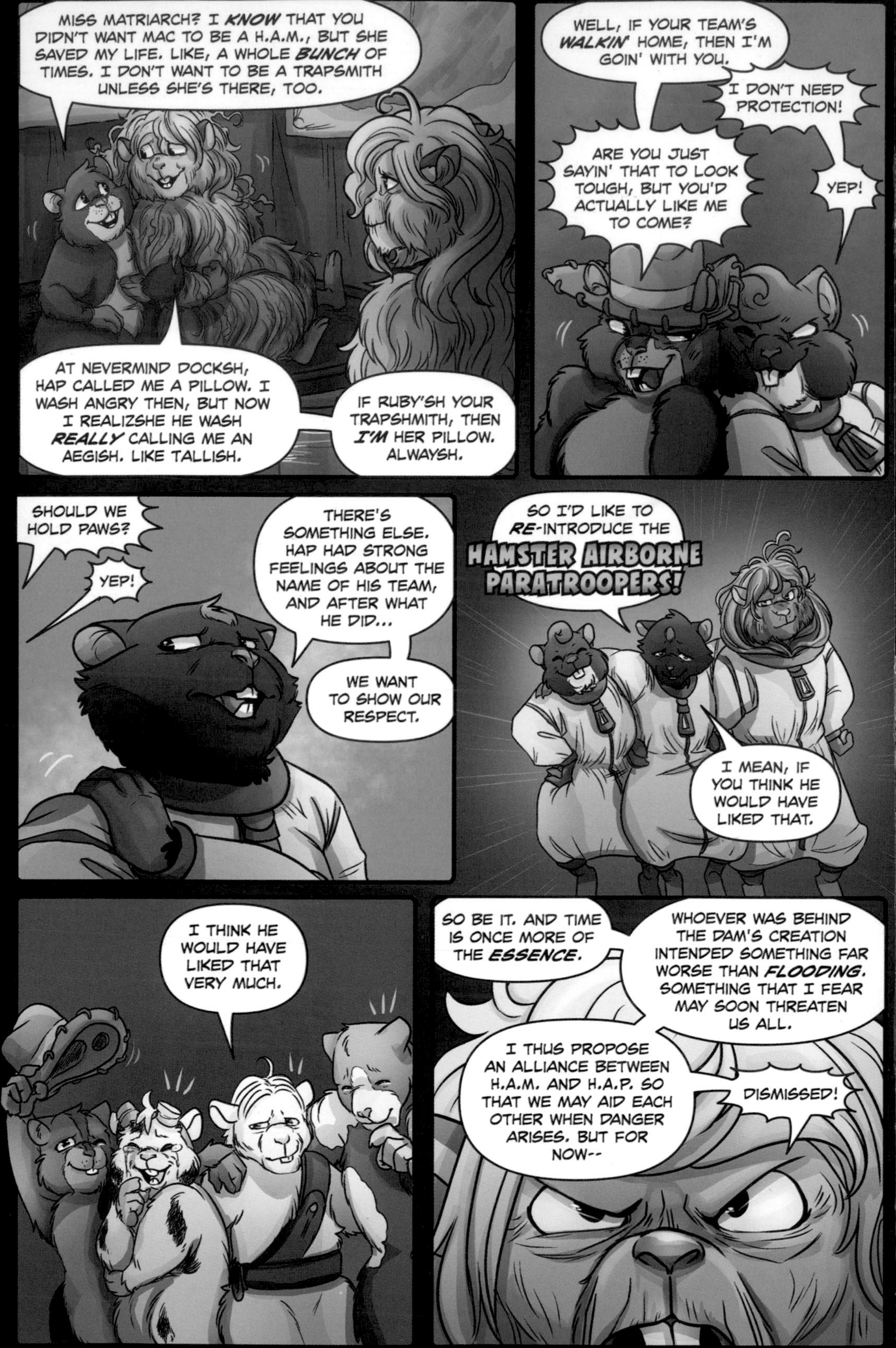
MISS MATRIARCH? I *KNOW* THAT YOU DIDN'T WANT MAC TO BE A H.A.M., BUT SHE SAVED MY LIFE. LIKE, A WHOLE *BUNCH* OF TIMES. I DON'T WANT TO BE A TRAPSMITH UNLESS SHE'S THERE, TOO.
AT NEVERMIND DOCKSH, HAP CALLED ME A PILLOW. I WASH ANGRY THEN, BUT NOW I REALIZSHE HE WASH *REALLY* CALLING ME AN AEGISH. LIKE TALLISH.
IF RUBY'SH YOUR TRAPSHMITH, THEN *I'M* HER PILLOW. ALWAYSH.
WELL, IF YOUR TEAM'S *WALKIN'* HOME, THEN I'M GOIN' WITH YOU.
I DON'T NEED PROTECTION!
ARE YOU JUST SAYIN' THAT TO LOOK TOUGH, BUT YOU'D ACTUALLY LIKE ME TO COME?
YEP!
SHOULD WE HOLD PAWS?
YEP!
THERE'S SOMETHING ELSE. HAP HAD STRONG FEELINGS ABOUT THE NAME OF HIS TEAM, AND AFTER WHAT HE DID...
WE WANT TO SHOW OUR RESPECT.
SO I'D LIKE TO *RE*-INTRODUCE THE
HAMSTER AIRBORNE PARATROOPERS!
I MEAN, IF YOU THINK HE WOULD HAVE LIKED THAT.
I THINK HE WOULD HAVE LIKED THAT VERY MUCH.
SO BE IT. AND TIME IS ONCE MORE OF THE *ESSENCE*.
WHOEVER WAS BEHIND THE DAM'S CREATION INTENDED SOMETHING FAR WORSE THAN *FLOODING*. SOMETHING THAT I FEAR MAY SOON THREATEN US ALL.
I THUS PROPOSE AN ALLIANCE BETWEEN H.A.M. AND H.A.P. SO THAT WE MAY AID EACH OTHER WHEN DANGER ARISES. BUT FOR NOW--
DISMISSED!

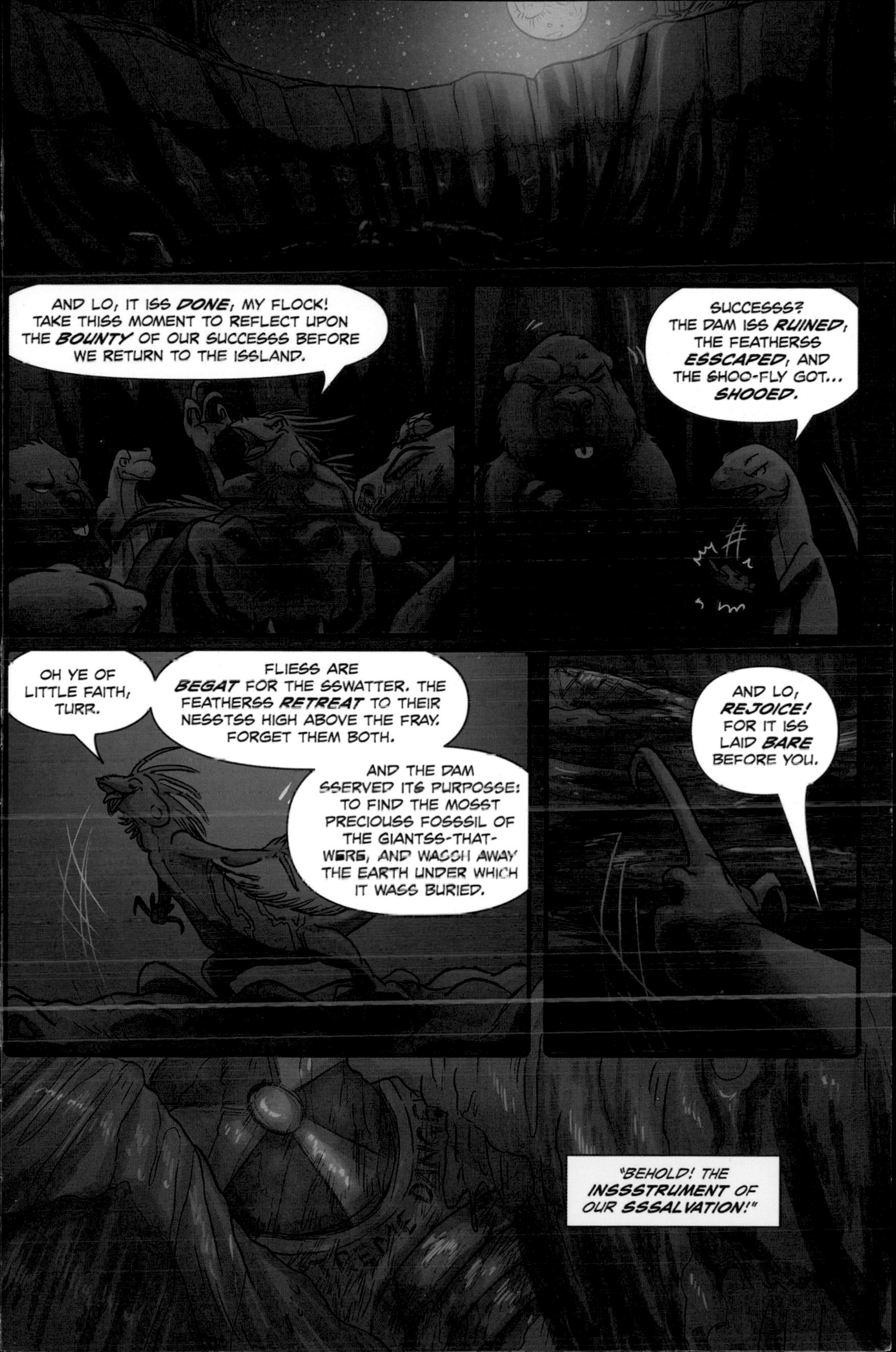
AND LO, IT ISS DONE, MY FLOCK! TAKE THISS MOMENT TO REFLECT UPON THE BOUNTY OF OUR SUCCESSS BEFORE WE RETURN TO THE ISSLAND.
SUCCESSS? THE DAM ISS RUINED, THE FEATHERSS ESSCAPED, AND THE SHOO-FLY GOT... SHOOED.
OH YE OF LITTLE FAITH, TURR.
FLIESS ARE BEGAT FOR THE SSWATTER. THE FEATHERSS RETREAT TO THEIR NESSTSS HIGH ABOVE THE FRAY. FORGET THEM BOTH.
AND THE DAM SSERVED ITS PURPOSSE: TO FIND THE MOSST PRECIOUSS FOSSSIL OF THE GIANTSS-THAT-WERE, AND WASSH AWAY THE EARTH UNDER WHICH IT WASS BURIED.
AND LO, REJOICE! FOR IT ISS LAID BARE BEFORE YOU.
"BEHOLD! THE INSSSTRUMENT OF OUR SSSALVATION!"

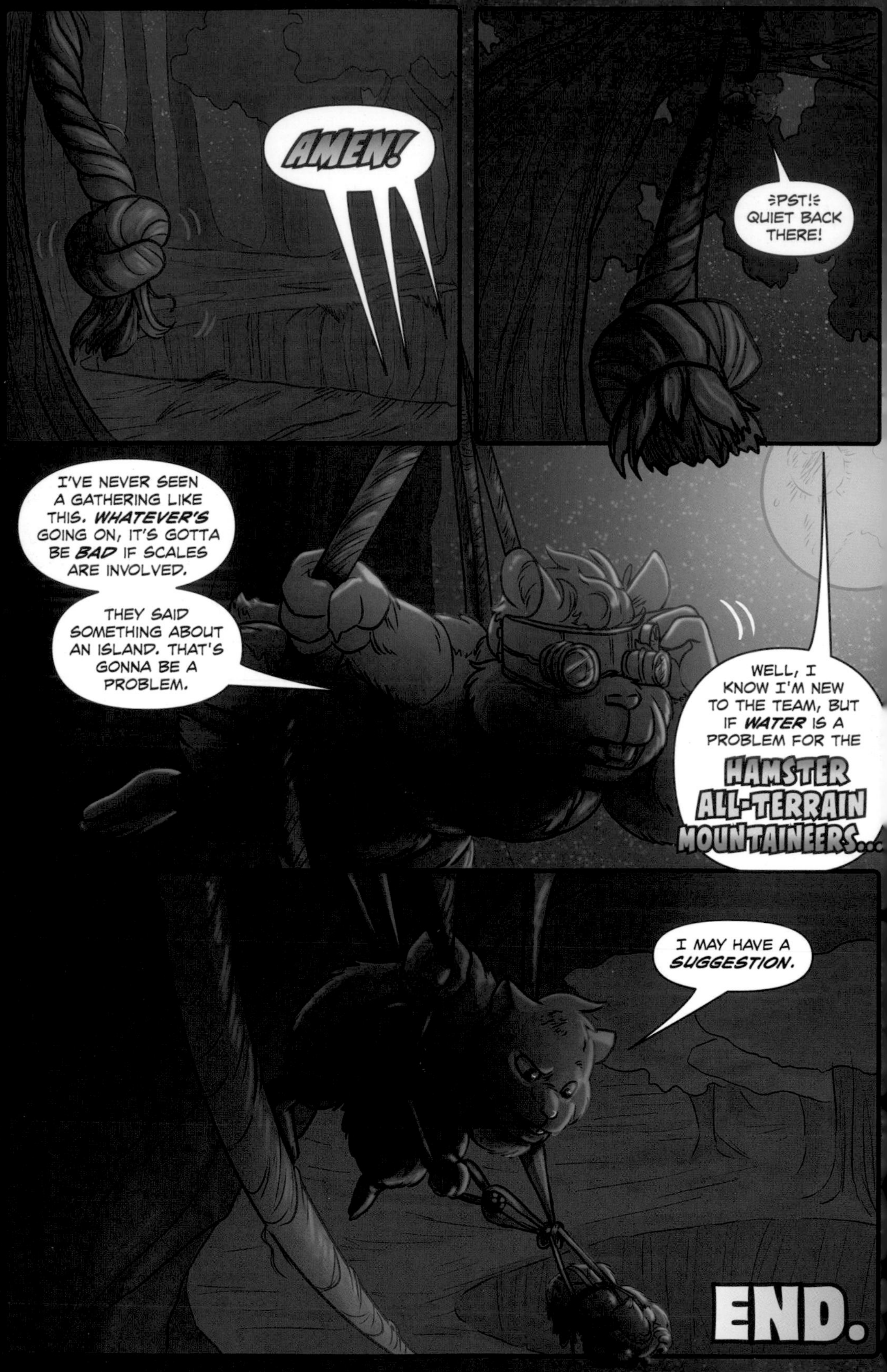

AMEN!
≠PST!≠ QUIET BACK THERE!
I'VE NEVER SEEN A GATHERING LIKE THIS. WHATEVER'S GOING ON, IT'S GOTTA BE BAD IF SCALES ARE INVOLVED.
THEY SAID SOMETHING ABOUT AN ISLAND. THAT'S GONNA BE A PROBLEM.
WELL, I KNOW I'M NEW TO THE TEAM, BUT IF WATER IS A PROBLEM FOR THE HAMSTER ALL-TERRAIN MOUNTAINEERS...
I MAY HAVE A SUGGESTION.
END.

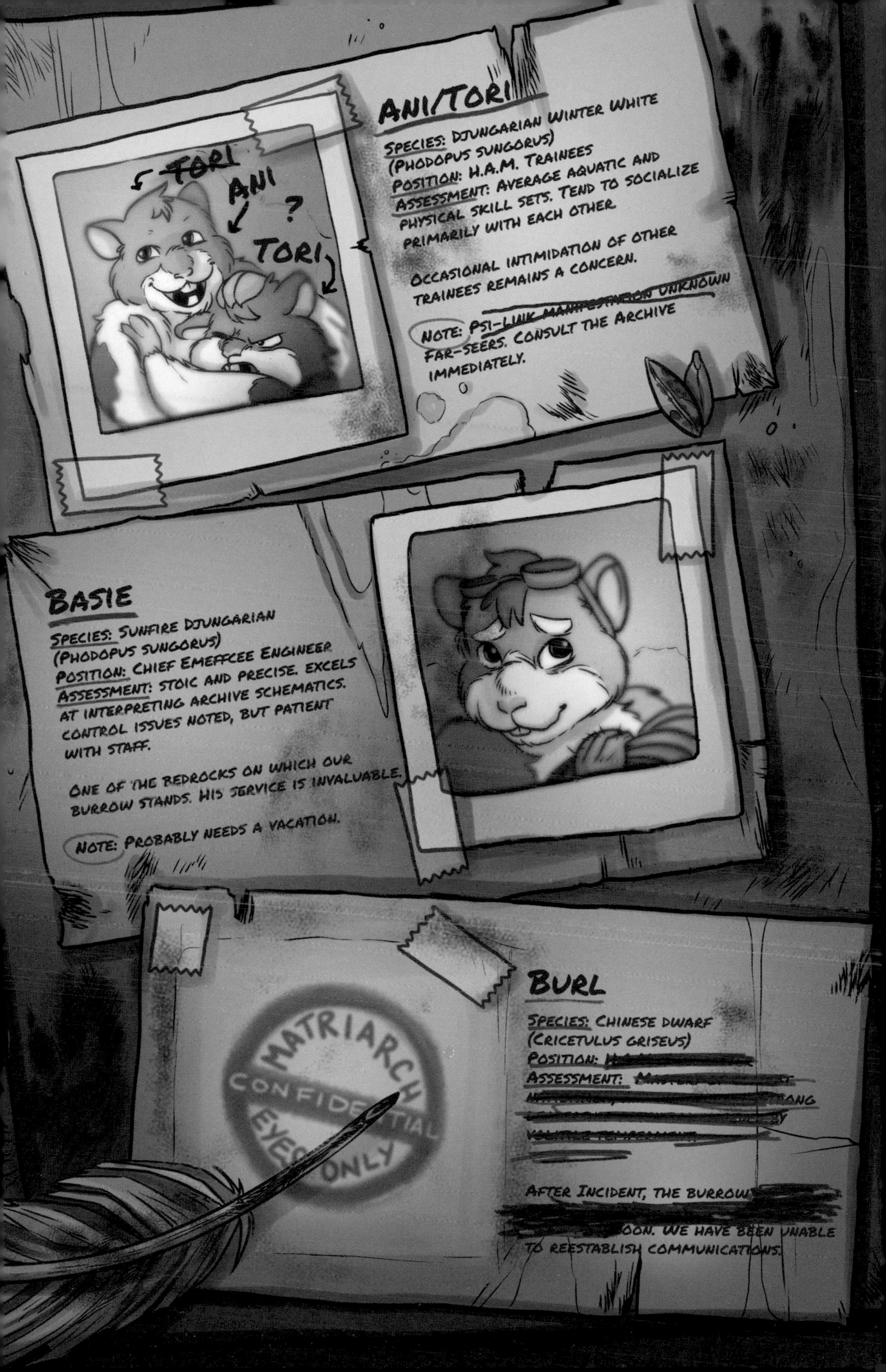
ANI/TORI
SPECIES: DJUNGARIAN WINTER WHITE
(PHODOPUS SUNGORUS)
POSITION: H.A.M. TRAINEES
ASSESSMENT: AVERAGE AQUATIC AND PHYSICAL SKILL SETS. TEND TO SOCIALIZE PRIMARILY WITH EACH OTHER.
OCCASIONAL INTIMIDATION OF OTHER TRAINEES REMAINS A CONCERN.
NOTE: ~~PSI-LINK MANIFESTATION UNKNOWN~~ FAR-SEERS. CONSULT THE ARCHIVE IMMEDIATELY.
~~TORI~~
ANI
?
TORI
BASIE
SPECIES: SUNFIRE DJUNGARIAN
(PHODOPUS SUNGORUS)
POSITION: CHIEF EMEFFCEE ENGINEER
ASSESSMENT: STOIC AND PRECISE. EXCELS AT INTERPRETING ARCHIVE SCHEMATICS. CONTROL ISSUES NOTED, BUT PATIENT WITH STAFF.
ONE OF THE BEDROCKS ON WHICH OUR BURROW STANDS. HIS SERVICE IS INVALUABLE.
NOTE: PROBABLY NEEDS A VACATION.
MATRIARCH
CONFIDENTIAL
EYES ONLY
BURL
SPECIES: CHINESE DWARF
(CRICETULUS GRISEUS)
POSITION: [redacted]
ASSESSMENT: [redacted]
AFTER INCIDENT, THE BURROW [redacted] OON. WE HAVE BEEN UNABLE TO REESTABLISH COMMUNICATIONS.

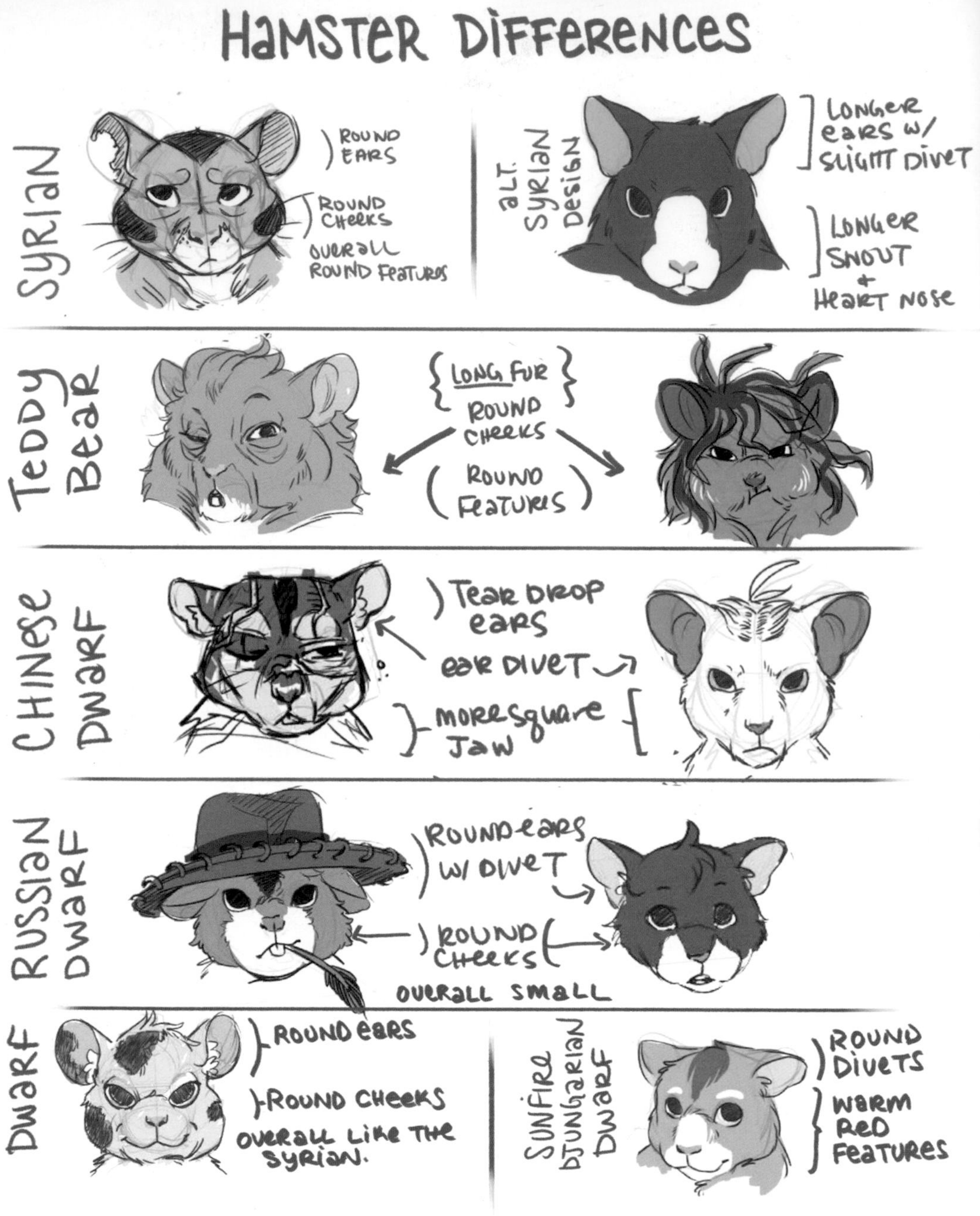
Hamster Differences
Syrian
Round ears
Round cheeks
overall round features
alt. Syrian design
Longer ears w/ slight divet
Longer snout + heart nose
Teddy Bear
Long fur
Round cheeks
Round features
Chinese Dwarf
Tear drop ears
ear divet
more square jaw
Russian Dwarf
Round ears w/ divet
Round cheeks
overall small
Dwarf
Round ears
Round cheeks
overall like the Syrian.
Sunfire Djungarian Dwarf
Round divets
warm red features

Why hamsters?

<u>*Emily*</u>: I've had pet rodents throughout life. I got my first hamster back in 2012 and she was a delight. Hamsters are adorable, soft, and dainty. They are quick, smart, and agile. They can be tamed, with patience, and even taught to do tricks. In spending time with my hamsters, each of them bonded with me and became my special little friend. And, of course, they are pretty easy to care for.

I've always loved tales of small creatures working together against the odds to succeed—as in *Watership Down*, or *Mrs. Frisby and the Rats of NIMH*. Like the characters in those stories, my pets have all had their own unique personalities. My first hamster, Ysabell Sto Hamsterlet (Izzy!), was a sweet, inquisitive little lady. I started imagining the adventures she had when I was not home; and this turned into Izzy sharing her thoughts on Twitter. One day, another little hamster replied to her, and a storytelling partnership was born ...

ORIGINAL CHARACTER SKETCHES

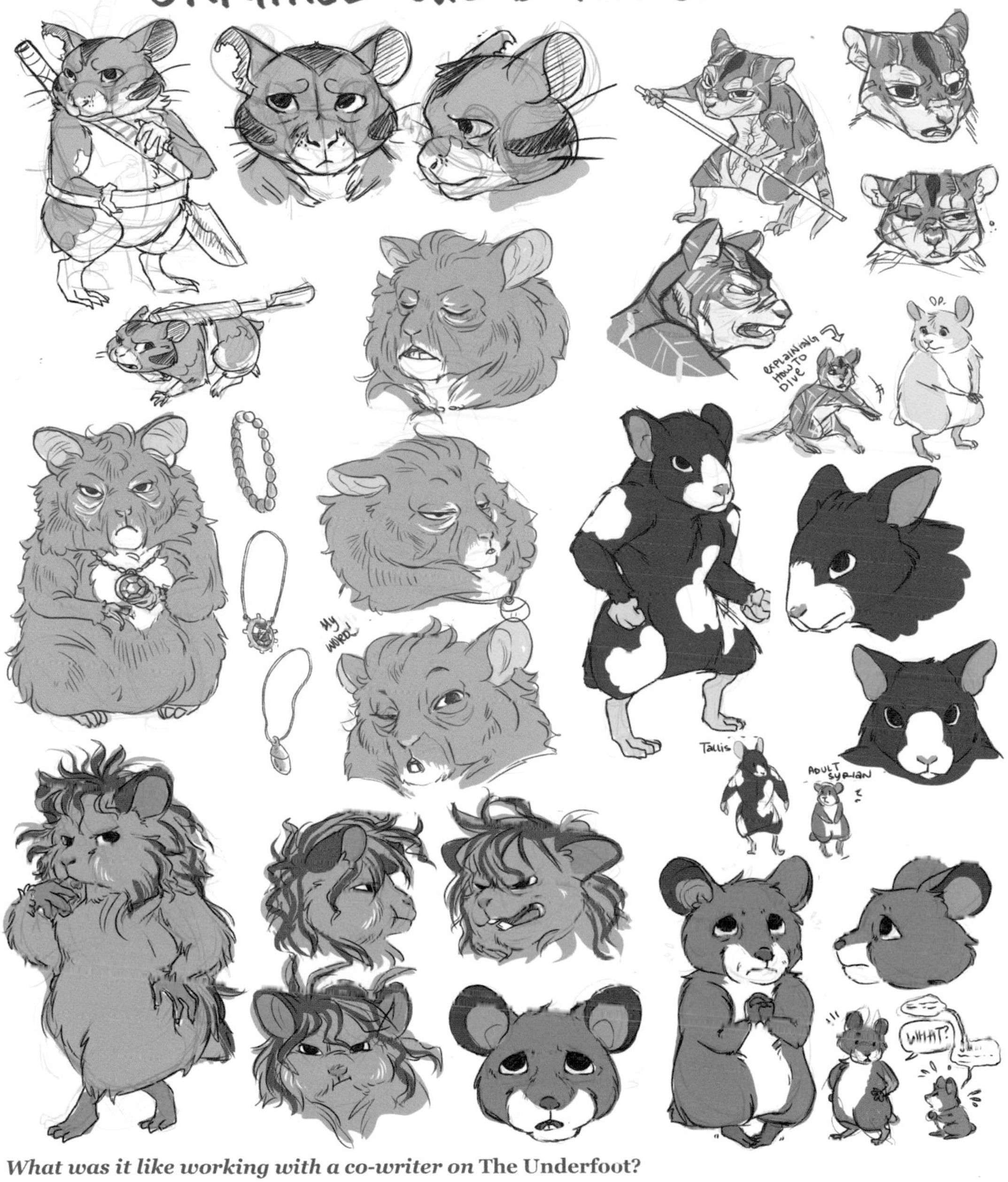
EXPLAINING HOW TO DIVE
MY WORD!
Tallis
ADULT SYRIAN
WHAT?

***What was it like working with a co-writer on* The Underfoot?**

<u>*Ben*</u>: I was nervous at first about collaborating with another writer. Would we argue incessantly over plot details? Would there be enough time to mansplain hamster sleeping habits?

But our process quickly became a refreshingly organic exchange of ideas offered, considered, accepted, and (often) discarded without ego or attachment. Our goal, always, is to tell the best story we can, for as broad an audience as possible.

It also helped tremendously that Lion Forge downloaded our collective consciousness into a glowing box of buttons and coils, from which scripts are printed and delivered to Michelle. They say this is now standard industry practice, and that we're free to re-enter our host bodies after volume three.

If anyone's reading this, please feed my cat.

ORIGINAL CHARACTER SKETCHES

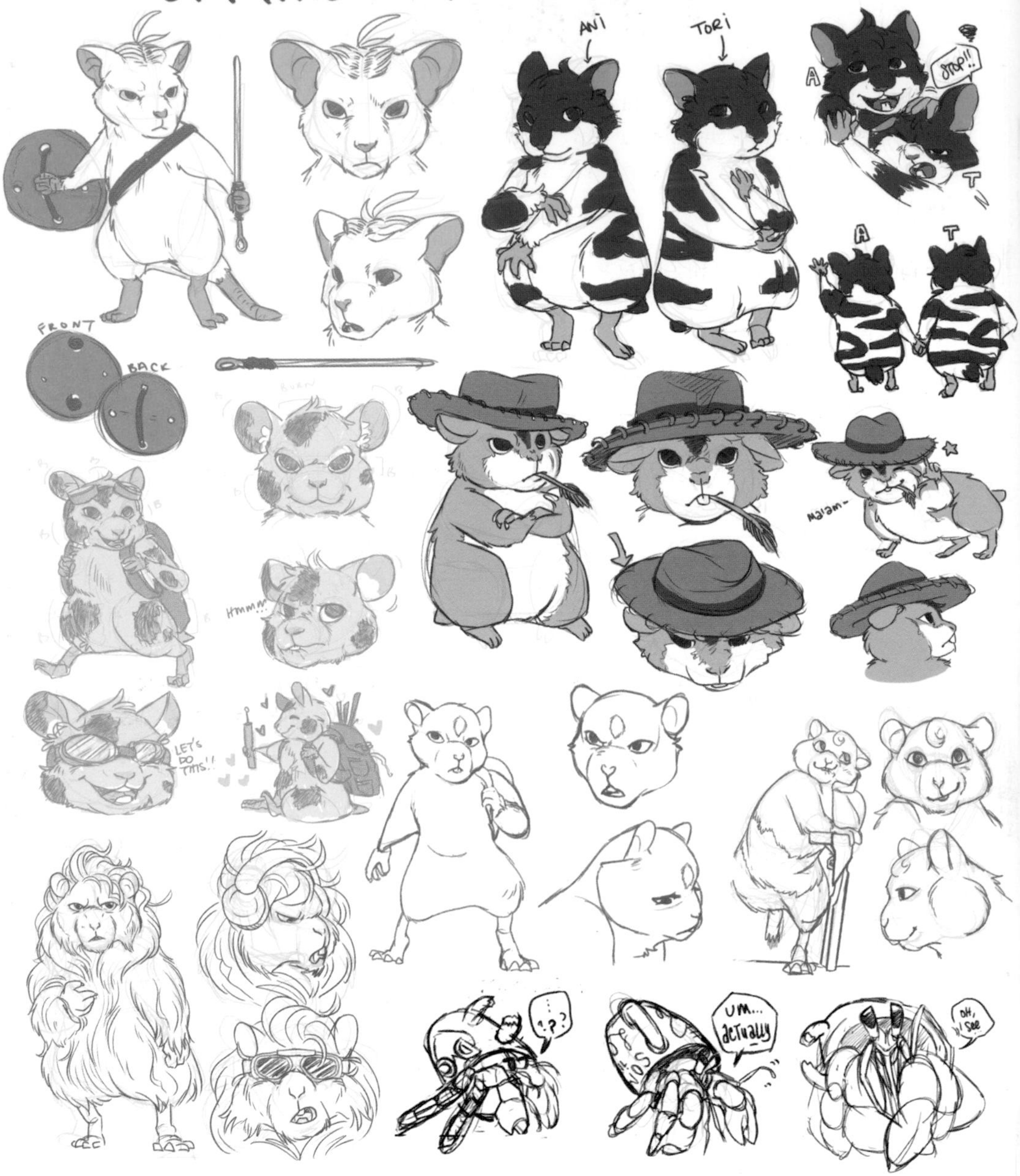
ANI
TORI
STOP!!
A
T
FRONT
BACK
LET'S DO THIS!!
UM... actually

What research did you do while creating the art for this story?

Michelle: Don't worry, Ben—I'll feed Fizzgig for you! As for the art, both before and after starting to draw *The Underfoot* I watched a *whole* lot of hamster videos online. I also took a few trips to local pet stores to watch them in action (and by action, I mean mostly sleeping). It finally clicked in my brain that hamsters kind of look like stick figures trapped in really poofy onsies cinched at the hands and feet. This helped me with their movement quite a bit.

As for other research, being an illustrator (especially in comics) means you have to be able to draw anything and everything. This requires the ability to cobble together references, and use them to turn your illustration into something believable and outstanding. For example: it takes multiple rounds of research and finding relevant images when creating a scene where a large fresh-water fish jumps over a hamster-driven boat made of an umbrella, children's toys, and a water bottle—because, let's be true, that hasn't happened in real-life . . . yet.

CREATORS

BEN FISHER is an attorney and author whose work spans a broad spectrum of genres and subject matter, but always with an underlying thread of humanity (and a bit of his trademark dry wit).

His father, a recipient of the NAACP Humanitarian Award, helped ensure that a thread of optimism was woven into even Ben's darkest tales, while his mother first set him on the story-teller path by giving him the *Dungeons & Dragons* "red box" while he was still in grade school.

He writes and performs "geek-centric" music under the name Tesla Deathray Survivors Anonymous, and his first album, *This Is Canon,* was released in 2017.

EMILY S. WHITTEN is an attorney, fiction writer, pop culture journalist and host, and media personality who also occasionally runs genre conventions. She has published columns and webcomics with the likes of ComicMix, MTV Splash Page, Reelz.com, and Movers & Shakers Unlimited, and has had recurring appearances on the *Fantastic Forum* radio and TV shows and the podcast *Made of Fail*.

Emily co-founded The North American Discworld Convention, and continues to assist in its management. She resides in the greater D.C. area, and in her copious spare time, she enjoys crafting and looking after her tiny hamster.

MICHELLE NGUYEN is an Eisner and Ignatz-winning illustrator and comic artist based in Portland, Oregon. She studied fine arts at the University of Puget Sound and Portland State University. She has previously contributed to *The Misadventures of Grumpy Cat and Pokey* and the *Elements: Fire* anthology.

THOM ZAHLER is a comic book creator and letterer. He created the Line Webtoon hit series *Warning Label* as well as the Harvey-nominated *Love and Capes, Long Distance,* and the time-traveling wine comic *Time and Vine*. He also writes and draws for IDW's successful *My Little Pony* series. He has lettered for numerous companies, including Warner Brothers, Claypool Comics, Antarctic Press, and more.

ADRIAN RICKER — Flatting/Coloring Assistance
ERIC ORCHARD — Maps

CARACAL™

ISBN: 978-1-5493-0289-3

10 9 8 7 6 5 4 3 2 1